EMPIRE OF OSHBOB

CITY OF ARTEM

By
Kevin Sinclair

Kevin Sinclair

Empire of Oshbob

COPYRIGHT © 2023 KEVIN SINCLAIR
All rights reserved

This novel is entirely a work of fiction. The names, characters and situations portrayed in it are the work of the author's imagination.

The Author has no medical experience whatsoever and is in no way offering dietary or health advice. Any situation herein, are purely of the authors imagination.

All resemblance to actual persons, living or dead, is entirely coincidental.

No part of this book may be reproduced or stored in a retrieval system, or transmitted in any form or by any means, electronic, mechanical, photocopying, recording, or otherwise, without the express written permission of the copyright owner except for the use of quotations in a book review.

For more Information email:

kevinsinclairauthor@gmail.com

First edition 2023

Kevin Sinclair

Empire of Oshbob

Contents

Partition 1 1
Partition 2 8
Partition 3 12
Partition 4 19
Partition 5 25
Partition 6 34
Partition 7 42
Partition 8 Unara 50
Partition 9 60
Partition 10 69
Partition 11 76
Partition 12 83
Partition 13 89
Partition 14 95
Partition 15 Unara 102
Partition 16 108
Partition 17 118
Partition 18 123
Partition 19 129
Partition 20 139
Partition 21 149
Partition 22 153
Partition 23 163
Partition 24 171
Partition 25 177
Partition 26 184
Partition 27 189

Partition 28	193
Partition 29 Unara	202
Partition 30	223
Partition 31	228
Partition 32	234
Partition 33	239
Partition 34	244
Partition 35	255
Partition 36	263
Partition 37	270
Partition 38	280
Partition 39	290
Partition 40	298
Partition 41	305
Partition 42	312
Partition 43	319
Partition 44	327
Partition 45	334
Partition 46	343
Partition 47	351
Partition 48	357
Partition 49	366

Partition 1

"Left flank! I said left! You stupid fucking orc," Sergeant Turner's whiny, panicked voice echoed through the comm in my helmet.

As usual, I ignored the useless asshole and kept moving down the main road of the derelict town. It must have been empty for a couple of hundred years at the very least. Plant life had made an aggressive effort at reclaiming the place, growing through cracks in the tarmac, and covering the buildings and decayed vehicles.

It was perfect for cover, which I exploited to close the distance to the creature we hunted. Despite Sergeant Turner's complaints, I was now only a dozen meters away from where it snuffled and snorted as it tore out Private Andy's intestines.

I did my best to blank out the continuing complaints through my helmet's speaker as I crouched behind the battered, overturned car. It was more rust than metal, but as I brought my breathing back under control, it gave me a few different options to get eyes on the two-meter tall, boar-like monster.

It was so entranced with its work, violently plunging its serrated tusks into our deceased team mate, that I took the opportunity while it lasted.

Gripping my plasma rifle firmly, I charged from cover. I made it around four steps before its black, hellish eyes turned on me. With no more need for stealth, I roared incoherently as its muscles bunched in preparation to pounce.

I held for the barest of moments, before unleashing a short burst at its planted forefeet. The move ruined its jump toward me and caused it to falter. Sadly, it didn't go down from the shot, and the distance became intimate in a few heart beats. I leapt to one side to avoid the same fate as Andy, but the Tier-Two leg mod creaked and seized up as I pushed off.

Kevin Sinclair

The leg itself was barely worth its rank and even at the best of times it occasionally struggled with my weight, despite constant repairs. Now it had seriously let me down and the stumbling beast cannoned into me.

While I managed to avoid being hit dead on, I was still thrown up into the air by one of its sweeping tusks. Desperate, and furious that Sergeant Turner was still yelling in my ear, I activated the claw hook on my Tier-Two arm mod. It was a mod that was only slightly better than the leg mod across general use, but the hydraulic loaded hook was damn handy for this sort of thing.

With a lot of strength and a little bit of luck, I slammed it into the monster's shoulder, managing to bury it deep into the tough hide where it caught underneath its shoulder blade. The anchor allowed me to drop onto its back and offered me the perfect opportunity for a little personal extraction before it was brought down *officially*. Letting the plasma rifle hang free, I pulled out the makeshift nanite extractor Tenev had sent me, and jabbed it in my foe's other shoulder, taking a healthy helping of its life force and giving myself a much better hold on the thing.

"What the hell are you doing, Osh?" Turner squawked again. "Shoot it, don't fucking dance with it!"

"Getting a good grip," I grunted, fighting desperately to stay on the now whirling, snorting hairball of rage.

The extractor beeped, signaling it was full, so I clamped my legs extra tight and swiftly slid the extractor back into the concealed compartment of my armored sleeve. I almost lost hold in that moment, as I was bucked from its back to be fully airborne, apart from the embedded hook.

Before I'd even fully landed, I'd managed to pull my hand cannon and insert four bullets into the back of its skull. Even I couldn't miss at this range, and those little metal pills had the desired effect and calmed the creature down.

Specialist Jacobs was first to make it to me as I put another four bullets into the same spot, and the monster drew its last ragged breath.

"None of us could get a shot on it with you getting tossed about like a ragdoll." He was a medium-sized human, and not the worst I'd had to work with by a longshot.

Empire of Oshbob

"Had no choice," I said, panting heavily from the exertion. "Damn mod seized up when I side-stepped."

"They might change it now. It's not right, them sending you out with Trash-Tier mods dressed up as a Two." As he spoke, he knelt next to the monster and pulled out the official extractor kit.

I agreed with his words whole-heartedly, but remained silent. Complaining never got you anywhere with the higher ups and even complaining to these guys was likely to get back one way or another. Then I'd never have a chance at getting an upgrade.

"Still," Jacobs continued as he inserted the extractor. "Good job at bringing it down. Back of the head's about the only place worth shooting these bastards. Unless you're using a missile of course."

As he laughed at his own joke, the others finally joined us—Turner coming in last, of course.

"We're supposed to be a team, orc," he snapped. "One more dick move like that, and *you're* off it."

"I don't mind if you wanna kill everything, Oshie," Corporal Maddock said, grinning and leaning against a large chunk of concrete that had once been attached to a nearby building. "Just as long as you don't mind me telling everyone it was me when I get back home."

That pulled a chuckle from me. The whole team was made up of humans, but Maddock was the closest to an orc. Big, brutal, and direct.

"You do what you need to do," I replied.

He grinned, but his response was cut short by Jacobs. "All done."

"Decent haul?" Turner asked.

Jacobs winced. His eyes flickered briefly toward me. "Light again, Sarge."

"Ah hell," Turner snapped, kicking out a loose bit of rubble along the road. "It's like the beasts are getting weaker. I'll let the top brass know when I get my arse kicked for taking longer to meet the quota. Could be that there's a bigger problem going on."

Maddock, huffed. "Quota bullshit. We're supposed to be fucking soldiers, not work orcs." He looked guiltily at me. "Shit. Sorry, Osh. Not you o'course."

I waved the insult away. Maddock wasn't bright, and he didn't overthink his words. The fact that he apologized was more than enough for me to be satisfied.

My main concern was that I'd obviously been getting too greedy, and I really didn't need reports of low nanite hauls making their way up the chain. Especially when all the other teams would be bringing in the same as always. "It's probably just a bad area. Let's move on. I bet the monsters are brimming a little further away from the city."

"No. We're done for today," Turner replied. "Let's head back to base camp and see what they have to say about what we've brought in. Then we'll have a look over the map and make a better plan for tomorrow."

"The sun's barely halfway to the horizon and you just said we had a quota to meet. It's not gonna look good if we head back now, is it?" I tried to keep my contempt for him from my voice, but by his offended expression, I'd failed.

"The day you're Sergeant is the day you can make that call, *Specialist* Oshbob. Maybe in a few hundred years?" he sneered.

"Yeah. Shut up, Oshie," Maddock groaned. "We've got Aska to get drowning in."

"The Aska will still be there in a few more hours, and if we do this, the first two are on me. You'll just need to drink faster." I spun on Turner and held out a warning finger to stop him from snapping at me. "If we don't meet our quota, there'll be questions asked. Those questions will be asked of you. You joke about the fact that I'll never be promoted past Specialist and you're right—I know how the higher ups work. So I know that a Sergeant on probation is gonna take a lot of heat. We're fit, we're healthy, and we're already here. Let's make the damn quota and save ourselves a whole load of heartache."

I wasn't exactly sure of Turner's story, but I knew that he didn't want to be in our dead-end little unit and that he'd had some difficulties which had put him here. All of those thoughts seemed to be passing over his face after my words.

"And you're buying drinks?" Maddock asked.

I looked back at him. "Yeah, first two on me, and I'll even pick your body up off the floor and dump it in your bed when you pass out."

Empire of Oshbob

"Mine too?" Private Gomez asked.

He was new, but he was handy, and he'd survived the longest of the newest privates. As much as I liked to be in a strong team, it was good to see humans being used as cannon fodder too. It made what orcs had to suffer a little more bearable. We weren't as alone at the bottom as I'd once thought.

"Sure," I agreed. "But I'm not buying you drinks until you're at least a Specialist."

Gomez beamed. "I'll get there and that's a promise. There's an eighty percent success rate if you make it past the first six months."

"Somebody should tell Andy that," Maddock said, pointing at our dead teammate.

"He only survived this long because he was a good runner," Gomez said. "He just ran the wrong way this time. May the gods of blood and chrome bless his soul."

I slapped Gomez on the shoulder, feeling a rare surge of pity for the man. "Tell you what, runt, if Turner chooses to continue, your first one's on me tonight. I'm feeling generous."

"You're serious?" he asked, jumping up, eyes wide.

Maddock started braying like a clapped-out generator. "Oshbob! You sappy bitch. That's the first time I've seen you shout a private around in the three years I've known you."

"Will you lot just shut it and get back to the AV," Turner snapped.

Maddock chuckled some more, and even Gomez risked a small laugh.

"I'll give Specialist Jacobs a hand with Andy's body," I replied, then headed over to our team's medic, nanite extractor, and covering fire extraordinaire.

He was crouched down next to the body of Andy, setting up the Vac-coff. It wasn't exactly a dignified way to go, but it meant that the body could be given an honorable send off.

I crouched down next to him. "Need a hand?"

"Sure. Just line the nozzle up with his hips for me."

I did as instructed, while he entered a code into the control panel of the meter-long metal box. A motor whirred and Andy's corpse was slowly sucked into the wide nozzle, bones, and all. Inside, it was thoroughly dehydrated and compressed to reduce the size and weight for ease of transport. Clear water flowed out of a weep hole at the side of the box nearest me. As always, I was amazed by how much water a body contained.

While the noisy contraption worked, Jacobs looked over with a sad smile. "I know what you're doing."

I fought to keep the annoyance from my face and my voice. I'd suspected he might be on to me, and after so long farming nanites under his nose, I supposed the only real surprise was that it had taken this long to notice.

"What's your plan with the knowledge?" I asked quietly.

I didn't need to add any threat to my words. I rarely resorted to violence with the other soldiers; I just wanted to do my time and get out of here. But both Jacobs and Maddock knew what I was capable of. They'd both joined the squad after me as Privates, and they'd seen the two unavoidable altercations I'd been involved in. They'd also seen me in all manner of battles with the beasts we hunted.

"Don't worry, Osh. I won't tell no one. Just figure you might need a hand. I reckon it must be lucrative, and well, I'll be leaving in a couple of years. If I survive that long. I could do with a little side hustle, make sure I have something worthwhile to go out to?"

"You got family outside you need to support?" I asked gently, though it was more for my own leverage than any consideration for him.

Disappointingly, he shook his head. "Not much in the way of prospects, either. You know my story. Taken in as a street kid."

I nodded. But I didn't know his story. If he'd told me, I hadn't listened. The woes and hardships of the constantly complaining humans only ever found deaf ears with me. But now that Jacobs was a threat, I had to listen.

"Figured I'd go the merc route if I'm honest, but even that's gonna need some creds. Decent gear doesn't buy itself," he said.

I rubbed at my chin and side-eyed the man. "There's not much you can do with the harvesting. But you keep quiet and distract the others on occasion, might be I can cut you in on some of the profits and even sort some work out for you on the outside."

That brought a snort from him. "You can sort work out for me? How? This through your nanite selling connections?"

Empire of Oshbob

"You could say that," I agreed. No one knew anything about my life outside, and I liked to keep it that way. While anyone from Portolans or around the adjoining neighborhoods would have heard of me, Artem was a very big place.

"Sure, then. I won't say no to a fix-up on leaving."

"Done deal then," I said, extending my fist toward him. He bumped it discreetly with his own and I spoke again. "I'm going to have to ease up on collection for a little while with us low on the quota. The nanite extractor vials I use are one shot deals. If I don't fill them up, I can't use them again, and I don't like wasting space."

"Understood," he replied. He looked about to say more, but the noise the Vac-coff provided as cover cut out. Its work complete with Private Andy's remains neatly packed.

"Let me get that," I said, sweeping up the disconcertingly light case from the puddle of water, ready to be stowed on the AV.

Kevin Sinclair

Partition 2

"There's a new sighting come in a few kilometers east," Turner barked from the front of the AV. "I've told command that we'll do them a favor and go deal with it."

His expression was stern as he quickly turned back to the pilot's cabin, avoiding eye contact with me in particular.

Once he was gone, the engines roared to life and we lifted smoothly into the sky. At least the AV's were well maintained, I thought, as I applied the cleaning and lubricating fluid meant for our weapons to my knee joint. After each application, it eased up, until it was moving freely again.

"Wanker," Maddock grumbled once he was certain Turner couldn't hear. "Hard to bullshit your way out of a low quota when all your men are willing to keep hunting."

"He's a funny one," Jacobs added. "Can't work him out yet, but I'm not convinced he'll last with us. Especially with Oshbob giving him palpitations every mission."

"He talks like a corpo," Gomez offered, to which we all nodded silently. I wondered if anyone who wasn't gainfully employed by a corporation had anything positive to say about them.

We all fell into amiable silence for the rest of the flight, checking and reloading our guns where necessary.

After around ten minutes, Sergeant Turner came back out of the pilot's cabin. "Rael is bringing us down now. Prep up and get ready to move. We've got a C rank to deal with."

"Is Rael coming out with us, seeing as we lost Andy?" Maddock asked cheekily.

Turner gave him the sour look his comment deserved before donning his helmet. Our pilots never left the AV's, and I wouldn't want them to either. If they went down, we were stranded.

"What's the point in hunting a C rank again?" Gomez asked. "We got next to nothing from the last one."

Empire of Oshbob

"I'm sure this one will be full of nanites," Jacobs answered, taking a few steadying steps as we hit turbulence on our descent. Gomez didn't look too enthused, but nodded acceptance.

We came down in another small town, and through the viewing port, we saw the beast immediately. It was half in, half out of an old storage barn. Its back end looked canine in shape. Most likely a mutated wolf or fox, and judging from its frame in the doorway, I estimated it to be around three meters tall.

Rael brought us down on the opposite side of town, and Turner set out a plan to take it out. At this point, I really wasn't sure why he bothered. I always worked on instinct, and so far, it had kept me alive. Maddock, technically my superior, though he'd been promoted above me a year ago, also preferred to work on my instinct too. Jacobs tried to follow orders, but he was coming around to my way of thinking as well.

"Maddock, Gomez. You get up on that building to the right of the road. Make sure you have clear line of sight of the street and the barn. I'll take position there," he said, pointing to a well-ruined tower bus, four floors high, that sat in the middle of the road, not far from where we stood. "I'll keep eyes on the whole playing field to give orders. Jacobs, Oshbob, you go up on the left buildings. Again, you need eyes on the road at all times."

"Sergeant," I said forcefully. "With all due respect, I am not built for derelict building gymnastics. I probably weigh the same as you four put together, and I include Maddock in that, and this leg has five Dexterity."

He looked shocked. "They gave you a leg with five Dexterity?"

"No. It's supposed to be ten, but my own leg is a seven, so I have something to compare it to. Trust me when I say it's no good to go up there."

Maddock chuckled. "Poor old Oshie, scared of heights."

I side-eyed him, which made him laugh all the more.

He held his hands up in mock defense and grinned at Turner. "Unless you want to make sure Specialist Oshbob doesn't make it back alive, you should probably put him on the street again."

Turner's face flushed slightly with anger as his plan was changed. "Okay. Go down the street, but we go slow and steady. No stupidity or heroics. And when we get back, you need that leg sorted out properly. If we hit quota from this, I'll bring up a new leg for you."

I maintained a neutral expression, but I was truly shocked that he made the offer to help with my leg issue. I was a long way from trusting the bastard, and even further from liking him, but this was a hell of an improvement.

"That would be appreciated," I replied with a short nod of my head.

With that said, everyone moved into position. I headed to the first decent cover—an overgrown bus stop—and waited for the others.

Soon I was moving down the street again, keeping to cover, but moving as swiftly as I could without drawing attention to myself. I wanted this over, because like everyone else, I didn't want to be here either. I just couldn't risk eyes on us for the wrong reasons.

Once I was in range of the shed, Turner told me to halt so I did as I was instructed, with the addition of a hurled frag grenade into the gaping hole in the roof to speed things up a little. "Grenade!" I shouted as it disappeared from sight.

Turner was already shouting at me as the grenade exploded and the creature howled in pain and anger. Then it leapt up, taking what was left of the storage shed with it. Which shouldn't have been possible.

As splintered wood and rusty metal was sent airborne, I was already backing off quickly. Something definitely wasn't right.

"It's a grower!" Maddock shouted from his position on the roof. "B rank at least!"

"Back!" Turner screamed. "We're not equipped for this."

As the dust and debris settled, the huge beast, which was undoubtedly wolf in origin, now laid eyes on me. Big, yellow, slitted pupils watched me with pure malice. It must have been closer to six meters in height now from its sudden growth spurt.

What was most concerning was that the grenade had hardly caused any damage at all apart from a painful-looking gash to its right shoulder and a cut to its face.

I decided there was nothing else for it and committed to a course of action I didn't take very often. I turned and ran as fast as my legs would carry me, scanning the street for some kind of escape option. Nothing called out to me as worth the risk, but

Empire of Oshbob

Maddock, Gomez, Turner, and Jacobs all thankfully opened fire on my pursuer.

It was a brave move, for the damn thing could easily leap on top of the two-story buildings if it had a mind to. Lucky for them, it only had eyes for my slow ass.

Desperate, I pulled out a stim and jabbed it into my torso in the hopes it would provide a boost of speed. Now I could hear the blood beating in my ears, as well as the snarling that was steadily growing in volume behind me.

Getting caught seemed inevitable, so I snatched another grenade from my jacket, pulled the pin, and tossed it a meter or so in front of me. Two seconds later, I was past it, and five seconds later, the monster wolf was over it.

I was catapulted forward from the force of the blast, and thudded into the ground a few meters further on. My back had been mostly protected from injury by the body armor I wore.

Rolling over, I looked back through the cloud of dust and debris, The wolf, somehow, was still on its feet. The shadow of it was moving toward me, though more slowly than before. Wriggling around, I managed to bring my plasma rifle around, and from my spot on the floor, I opened fire, joining my friends as they continued to rain down pain on it.

When it emerged from the aftermath of the explosion, it was in a bad way. Its guts hung out from its belly, and it limped badly as it was eviscerated from the sides, but it still made one last concerted effort to lunge at me. Despite only having half a face left, its jaws still worked incredibly well. I pushed the rifle into its open maw, and it chomped down on both it *and* my arm, crushing metal and motors as its jaw tightened. With my free hand, I managed to get my hand cannon free and raised it to point directly in its remaining eye and into its brain.

It was weakened, but still, it didn't die. Not until Maddock appeared at my side and hacked into its neck with his plasma sword. A gout of hot blood covered me and the wolf's incredibly heavy body fell on top of me.

Maddock knelt down by my head, a huge grin on his face. "You can keep your C rank pig story, Oshie. I've got a better one now."

Kevin Sinclair

Partition 3

"He's only got a fucking promotion," Maddock ranted, slamming down his beer. "Didn't even want to fucking go, and did sweet fuck-all to kill the damn thing. Yet that weasel bastard gets a commendation and a promotion."

I shrugged, leaning back on the only sofa in the barracks capable of taking my weight.

"Glad he's off our team," Gomez replied. "No time for him."

"But better the specter you know," Jacobs grumbled. "Who's gonna take over now?"

"They might give it to Maddock?" Gomez suggested hopefully.

"I got too many disciplinaries. We'll probably get another buy-in, low-level, corpo tosspot looking for some easy ranks and combat time behind the safety of a trustworthy team."

"Can't believe we'd ever be called trustworthy," I finally chimed in. "But you're probably right. Merit's worth about as much as a goblin hand-job."

They all laughed at that, before Maddock clapped his hands together loudly. "Come on then, you miserable bastards, let's get to the club. Oshie still owes me two Askas."

We drank heavily in bitter honor of Turner's undeserved promotion. As the base bar closed, I helped Maddock and Gomez to bed as promised, then headed outside and around to the back of our quarters with a dwarven cigar.

My time back in the military had done very little to ease my hatred of humans and elves, despite the select few humans I tolerated well. But in all my time stuck here, I'd not seen a single dwarf. Which was a shame because they made the best cigars and booze.

At the rear of our quarters were a few old tires that had served as a comfortable seat for over a year now. I eased myself on them, lit the cigar and lay back to wait for Leo's drone.

Empire of Oshbob

"See. I told you he'd be here," a nasally voice said.

I turned slowly toward the direction it came from. Five silhouettes were walking toward me. I assumed they were all human at first, but I caught the faint woody smell of an elf that passed even through the floral soap they smothered themselves in. I eyed the group more carefully now.

They finally stepped into the light of the nearest flood light. I took another long drag from my cigar, then turned to look up at the moon again. Attacks weren't uncommon on base, and high-ranking officers against an orc would be quickly swept under the rug. Unless, of course, that orc caused any noticeable damage.

"What you doing out here?" one of them snapped. He was an officer, but I didn't recognize him as being in my unit's chain of command.

I waved the cigar at him in answer.

"You'll speak when you're spoken to, green skin."

"Smoking my cigar," I drawled.

"Smoking my cigar, SIR!" he snapped again.

"Sure," I replied and took another drag, before adding, "Sir."

"We've had reports of you coming out here every night and of a drone coming to meet you on occasion. There have also been reports of tech going missing. What are you sending out from here?"

While I did come out every night, the drone only came to me once a week, so someone had been filling him full of bullshit. "I come out here every night to smoke my victory cigar for surviving another day. A drone comes once a week to deliver my new supply."

"Expensive habit for a specialist," he snapped. "And against regulations. Are you not familiar with barracks rules?"

I nodded slowly. "Sure I am. For a while, I even abided by them until I realized no one else was. Officers and privates alike. You'd be amazed at some of the things I've seen getting delivered to base. Some really filthy stuff too. Especially among the officers. Lower ranks normally just stick to the booze and drugs, sir."

"What are you implying?" There was a dangerous tone in his voice.

I shook my head, a wry grin forming on my face. "What are you implying, sir? You want me to stop my *one* vice? My cigars?"

He eyed me suspiciously. "I can smell a great deal of alcohol on you, so it's hardly your one vice."

"Gods above. You're counting alcohol as vice now? Honestly, if you'd seen the things I'd seen with these reconnaissance optics I've got, which record everything I want them to," I added, my words loaded with meaning, "you'd get so drunk you wouldn't come up for air for ten years."

He bristled at my words, and so did the others.

"Is that some sort of a threat, orc?" the elf on his shoulder asked.

I met his eyes and smiled. "Why? Guilty conscience?" As he bristled, I took another drag.

"I'll see you court martialed for that!"

"What for? The cigars?" I asked innocently.

"At the very least," the high-ranking human answered. "Are you expecting a shipment of cigars this evening?"

"Could be."

"And they come at midnight, is that correct?"

"I wish. My supplier's not that efficient. Could be sitting here for hours yet, or it might not even be tonight. I lose track."

"It's almost midnight, we'll wait and inspect the contraband as it arrives."

"If you want cigars, just ask. I can always have more delivered. Creds up front, though."

"You think we need a stinking orc to provide our luxuries?" the elf scoffed.

"Fine by me. I don't much like doing business with elves, either. If you think I stink now, I feel so dirty after these dealings that I need a hot shower for my soul afterward."

"You dare!"

"Dare?" I asked curiously.

"You insult the elven race!" he said, reaching for his gun. "I demand honor!"

"You insulted the orc race first. You sure you want to go down this path?" I asked, hopping down from the tire seat.

"He does not," the human said, before spinning on the elf. "Dueling with a specialist? One with a broken arm, and an orc too! What honor do you expect to earn from such an encounter?

Empire of Oshbob

They're animals. Would you be insulted at a dog for barking at you?"

The other elf laughed, and turned his relieved eyes on me as he re-holstered his pistol. "You are lucky today, dog."

I took another puff and finished the cigar. I flicked it at the ground between us. "If you don't want cigars and you don't want to have me tried for admitting to receiving cigars, then it's past my bedtime. Excuse me, sirs."

The elf—a lieutenant, I realized as I passed—didn't even try to stop me. I imagined the threat of the things I'd seen with my recording optics was all too worrying for him. While Artem Military was as corrupt as anywhere else in the city, it still needed rules, and even well-thought-of officers had fallen foul of those rules on occasion.

He would more likely arrange an accident for me. It wouldn't be the first time someone had tried to get me out of the military. I'd just have to be on my guard for a few weeks.

I chuckled to myself as I closed the barracks door behind me. If they did wait for the drone, they were going to be disappointed. I'd had an extension installed on my keystone which allowed me to contact Leo. Just short messages and only one way; otherwise, they could be tracked, but I'd been able to put him off for this evening's delivery.

I eased myself on to the bed, troubled but pleased I'd evaded whatever trap those fuckers had in store for me.

I awoke with a shoulder shake. It was Jacobs. He never got as drunk as the others, and was always up first.

"Captain Arite wants you up at his office now." His expression was one of worry, which in turn worried me, especially after last night's midnight meeting.

"Do you know what he wants?"

Jacobs shook his head. "Just got a message for you to go up immediately."

That wasn't good. I pushed myself up awkwardly from the bed, overbalancing a little with my seized-up leg-mod and my mangled arm, then quickly got dressed.

Captain Arite was our commanding officer on the huge city base. Another human, which in all fairness was better than an elf, but he still didn't like me and had passed me up for promotion after promotion, despite my achievements and willingness to learn and take all training courses. Admittedly, because it would be easier to ship nanites off the base the higher the rank I was rather than any desire to excel in the military.

I knocked on his office door, fearing the worst, so I was taken aback by his jovial greeting as I entered.

"Oshbob! Good to see you. I've two things to discuss with you."

"Okay, captain," I replied, completely wrong-footed, but trying not to show it.

"First thing. Despite Turner's general loathing of you, he actually spoke highly of your part to play in killing the B rank wolf." He stopped for a moment to look down at his Datapad, and began reading a statement from Sergeant Turner. "If not for the bravery of Specialist Oshbob's in drawing the attack, and Corporal Maddock's well-placed plasma sword attack, I would never have been able to take the killing shot."

Arite looked up to me with a broad smile. "He also said you were unruly and difficult to command, but he feels that in his short time in charge of your unit that he's managed to make you almost civilized and recommended you for a promotion to corporal. So, congratulations. You are now a corporal."

I stared blankly at him, still trying to process the information. When Maddock had been made up over me, I'd lost all hope of going further. Along with the trouble I'd encountered last night, I was expecting to be demoted if anything.

Arite continued talking, which served me well as I recovered from the bombshell.

"Which means, when you go and get that arm fixed, you can pick from the Tier Three arm mods.

I nodded, more relieved at being able to choose from a higher Tier mod going forward. That would increase my survivability by a wide margin. I hoped I could swing a new leg while I was on, but I left that request unspoken for now. What I was most curious about was how my promotion would work.

"Two corporals in one squad. How does that work? Is Maddock getting a promotion too? Are you gonna let him lead?"

Arite laughed. "Good gods, no. I think Maddock has reached the pinnacle of his military ambitions. There will be a new sergeant installed along with two fresh new privates to train up."

"I see," I replied shortly, wondering where this was going. To his credit, he didn't keep me hanging on the hook for too long.

"That does lead me nicely to my second point. You…" he said, then looked out the window of his office, before lowering his voice, "…are an orc. And while I'm indifferent to your race, I'm in a minority. You're being watched by the wrong people and they want you moved on."

"The men last night?" I asked, already knowing the answer. "Why were they snooping around?"

"Don't ask me. I've told them you've been a solid soldier for us." He scratched his head looking uncomfortable. "Could just be that you're an orc. Lots of the higher ups have tight links with the corporations that sponsor the military. Most of them have second jobs in the corporations themselves. So who knows what their real motives are. I'm pretty sure MCorp would banish all orcs and goblins from the city, full stop."

I blew out my cheeks in a long, disappointed sigh. "Where am I going?"

His brow wrinkled as he pretended to need to look at his Datapad again. "An outpost. One of the wild bases. Don't know the exact Base designation, which means it's a classified one."

My eyebrow raised as my heart sank. "Lots of A Rankers out there. I thought only APS messed about that far out."

"APS and some elite units." He cringed as he said the last words.

"You mean expendable," I growled low and slow. "Let's not beat about the bush. The promotion is a joke. This is a death sentence."

"Well, Oshbob. That's up to you, isn't it?"

"No. It's up to whatever arsehole I'll have commanding me. And if they're anything like Turner, they'll be well away from the fighting. Maddock finished that fucking B rank. I doubt Turner's ever finished a full plate of food."

He grinned at that. "I thought as much." Then he shrugged, a serious expression returning to his face. "For what it's worth, I'm sorry. I hear your concerns, but my hands are tied. Go get your arm and choose a good one. It might help. Then go say your goodbyes—you're shipping out tonight."

Partition 4

As Captain Arite had suggested, I headed straight to the Military Carver. He was stationed in the same building, so it was worth getting it seen to immediately. The carver was a grizzled human. He may have even had a little dwarf somewhere in his genetics considering how broad and hairy he was.

He eyed me speculatively as I entered. "Orc! It's been a while, hasn't it? I expected you to be trashing mods weekly."

"Is that why you fitted this cheap shit on me?"

He chuckled and rubbed his belly. He thought it was so funny. "Didn't think you'd notice. There's a reason the insult 'orc brains' exists."

"There's a reason everyone is secretly terrified of us as well."

"Aye, there's truth in that. Come on in, then. I've been feeling bad about the shit I tacked on you last time. You've done well here, and I've heard about the bullshit they're pulling on you." He lowered his voice. "And thanks for those mods you got for my kid. Damn military wouldn't do shit for me, but with that new liver, there's no stopping my youngest now. He's apprenticed at MCorp believe it or not. Could make something of 'imself yet."

"Glad I could help," I grumbled, still reeling from the changes ahead. "Can you sort this leg out for me too?"

He winked, sidelong. "I'm not supposed to change anything not busted, but let's have a look at it and we'll see what we can do, eh? You can have a look through the arm stock I've got available for you and choose while I pull up some leg-mods you can swap out for."

"When you say, *'available for you'*, you mean specifically me, don't you?"

He adopted a sheepish expression. "That there is a list of the worst Tier Threes I could find to show you. Orders from above. You get me?"

"I'd expect nothing less."

Kevin Sinclair

The first one listed filled me with despair at what was to come:

Full Arm (Right)	Tier: Three
The Mil-Co Hammer is a mainstay in mods designed for those with a rugged lifestyle. Falling rubble, stray ballistic shots, or a need to make a beautifully shaped dent in a variety of substrates, the Mil-Co Hammer is the arm for you. Strength: 15 Dexterity: 6	
Durability: 100/100	Slot Cost: 3

The second one was no better.

Full Arm (Right)	Tier: Three
The Mil-Co, Special Edition: *Crane Operator* provides a full range of upper arm motion and with incredible grip strength. (Mil-Co accepts no responsibility for arm failure prior to grip failure) Strength: 15 (Hand: 18) Dexterity: 4	
Durability: 96/100	Slot Cost: 3

"These are awful. You know I had a Tier Three before I was brought here, right?"

He smirked. "Keep reading."

I sighed.

Full Arm (Right)	Tier: Three

20

Empire of Oshbob

The Takemoto Multi. When your work and life demand the best, over enhancing any single attribute is a short trip to failure. The Takemoto Multi provides ability across the board. Strength: 14 Dexterity: 14	
Durability: 96/100	Slot Cost: 3

I ogled at the stats. I wouldn't even know what to do with that much dexterity. I wondered how it would affect my accuracy with a rifle first and foremost. "Is there any point reading on?"

He gave an imperceptible shake of his head, then replied, "That's up to you. If you see a winner, then go for it."

Accepting that not looking at the other four options on the list would be foolish, I wasn't surprised to find that they were all truly terrible.

"Wow. You weren't lying, were you? There's some real shit here. How is it even classed as Tier Three?"

"No idea. Somebody must be fudging the documentation."

I flicked back through them. "Gimme three."

He nodded. "Best of a bad bunch, I reckon. I can give you the leg to match?" He gave me a little wink.

"I suppose so," I replied, feigning dejection.

As I lay back on the table, I made a mental note. *Rare acts of kindness to people with a little power can pay off!* I couldn't even remember why I'd offered to source and supply a new liver for him last time I was in here. I didn't have much time to mull over the act as the anesthetic kicked in.

Coming around fuzzy headed, I knew the work had been done, and done well as I could hardly feel any pain around the attachment site. I accessed my keystone and brought up the stats.

Identification: Oshbob				
Species: Orc		Bonus: None	
Mod Capacity: 26		Mod Capacity in use: 8	
Stat	Current	Description	Mods	Quality

Kevin Sinclair

	Points			
Dexterity	6	Governs agility and movement.	Right Leg Cost: 3 Strength: (14) Dexterity: (14) Right Arm: Cost: 3 Strength: (14) Dexterity: (14)	Tier-3 (Professional) Tier-3 (Professional)
Mental Power	11	Governs swiftness and fortitude of the mind		
Perception	9	Governs an individual's senses and connection to the world around them.	Altro-Recon Cost: 2 Peception:10	Tier-2 (Basic)
Strength	15	Governs physical strength and damage dealt	Right Leg Cost: 3 Strength: (14) Dexterity: (14) Right Arm: Cost: 3	Tier-3 (Professional) Tier-3 (Professional)

Empire of Oshbob

			Strength: (14) Dexterity: (14)	
Toughness	15	Governs the body and internal fortitude		

I'd be unbalanced all to hell with the right-sided Dexterity, but it was a solid upgrade and I'd once proven that I could compensate.

"Thanks, doc," I said, jumping down from the table. "Sounds like I'm heading into the shit, but this is gonna help a lot."

"Go easy on them for a few days if you can. Don't want you sprinting off and having to come back in for facial reconstruction. Though… it might improve things."

"I'm sure it would," I replied back as I headed for the door. "But I got over any shame I was made to feel over my race a long time ago."

He chuckled at what he thought must be a joke, and I headed out of the door.

Our quarters were empty when I returned, and from what was missing, they hadn't just gone for dinner. There were only three of our squad left with Turner gone and me out of action. They couldn't have sent them back out already, could they? Or had they already had replacements lined up.

What does it matter? I thought to myself. *Not as if they're true family. Just people I've been stuck with.*

Yet it hurt. We'd been close. Maddock had been an utter arsehole from the start, but he didn't care that I was an orc. He was equally obnoxious to everyone he met. Jacobs was reserved, but he was solid and reliable, and he'd never caused me any issues. Hell, even the new guy Gomez only looked at me with fear and respect. I growled to myself as I thumped down on my bed for the last time.

How was it that I kept making bonds with human scum? Even both my hackers, Leo and Meli, were human. Asala was human!

Kevin Sinclair

I'd protect them all to the death, I knew I could trust all three as much as I could trust anyone. But it was hard. For as many humans that I liked, there were a hundred behind them ready to throw a slur, or see me and my kin burn. At least elves kept it simple. They never gave me reason to like them. Every meeting reaffirmed the stereotypes about them.

I pushed the pointless thoughts down and sent Leo a message to explain what was happening.

> They're moving me to another base. Its destination is classified, so I'll let you know once I'm there.

Leo couldn't reply, or it would be picked up. But a short, outward bound message from me would never be caught.

With that done, I moved to my locker and grabbed my kit bag, filling it with almost everything I owned here. Then I dumped it on the bed and wandered over to the kitchen. Leaning down to the refrigerator, I opened the bottom drawer filled with beer and slid it all the way out, crouching to cover my movements.

With a swift yank, I detached the small lock box from the back of the drawer, marveling at the increased Dexterity with which I'd completed the task. Then I slid it up my long sleeve where it stuck to the magnet embedded there. Finally, I pulled out a beer, and with a flick of my new thumb, I discarded the cap and drained it in one.

Throwing the empty into the sink, I grabbed another four and headed back out to sit on my favorite couch. There, I drank them slowly, hoping to see the guys before I left, but knowing full well that whoever had set this up wouldn't allow me that luxury.

I didn't know who was involved yet, but I would find out sooner or later, and they'd go on the ledger in my mind, reserved for those who had crossed me. It could be a few weeks, it could be twenty years, but for as long as I was alive, I'd see to it that everyone on that list would pay.

Some might call it petty. But not me, an orc had to have a hobby.

Empire of Oshbob

Partition 5

It was a long flight to the wild base and our aircraft was tiny. Up front there was a pilot and co-pilot—otherwise known as a guard even though this was just a transport mission for a respected soldier. In the hold, because that's what it was, there was me. Crammed into the tight space with a flap down seat designed for someone far smaller and far lighter than me.

None of this made my disposition any happier and I silently seething at the turnaround. At how I hadn't gotten to see any of my unit before leaving.

Something was amiss for me to be yanked away so suddenly and I had no doubt elves would be at the heart of it.

When the pilot's voice came over the speaker I was pulled out of my blood and revenge filled overthinking loop.

"We're coming into Base 317. Get ready to disembark, corporal. We're touching down and taking off. That's all."

I continued to sit in silence, I had all my gear with me, and nothing else to do until I landed. This ship didn't even have a viewing screen, which again, I suspected was intentional. At that thought, I moved over to the door separating me from the pilot's cabin, and peered through the narrow visor to see if I could get an idea where I was headed.

My new home slowly came into focus: a disk at least a kilometer wide, suspended on six giant legs of steel. Those legs were in turn surrounded by a hefty reinforced concrete wall, covered in electrified mesh.

I scanned the layout as we made the final descent and committed what I could to memory. At the very center of the disk stood a huge central command building with multiple smaller buildings tightly clustered all around it. After that were long, wide hangers that stored the assortment of ships and Aerial Vehicles the soldiers here would use.

Next came a ring of clear space, wide enough for those ships to take off from and for soldiers to carry out drills, as evidenced by the units currently doing drills. Finally, came the accommodation. It was easy to spot. Long rows of huts formed the outer rim.

I returned my attention back to the formed-up soldiers in the bare space, and my attention snagged on a team of APS soldiers marching out from a heavily armored AV. It was my first time seeing a unit of them in real life. I'd seen the suits, and I'd seen the videos of them in action, but there generally wasn't any need for them to come into the city.

They marched in step heading for one of the hangers, and then my vision was obstructed by the co-pilot's body. I stepped back as the craft touched down.

The pilot's cabin door opened a moment later. "Off you get then, corporal. Enjoy your new home.

The statement was delivered flat and emotionless, and though I couldn't sense any malice or even sarcasm as he spoke, I couldn't help feeling, I wasn't going to enjoy my new home at all.

As I walked down the ramp into the dry, warm evening air, I was immediately accosted by a tall, broad human with a voice almost as coarse as my own. On his sleeve, he wore the crossed rifles of a captain's insignia.

"Corporal Oshbob! Welcome to Outpost 361," he announced. "Don't get many full-blood orcs with that kind of rank. In fact, I think you're the first one I've heard of."

I offered a respectful salute in an effort to start things off on a positive note. Two years left. Only two years left.

I regretted the effort moments later as his mouth opened again.

"I suppose you think that makes you special? Well it doesn't. Out here, you're a piece of shit. A corporal in a Scrub Team is worth about as much as a fresh-faced private just out of his basic training anywhere else. Your job will be to mop up anything the APS don't take out. They're the business end of the deal here. Don't get in their way. Don't talk to them."

I raised an unimpressed eyebrow at his delivery of my new station, but he neither noticed nor cared as he continued.

"Stay in your quarters until you're called over the PA. There's a kitchen in your quarters. Supplies are delivered once a week. Your new teammates know the script." He pointed past me. "Barrack 16.

Empire of Oshbob

If I see you again, it's probably because you did something wrong. Don't let me see you again. We don't tolerate no dumb shit here. You understand, orc?

I eyed him and remained silent.

"DO YOU UNDERSTAND ME, ORC!" he yelled in my face.

"I worked hard to reach corporal. While military code allows a certain amount of freedom with how you address privates, you *will* address me as Corporal Oshbob, or I will report you to our superiors. *Sir.*"

He laughed, long and hard. It took a moment for him to speak again. "Oh, I think I'm gonna like you, orc. You're real fucking funny." His voice suddenly accelerated, and increased in volume again. "You wanna wind up dead before your first assignment, you keep up with the attitude. I pop out tougher shits than you on a daily basis, and even though I've got more respect for them than I do you, I still have no qualms in flushing them."

I nodded as he spoke, then replied calmly. "At this moment, *I* have more respect for your shits than I do for you. Show some professionalism, captain."

His face reddened—my favorite color for human faces. His mouth opened and closed a few times, and while he tried to come up with a fitting response, I turned and started walking away to barrack 16.

"Don't you walk away from me until you're dismissed, orc! I'll have you court martialed."

I turned and grimaced. "I'm only going to say this once: people always underestimate me. But the first thing I did when I was brought back into the military was to learn all of the rules. More than that, I took the effort to *understand* them. Sure, there are rules that can be bent and rules that can be broken. But it doesn't matter which major city barracks or outpost we're at; one of the most basic and readily enforced rules is that rank must be acknowledged.

"So, until you recognize my hard earned rank and use it accordingly, I don't recognize your authority as a commanding officer. I expected to meet a lot of people like you as I progressed through the military, so while my optics are poor for most things, what they can do is record. If you wish to pursue this overly aggressive method of putting me in my place, then by all means do. But when it comes to actual repercussions for me for ignoring everything you say, the recording of this conversation will be replayed in its entirety, and your lack of due respect will be taken into account."

My optics didn't really record, but it was one of my favorite lines. Especially the reaction of superior officers when I told them. Except, the captain, who hadn't even bothered himself to introduce himself yet, didn't react as usual.

"This is a top-secret base, corporal. You'll need to have those removed if they're capable of recording potentially sensitive information. I will send one of our base's carvers over to see you."

It wasn't lost on me that he'd slipped in corporal. "Don't bother. The eyes don't record. Standard Milco recons at Tier-Two, x5 zoom and thermal imaging. That's it. You can check my records if you like. All my mods are military issue."

"So not just an orc, but a bullshitter too? Looks like I'll have to keep my eye on you after all." He spun on his heel, then stalked off toward the command buildings in the center.

I watched him go for a moment, and nodded. That didn't work out too badly after all. Now to check out my new home.

It was well lived in, and nowhere near as clean as the quarters I'd just come from. There was also a very strong, very familiar scent. orcs. If not for the vague, less pungent scent of human, I would have suspected this was another death sentence. It could still be, but as I lay on the one unused bed of the eight, my mind began to work over the situation and it hit me. Half-orcs. Perfect for dangerous work, but too respected to be used as Deaters.

After stowing my meager possessions in the cabinet by the bed, I sent another message to Leo.

> I'm at a place called Outpost 361. It's damn hot, so North. Don't bring a Drone into the base. It's high security. See what you can find on the people here.

With that done, I napped for a while. I wanted to be alert for when my new teammates arrived. With half-orcs, I expected it would need an indelicate touch.

Raucous shouting and cursing woke me up. The door swung open a moment later, slamming against the bed behind the door. A strong, sharp-eyed half-orc strode in. He was a sergeant, which surprised me, but also gave me a little hope. His eyes fell on me immediately.

"Well, well, well. What have we got here gang? Looks like a full-blood dumb-dumb." He marched eagerly toward me, and loomed over my bed.

Five other orcs came marching in behind him all looking equally eager to roast the new guy. I remained where I was, looking more relaxed than I felt.

"So they think they can just send some city soldier out here as a corporal in my unit, do they? Well I've got news for you. My guys here have all proven what they can do. They follow orders from me and me alone. As far as we're concerned, you're another private coming in from the bottom."

"I'm a corporal. I'll follow your commands within reason, but you won't be treating me as anything other than my rank demands."

A few of the half-orcs jeered at my words as the sergeant barked again, "I'll treat you however the hell I want to treat you until you've proven you're worthy of better."

I noticed one of the half-orcs behind the sergeant looking awfully pale and not joining in. He clearly recognized me, though I didn't know him.

"Er, Sir," he mumbled. "Maybe not this one for roasting. I think he might do the team good."

"The hell you talking about, Nozz? You know him or something?"

Nozz nodded, reluctantly. "You know how I was telling you I had to leave Portolans when the new gang lord took over?"

The sergeant's head bobbed along, but his eyes remained on me. "Is this one of them that kicked you out for being a half-orc?"

"No. He *is* the gang lord."

The sergeant's eyes narrowed. His head flicked around to Nozz. "Then what's he doing here?"

"You do know I let your people back in?" I asked Nozz as he stammered over his superior's question. "Just had to have a shake up to iron things out."

Nozz nodded. "I heard. When I get the chance to communicate off base, I call home. I still have links with the others. Don told me there was a place for me when I get out?"

"There is," I agreed, then looked back to the furious sergeant, who was staring at Nozz now with undisguised anger.

"What in the ten green hells is this bullshit? Who's this guy supposed to be?"

"You've never heard of Oshbob?" a strong female voice asked from behind the Sergeant.

"Oshbob? What kind of fucking name is that?"

"It's an orc name," I said finally, moving to get to my feet. My new sergeant paled as I now loomed over him.

"God damn," someone further back hissed. "He's as big as I'd heard."

The sergeant tried to stand his ground in front of me, but had to take a few steps back to give me some space. He now looked at me sourly. "If you're such a big deal, why are you here?"

"Have you really not heard the story?" Nozz asked. "About the gang lord of Newton, and the mech suit?"

"The stolen training mech? The one that got busted in a gang war?"

Nozz shook his head and pointed at me. "There was a gang war, but it was Oshbob who fought the mech."

"Must have been a useless mech pilot then," the sergeant said, returning his steely gaze on me. "No way a man can beat a mech."

"Used an EMP, I heard." Nozz said, looking at me for confirmation.

I nodded as the Sergeant continued.

"There you go then! He didn't beat it, did he?" He punctuated the point by poking me in the chest. "And he's no gang lord now. Just another meat shield for the APS."

I put my hand on his shoulder and met his gaze. "We can play nice and we can all get through our service together the easy way, or you can fuck around with me and find out exactly what I am now. I get out of here in two years, so I'm on my best behavior which means, I won't just snap you in half if you push me any further. But I can promise that you won't see the year out."

He surprised me by laughing. "You know the turnover of half-orcs in this unit? If I see the year out, it'll be a bloody miracle.

Your threats mean nothing to me." He bashed my arm away and set himself for trouble.

I nodded thoughtfully. "Fair point. In that case, any family, or friends you have waiting for you outside won't see the year out, and I'll make sure you survive for as long as I'm here."

His eyes widened at those words. He finally didn't know how to respond.

Nozz put his hand on the sergeant's shoulder. "He'll be a good team member, trust me."

That seemed to snap him out of it. Shaking free of the hand, he squared up to me again. "You think you're a real big deal, huh? You don't think I know people outside? You wanna start something, I'll see to it that your family and friends don't make it past the month!"

"Go on then. Set them away and I'll do the same. Do you want recordings of your loved ones' last moments? Might make a good keepsake."

"What?" he asked as if he'd suddenly lost the thread of the conversation.

"I'm sending a coded message to my hackers now. They are very good, and I'd be surprised if there isn't someone paying visits this very night. So you'll have to be quick and tell me if you want the recordings."

"What? I..." After a spluttering attempt at a response, he suddenly came back to his senses and lunged for my throat. "Call them off, you bastard."

I blocked his attack and pivoted on my new leg, using his momentum to throw him on the bed. The bed broke in half.

"You do your job and we won't have no problems, *sergeant*. I'm here to serve out my time and go home. I'm not here for your entertainment. Do you understand?"

He scrambled up as I spoke and resumed a fighting pose. This time, he didn't come after me again.

"Have you got kids?" he asked.

"Are we supposed to be bonding now, or are you fishing for something to use on me?"

"No," he growled. "I just want to know who I'm dealing with. Did you send the message?"

"Not yet. On both counts."

The sergeant let his fists fall. "This didn't go how I expected. We normally rough up the new recruits. It's a bonding thing."

"I can see that. Probably best not to do it to those coming in at corporal level. Though I doubt you would have done it if I wasn't an orc."

He shrugged. "Maybe." He paused, looking thoughtful, then spoke again. "How the hell did you get to be a corporal? I've been serving damn near twenty years, and I only made sergeant last year and that's rare enough."

"Let me guess, you got sent here to be a sergeant?"

His brow wrinkled up as he thought about it. "I take it you just got made up and sent here?"

"You take it right," I replied tiredly.

"We thought they'd make Specialist Theta up to corporal. She's been here longer than me."

"That's because I'm the toughest here," the muscular woman added.

She was as big and as wide across the shoulders as any of the men but one, yet she was undeniably a woman. She wore her long, purple-streaked black hair braided tight against her skull, and a long plait hung down her back almost to her waist. She even had small tusks which weren't always evident in half-orcs.

"You look tough," I replied sincerely, and she beamed a wide smile.

I turned back to the sergeant. "We good, here?"

"You'll leave my family be?"

"You have my word that if you don't cause any trouble for me, your family will be safe from harm. I take no pleasure in having kids killed."

"But you'd still kill them given a reason?"

"Without a second's hesitation. If your actions end up getting me killed, there's a lot of people who I care about, from young to old, who'll suffer. I can't let that happen."

He extended a fist. "I'm Sergeant Umak."

I more than happily bumped it with my own. "Corporal Oshbob."

"You best take Monek's bed. Just swap the frames," he grumbled and made his way to his own bed.

"Drinks?" Nozz suggested.

"You better fucking believe it," Umak replied sitting down heavily.

I dragged the frame over, watched by sad eyes. "So what happened to Monek?" I asked as I swapped the mattresses over.

"Ambush. Arachnid types. About eighty of the bastards, and all of them over a meter tall."

"You kill them all?" I asked.

He shook his head. "About a quarter. APS decided to come back and help us out."

"After deserting us," Nozz said, handing both me and the sergeant an ice-cold beer.

"Deserting you?"

"Aye, they go out for the big stuff. We support them by clearing up around them, but this time, they knew we would be hard pressed when the arachnids ambushed us. But their full team still kept moving after the A Ranker. They and the other Scrub Team could have easily helped, but no, they kept on moving. We ended up pinned down for over an hour until they were finished."

I rolled my neck and groaned contentedly as it clicked a few times. "So they're assholes and they don't mind us losing people."

"Exactly," Nozz said.

Umak fell silent as he replayed the events of the day over his beer. He finally spoke again. "We need to work on defensive formations. We should have done better, and that's on me."

"Bullshit, Sergeant. Them bastards spread us out so we hardly had a chance," a lean, mean yet slightly comical looking half-orc said. He had an odd mouth twitch as he spoke and a shock of white hair that grew straight up, but only in one circular patch on the top of his head. He then looked at me. "I'm Froom by the way. That's Agga," he said, pointing out the biggest of the group next. "Last, and definitely least, is Private Lanris. He's the newest after you and he don't talk too much on account of 'im thinking he's better'n us all."

Lanris cast an irritated look at the white-haired soldier. "Fuck off Froom. I just don't talk shit all the time."

I chuckled at the interaction, though I wasn't in the least bit surprised to hear there were problems with how my new team was treated by the higher ups. I did feel a sense of camaraderie with them as they did the only thing they could do about the unfairness of it all. They sat and drank the rest of the evening away until, one by one, they dropped to sleep.

Partition 6

There seemed to be no impetus to move the next morning. As light streamed through the windows, most of the others groaned, rolled over, or put a pillow over their heads to block out the light. Some did all three.

"Not like the city bases, then," I mused. I was more than happy to lounge a bit longer. The less time spent fighting or stressing about something or other, the better it was for my chances of survival.

Nozz was the first out of his bed. He walked past mine and came to a stop. "You know where the mess hall is, sir?"

"I don't, but I could eat. The captain who welcomed us said to use the kitchen in our barracks."

"That's because he's an asshole. It was Captain Parraway, I assume?"

"Never gave me a name. He was a big human, gruff and irritable."

"Yeah, that's Parraway. Don't get me wrong, they'd love it if we ate in our quarters. That's why we keep getting supplies, but everyone else eats in the mess hall, which means so do we."

"Good enough for me, Nozz. I'm not much of a cook, so lead the way."

The mess hall wasn't in the main building area. It was one of the surrounding long huts given over entirely to feeding soldiers. There were a number of people already eating, and they looked up to scowl at us as we entered.

"Is that just for me?"

"It might be a little spicier than usual, but that kind of greeting is reserved for the entirety of Scrub Team 4."

"That us?" I asked, having never heard the designation before.

"Yep. There're five APS units stationed here, and twelve Scrub Teams. Two Scrub Teams go out every time an APS gets a call for an A Ranker."

We came to the serving station, and our conversation filtered out while I took in the delights. It wasn't half as bad as I expected, with a good range of decent, if synthetic, looking food.

"What do you recommend, Nozz?"

He was interrupted by an announcement over the PA.

Alert. Scrub Teams 3 and 4 report for duty.

As the rattling speaker fell silent, he answered my question as if nothing had happened, "I recommend the eggs, the roasted schmeat, and the mixed roots. The roots are grown in a hydro-farm under the base. You can taste the difference between them and the other stuff."

"Sounds good," I replied, wondering at the lack of urgency to go and report for duty. "Shouldn't we get moving?"

He waved my concern off. "Nah. The APS will sound an alarm for us when we're set to go. We have an hour from that point—plenty of time to get our act together."

I scooped from the dishes he'd suggested, looking forward to the roasted schmeat in particular. It had a gravy that had a rich, savory scent that was about as good as anything I'd inhaled since rejoining the military.

The thought brought a question to mind. "So you said you joined the military after I took over in Portolans, does that mean you have seven years left of service?"

"Closer to six now," he said with a grimace. "They really need to start offering shorter terms of service."

"I hear you there. And they don't like you leaving halfway through for a break." A wry grin split my face as I thought about my return and how lucky I'd been that Harold had intervened.

By the time I was halfway through my pile of food, Umak and the rest of our team came into the canteen, loud and raucous, upsetting the rest of the diners. That brought yet another smile to my face. I'd never get a team of orcs to work with, but I had to admit that this was the next best thing.

They all grabbed plates of food, getting almost exactly what Nozz had suggested to me, before sitting around our table. Theta sat right next to me, shoveling a fork full of food into her mouth before pointing at my plate.

Empire of Oshbob

She at least finished chewing before speaking. "What did you think of the fodder?"

It was just as well she pointed at my plate, or I'd have no idea what she was talking about. "It's good. Better than the last base."

She nodded as if she'd won a personal victory and dove back into the meal, eating quickly but not in any great panic despite the call to report as the second call blared out across the PA:

Scrub Teams 3 and 4, fifteen minutes remaining to report for duty.

With a large belch, Umak slid his empty plate away from him. "Time to go."

I followed them out of the mess hall and across the yard to where one of the chunky AV's stood on retractable footpads. We headed straight past it and into the hangar where six APS in their mighty, beige-colored mech suits were checking their weapons.

Umak led us right to the back of the hangar, to a room filled with lockers and pegs. Umak pointed to a large locker with the number two on it. "That's yours, Corporal Oshbob."

I headed directly over and opened it with slight hesitation. Inside was a set of dark gray full-body armor that looked like it would fit me perfectly. I first picked up the helmet; its reflective glass visor was down. It had a different design from the ones I was accustomed to, seeming more durable, and a button press on the side caused the visor to retract into the helmet—a feature that was similar to previous helmets I'd worn. I tried it on to see if it was big enough.

As it slid over my head easily, I felt a nudge in my ribs. It was Theta. "Put on your overalls first, big fella," said Theta, already in her overalls and grinning like a drunk goblin.

I removed the helmet and returned her smile. "Just checking. It's rare that I get anything that fits without a battle with administration."

"I can imagine. You could push a small moon off its orbit with that head," she quipped, before sauntering off to continue with her own armor.

A quick glance around told me that I was already falling behind the others who were gearing up with efficiency. With the aid of my newly acquired right arm and the Dexterity it provided, I set about catching up.

Once fully armored, I looked back into the locker to examine the weapons stored there: a rifle, a handgun, and a long knife. I picked up the rifle first:

Plasma Assault Rifle: Nilsamun RRS-14

The Nilsamun RRS-14 is a staple in militaries worldwide—for good reason. It is lightweight, has an easily activated mag clip for stowing anywhere on the appropriate armor, offers excellent accuracy, and provides impressive stopping power at medium range. It's one of the most reliable, mass-produced guns in existence.

Primary Attack: Standard fire rate, five-shot bursts of plasma projectiles with a fire rate of 0.05 seconds per shot, followed by a 2-second cooldown.

Special Function: Thanks to the Nilsamun's patented solar recharge technology, an operator could theoretically have an endless supply of ammo as long as there's sufficient light and the plasma cells are not drained entirely. Fully drained plasma cells need recharging at a suitable charging station.

I had used the Nilsamun RR-14 at the city base. It didn't have a recharging plasma cell, but that was hardly surprising given the city's general lack of sunshine. I moved on to examine the handgun next:

Ballistic Hand Cannon: Artec Deliverer MQ-10

The Artec Deliverer provides low-tech solutions to high-tech problems. With enough short-range stopping power from its armor-piercing ballistic rounds to put a rampaging, armored orc on its arse, you know you've got all bases covered when paired with a sturdy plasma weapon.

Empire of Oshbob

I was far from amused that orcs were used in the description, but I had to admit, it made the gun sound powerful. Last but not least for the weapons, I cast my eyes over the long knife:

Viber 3.1

This simple yet effective knife is ideal for both stabbing and slashing. With the addition of ultrasonic vibration, it can deliver precise and deadly attacks to unarmored flesh.

Aside from the weapons, there was also a small package with 'Survival kit 4 of 8' written on the dark blue wrapping.

4X Geodome

A pop-up shelter featuring a double-wall design for excellent insulation against extreme temperatures. 9 square feet of living space (suitable for up to eight).
The 4x Geodome solidifies once fully expanded. This provides an extremely stable structure even in high winds, as well as a strong protective barrier against slashes, cuts, and punctures. All material used in its construction is inherently flame resistant, protecting against thermal hazards up to 600 degrees Fahrenheit.

I hoped I never needed it, but it was good to have, and so lightweight that I would hardly notice carrying it. I placed the shelter in one of the empty compartments on my belt, then checked on the others. The rest of my new unit were waiting patiently for me.

Agga, the biggest and most scarred among them, slapped my back as I followed Umak out of the locker room. He had a deep voice and spoke slowly, "Normally, I'd give the new guys a survival pep talk, but I don't think I'll bother with you." He slapped a grenade in my hand. "Don't forget this."

"Only one?"

"It's all we're allowed."

"Then it'll have to do."

Agga fell silent. The mood had shifted; everyone was serious now, marching in a strict single file. We boarded the Balor AV, sitting on a long bench across from Scrub Team 3. They were all human—big and rough-looking for their kind, but still small compared to orcs. They chatted among themselves, barely acknowledging us beyond a few scowls.

A voice came over the ship's PA as the back door raised.

This is Colonel Azash. I'll be coordinating the operation today.
Keep your eyes and ears open, and your weapons ready.
Take off in 3, 2, 1…

Once airborne, Umak finally spoke, "When we get off the AV, the APS go first and move towards the target. Their passage usually brings out lower-rank monsters. Anything under a B rank, we'll be expected to handle. One of the Scrub Teams shadows them at around two hundred meters. The second Scrub Team follows at around six hundred meters, depending on the terrain. Some days are easier than others. Some days nothing shows up at all."

"Which is more difficult? Following the APS or bringing up the rear?"

"They're all dangerous when you're a useless fucking orc," one of soldiers opposite us snapped, their voice distorted through their helmet's speaker.

I noted the number on their armor. Number 5. I couldn't add every orc-hater to my mental ledger list, or I'd have near enough the whole city to kill. But I'd certainly keep an eye on him. For now, I ignored him as Umak replied.

"The rearguard has it the worst—less chance of assistance if shit gets bad. That's where we're seven times out of ten."

"Figures," I replied, expecting no less.

It wasn't long before the AV landed again. We were blind inside, and I was grateful for the helmet visor as we headed into the harsh sunlight beating down on the barren, dusty landscape.

"We'll be around a kilometer away from the sighting," Theta said for my benefit over the group channel of our helmet comms.

As we disembarked, Umak led us off to one side of the ramp while the other team moved out and stood on the opposite side to make way for the APS as they stomped off the ship, carrying an impressive array of heavy weaponry. Around twenty drones shot out above their heads and set off down the valley that stretched out before us. The APS wasted no time marching off after them.

We stood silently, waiting. Until a few minutes later, Corporal Azash's voice came through my helmet.

Scrub Team 3. You're up.

I watched with interest as we trailed after the APS, then finally took in the landscape around us. It was hellish, that was for sure. Even the few sporadic shrubs looked miserable as they clung to life in a landscape that perfectly mimicked the beige armor of the APS. Unlike our graphite-colored armor, which I'd thought looked sleek back at the military base. Now, I had my doubts.

Scrub Team 4. Follow in. Stay alert. The drones are picking up movement in the valley wall to the East.

Finding myself in the middle of our squad, I scanned the rocky hillside that ran along our intended path. There were no obvious signs of life to my eyes, but I still felt uncomfortable that we were in a line formation when any threat would approach from our flank.

The other Scrub Team was moving in the same formation, so it must be one of those habits that formed over time. Today probably wasn't the day to start suggesting changes. Instead, I kept my eyes glued to the eastern ridge line, determined not to be caught off guard.

A loud, piercing beep sounded from behind us, and we all spun toward it. Almost the moment we did, a horde of Arachnids came pouring over the top of the *western* ridge—the opposite direction to where we'd been warned. What created the beep to alert us, I had no idea, but it had probably saved our lives.

"APS and Scrub 3 are gone," Theta said through our private team channel.

"Same as yesterday, then," Umak growled. I then heard him speaking over the command channel only he had access to as the rest of us opened fire.

Kevin Sinclair

Close to a hundred Arachnids almost on top of us. A mix of C and D Ranks.
Support needed.

I couldn't hear the reply, but Umak's next words on our channel were telling.
"APS and Scrub 3 are already engaged. We're on our own."

Partition 7

Umak's estimate was high, not that the difference between eighty and one hundred Arachnids all intent on killing us made that much difference.

Nozz was the first to throw a grenade, prompting the spiders in its vicinity to leap forcefully away. Their leaps were impressive, but the most terrifying thing about the move was the indication of intelligence. The spiders recognized the grenade.

Still stupid spiders though, I grumbled.

Theta was about to throw hers, and I shouted across the comms on instinct. "Only throw in twos! Aim at the edge of the group. Theta, I'll go with you."

"When?" she shouted, still firing her rifle.

I quickly detached the grenade from the pouch on the belt at my waist. "Now! Go left," I yelled back once I had it ready to hurl.

She did as I asked, though she aimed a little too far to the edge of their group. It still had the desired effect as the Arachnids jumped centrally and got in each other's way in their desperate bid to escape the blasts.

While the others all focused their fire into that central group, Umak threw his grenade a moment after ours. It was the perfect throw, landing in the center of the now condensed group. The destruction was devastating, yet around forty arachnids survived the blast, and we only had two more grenades left from Agga and Froom, who had his in his hand ready to throw.

"Hold it!" Umak barked out. "They're on the ropes now, but there might be more."

I agreed with the call as the Arachnids were down to less than twenty now and our guns were making short work of them.

When the last of them fell, Umak spoke again, "That was much easier than last time. Good work, everybody, and good shout on the grenades, Corporal Oshbob. It was quick thinking."

"You getting one into their center was quick thinking. It worked perfectly."

"If it hadn't, we'd have been screwed," Theta offered absently. She was completely right. Fighting those kinds of numbers with just our rifles would have been close to impossible.

"Come on," Umak said. "We still have a job to do. Let's move out."

"What about nanite extraction?" I asked.

"Ha! Have you seen anyone with nano extractors?" Agga said. "The drones come in to do that."

I grimaced at the news. Then I looked back at the Arachnids, considering just taking some in front of the others. I only had two vials left to fill and a bunch to send back to Artem when Leo's drone finally got here. At that thought, I looked back up to where the noise warning us of the spiders had come from.

Just above the ridgeline, I saw a drone hovering there. Eager to go to it, I was tempted to take the nanites and sneak off, if the others would cover me, but I knew it was too risky. I didn't know them well enough, and I had nothing on anyone yet for blackmail should I need it. Then there was the issue of the drones returning for the nanites; while there was nothing watching us now, we had been generally well observed until the fight with the Arachnids.

In my moment of thought, Froom roared out. "Incoming!"

I spun and looked in the direction he pointed. I had to do a double take. I saw a few loose rocks bouncing down the slope as if they'd just been disturbed, but there was nothing there. Then I saw it. The shadow of something big.

"The fuck is it?" Nozz asked.

"Shadow beast," Theta answered, uncertainly.

Umak didn't answer. Not directly at least. He was speaking through his command channel, and it seemed he was the only one among us who recognized what it was. "We need back-up here now! We've got a Syniat Lasat approaching our position."

At his words, the other half-orcs paled and started backing off.

"Don't turn your backs," Umak warned with a feral growl. "That's what it's waiting for. It'll run us down and tear us apart, armor and all."

"How did they miss a Syniat"? Nozz said in a hushed tone.

Empire of Oshbob

"How do you think?" Umak growled, raising his gun. "Fall back slowly."

I followed the command, but had to ask. "I've not heard of a Syniat Lasat before. What is it and how is it invisible?"

"Not invisible," Umak said. "It's the shadow."

I frowned and looked closer. As soon as he said it, it became obvious that nothing, invisible or otherwise, could be casting the shadow it made. The sun was in the wrong direction for a start.

"Should we shoot?" I asked.

"Not yet. Range is still shit, and once we open fire, it's gonna come fast. Anyone with grenades left, get them ready."

Agga and Froom did as he asked.

Umak saw this and spoke again. "On my command, toss them. Froom, aim at the beast. Agga, throw short. Ten meters. Everyone else, open fire the moment it leaps."

The next thirty seconds seemed to take an age as the Syniat slowly closed the distance. Its shadowy, semi-transparent coloring seemed to intensify in shadow and reduce in bright light. Umak waited until it got within fifty meters of us.

"Grenades!" he hissed.

Froom and Agga threw. We fired a moment later. The Syniat pounced forward, almost directly into Agga's grenade and our wall of plasma that followed.

Its camouflage dropped to reveal a huge black cat, maybe six meters tall, complete with long, dark gray spikes around the base of its skull that descended in size as they ran down to the middle of its back.

It yowled as it came under attack, the flesh on its forelegs badly damaged from the explosion. It leapt off to one side, disappearing again, injured but nowhere near dead judging by the way it moved.

"Don't suppose anyone has any more grenades, do they?"

"One each a mission. That's it," Umak said. "Unless we can make it back to the ship. But..."

"But what?"

"We'll be tried if we don't keep moving to support APS. Especially if that thing blindsides them and we ran."

"Tried?" I asked disbelievingly.

Agga, mistaking my response for ignorance rather than amazement, explained. "Tried for cowardice. With the way these things work, we'd be found guilty and executed as well."

"It's there," Nozz said, pointing up the slope to our right.

I followed his finger to see the last of a dark shadow disappearing from sight behind a boulder.

"Let's keep moving," Umak said. "Circle formation, stay on the ball. Focus on the area in front of you only, unless we spot it."

All we saw for the next couple of minutes was the occasional rubble slide to the slope on our right, which was enough to know we were still being stalked relentlessly. The tension ramped up the longer it went on for, and when the signs of it disappeared, it was in some ways worse.

"Has it gone?" Froom asked.

"Hardly," Theta replied first. "It's my first time seeing one, but I've heard all about them. The Syniat don't stop hunting their prey unless they think they can't kill it."

"Maybe it knows it can't kill us then," Agga replied hopefully.

"Bastard!" Lanris screamed, firing his gun up the slope behind us.

In a depressing reply to Agga's statement, the deadly shadow had appeared halfway down the slope on our other side.

"It must have dropped back and sneaked around, and we'd missed it," Theta growled between bursts of plasma from her own weapon.

It dodged much of our fire, hurtling down the steep slope on fully healed legs. We were in the deepest of shit.

"Back!" I yelled on instinct.

But Umak continued to hold the line.

"You need to move back," I growled low as the Syniat stalked down onto the flat ground almost impervious to our rifle fire as it healed almost immediately.

"Where to?" he replied, distantly. "We're done."

"Every second that passes gives APS a chance to back us up," I snarled, not ready to die just yet.

"They're not coming," he snapped. "I told them, and they're still not here. No Scrub 3, no drone or air support. I've heard of shit like this happening before. We're not supposed to walk away from this." As he finished, his face turned sour.

Empire of Oshbob

"You think it's because of me?"

"I think you showing up just as we lost someone yesterday in similar circumstances is pretty convenient. Normally takes days if not weeks to get a new body in. Yesterday they were happy for one of us to die before they helped us. Today…"

"Then I'm sorry. But we're not done yet. I'm gonna back off. You need to do the same, but keep it focused on you guys. Not me. I'm going to try something."

I didn't give him a chance to ask more questions on my plan as it was barely fully formed in my mind and we didn't have the time.

I practically ran backward. The eyes of my new team watching me with confusion and derision. They all thought I was running away. I probably should have. But I wasn't into letting teammates down until they crossed me.

I finally reached an outcropping of rock from the slope, around ten meters in height. Without a word, I slipped behind it, then stowing my rifle against my back on the mag clips there, I climbed up the backside of the jagged obelisk, attempting to remain unseen as I did so.

Now I just had to hope that they made it this far. Once I got into position, I removed the nanite extractor from my armored sleeve and loosened the vial in its chamber. Not enough to stop it from working, but enough for easy removal.

Next, I placed the last, empty vial in my mouth and gently gripped it behind my tusks. They were durable containers, but this was potentially a one-way ticket to a mouth full of glass. Still, with options limited, I lay like that and waited for my new unit to pass.

They looked beyond desperate when they finally came into view. I shuffled forward to finally peer over the top of the outcropping. It was there.

With a silent prayer to any god that would listen, I got my feet under me and leapt out into the open air. Free falling for the briefest of seconds, I smacked into its bony but well-muscled back, managing to avoid the worst of the spikes and sort of flattening the ones I landed on. I grabbed one of the bony protrusions in front of me for purchase; it thrashed as I landed. With the additional purchase of the nanite extractor into its ribs, I managed to keep hold and not shatter the vial in my mouth despite a couple of close calls.

A beep from the extractor heralded the really tricky part of my plan. Removing the full vial with a few awkward flicks of my thumb, I had no choice but to just let it fall to the ground. I kept my eyes on it as it fell so that I could retrieve it later. *If* I survived the next few minutes. Unfortunately, it bounced off the beast's shoulder and ricocheted out of my line of vision. With an irritated growl, I set about trying to push the new vial in with my mouth. Suddenly, holding it *behind* my tusks seemed like a bad idea.

It took far too long, but somehow, with more tongue work than I'd ever done before, I managed to get the screw fitting of the vial to catch hold. The rest I was able to do with my thumb.

As I pulled out more nanites, I could feel the moment the Syniat began to panic. Its head thrashed around to snap its foul-smelling jaws at me. Its camouflage was completely gone.

"You messed with the wrong squad," I snarled as the extractor beeped.

It answered by dropping to the floor and rolling in an attempt to crush me. An attempt which was successful, causing me to lose my grip and the extractor, as I was smothered into the hard dusty ground.

It soon rolled off again, the sounds of gunfire much closer, and the Syniat screeched an ear-splitting howl as it now tried to back off.

Through bleary eyes, I saw that it was taking heavy damage from the plasma fire now. I pulled my own gun around, and from where I lay on the ground, I joined in the onslaught.

The Syniat gave up its slow retreat and made a run for it.

"Aim for the legs!" Umak barked out.

I obliged and lowered my own line of fire with the others.

The Syniat faltered, then it fell to the ground, using its face as a break. I dropped back and heaved a sigh of relief as the others continued to unload on it, when I remembered the extractor, and the vial. If anyone else found those… I'd be in the worst kind of trouble.

Picking myself up, I limped over to the beast with the others. They'd finished it off now, and they were all cheering and patting me on the back for my part in the attack.

Empire of Oshbob

I ignored it all. I only had eyes for the beast and the extractor, but it was gone. I scanned around its corpse, then back where it had landed on me. Nothing.

I walked back despite their shouts and celebrations to see if I could at least see the missing vial. But there was no sign of it anywhere. I'd messed up badly. To make matters worse, the drones responsible for the extraction chose that moment to turn up, all buzzing toward the dead Syniat.

I saw Umak watching me closely and had a sudden pang of worry.

"Where is it?" I asked, storming over.

"Where's what?" he asked innocently, while nodding behind me.

I turned to see the Balor AV coming in to land. As the ramp lowered, two high-ranking men walked down, fully armored.

"Sergeant Umak. We heard you were in trouble, so we came to help. It seems you had everything in hand after all?"

"An A rank Syniat attacked us, commander," Umak snapped back with a salute.

"A Rank you say? And exactly how did you kill it?"

"Seven grenades and almost our full complement of ammo along with some quick thinking and excellent training, sir."

"I see…" The commander fell silent for a moment, I suspected listening to someone else in his comm. "The drone extraction report is in. It seems there is a more sensible explanation for why a squad of half-orcs was able to kill an A Rank. It seems the Syniat was dying anyway. A very low nanite yield suggests it was old and near the end of its life. Still. Good work, Scrub 4."

With that, they turned and headed back onto the ship. We watched them go until Umak sniggered and lifted his visor. "Old my big green ass. Cut your comms, corporal."

I did as he asked, lifting my visor so that I could respond to whatever he had to say.

"That was an impressive idea." His grin deepened. "So what's our cut?"

"Today, your cut was surviving. Next time, I'll see what I can sort out."

"Pffft," he said, handing over the extractor as inconspicuously as possible. "That's a shit deal. What does *sort out* mean?"

"It means I'm not made of money." Which wasn't exactly true. Portolans was thriving both legally and illegally. "There's lots to juggle out there, but I can give you a cut of what we get going forward, providing it's more than I can get by myself. Beyond that, what do you want when you get out?"

He shrugged. "Dunno. Haven't much thought about it."

"Well, I always need good fighters, so there's always work for you."

He looked around as if to see if anyone was listening, then looked thoughtful, before seeming to decide something big. "I'm sick of fighting, sick of killing, and sick of being in danger. But there ain't much work for a half-orc that doesn't involve those things. You got anything quieter?"

I slapped him on the armored shoulder. "You better believe I have. You name it, I can probably set it up for you. Or you can discuss it with my business partners once you're out."

He nodded, a wistful expression on his face. "I'll think about it."

As he spoke, Theta came up and discreetly handed me a vial. "I'm happy to fight when I get out of here. As long as there's good money in it."

I grinned at her. "Then you're speaking to the right orc."

"What now? Do we follow after the APS?" she asked.

"Slow walk," Umak replied with a knowing smile.

As we set off down the valley, I felt good despite being pockmarked with wounds from the Syniat. We hit a leisurely pace, which meant I could scan the air for the drone I'd seen. Unfortunately, only military drones showed their presence now.

Leo would be long gone.

Partition 8
Unara

"What do you mean you can't really reach him?" I snapped, getting up close and personal.

Despite having filled out and grown up a lot in the last four years, Leo still shrunk back from my wrath.

"Unara!" he said, hands up in defense. "The security in this new base is insane, and whenever they go out, he's surrounded by people and surveillance drones *all* the time. I could have easily got to him, but our cover would be blown, and that wouldn't be good for him. But trust me, I'm working on it."

Those words… I hated those words. *Trust me*. I had a sudden and overwhelming urge to slash his throat. I knew he'd been diligent in his duties, always reliable *and* he utterly worshiped Oshbob. The likelihood of him betraying us was small. Even so, there was always a chance of betrayal, and if it came, I'd be ready. We had Meli watching him, while he watched her. They tested each other's security constantly, looking for anything off. So far, neither had any complaints about the other.

But out of everyone in our little empire, I only trusted Oshbob one hundred percent, and I *really* needed to talk to him. I kept all of that inside and let my hand fall away from my knife. "Focus on reaching him, Leo. Nothing else matters. Don't let me down."

"I won't, but what about…"

"I can deal with whoever's trying to track me down," I snapped. "And if I need any help, I'll use Meli."

He offered a conciliatory smile despite not having done anything wrong.

I felt my blood rise again and decided I better get out of there quickly before an accident happened. "Just get us in touch, or I'll put Meli on this, too."

Without another word, I stormed out of his office with an overwhelming urge to kill someone. Luckily, I had an idea where to find a victim. I just needed a few tools for the job first.

An hour later, I fought my way past an army of hardworking goblins and orcs carrying metal sheeting and fixing it to the tunnel walls with high-tech bolt guns that just looked wrong in their hands. I was tempted to stealth past them in my current mood, but I knew how much they liked to see me, so I headed down the center in full view.

Shouts and greetings rose up immediately, then a scream as one of the goblins bolted his feet to the ground.

As other goblins rushed to help him, the orc foreman Berrik came over to greet me. "You here to check on us?"

I shook my head. "I wouldn't know what I was looking at anyway. Where's the construction crew from Asala?"

"They only work eight-hour shifts. We leave all of the technical shit to them and just do most of the heavy lifting. Some of the boys are getting good at the work, though. Might not need the stuck-up humans in time."

I frowned at the thought of it. "I'm not happy with them down here anyway, Berrik. If your guys can learn, then I'd be much happier. There's still a lot more work to do to link things up."

The big orc grinned. "I reckon we can do that. Though, you're shit out of luck with the security systems and doors. I'd need ten years of schooling and a set of instructions just to read the instructions for one of the doors getting installed."

"Luckily, we've got people we really trust doing the security. Otherwise, we'd have to kill them afterward."

Berrik laughed uncomfortably at the thought, and I bid him farewell, continuing on to the entrance to Harold's shop. It would be part of our new network, sealed off from the rest of the Undercity along with access to both my new home and Asala's.

Hitting the intercom, Harold's voice came out of a hidden speaker. "Ah! Unara, my dear girl. Is everything okay?"

"No," I replied sullenly. "I need to talk, and I need a scope."

He buzzed me into the basement as he replied. I heard his voice through the comm telling me he was up in the shop, but I was already past it and halfway to the stairs.

Empire of Oshbob

Harold lounged in his worn, fake leather swivel chair, facing the door as I entered he raised a glass of whisky and smiled. It was a pasty, strained expression, but that was his normal these days. He'd lost a lot of weight in the last couple of years, and Asala was constantly worrying over his health, but the tough old human insisted he was fine and wouldn't talk about it anymore. I'd quickly learned never to mention it, but I hoped Oshbob could speak some sense to him once he returned.

Jumping onto the counter opposite, I sat and watched him closely for a few seconds before speaking. "They moved him. Gave him a promotion and then sent him off to the wilds in something called a Scrub Team. We haven't been able to get in touch with him since."

A deep frown crossed Harold's face. "A Scrub Team in the wilds, eh? That's rough." He paused, looking pensive for a long moment. "I'll have a chat with my contacts. See what I can find out. You think it's connected to what's happening with you and Asala?"

His words hit me like an avalanche. My jaw tightened while I thought over his words. "Goddammit, Harold. I didn't even think Asala's troubles were connected to mine. But you're right! They could be and I should have seen it."

He nodded and took a drink. "Awfully big coincidences otherwise. Assassins turn up for you. An increase in attempts to hack the company systems. Not to mention the infiltrators that have been raked out. Then Oshbob sent well out of the way where you can't get in touch with him? Somebody's making moves, Unara."

I slid off the counter, unable to sit any longer. "Whoever it is, they're gonna wish their mothers never squeezed them out."

"You should go and see Asala. See what you can work out together. She'd appreciate a visit, and I don't like the idea of her being in that tower all alone at night."

I shook my head. "We're trying to wipe all traces of mine and Oshbob's involvement with Portolans Security, and I've no doubt there'll be people watching the tower. In fact, tonight, I'm banking on it."

"Which makes me even more nervous," he grumbled. "I'll feel better when you've got this new tunnel system locked up and she's safe in her new home."

"As will I. But that tower's like a fort. Especially with the new AI."

He took another drink and grumbled. "A system worth that much must be damn near unhackable. But it won't stop a physical attack. I know her security team are top shelf, but…"

"I was going hunting tonight anyway, Harold. I'll start closer to the tower. See who I can find."

"So that's what the scope is for? Why not just take a sniper rifle? Better yet, get some optics with a decent zoom."

I glowered at him, and he looked rightfully ashamed.

"Right, right. I'm sorry. My damn mind isn't what it once was."

I waved it off. Everyone who knew me well knew that I'd never get my eyes changed. Not just because Oshbob had asked me not to, but now I knew they were hackable and could be affected remotely. There was no way I'd make that *upgrade*.

"It's fine, Harold, but if I shoot, even silenced, it's gonna be picked up and I'll give myself away. I want to get up close and personal this evening and get some answers about what's going on."

Heaving himself up from the chair like the old man he was, he offered a sad smile. "Let's have a look at what I can do for you then."

After a few minutes raking around his shelves and drawers, he came back with a hunting scope.

"That should do you. It's mid-range, but about the best night scope I can give you today. You'll be able to see a fly fart at anything under a thousand meters with that."

I took it from him gratefully and inspected it.

"And, Unara…be careful out there. You don't know who it is yet and how much they're willing to put on the line to bring you all down."

"Whoever it is, they'll die just as cheaply as anyone else."

I let him rest a hand on my shoulder. It was hard, but I tolerated it because I actually liked the old man. He'd saved Oshbob, and he'd helped us a lot in the early days. Unlike Raven, he didn't want anything other than a job for his granddaughter, and if I didn't miss

Empire of Oshbob

my guess, to be part of something interesting. He still didn't get total trust, but he was close. I'd give him a 96% loyalty score.

"Oh I've no doubt who needs my sympathy tonight, but I still need to say it. Be careful."

I was pleased to be back out of the shop, alone in the dark again. It was only in the shadows where I truly felt at peace, and once my eyes acclimatized, I set off, moving fast and as silently as possible toward Hi Shine Tower.

Granted, the apartment block was part of our legitimate business now, but it was also one of the best vantage points in the district. And while it had taken some work, there was a network of cables, pipes, and handholds that allowed someone agile enough to run, jump, and climb for miles across the city skyline. The only real difficulty was getting to the roof without being spotted.

Half the building was filled with our people now. Most loyal, but not all could be trusted. None of them would see me in the service lift reserved for gang use only. Not even the security guards who monitored the building. At most, they'd catch sight of a hooded figure here and there, but they would know it was me. It annoyed me to be watched, but it couldn't be helped.

Despite no one else being able to use the elevator, it still took an eternity to reach the top of the building. When it finally came to a halt, the doors opened with a squeal that set my teeth on edge. And on seeing the coast was clear, I pulled a dagger out, and at a low crouch only possible due to my Tier-Four spine, I stepped out. The moment I exited the door, I sensed a presence to the left, so I moved to the right, quickly and silently.

Hiding in the shadows, I waited until the elevator doors closed and the carriage descended.

A massive half-orc stepped out from behind the elevator, scratching his head and looking at the doors.

He must have been speaking across his keystone, as he had a far-away look in his eyes. While he was distracted, I slunk behind him, leapt into the air, and snaked my arm around his throat, knife pressed to skin.

"Why were you hiding around the corner from me?"

"Hey…" He gulped. "Unara! Didn't know it was you. Just saw a hooded figure on the cams."

I dug the knife in deeper. "You knew it was me. That, or you're so stupid you don't deserve to live."

He didn't try to fight or free himself. That was a good sign that he had some sense. "Okay. Okay! I wanted to see if I could surprise you. You're always sneaking up on everyone."

"Stupid," I whispered in his ear and jumped off his back, speaking more loudly. "Not stupid enough to have your throat slit. But still very stupid."

"My da is currently explaining the exact same thing through my keystone as we speak."

I grinned at the ridiculous half-orc. "It was funny, though. Did you really think you could sneak up on me? You breathe louder than most people talk. You should stick to your strengths, Dondo."

He turned to face me, rubbing his throat, but still had a wide confident grin on his face. "Yeah, but Artem loves a trier."

I shook my head. "Artem only loves a clever trier, not an idiot."

"Hmm, maybe. But I'm still a work in progress."

"You're nineteen? If you're still an idiot now, there's really not much hope for you."

He looked hurt by that, and I had a pang of guilt. He was generally a good guard but he also had a dangerous enthusiasm to learn and develop that was likely to wind up getting him killed. Or worse, someone he was with.

"You want me to take you to my da?"

"I'm not here to see anyone today. I have some work to do up above."

His eyebrows climbed his face at that. "Anything interesting? You want some company."

"No, Dondo. This is going to require stealth, and you've just proven you're about as stealthy as a toothless goblin eating soup."

His face fell again, but not so far this time, and he looked like he was working on a witty reply. I quickly made my way to the roof ladders before he could make it any worse.

On the roof, it was fully dark now. Or as close to dark as the Artem skyline ever got. Neon lighting caused the near constant mist to glow. Perfect for hunting and perfect for my current disposition.

Keeping low and moving in the shadows, once I reached the parapet wall, I used the scope, focusing it on the general area of the

Empire of Oshbob

Prestige first. The building itself was obscured by those around it. But those buildings were most likely where the assassins hunting me would be lurking.

I saw nothing in the immediate vicinity, so I moved toward the giant glowing tower of Portolans 360. It was brighter than anything else around it, and while I felt a sense of pride that it was ours—that we'd fought and bled and took it and now it was the Jewel of Portolans—I also shuddered at Harold's words at how much of a target it presented.

From my vantage point, I saw no sign of our mysterious enemies, but if they were any good at all, I wouldn't have expected to.

I moved methodically to the midpoint between the two buildings, using every ounce of cover available, and remaining completely silent as I searched for anything unusual. It took three hours before the thermal imaging gave me a target. At first, it was hard to be sure of anything about them, other than that they were hunkered down in a static position.

I called Meli on my Keystone:

"Unara, what's wrong?"

"I'm out hunting my hunters. I've found someone who looks like they're watching the 360 tower, so I'm going to go check them out, but if they move while I close the distance, I don't want to lose them."

"No problem. Ping me your location and I'll send a drone."

I made sure both of our hackers couldn't track me now, but that I could give them my location in a heartbeat if I needed to, and with a quick thought, I gave her my position.

"Got it. The drone's on its way. I'll keep it in Dark Mode, but I'll be watching if things turn sour."

"Perfect."

Ending the conversation, I set off running, taking a roundabout route that would give me the best cover. I checked every second building to make sure my target was still there.

It took me a disappointing twenty minutes to get to within a few rooftops of my destination when I stopped. The figure was still in the same position as I had first spotted him. Clearly up to no good, but as it so often did these days, paranoia had been playing on my mind as I made the journey.

Now, as I closed the distance, I caught a faint scent. A smell I hated more than most. Elf. I came to a halt, and hid myself completely in the darkness.

"*Meli,*" I hissed through the keystone. "*I'm certain there's an elf on this roof. There's no clear line of sight to either the Prestige or the tower from here, so I think the one I spotted is a lure.*"

"*Gotcha,*" Meli replied. "*Sending more drones now. Will you wait for backup?*"

"*No. And just send assault drones. I'm going to see if I can find and kill the elf on this roof. We'll go from there.*"

I cut the call, and rather than pulling out the scope, I pulled out my hunting knife and sniffed the air to tell me where the bastard was hiding. Moving slowly and trying to gauge the wind direction, I finally caught sight of a flicker of movement among some duct work.

A quick check through the scope told me what I expected to see. His body heat was shielded. He came up entirely black, as did his sniper rifle which was aimed directly at the more obvious assassin.

With an internal growl, I stalked forward with all the care and patience I possessed. I should have waited for the assault drones. I should have called for backup, but I was furious at the lengths these bastards were going to, in our own district. I'd very nearly been ambushed, despite my best efforts; now I was going to make them pay.

Climbing silently to the top of the ducting, I felt exposed, but as I appeared above him, and with his eye glued to the sight of his rifle, he never saw me coming. Luckily, I saw the thickness of material around his throat. He had some kind of lightweight armor. The only skin on show was his mouth… I could work with that.

With a controlled fall rather than jump that might create unintended noise, I landed on his back. As he opened his mouth to scream, he presented the only opening I could see available. I rammed the knife upward into the roof of his mouth and held on as he bucked and squirmed in his prone position on the floor. He wasn't going anywhere. Unfortunately, his last act before he dragged out his last breath was to fire his gun.

There was a moment of calm in the night before all hell broke loose. From around six different positions, gunfire tore out through the night sky. A moment later, even more guns fired as the assault drones attacked those shooting my location.

I grabbed the sniper rifle and moved around the roof and out of the danger zone. Once as safe as I could be, I raised the gun and inspected quickly.

> *Rail Gun: Death-Slide-4 Stealth edition.*
>
> *The Death-Slide-4 Stealth edition is a special edition version of the world-famous Death-Slide. Made by Takemoto industries, this version boasts state-of-the-art frictionless rails and incredibly lightweight ammunition that fragments on impact, creating a small entrance wound, but sufficient internal damage to bring down all sentient races and up to Rank C creatures with a well-placed shot.*

It was a very good gun. Top of the range if I wasn't mistaken. I found a target immediately, took a breath, waited for his head to peer around the roof entrance of the building he'd taken position on and bang.

The recoil was practically nonexistent. The armor the man wore did nothing against the high-powered bullet I'd just put into his head. He dropped and I moved again.

The others up here were so busy defending against Meli's drones that they couldn't focus on me. I had time to take out two more shooters before the night fell quiet again. I continued to watch from my hiding spot until my keystone beeped. Meli.

"Unara? Are you okay?"

"I'm fine. Did we get them all?"

"By my count, four got away. I hope you don't mind, but I've called Bagri to send a cleanup team."

"Not at all. Now we just need to work out who the hell they are. I wished I could have taken one alive."

"No need. I'm running facial recognition on those I killed right now. Give me a moment and I should have something."

I slowly stood from my spot behind the lift motor housing I'd taken cover behind while I waited.

Meli's voice suddenly burst back into life. *"I... we got a hit. It's not great. They're all elves, and the last record I can find on any of them has them working for the Armed Brigade. But that was over two years ago. They've been dark since."*

"*Keep looking,*" I practically hissed back, resisting the urge to smash the rail gun against the ground.

Empire of Oshbob

Partition 9

Three days and I still hadn't seen Leo's drone again. Whoever was trying to kill us, or me, hadn't executed another plan yet, but that didn't mean one wasn't coming. The only time unobserved was the short period of time between leaving the ship's line of sight, and before we reached the area the support drones covered for the APS team. It wasn't a big window, and so far, it had been filled with monsters to kill.

I'd kept my eyes open, scanning the horizon constantly in the hopes that Leo's familiar drone would appear, but it never did.

What did appear was a particularly annoying drone that flew into my forehead. I slapped at it but it had already flown off. With a grumble, I trudged on until it hit my head again. And again. My flailing efforts to kill the belligerent thing were doing more damage to me than they were to it. Then it started flying side to side, just out of reach.

I felt stupid. I should have noticed earlier. It was a tiny fucking drone. Once I stopped, it stopped, then flew slowly off to my left and waited. I nodded at it then turned to Umak, who was looking at me oddly.

"You okay, Oshbob?" The others were all smirking.

"Seems to me like the heat's getting to our favorite full-orc," Theta added.

"Real funny. I saw movement up in those rocks," I said, pointing to the left. "I'd like to go check it out. Make sure there's no ambush or something to attack our rear."

Whatever his first instinct was, he stifled it and looked up to the rocks, chewing his lip. "Well, if you think there's a danger up there, corporal, go investigate. We'll cover you from down here."

"Shouldn't…" Agga began, but Umak halted his words with a hand signal. He then muted our squad channel and raised his visor.

"I take it *you* have to check, corporal?"

I offered him a thumbs up and realization dawned on the rest of the squad that I was up to no good.

Umak lowered his visor and unmuted the channel. "If Corporal Oshbob wants to prove himself, let him go and check. Just cover him well. I don't want to lose any more men, you got it?"

A chorus of, "Got it, sir," came back in response.

They all spread out behind me, and I made my way after the fly. It led me toward the rock cluster I'd pointed out to the others, and by some fluke, landed among the rocks.

It flew through cracks between them, causing me to lift a few rocks away. Then I found it. The much larger, familiar drone was hidden just below the surface.

"You clever little bastard," I growled, a wide grin splitting my face as I moved the last couple of rocks.

"I don't know whether to be offended or pleased," came Leo's voice in answer.

I signaled for silence from him before muting all of my channels. "You've got about ten seconds before I have to unmute everything or risk having questions asked. And well done for getting to me. Good thinking with the stealth drone."

"No problem. Unara would have killed me if I didn't get in contact with you soon."

I smirked at the thought, then felt a pang of worry. Unara probably would kill him too.

"If we're having such a hard time meeting up. I can just send you a message every time I'm full up with nanites. Or we can switch to every three weeks?"

"Whatever you think's best, but do you mind explaining that to Unara, Oshbob? Seriously, you need to tell her the new itinerary."

I laughed. "That bad, huh?"

"Worse. We've been having trouble here, and with you being moved…"

"Time, Leo. I need to know but…"

"I know! There's a communication device in the drones storage compartment." The top of the drone opened up as he spoke. "Take it with you to communicate. I'll take the storage drone away once everyone has gone from the area."

"Can I sneak this one into our base? It won't give me away will it?"

Empire of Oshbob

"It should be fine. Just don't get caught with it."

"Of course, and speak soon."

I unmuted my helmet and looked over the insides of the drone. Twenty-four cigars. The top twelve were actual cigars and were meant only as a cover for the hollowed-out ones underneath, but I found myself unusually glad to see them when they arrived. Sweeping them out and putting them in my storage compartment, I then removed the empty vials from the remaining twelve and replaced them with the filled ones.

It was normally a nuisance to do the task, but this time, it happened so much faster with the increased dexterity of my right hand. I finished by shoving the small communication device inside my armor rather than the storage compartment in case either one was discovered.

With that done, I covered the drone with rubble again and then headed back to my squad.

"All clear!" I shouted as I approached. "Whatever was there has gone now."

"Not like you to get spooked, Osh," Theta said. I couldn't see her face, but I knew she was grinning.

"We need to move fast and make up the ground between us and the APS," Umak added. "Fine to fall behind if there's something to fight, but we'd have a hard time explaining this one."

We set off at a steady jog to catch up. There were a couple of Arachnids about, but only small nests, and they ran once they realized we meant business. As we approached the APS battle ground, we got the call that the A Rank had been dispatched.

Umak sighed with relief. "Now that's how these things should go. This is how they *used* to go."

"Well let's all pray to the old gods for another day like this tomorrow," Theta said.

I snorted. "I don't think that's how the orc gods worked. Saying shit like that will almost guarantee a mighty battle if they're still listening."

"Yeah, but they're not listening, are they?" she replied testily. "And even if they were, they wouldn't listen to a half-breed like me."

It was Nozz's turn to laugh this time. "You can fuck tight off with the self-pity, Theta. Dead gods might not listen to you, but you get a lot more opportunities than full-orcs do."

Agga interrupted the bickering. "Aren't we due a day off? I feel like we're due a day off."

"Soon," Umak agreed. "We are overdue."

Back at base, the others all hit the showers, but I didn't want to risk leaving my gear unattended. Even though I was feeling good about my squad mates now, with the exception of Lanris who was just too damn quiet, it wasn't worth the risk. So I sat back and waited. Feeling oddly relaxed with the knowledge I'd be able to speak freely with my people soon.

We headed back over to the barracks area, and they all left me to go to the canteen while I headed back to the barracks with a promise to join them soon. The moment I was back inside, I hid away my contraband and empty vials in the ceiling vent, then lay back on the bed with the communicator.

"Hey Oshbob!" came Leo's chirpy voice. "I've been tracking your movements and scanning the base you're in the best I can without risking being detected. I'd estimate we have fifteen minutes maximum before their systems pick up on the signal, and I'm reckoning around another five minutes after that before they track it down. So, if it's all right by you, I'll cut the connection at thirteen minutes, just to be sure."

"Sounds as good a plan as any. How have things been? You said there was trouble?"

"There is. Someone's been targeting 360, heavily. Trying to hack into their systems and a bunch of other stuff, but I'll let Asala and Unara tell you all about that. Suffice to say, on the hacking side, I've been working with Meli's team from down here to keep them at bay. But now that the new AI is installed, it's so much easier, and they don't need my help with that side of things anymore."

"Good. I'm glad it was worth the investment. But, Leo, you really should move out of that unit. It's not good for a human to be underground so long."

Empire of Oshbob

"I get out once a day with the new exit," he assured me. "And I'm happy, so don't worry about me. At the minute, it's you and Unara we need to worry about. I'll push you on to Asala next."

"Not Unara?" I asked, puzzled.

"No, she wants to go last so that she can have every last minute. We've both been warned to keep things brief."

I smiled in spite of myself. "Fair enough. Pass me on."

"Okay. Speak to you next time, Oshbob."

His voice cut out and Asala's soft monotone voice took over immediately. "Can you hear me?"

"Asala. I can. Are you good?"

"I'm mixed. Business is very good, but my uncle is unwell and someone is attempting to undermine our business."

"Wait, wait. One thing at a time. Harold is unwell? What's wrong with him?"

"Neural degradation from the military hardware as best as I can tell. He keeps insisting that he's fine, but he's not."

"What can we do for him? Surely there's an implant or some kind of medicine."

"Getting him to admit there's something wrong and agreeing to help is the first step. We can't make him do something he doesn't want to. You know how he is."

I nodded to myself. "I do. Next call, make sure he's linked in. I want to speak with him. We'll find a way to heal him, whatever it takes. Do you understand?"

"I do, and thank you, Oshbob. I wouldn't have expected anything else from you."

I wasn't sure what to say to that, so I moved the conversation on. "Is there anything else I should know about? I hear the AI and Meli have the hacking under control."

"It's much deeper than that. We have had new, well-vetted employees turn out to be infiltrators. So far we haven't been able to track down who they are working for. We have a couple held in our cells in the 360 tower, but they're not giving anything up, and our interrogators are being thorough. It seems they are prepared to die either through misguided loyalty, or they have been offered something more valuable than their own lives."

"Just kill them, then. Don't bother wasting your time questioning them anymore. There's always other ways to find out who it is, and when we do find out, they're going to be sorry."

"I see. That is rather ruthless, especially when we are attempting to remain a clean and wholesome company, but… we have excellent lawyers who can make almost anything we want to throw, stick." She fell silent for a moment, thoughtful, so I didn't interrupt. "And if we keep finding and killing their informants without preamble, they are far less likely to send more."

Though it was hard to tell with the tone of her voice, I sensed she was excited by the idea.

"Thank you, Oshbob. You always know exactly what to do."

I couldn't help but laugh. "I have no idea what to do, Asala. I just have a motto that doing anything is better than nothing. Killing their people sends a clear message. Sure we want the public to think 360 is wholesome, but our competitors? Hell no. They need to know we'll burn them to the ground if they fuck with us."

"Agreed. I should really go now as Unara is waiting for her turn, but before I go, as you were so helpful with the infiltrator problem, we are still buying up any low-cost properties within Newton and Turan, ready for when we make our move. But recently, we're being hampered with our efforts here. When we started, on average, we were picking up properties at auction for between fifty and eighty percent of their market value. Over the last year, that average has crept up steadily. Our company policy was to stop at eighty-five percent of market value. We've had to move it up to ninety-five percent, but even at those prices, we're only winning about a quarter of the properties we go in for. Last year, that number was around two-thirds."

"You checked out who's buying them?"

"We have. It's mostly the same property developers and the occasional new hopeful that we've competed with since we began three years ago. I've personally traced each property we've missed out on, and they are still in the hands of those individuals or small-time companies, and they all still own the properties. None of them have the clout to cause us problems or send assassins after Unara."

"They fucking what?" I growled, sitting up in my bed, fist clenched and ready to run to Artem if I needed to.

"She is fine, and… her assassins are not. But I should let her tell you all about that. She is waiting."

"Thank you, Asala. And I'll think on the property situation, though I've got no idea what the answer is, other than more violence."

"Thank you again, Oshbob. Stay well."

I was about to reply, when Unara spoke, her voice energetic, frantic almost.

"Oshbob! I nearly came out to find you. If Leo never got to you soon, I was going to."

I laughed. "Thanks for the concern, but I'm all right. Got a squad of half-orcs here, and they're not a bad lot. Somebody's definitely trying to get me out of the way, though. If they're trying to kill me, they're attempting to make it look as accidental as possible. I'm more worried that someone's trying to kill you, and bring down 360."

"Don't be. Neither of those things will happen. When they come, the only thing they'll achieve here is their own deaths."

"Can you defend the district against them?"

"We're managing well so far. I'm in the process of rounding up every elf in the district."

I waited for more, but she stopped speaking. "And?"

"What do you mean, and?"

"And what are you doing with every elf in the district? I'm guessing it's not tickling them."

"Well, no, Oshbob. I'm killing them."

I winced. Not that I was against killing elves because I really wasn't. "And you don't think that will bring even more trouble?"

"I'm doing it with great secrecy!"

"But we're the only criminal enterprise in Portolans. Whoever they are, they're going to know it's us. What if it's someone like Living Earth? Do we really want to be goading those bastards into attacking us with everything they've got?"

She was silent for a moment. "You think it's Living Earth?"

"Hell, I hope not. We're not ready for that kind of heat. I dunno if we'll ever be, but slaughtering all the elves of the district… If Living Earth or any of the other elven corporations catch wind of it, then we could have a hell of a lot more problems on our hands than what we have now." I took a deep breath. "It doesn't strike me as a good idea."

It struck me as a ridiculous idea. Like getting in a cage with a Rank A and repeatedly poking it in the eye with a stick. But I didn't want to say that outright.

She sighed. "I thought it would bring whoever we were facing into the open, but you're right, it could create even more enemies, which we really don't need right now."

"And the main ACE headquarters," I added. "If they come for us, district ACE will have no choice but to come after us, and we really don't need that kind of heat."

"I get it. I get it."

Relief washed over me. If she listened and I was lucky, there might still be something left of Portolans when I returned.

"What if I kill elves in Turan and Newton as well?" she added, proving that she hadn't really grasped what I was driving at.

I was about to say it as straight as I could and insult be damned, but I stopped. It wasn't actually a horrible idea. In fact, providing it wasn't full scale genocide, it could even give us some leverage against whoever was coming after us.

"How're our links with the new gang boss in Newton?"

"He's behaving himself for now. We've spoken a few times, and he says he's willing to let the past drop."

"Okay, then do it, but not you. Send someone else and don't let them be seen. Only send people you trust to keep their mouths shut and be discreet."

"What about Turan?"

"Leave Turan alone for now. It provides distance and it keeps Burrel guessing."

"Oh he's guessing alright," she chuckled. "He's always trying to cut deals with us and never gets anywhere."

"I bet he is, the little snake. I'll go cut a deal with him once I'm out. Until then, let him stew. And, Unara?"

"Yeah?"

"Let's talk about you for the few minutes we've got left. How are your new mods coming along?"

"Great. I got a special coating on my skin that makes me blend in when I don't want to be seen. It's attached to my neural link and it's pretty neat. I definitely could have made it to you without being spotted. I'm still thinking about coming to see you at some point to show it off anyway."

"Don't," I said forcefully. "I don't want you anywhere near the military if I can help it. As soon as I'm out of here, I'll never look back. Keep some contacts. Use ex-soldiers, sure. But I won't be going near a base again. Not even to steal their shitty mods. Though, the new Tier-Three upgrades for my arm and leg are decent enough. Even if I was sent out here as a death sentence."

"Do tell!"

"Yeah. Don't get your hopes up. Even at Tier-Three, military spec doesn't mean better. Hell, I think it just means it's been repaired more than normal. The tech here keeps breaking constantly."

"We'll have you home soon and fitted with some top-of-the-range gear. I'll shop around before your time is up."

The mention of time reminded me that we had a limit. I checked the timer. A minute remained. "Okay, Unara, almost time to go, but stay safe. Try not to draw too much attention to yourself, and once I'm out of here, we'll burn them all down together."

"You don't trust me to do it myself?"

I laughed. "Hell yeah, I trust you. But we're playing a dangerous game here, and if you're gonna get yourself killed, you're gonna do it with me at your side and we're gonna go down in a blaze of glory!"

She chuckled back. "Okay. That I can get behind."

I didn't get a chance to say anymore as the automatic timer cut us off. I cursed, then quickly stowed the communicator up in the air vent. It had been good to talk to the three of them, but the uncomfortable knot of concern that sat in the pit of my stomach had tightened.

Kevin Sinclair

Partition 10

"What's this all about?" I muttered across to Theta.

She yawned and rubbed at her eyes despite her anger. "No idea, but it's supposed to be our day off, so pulling this goblinshit is... well, it's goblin shit. Eight in the morning and we're lined like trainees for inspection."

"Shut it, you two," Umak hissed, nodding over to the central command building.

Three figures emerged, all dressed in the regalia of high-ranking officers, led by Captain Parraway who was the only one I recognized.

They marched across the parade ground toward us with purpose. It wasn't until they came to a stop that I noticed one of them was actually an elf. Just tall and broad for his kind, and if I didn't miss my guess from his uniform, he was the base commander. They all wore haughty expressions, but his was the most arrogant.

Parraway was first to speak, snapping out his words in clipped unpleasant tones. "Base Commander Wendel has questions about your recent altercation and the successful defeat of a fully grown Syniat Lasat."

We all waited silently for more, but the three men just stared at us as if waiting for one of us to crack over something.

Finally Umak spoke. "What do you want to know?"

The other human of the three—not Commander Wendel, I noticed—stepped forward. The insignia on his chest of two golden wings marked him as a colonel.

"From the glimpses and information put together from the drones and *other* sources, there appears to be a common agreement that this Syniat was fully competent. Neither old, nor injured prior to its attack on your squad. Yet the amount of nanites harvested from its corpse were unusually low. Around two-thirds of what we would normally expect to see."

Empire of Oshbob

Externally, I made every effort to look neutral and uninterested. Inside, I felt myself tensing up. I'd risked a lot exposing myself to my new teammates, now I was about to find out if I'd made a horrible mistake.

"It was self-healing, Colonel Thile," Umak said. "And it had to heal a hell of a lot with our grenades and rifle fire. When Corporal Oshbob brought it down, diving from the bluff, we didn't let up on it. Between the seven of us, we managed to hurt it faster than its healing could work. Eventually, it's power began to wane until it wasn't healing at all. That's how we managed to kill it. Teamwork and determination."

The colonel didn't look convinced, nor did the still-silent base commander behind him, who devoured every word Umak said like a starving man would a slice of spoiled meat.

The colonel spoke again, with a dangerous edge to his voice. "Many of our APS teams have taken down Syniat Lasats with healing powers, and a reduction in nanites have never been noticed."

"Begging your pardon, sir," Lanris said.

My heart sank. If I suspected that anyone would throw us under the mag-rail, it would be him. I fought not to clench my fists as he continued.

"But APS are well known for using excessive force. Do they ever need to wait until a Syniat has ran out of healing power?"

"That is something to be assessed. Either way, Scrub Team 4, however you managed to kill it, your group's competency has been noted. Do not be surprised when you're chosen for more dangerous assignments."

"Is that wise?" Umak asked. "That's the second time we've been hard pushed to survive. We were lucky against the Syniat and it's been noted, by us, that the APS didn't come to help out. Next time, we might not be so lucky."

I was surprised by how much Umak was going at this, but I had to be happy that his righteous anger was taking the heat away from the missing nanites, so for that I was grateful.

"The APS were dealing with a Terad," the colonel snapped back. "Your job is to make sure *they* aren't overwhelmed. Not the opposite."

Umak planted his hands on his hips. "It was my understanding that the APS dealt with A Rank beasts, and we *supported* them."

The colonel and Captain Parraway looked as though they were about to explode on Umak. I couldn't stop it, but I could at least support him.

"And I was led to believe, from the countless hours of training I've been through in Artem Military, that when we go out to risk our lives, we're a team. And as a team, we're supposed to make sure *everyone* survives, whenever possible."

All three faces turned on me. There wasn't a pleasant expression among them.

"Ah! The orc corporal of great renown," said Colonel Thile. "The one who inexplicably brought the Syniat down on his first outing in the wild lands. Even here, you are incapable of keeping a low profile. I would think the fewer people taking notice of you would be in your best interests, but here you are in the center of controversy again. People are taking notice of you, corporal, and that is not a good thing."

I seethed at his words. To my ears, he all but admitted they'd been trying to kill me. Smug bastards. I decided to go all in. "Will their notice keep me alive from whatever games are being played to see me dead?"

That took them by surprise. The commander was first to react, and to everyone's surprise, it was with a laugh.

"Ah, the directness of savages. Even when they are confused! It never ceases to be amusing how simple you orcs are."

I faced the elf, shoulders square, proud and calm. "So we weren't set up? Left to defend against a creature that should have killed us all if not for a little luck and a lot of bravery by these fine half-orcs?"

"Preposterous," the colonel answered. "Who would bother themselves with the effort that would take for… orcs." He looked at the others in the group, showing the half-orcs that they were fully included in his derision.

"I don't know, yet," I replied as calmly as I could. "But I'll find out, and they'll pay such a heavy price that they'll wish they were dead."

"Is that a threat!" the commander said in an unexpectedly high voice that all but proved his guilt.

"A threat? Unless there's someone here guilty of trying to kill our team, then no. It was just intended as a statement of fact."

Realizing he'd overplayed his hand, he calmed a little and offered a smug smile. "It's incredibly difficult to take revenge when you're dead, orc."

It was my turn to smile, but I remained silent.

Parraway turned back to his two superiors, and the commander offered a nod. Then with a quick bark, we were dismissed, allowed to go back to our quarters to enjoy the rest of our day off under the dark cloud of our commander's distrustful eyes.

"Well that was fucking horrible," Nozz said. "And they pretty much admitted they were trying to kill us."

"I picked up on that too," Theta said wryly while Umak thumped down on his bed looking distraught.

I brought my hands together in a loud clap to get their attention. "The thing is, they were already trying to kill us off before we knew about it and we survived their best effort. If they can't take us out while we're ignorant, then I think our chances are good. I know I fully intend to live, and I intend to get my own slice of revenge one way or another, but what I'm not going to let do is let them spoil my day off."

I slid the smokable cigars out from under my bed. "I hope someone has something to drink."

"It's nine in the morning!" Lanris said.

I nodded sagely. "I know. We've missed at least two hours of daylight already!"

Nozz whooped with joy, pulling a hidden bottle of knockoff Aska from the back of his locker. "If we have a whip-round, I'll go get more."

Theta pulled out a bottle of purple-hued liquor from her locker, followed by Agga producing a terrifyingly large plastic bag filled white powder from his.

"I'm all in on the drink and cigars," Umak said. "But you can put the damn Char away, Agga. I want to keep some of my wits about me."

Agga shrugged with a wide grin. "It's there if anyone wants a blast. Clear the pipes."

For the following week, we were sent out every day without fail. We also had a new team member of sorts—a drone that followed us high in the sky, offering no help but watching everything we did. That consequently meant I'd managed to get zero nanites. It didn't actually matter. Business was booming in Portolans, and this was just my way of contributing still, and also giving a middle finger to the hierarchy. What was more of an irritation was the constant danger.

As our name was called out on the tenth successive day, Umak roared in anger and put his meaty fist through the wall near his bed. It was futile, but I understood. They were grinding us down. Something big was coming. We could all feel it. Except perhaps Agga.

"At least they haven't tried to kill us again."

Umak ignored him and turned to me. "I think you coming here was both the best and worst thing that could have happened to us."

I shrugged. What else could I do apart from keep my wits about me and try to keep them all alive.

We trudged out for breakfast, with heavy feet and hearts, going through the motions. I tried to pick up any clues from the commanding officers and the other teams as we got ready and boarded the AV.

Nothing stood out to me until we came into land. Through the viewing screen, I saw another valley network, much like the one where the Syniat had attacked us.

The AV landed in the lowest point of the valley and we all marched off as usual. As Scrub Team 2 followed after the APS, Theta turned off her comms and lifted her visor up.

Catching my eye, she pointed up. "No drone."

I scanned the horizon, she was right. We weren't being observed. Quickly muting my own comm, I lifted my visor. "Everyone. This is it."

One by one, they cut comms and raised their visors.

"This is the set up," I continued. "Be on your guard. Keep an eye out for defensible positions we can retreat to. Caves, bluffs, anything."

"Move out in a circle formation," Umak added, looking up to each ridgeline suspiciously. The rest of them nodded grimly, but remained silent as they reactivated their helmets.

Empire of Oshbob

It was just as well they did as a communication came in from Colonel Azash.

"Scrub team 4, follow in until eight hundred meters, then form a rearguard. Lepto-gigantis reported in the area."

Even with visors down, we each managed to convey that *yep, we're being fucked* look.

Umak responded to the communication. "Leptos? And you want one team in a valley to deal with them, Colonel Azash? They nest in the hundreds. Sometimes thousands."

"Why are you here if you can't clear a few Leptos?" the colonel replied with obvious enjoyment. *"Do we need to send in an elven or human squad to get the job done properly and have you all demoted?"*

As Umak responded as professionally as he could, my mind worked over the problem and how best to face the Leptos. They were relentless, rat-like creatures. Like the Arachnids, they stood around one meter tall. But they were around three meters long, with wicked teeth and claws. They could climb, they could swim, and they swarmed their enemies. The only thing they didn't like were predators bigger than them. Which definitely wasn't us.

As that thought washed over me, the commander spoke again, *"Scrub 4. What are you waiting for? Move, move, move!"*

"What we gonna do?" Nozz asked.

Umak shrugged. "Move. And if anyone has any ideas, I'm all ears."

"We need to know how many we're dealing with first," Theta replied. "A hundred, two hundred, we've got a chance. Any more and we're screwed."

"If there's more, then there's only one answer," I replied. I had to speak through the comms, so I didn't want to give away my intentions. "We get to high ground. The nests will be lower than us. That should give us half a chance."

They looked at me expecting more. I tapped my helmet and hoped they'd just trust me.

"The ridge on our left looks to have the least dips and troughs," Umak offered. "Let's hit our checkpoint then head up?"

"Agreed, sergeant," I replied, and we set off into the valley, hugging the base of the ridge to our left.

The command came after a couple of minutes. *"Hold your position, Scrub 4."*

"Understood," Umak replied, then used the group channel. "Required position is eight hundred meters. Keep that distance," he warned, then set off up the side of the valley, weapon primed and ready.

I expected to hear a complaint from command that we'd moved, but none came. I suspected they were trying to make our demise as innocent looking as possible should there be an investigation afterward. That thought gave me a little confidence. Whoever was pulling strings, even if it was someone from a major corporation, wasn't all powerful within the military even if they could insert their people into positions of power when they needed to.

Empire of Oshbob
Partition 11

From the top of the ridge, we got our first signs of the Leptos. A group of around twenty at the base of the valley were moving to where we had been.

Finally, Umak received a communication that he put through to us all.

"Scrub Team 4. Why are you heading up the valley side? We need you back down, drawing the Leptos away from the APS."

"We can draw them away and kill them just as well from up here," Umak replied. "We'll be much more effective and in a far better defensible position."

"You're not supposed to be defending yourselves, you fucking idiot. You're supposed to be killing Leptos so that they can't attack the rear of the APS team."

"So you want us to go against all of our training and let ourselves get overwhelmed and killed in the base of the valley so the APS can kill a Wraith Fox?" Umak asked.

I looked down the valley at the steadily increasing numbers of Leptos. It was bad.

"If you get overwhelmed and killed, then that's because you're not good soldiers. Nobody will be surprised."

"Perhaps we just need better training," Umak replied. "How about you come here and show us how it's done?"

"Stick to the plan, Sergeant Umak, follow the line of approach laid out, or you will be held accountable for your team's actions today and stripped of rank."

With those words the communication was cut. Umak looked at me with something approaching terror in his eyes. "We need to go down."

"Do we? If a commanding officer gives you a command that makes no sense and puts you in unnecessary harm, then you are permitted to make a judgment call. You've explained the situation and you're right. Those Leptos won't even fucking scratch the

APS, they'll decimate us. I know it's gonna be hard if we disregard the order, but if we follow it, we're dead."

"Damn it, Oshbob. I'm a year away from getting out. Getting out as a sergeant! I'll get a good pension. Not great but…"

Rather than messing around with comms and visors, I pulled my helmet off and glared at Umak. "You go down there, you're never getting out. This valley will be your grave. We can't fight that many Leptos, but we can fight a disciplinary."

He opened his visor, "Fight the military. Are you mad?"

I shook my head. "They're run by corpos. Corpos like profits, and as sly as they all are, they still need to have rules and they still have to follow them. Because if they don't, their competitors won't, and they really can't be having that. Trust me," I said with way more confidence than I felt. "If they push us on this and it goes to court, they won't have a leg to stand on."

"If you have a lawyer!" he snapped. "You know how much a half-decent lawyer costs? I won't even be able to defend myself. If I die… at least my full pension goes to my family."

"If it goes to court, I'll provide the lawyers," I promised. "And if you don't like this part of the plan, you're gonna hate the rest of it."

He groaned. "What have you got planned?"

"What are the APS hunting?"

"A Wraith Fox," Theta said with way more excitement than was needed. She'd already clicked onto what I was trying to do.

Umak still looked confused.

"And what do Wraith Foxes hunt?"

Realization dawned on him. "Leptos! It was probably hunting them before we came!"

"It was definitely hunting," I said, pointing at the swelling mass of Leptos at the bottom of the valley.

"What's going on?" Agga asked, sounding completely confused.

Lanris hissed at his side. "We're gonna lead the Leptos to the Wraith fox and try not to get torn apart by both of them."

"Exactly. Make sure to kill plenty of the Leptos as we go. We need to back up our side of the story. Let's make it look like we're being pushed back."

"Crafty bastard," Umak muttered, looking sick.

Empire of Oshbob

"They're coming up," Theta warned, then fired a short burst from her rifle.

Her attack seemed to have the exact opposite result that we were looking for, and the Leptos sent up a screech of enraged joy. Worse still, more Leptos burst from concealed holes in the scrub beneath us. The trigger-happy Theta looked suitably guilty at what her early attack had brought about.

Umak didn't care and yelled out orders. "Hit the front line only! Slow their advance! Bunch 'em up where we can and then frag the stinking fleabags when there's enough of 'em together."

It was a good tactic, and we unleashed hell on them. Screams of pain filled the air for a time, but the Leptos spread out rather than bunched together. Not only was it not worth throwing grenades, but all hopes of a slow retreat were dashed as the Leptos threatened to get behind us.

"We need to run!" Umak shouted.

I applauded the call, and the seven of us turned and legged it along the ridge toward the APS location.

It was probably Umak's intention to stop running at some point, but the Leptos were so fast it wasn't an option. There were thousands now, and while we'd managed to draw most of the snarling, slavering monsters in a long thick line, some were still racing along the ridge below us in a desperate attempt to loop around and ensnare us.

Umak shouted, "Cover me." Then he slowed into our ranks to hurl a grenade, promptly matching our pace again after.

A risky glance back told me that the grenade had hit the front of the line. Not the most effective for numbers killed, but the explosion of deadly shrapnel injured a good number and slowed their approach for a brief moment.

We tried to keep the pace as each of us took turns to throw our grenades. It was inevitable we would fail, but the damage we caused was enough to slow the Leptos even more as we continued to cover ground.

Umak left our squad channel open so that we could all hear the orders being screamed at him through the command channel.

"Scrub 4! Hold your position. You're going to ruin the mission!"

"Can't hold. Overwhelmed. Need assistance," Umak grunted in ragged breaths.

"No assistance available. Hold your position and fight. APS will provide assistance when they've completed their mission."

We did not hold our position. We continued our desperate, staggering retreat across the ridge top, until all of our grenades ran out and the APS were in sight—or more crucially in this case, the Wraith Fox they were fighting.

In truth, fighting was a stretch of the imagination. The APS were all protecting their precious suits from its steel-like claws by hiding behind any defense they could, while taking the occasional potshot at the furious beast. Not one of them had their famed plasma swords out despite it being very obvious in my brief glimpse that they could have charged and ended the battle in seconds.

The commander was screaming through Umak's comm now, and I couldn't help but be impressed with how calm he remained, completely disregarding the spew of venomous threats.

"Go down!" he yelled, waving us toward the APS battle.

We followed smoothly, racing down the bank, firing at those Leptos who'd been trying to cut us off.

We couldn't do nearly enough damage to break through in the time we had, so with a desperate move, I raised my rifle and took aim at the Wraith Fox, still around three hundred meters away. Even if I wasn't bounding down the hill, jolting around like a bag of hammers in a hurricane, I probably wouldn't have hit it. But the fresh fire along with my rage-filled roar as I pulled the trigger got its attention.

When it laid eyes on us and the marauding Leptos, its predator instincts took over. With a yip of eagerness and terrifying speed and agility, it lost all interest in the APS and dashed toward us.

The APS troops finally tried to take the fight to the creature, but it was too late. The fox was far swifter than the heavily armored mech suits, and it stretched out a lead despite their best efforts.

"Bear to the right!" Umak thundered.

It was the only option left to us now before we were ripped apart from any number of sources, and as one, we all set off along the embankment, away from the Wraith Fox, the APS, and with a quick glance back over my shoulder, the Leptos who had fallen into panic.

The Wraith Fox seemed to be blind to the continued danger of the APS as it reached the first of the Leptos and lost itself in a killing frenzy. While the danger had technically increased, we were suddenly free of any real trouble.

"Umak!" I shouted.

I didn't need to say more. At the sound of my voice, he turned back and saw that we were clear of most of the danger, and the APS were entering the fray, attacking both Wraith Fox and Leptos.

He held up a hand to bring us to a halt. "Form up, let's offer some support."

Within seconds, we were all facing back the way we'd just come, picking our targets while the APS finally brought out their plasma swords and herded the Wraith Fox between them. Its seconds were numbered now.

"YOU'RE ENTIRE SQUAD IS GOING DOWN FOR THIS!" came the commander's voice through Umak's helmet and along our comms.

Our sergeant looked grim as he replied. "We fought and killed hundreds if not thousands of Leptos. Your orders would have seen us all killed unnecessarily. Next time, give better orders."

The commander responded but Umak was already barking out orders to us. "Move back in. Defensive line! Kill anything that isn't ours."

We did as he asked, focusing on doing things as professionally as we could despite the dire threat from command. I, for one, was very pleased with how the day had gone. Despite the odds set against us, we'd survived again, and now, Asala and the lawyers from 360 could get involved. If things went well, we'd probably be left alone after this, and we might even flush out whoever was gunning for us.

Soon there was nothing left alive. As the last Lepto disappeared, the Balor AV came sweeping down to pick us back up. This time was a little different. The moment it touched down, Colonel Azash came marching off with another five soldiers.

The first thing I hadn't realized was that he was an elf, having never met the man who wanted to send us to our deaths. With recent revelations, it didn't help. I knew that not every elf in the world worked for Living Earth, but I couldn't look at one of them without suspecting them.

"You're all under arrest!" he shouted as he marched up the Lepto-strewn hill, swerving around corpses in his self-righteous dash toward us.

"You'll need to tell us what the charges are first," I replied with suppressed anger.

"Oh I'll tell you," he said, finally reaching us. "Scrub Team 4, you are being arrested for insubordination and endangering the mission!"

I looked down at his deep crimson face and shook my head in disappointment. "It seems to me that the only thing in danger throughout that entire mission was our squad. Yet we haven't lost anyone, the Wraith Fox is down, and there are easily over a thousand Leptos to drain of nanites. That seems like a very successful mission, working from my understanding of success."

"Just leave it, corporal," Umak said, placing a hand on my forearm as Colonel Azash's face grew darker.

He ignored Umak and turned to the approaching APS. "Arrest them! Take them into custody. All of them!" He then looked back at us. "We'll have this out, back at base. You'll pay for your choices today."

"So will you," I replied evenly. "Gross negligence is frowned upon, so I hear."

That seemed to calm him if anything. He produced a horrible sneer. "You think anyone will listen to your snuffling and grunting?"

"No. I don't suppose they will listen to *me*," I replied with a shrug. "But we have the right to legal representatives, and if you push this, I'll have mine push back *all the way*."

The APS nearest me thumped me in the stomach with his gun. His voice came out emotionless and robotic through the massive helmet he wore. "Remember your place, you green pig."

Azash was laughing now. "I must admit, for the entertainment value alone, I'm fascinated by how you think this is going to play out! Legal representatives indeed. Do orcs practice law?"

I fell silent at his mockery and let myself be led off by the APS who'd hit me, taking note of the number on his suit of armor. I then sent a message to Leo to make sure there was recompense for the insult.

Kevin Sinclair

Partition 12

My hopes of being able to contact home were dashed. Even in the military, where calls to the outside were both heavily restricted and monitored, I expected to be given my call. Instead, we were thrown into separate cells, dark, bare, and stinking of pure sewerage from a toilet that looked not to have been flushed for the best part of a century.

Despite everything, I couldn't not take a minute to at least try and flush it, but as I'd suspected, nothing happened. I imagined the guards watching through the surveillance cameras, laughing, then pushed those thoughts from my mind as I eyed the stained mattress.

Shaking my head, I picked the cleanest spot on the floor and sat down with my back against the wall. I'd sent a stream of short messages to Leo, outlining what had happened and what I would need. Not being able to receive a reply on the keystone modification was starting to feel like a huge oversight. Though I understood the need for it.

Now it was just a waiting game, so I closed my eyes, and thought of all the different people I had to kill in the coming years and how I would do it. My imagination didn't stretch far. No elaborate deaths played out in my mind's eye. There were just a montage of faces and so many punches.

I must have entertained myself for hours, when the lock in the door activated and it swung open to admit a guard with a rifle.

"Up. You've been called for questioning." He spat the words out as if it left a bad taste in his mouth just speaking to me.

Ignoring his vehemence, I pushed myself up from the floor with a heave and a groan, far stiffer than I'd expected after our afternoon run.

"Who gave the order to ignore the commander?" Azash asked almost as soon as I sat down in the interrogation room.

Empire of Oshbob

"Colonel Azash," I said slowly, but respectfully. "As I informed you on the battlefield, I will be pressing a complaint against you for your negligence during our mission. The only reason I've been unable to do so is because you have continued your negligence and deprived me of any form of communication. Which, I might add, is another offense. With that in mind, I believe the protocol is to assign another officer to the handling of this investigation."

"You think you're smart, orc?"

"It's Corporal Oshbob, and no, not particularly," I answered honestly. "But I am used to being screwed over by people with a dislike for orcs, so when I reentered the military, I made the effort to read and learn as much as I could about military procedure to protect myself where I could. We do all have rights, don't we? Even orcs?"

He fell silent at that. The other officer, a prison sergeant, looked uncomfortable as I spoke, but he remained quiet too.

Azash snapped out of it soon after. "Who gave the order to ignore my command?"

"Nobody gave an order to ignore you. But as trained and seasoned soldiers who were involved in the specific battle, we all had to make judgment calls. If you were there, you would have made the same decision."

"No!" he said, slamming his hands on the table. "I would have died with honor."

I stared at him for a long moment, before responding. "So you admit you left us to die?"

He blustered at my reply before responding awkwardly, "That is not what I said."

I turned to the prison sergeant. "I request to be questioned by someone impartial as is my right. And I request for my legal counsel to be present before responding to any more accusations."

He nodded, then turned to Azash. "We have to do this. He's right on that at least, and this is all recorded."

Azash paled, though he must have known it was being recorded. "Very well, Sergeant Estar. Escort him back to his cell. I am certain we can arrange someone beyond reproach for this investigation." Then he turned back on me. "Know two things. If I was there with you, we would have stood and we would have held. And secondly, this stall for time isn't going to help you."

Kevin Sinclair

I met his eyes, but said nothing, much to his irritation. The prison guard led him out, and I was soon escorted back to my cell to wait again.

I slept in my sitting position, but when I was woken by the cell door opening, I felt refreshed and ready to face the day.

The guards led me back to the interrogation room without any fuss, where I was greeted by Sergeant Estar the prison officer and none other than Base Commander Wendel. The look of malice etched across his full expression, from his narrowed eyes to his thin-lipped scowl, was clear to read. My chances at reason and fairness had not improved with this elven asshole. I consoled myself with the knowledge that I'd at least annoyed Azash.

"We are recording. Do you understand?" Estar asked.

"I do," I replied neutrally.

"You seem to understand a lot, orc," the commander replied.

"That's Corporal Orc to you," I replied simply. "I'm getting tired of reminding officers how they're supposed to address those under their command."

He bristled at my correction, so I made it worse. "Respect works both ways. It's in the AMC handbook."

He slammed his hands down on the table, ignoring my words. "You are causing a lot of issues here on my base."

I shook my head. "I've caused no issues for you. Unless you're involved in the attempt to wipe out my team? Otherwise, I've done only my duty."

"You really do think a lot about yourself, don't you?" he asked with a forced smirk. "*Your* team indeed! "

"Yes, my team. The team of which I am part of. I don't know why you're trying to play with my words and pretend they mean something they don't. If we have to continue with this bullshit shakedown, can you please stick to the facts?"

There was a sharp intake of breath from Wendel. "You dare speak to your betters this way?"

I couldn't fight the frown on my face as I leaned forward. "You're not better than me. You just have a higher rank within the military, either through birthright or service. And I haven't said anything that should offend you yet. Tell me the charges, and I'll disprove them."

Empire of Oshbob

The commander sighed. "Your guilt is assured."

"By whom? As a citizen of Artem and an officer of its military, I have the right to be judged by an impartial jury once all of the evidence has been collected and heard."

He laughed. The prison guard didn't. "You won't see a jury, you fool. We have irrevocable proof!"

"I'll let my legal counsel decide that. Where is my legal counsel by the way? Because I'm fairly certain by law that you aren't supposed to be questioning me until I'm represented."

"I'm your legal counsel," Sergeant Estar replied grimly, shifting uncomfortably as he spoke. "I have all the necessary qualifications and requirements to act as such."

"No. You really don't," I replied equally as grim, drawing out each word to lend them weight. "You would need my consent, which I refuse."

The commander laughed victoriously. "Then you refuse council! A foolish decision, but your recorded decision, nonetheless. Your official trial will be held in twelve hours."

"You will not let me contact any one as is my right?"

"Oh heavens no. You've caused enough trouble."

"And you do realize that is illegal and you have it all recorded?" I replied, eyeing both of them.

"Not if nobody knows about it," Wendel replied.

"These recordings will never be heard again," Estar added.

"I hope you both know what you're doing. Because I'm going to tear you both a new asshole over this, legally speaking, of course."

"Guards!" Wendel yelled.

Four of them rushed into the room.

"Take him back to his cell." He then snarled at me. "Twelve hours, orc."

All four laid hands on me and attempted to drag me from the room. I had no intention of resisting, but I figured I'd make it as difficult for them as possible and forced them to haul me up and hold my entire weight until I was deposited in my cell once again.

Three hours later, the cell door opened again. The features of the guard framed in light were obscured by shadow, but I could hear the tension in his voice as he spoke.

"Follow me, corporal."

I stood and followed without a word. He led me to a different room this time, one where a suited man and woman sat, with serious expressions. I took the seat across from them while the guard stepped back to take a position against the wall to the side of the door.

I eyed the two suited people across from me and the woman smiled.

"We're from Turner and Syalas Attorneys."

I recognized the name immediately. It was the law firm that took up the three floors under Asala at the tower. It was now a subsidiary of 360, but that information was kept as quiet as possible, discoverable only with a lot of digging.

"I'm Terese Sloan and my associate is Caleb Price. We are here to represent you."

"Am I glad to see you two. I was starting to worry. What can you tell me about what's happening out there?"

"We have contacted the Regional Major General about your case, and it is being moved up to be heard in the Luas court. You will receive an unbiased result from there as the jury will be made up of officers who owe secondary allegiances to a range of different corporations. Whatever internal battles are going on within this base will be swept aside for the hard facts. We have spent years developing our portfolio of contacts within the military to ensure smooth legal practice regarding all of our clients."

"I need you to take on the rest of my team, too," I replied in a tone that brooked no argument.

"Already done," Caleb replied. "Though it will be a while before your sergeant can be tried as he is recovering from an incident in custody which will surely result in an interesting settlement claim or compensation."

I nodded along as they spoke. "So what happens next?"

"We're awaiting to hear word from your accusers as we speak," Terese answered. "In the meantime, we should discuss a few details of the case."

"Happily," I replied, leaning back in the chair and regretting the decision as the chair creaked ominously.

I spent around five minutes covering the lead up to the last mission before starting in on the details of the following day. I was interrupted by a guard I hadn't seen before, poking his head in the room.

Caleb was about to chastise him, but instead smiled as the guard spoke.

"All charges against Corporal Oshbob have been dropped."

I didn't smile. Turning back to the attorneys, I glowered. "Not good enough. I want to raise charges against the base commander. Wendel."

Terese shook her head. "We can. But I would strongly advise against it. Perhaps the mission commander?" She rustled through her notes. "Colonel Azash? The one who gave the instructions for you to go into the valley against all military sense."

"Even if it was those above him who gave him his orders?"

"That's not a nest you want to go poking around in. It would be incredibly difficult to achieve a positive result. The military has laws, and they are law abiding. But going after high-ranking officers is a sure-fire way to draw attention you really don't need if you want to make it out of here alive."

Caleb nodded in agreement. "Personally, I would suggest you don't even go after the colonel. I imagine everyone involved will currently be dealing with their own fallout from this. Heads will no doubt metaphorically roll."

I didn't like it, but I understood it. "Very well. I'll leave it be."

Kevin Sinclair

Partition 13

Anger still had a hold of me as I booted the door to the barracks open. That was it. They slunk away, no questions answered, and no punishments, leaving them free to try again.

Five heads spun to look at me. Everyone was there but Umak. He was apparently still in the infirmary after what sounded like a severe beating.

They all spoke quickly, but Theta was first to me. "You're back? What the hell's happening, Osh?"

"Nothing," I replied simply, walking past her to sit on my bed. "All charges are dropped. Everything is apparently back the way it was before, apart from the fact that Umak has been injured. Have any of you heard anything from him?"

"No, we're just sitting here waiting for news," she said miserably. "We were told only you and he are being held accountable, but that we weren't allowed to leave the barracks until it had been resolved."

I shrugged. "It's gonna be swept under the rug now. It's not an awful result, but it's not great either. We're gonna have to be on our guard."

"Bullshit," Agga grumbled.

"Damn right it is," Nozz added. "One of them stuck up bastards should be made to pay. I mean, they tried to bloody kill us! Did you see how the APS were fighting against that A Ranker! They were just hiding, they weren't even trying." He booted his bed, flipping it over with the force of the kick, then wincing in pain he hobbled over to the couch to nurse his bloody shin. "They're all in on it. We need to get transferred."

Lanris snorted. "We've got no chance of that happening. That's not how the military works. They might hold off for a month or two with their attacks, but they'll be back to see us dead."

"How the hell do you know that," Nozz growled, more for the pain in his shin than any annoyance at Lanris.

Empire of Oshbob

I was, however, very interested in the answer. Lanris was quiet, he'd warmed up a bit lately, but there was still something not right about him.

He sighed at Nozz's question. "I have family in the military... My mother is a city guard commander."

Theta spun on him. "You're joking, right?"

He shook his head. "Only reason I joined. But... we fell out, and I, thinking I was clever, moved out here to be away from her. I tried to get a transfer back when I saw how many people we were losing. She tried to help but they wouldn't let me go. Once you're out in the wilds on one of these hidden bases, you stay here until you die or finish your service. Unless you're an officer."

"Well shit," Theta said, lying back on her bed. "No wonder you're always a bit weird."

"I'm not weird," he protested.

"Sure," Agga chuckled. "Only damn half-orc I've ever seen with a stick up his arse as straight as yours."

As they spoke, I was watching Lanris carefully, considering whether to kill him or not. Last thing I needed was someone passing on my secrets to other people in the military. I knew from the start there was something off about him.

"I'm not a half-orc," Lanris snapped. "I'm a quarter at best, but I'm proud of my orc heritage," he said quickly, turning to me. "And I see how you're looking at me, corporal. I swear, I've never told anyone about what you're up to and I never will."

"I agree with Theta and Agga," I said calmly. "There's always been something about you that's been a bit off. You have a stick up your arse. I'm glad we know why. You swear to me you won't sell me out?"

"I swear."

I found myself grinding my teeth together before I could utter a reply. "Thanks for letting us know why. You can loosen up now?"

He nodded, looking the whitest shade of green I'd ever seen.

"Your dad was a half-orc?" I asked.

"From what my mother tells me, yeah. She doesn't talk about him much."

"Okay. At least we know now." I stood up, drawing all of their attention with the sudden move. "I'm going to go to the infirmary to see the sergeant."

"We'll come," Nozz said.

I shook my head. "We all go separate. Too much otherwise, and I need information."

I saw their crestfallen looks and felt a pang of empathy. They all respected Umak, loved him even, and I understood why. He was a good leader, and as solid a half-orc as I'd ever met. "We can go in twos. Nozz, come with me. The rest of you can take it in turns after us."

They accepted my orders far easier than I expected. But after all we'd been through together, I supposed I shouldn't have been so surprised.

The infirmary was in the main base. As we crossed the parade and landing strip, all eyes were on us—some with anger, some with confusion, others intrigued. We ignored them all.

Entering the building, we were stopped by waiting guards. They'd watched us approach with wary expressions, barely concealed anger. I wondered what stories had already been spread.

"What do you want here?" the human on the right side asked, his gun pointed at my chest.

"We're going to the infirmary to see our sergeant," I replied, stifling the warring emotions pushing to break free.

"No visitors permitted."

"On what grounds?"

"On the grounds that the base commander said so," he snapped.

"Well unfortunately for the base commander, even he has to follow rules, and as I'm the sergeant's direct reporting officer, I have the right to see him. Stand aside."

"He is under arrest," the other guard said, stepping forward threateningly.

"No, he's not, and you have no right to stop us entering our command building. Step aside or—"

The first guard interrupted with a sneer, "Or what, orc."

I threw an uppercut into his armored stomach aiming for the wall behind him. The armor protected against penetration but it did nothing to protect against force. He lifted off his feet and clattered into the wall.

The other guard tried to shoot, but I was already moving into him, knocking his gut to the side with my descending right elbow and sending a strong straight left to his armored chin. His helmet spun, and in his moment of bewilderment, I snatched the gun and threw it to Nozz, who caught it in a muddled panic.

Then I grabbed the gun from the guard recovering on the floor.

There was shouting across the base now from those who'd seen the altercation. The two guards were trying to get to their feet.

"I suggest," I growled forcefully, "that you read up on the rules of our base and the military in general. Get inside now."

The first guard to speak tried to lunge for the gun. I stepped back so that he over-extended and stumbled into me. Then I smashed him to the side of the armored helmet so he fell to the floor, where I kicked his head again.

When he finally came to a stop from his little game of head pinball, he lay still, unconscious.

I grabbed his armored chest and threw him through the door, then turned to his fellow guard. "Go get the base commander. Let's clear this unwarranted assault up, eh?"

He ran off into the building while I turned to those who had come running over. "We were unlawfully refused entry to see our sergeant. We've been cleared of all crimes, and whether you hate us or not, tread carefully because I promise you that the law is on our side here."

"Fuck the law. You don't get to go around doing what you want," a big human said. "Down on the ground now or I'll shoot."

"Threaten me again and I'll shoot first," I replied coldly. "Neither of us has armor, who do you think will last longer?"

He was saved from answering by a shout from the window above. "Let them through!"

I looked up to the window to see Commander Wendel leaning out. I was both surprised and unwilling to let the opportunity go begging.

"Come on, Nozz."

My terrified squad mate nodded eagerly, and we entered the building properly. As we marched down the empty corridors, I wondered if we'd see Wendel again, but we reached the infirmary without seeing a soul.

Umak was a mess, bruised and beaten and missing both arm mods and his left eye. He still managed a smile as he noticed us.

"Some fine string pulling you did there, corporal."

"You're welcome, sergeant. How are you feeling, though?"

"Like shit. But, believe it or not, I'm getting the care I need now, and some shiny new mods. I've been assured they'll be of better quality."

"Why did they mess your mods up?" Nozz asked, just as confused as I was.

"I dunno what they were thinking." He lowered his voice before he continued. "I hear they're moving the base commander on."

"That would be good," I replied, feeling a small surge of hope for an easier end to my final two years. "What about Azash? He's as much of a problem."

"I don't know, but I can't imagine them putting him as our mission commander again. I think we'd have the right to refuse from what I gather. We'll have to see what the new base commander has to say."

"Yeah," I drawled, unconvinced. "If it's another elf, I might just kill them off the cuff and have done."

Umak laughed. "You did good, Oshbob. I think we're in the clear."

"You're only saying that because you have less than a year to see out before you're off," Nozz said lightheartedly.

"Exactly! Even I can survive that long with you lot. And I have a nice compensation nest egg now, so I won't even have to go begging to our resident gang lord here for work."

Nozz shrugged. "There're worse things for a half-orc to have to do. Oh by the way. Lanris is only a quarter orc and his bloody mother is only a city base commander!"

Umak smirked. "He told you then. I'm glad. He's a good kid. He was worried about how you'd all take it. Especially when Oshbob turned up."

It was understandable. The more I thought about it, the more I accepted that I would have kept that information to myself as well.

"He's good with me. You all are." I touched the fingertips of my right hand to my chest and then to his. His eyes widened and I grinned. "You know what that is?"

He nodded. "I was brought up by my father. The Onia is the highest sign of respect an orc can give."

I nodded. "I'd only offered it to three others in my lifetime." I turned to Nozz and repeated the gesture. "Five now."

"And it means respect?" Nozz asked.

"More than that. It means thanks, peace, and togetherness. One of the few things we've kept from our past."

"Then I'm honored," Nozz said, copying the gesture.

I bristled a little at the sight of a half-orc doing it, but I crushed the foolish pride. He meant it as it was intended, and despite my early hatred of half-orcs, I couldn't keep that up now I knew so many good ones.

We talked for a few hours together until one of the base carvers came in to fit Umak's first replacement mod. He chased us out respectfully, and I was happy to go.

Kevin Sinclair

Partition 14

Three long days were spent between the barracks and the mess hall. We weren't alone. It seemed there were hardly any missions leaving the base. Our reception in the mess hall was extra frosty, but no one mustered the enthusiasm to speak with us or even shout an insult.

Yet as strange as the atmosphere was, it paled in comparison to the arrival of our new base commander at our barracks along with Captain Parraway, and Umak.

It was dark out and we were all lounging in our beds at the time, though even I jumped to attention when they entered. Though it galled me deeply to do so.

"So this is Scrub Team Trouble?" he said, eyeing us all sullenly. He was a human of medium height, with a short, well-groomed beard that matched his brown hair, though with more gray.

"Sir!" the rest of the team answered. Not me, but he didn't notice.

"My name is Commander Gullan. I'm sure some of you will have abilities you shouldn't have, to check on things you shouldn't be able to." He eyes landed on me. "Stories percolate around the grapevine, so I'm gonna to tell you something important to address the A Ranker in the room. I don't fucking like orcs. That goes double for half-orcs. Don't like you. Don't trust you. Don't want anything to do with you. But! Even I can admit that you make good soldiers. You probably know the corporations have a big say in Artem Military, and they do, but I have no affiliations with any of those that have caused trouble for you in recent history.

"I've looked over all of the data from the incident myself, and I'd say you handled the situation impressively. Your sergeant, despite being of orc blood, is an intelligent soldier with a keen battle sense. I have brought with me a new mission commander, Colonel Poulson. He is not a micromanager. You will be given instructions to protect APS from little shithouse monsters while they're busy with A Rankers, that is all. Keep good communication lines, and if you find yourselves overwhelmed, we will assist, even if that is through extraction. Do you all understand?"

"We do!" Nozz said, overjoyed to have Umak back.

"Good. The second thing we need to cover is that the intelligent sergeant with a keen battle sense isn't this guy here," he said, pointing his thumb toward Umak. "Though he's probably not a complete idiot after everything that's happened. He's demoted himself to corporal. You have a new sergeant."

That brought angry mumbling from around the room.

"I really, really hope you enjoy working under him and that he keeps you fucking savages in tight order, because I will take no shit from you. I won't try to have you killed—I'll have you demoted and sent to be dealers."

My heart sank at his words. Not only did I want to break his neck for calling us savages but I also knew that whoever the new sergeant was, it was a set up.

It turned out, I wasn't always right. Or at least, I really hoped I wasn't this time.

"Oshbob," he said, marching over to me. "You're now a sergeant. This is the only ceremony you're getting."

He handed a case over to me that I hadn't even noticed he was carrying. I took it, trying to remain neutral.

"Do a good job, sergeant. Don't cause any shit for me and look after those APS like your life depends on it. If you manage to do that, then we don't have to speak again, and I think we'd both prefer that. Yes?"

"Yes, sir." I saluted.

The asshole smirked, then spun on his heel and left our quarters.

"What the hell's going on? Umak?" I half-shouted, throwing the case on the bed. "You demoted yourself?"

"I did. I don't want the responsibility and it was you who made the plan. You who saved us again out there. And it was you who got us all out of trouble back here. If you're not already the squad sergeant, then I don't know who is."

"What about your pension?" Nozz asked, eyes wide.

His stern expression creased into a smile. "Not to worry, Nozz. The compensation I've received for the beating is more 'n enough to see me right for a long time. Now open the case, Osh."

I looked at the black plastic case skeptically before undoing the clips. Inside, there were eight badges for my uniforms along with four bottles of Aska and seven cigars. I looked up at the others, and they were all grinding like drunk goblins.

I met each of their eyes retaining my neutral expression. Then I rubbed my hands together. "Fuck it. Let's enjoy the moment while it lasts."

I threw a bottle to Umak, then one to Agga and one to Theta, before ripping the cap off the last one and taking a long swig. I then passed it to Nozz, who took it gratefully.

"Does that mean you're the first ever orc sergeant?" he asked.

"I neither know, nor care," I replied, scooping up a cigar. "There's no honor in anything these bastards do. I'm here to serve my time, stay alive, and if I can turn a profit while I'm here, then you bet your ass I'm gonna."

I was surprised by the level of enthusiasm my words brought from them as they all cheered.

A couple of days later, our schedule returned to normal. Four days out, three days off. True to his word, Commander Gullan left us entirely alone. Colonel Poulson, who I had only seen briefly, had very little to do with us other than to give me basic orders. Nothing suicidal. The strangest part of the whole thing was having Umak as my corporal now. I still treated him just the same as I had prior.

In fact, the biggest difference now was one change that I made much to everyone in the squad's displeasure. We all trained on our days off now, drilling a dozen different formations, from aggressive to defensive, and just as importantly, how to run away effectively when escape was the only option. Though, as Nozz and Agga both pointed out, that was one area we were pretty handy in. That didn't stop me from pushing them.

One very useful side effect of the change in command was the degree in which we were being watched. It meant that when Leo's drone came again for my nanites, I could speak to everyone without too much worry.

We still had to keep a time limit on how long I spoke, but I took great delight in my first communication home as a sergeant having beaten the attempts against me, comprehensively.

Empire of Oshbob

Leo spoke first as was usual, but passed me onto Harold almost immediately.

He began with an unpleasant sounding wheeze before he spoke. "Well, well, well. I hear someone made sergeant."

"I did, for what it's worth. I'm more worried about why you haven't gotten any help for what's wrong with you."

"Look, lad. I don't want to spend much time on this, okay? So let's get it out of the way so that we can talk about all the other things going on. The top and bottom of it is that I'm dying. I know both Unara and Asala will want you to speak with me about it. Don't bother. I've seen specialists already, and it's because of the sniper mod I had when I was in the military. The ones we got back then were faulty.

"I've spoken to the people in the military, they're doing research on the damage they caused, but right now, there's nothing they can do about it. My nervous system is degrading and it's irreversible. You can try to help me all you want and you'll be wasting both our time. The last thing I want is to be prodded and poked and god knows what else in the little time I have left. Asala is doing well and it looks like you're going to be okay too. That means I'm happy. I had a good life, I helped you and was part of something really special in our district, I can die happy."

It was so much to take in. Everything in me screamed to talk him out of it. To encourage him to fight for every last second. To not lose hope. I wanted to make promises that we could find a cure. But I also trusted him. I respected him, and most of all, I heard what he was saying. He was done. He'd fought his fights, we'd achieved his goals, and he was happy. Who was I to try and guilt trip him into taking therapy and having implants that probably wouldn't work and that he didn't want?

It took me a long moment to process everything, and when I finally opened my mouth to answer, all that came out was, "Okay."

"Ha! I knew you'd understand." He then broke into a coughing fit for a few seconds before continuing. "So, with that out of the way, the next thing I need to talk to you about is my shop. We're linking it into the safe-zone in the Undercity, so whoever it goes to after me will need to be someone you trust."

I hadn't considered that before, but he had a valid point. "I just assumed you would pass it on to Asala. Is there someone else?"

"I want you to have my shop, lad."

"What?" I asked, utterly baffled.

"You know as well as I do that it's one of the safest places in the city. There's quality tech in there that they don't even make anymore. Unless any hostile hackers are over sixty, they probably haven't even heard of half the protocols the systems running. And let's face it, when you're out, you're always going to need a low-key meeting point, even when dealing with those you trust. You can say no, but it's still yours."

"You should give it to Asala," I protested. But Harold would have none of it.

"It's useless for her. What would she need it for? Bah! I'm decided. It's yours. I'm closing up over the next few weeks, and I'm going to go live with Asala. I'm not much use anymore, but with all the trouble going on, I'd feel better being close to her. At least until she's in her new home."

"Then thank you, my friend," I said, feeling horribly emotional. "Will you be moving in with her?"

"Until it's time, yes. I don't want to be a burden to her. She's got a lot on her plate."

"You'll never be a burden, Harold. I'm going to make sure you're looked after even if you won't get tests and help."

He was silent for a moment, then his tone changed from morose to typical upbeat Harold. "Right, good to talk to you, lad, and well done on everything. But there's others waiting to have a word. See you soon."

And he was gone. The line went dark for a few moments, then Asala's voice came on.

"Would he listen?"

"Hello to you too, Asala. And no. He won't listen. Do you know he's giving me his shop?" Silence. "I told him to pass it on to you."

"He won't," she said quietly. "And yes, I knew. He wants to come here in the tower until I move into my new home."

"How are things with 360? With Unara too. Are you both still being targeted?"

"The physical presence has waned after her war on elven kind in Newton and Portolans. Though from what I gather, Portolans ACE are getting nervous if it continues. As for 360, we're still receiving regular hacking attempts, but they aren't so much of a problem. Our biggest issue is still our real estate push in Turan and Newton. Fewer properties are going to auction now. They're being actively bought as they come up for sale. Again, from the records, they're being bought by a wide range of buyers. Meli is working overtime on finding a common link, but they're all semi-wealthy with very well protected accounts. The only common link we've found is Kenneth. The new Newton gang lord."

I felt a swell of anger. "I thought the Newton gang lord was in our pocket? What's he up to?"

"While the district gang lords are not my area of expertise, and I too thought the Newton gangs were subdued, the ACE reports from Newton write off recent building and business damage as non-crime related, which is how our own ACE cover up gang business."

"So the gangs in Newton are fucking up the buildings and someone else is buying them up before they get to auction?"

"Exactly. The link is tenuous at the moment, but we're working to nail it down."

"Have you spoken to Unara about it?"

"We've discussed the possibility of the matter. I'll pass you over to her now."

"Thank you, Asala. We'll get this sorted out."

"We do have a wide range of buildings in Newton now, so it's not essential to continue our buy up. My only real concern is that someone is targeting assets we desire and they are doing it in a purposeful way to cause us trouble."

"Yeah, we'll sort it out. One way or another."

I moved swiftly onto Unara. Her voice was surprisingly bright. "Oshbob! It's so good to hear you. I've heard all about the attempt to kill you and got a full report from the lawyers over what happened. You're a sergeant now?"

"I am. Hopefully that will keep me alive. Things have settled here, but it sounds like it's getting worse there?"

"Not so much on the streets. There's been no more attempts on me for over a week, but did Asala tell you about Newton?"

"The gangs are helping whoever is fucking with us help them buy properties?"

"Yep. I'm planning on having a word with Kenneth, but I've held off to speak with you first."

"No, it's a good idea. Contact him and keep it friendly. See if you can find out who's paying him to turn the properties over. Keep it sweet unless you think he knows he's screwing us over. There's every chance he doesn't."

"I can do that. Though he griped about the amount of orcs moving to Portolans, he hasn't been any trouble otherwise."

"That's good to hear. How's the work coming along underground? The sooner we get Asala safe, the happier I'll be."

"It's gonna be another six months at least. We're focused on the tunnel system first. I expect that whole underground area to be locked up tight in around two months, then we can get to work on the living quarters."

"That's not so bad, I suppose. What about…"

A shout from behind drew my attention. I turned to see a drone heading in our direction.

"Drone. Gotta go," I snapped.

Leo dropped his to the ground. I heard Unara's voice as I walked away.

"Stay safe."

"You too," I replied, heading back to my teammates.

Whether she heard or not I didn't know, but the drone was overhead now. It flew around the area a couple of times before moving off to the west, and we continued on our route, scanning the surrounding land for danger.

Empire of Oshbob

Partition 15
Unara

I came up from a sewer grate out the back of the garage and moved swiftly to the extractor vent for the spray shop in Kenneth's base of operations. Covering my face, I worked off the grille and slid inside before climbing my way up into the ceiling space.

I only wanted to see Kenneth, but I figured I might as well snoop and see if I could hear anything of interest on the way. It was mainly just clanging, banging, and metal cutting, which allowed me to move quickly toward his office. There wasn't much chance of being heard over the racket below.

I eventually came to the part of the roof space that went above the offices. Here, there was a concerted effort at security, a camera pointing along the vent.

"Leo. Is that camera down yet?"

"It's looped, you're good to go through. The charged section of duct is going down... now."

I didn't bother to reply as I focused on my task, crawling forward faster than most people could walk. I passed the camera and reached the section of duct Leo was talking about. There were two dead rats in the stretch, flies buzzing around their bodies, and a bitter smell.

They must have had to clean the ducts regularly with their security measures.

I finally made it to the grille that overlooked Kenneth's office. He didn't have nearly as much security as he ought to have as the gang lord of Newton, even if he was a puppet one.

I waited for around twenty minutes watching his actions. He didn't do much. Made a few calls, hacked on a keyboard with thick, grease-covered fingers. He was a big human, with a scruffy brown beard and a bald head, full of muscles borne of heavy work.

Just as I felt I wouldn't get anything useful from watching any longer, another man entered his room. I couldn't see them, but it hardly mattered as long as I could hear. I allowed myself a small smile as the shouting began.

"Four fucking buildings, Lal. What the hell happened?"

"Does it matter, boss?" the other man said confidently. "Can't you just charge the buyers more for the work?"

"That's not how this works! They tell us the building, we make sure they can get it. And what makes you think I want them buying all of these buildings. I want to know who's moving into my district, and I don't like not knowing."

I cursed that it seemed like Kenneth was in the same position as we were. But he was getting paid to be in it.

"Can we not buy them? It's how Grant got rich, right?"

"Yeah, and look how that ended up. Too big for his own boots. Just stop fucking up, Lal. It's hard enough keeping ACE sweet when we do it right."

Lal snorted back some phlegm but swallowed whatever he produced. The sound got under my skin so much that I wanted to jump down and punch him in the throat instead of lying there listening.

"It won't happen again, boss. Maybe we should ease off using fire for a bit?"

"About the smartest thing I've heard you say since I've known you, Lal. Maybe hit pipework, water, gas, whatever. Fuck electrics up, smash their roofs in when it's raining. Anything… I don't know. Just stop burning half the streets, though."

"Got it, boss."

I heard the door open and close, and watched Kenneth as he hit a key on his keyboard which filled the room with bass-heavy synth music. Then he leaned back in his desk chair, rubbing his face tiredly.

I lifted the vent silently away, then dropped into the room behind him. I landed lightly, the music covering the patter of my feet hitting the floor. When he removed his hands from his face and took me in, he jumped in his seat, his hand going to his chest.

"Fucking hell, Unara, my heart damn near exploded." He seemed breathless for a moment as he recovered.

Empire of Oshbob

I stood and watched and waited for the dramatic display to die down.

He finally managed to turn the music off and regain his composure. "Whatcha you doing here?"

"Wondering, mainly," I replied, placing my hands on his desk and meeting his eyes. "Why are you burning buildings down in Newton?"

"You heard about that, eh?"

"I did hear."

"So what's the problem? Nice little side hustle to bring in the creds. All of our deals are still in place."

"We have a vested interest in Portolans, though, don't we? How much are they paying you?"

He raised his hands and shrugged. "Depends, don't it? 10k for an empty building with an owner in need of some persuasion. 30k for one with an owner or tenant still occupying."

"That's a lot of creds. Where are they coming from? Who's giving you the money?"

"Whoever buys the building. Different every time. There's some kind of syndicate going on where people who want to buy into the area are put in touch with me and they pay for the building to be *cleared*."

"It must have started somewhere. Who was the first to speak with you?"

He winced. "I can't rightly remember now. A suited guy—human, about a month. He came into the shop, didn't give no name or anything. Just made the offer. Said people would be in touch if I was interested."

"Any ideas on where the syndicate might be based? You got a list of names of those who got in touch?"

He shook his head. "No names."

I pulled my dagger and slammed it into his desk, burying an inch of the blade. "Then how do you know it was the people who went on to buy the buildings who gave you the money?"

His eyes flicked down to the knife and up to me nervously, but I saw the hint of anger there. He wanted to hit me. It was as clear as day in his glassy eyes.

"Different account numbers each time. Paid when the people told me they were gonna pay."

"That still doesn't mean it was the individuals."

"Why's it matter so much? What's a few buildings in Newton mean to you?"

"I want the account numbers, and I want a list of the buildings they belong to. Has anyone moved into the buildings yet?"

With a rub of his brow, he sighed. "No occupants in any of them yet. Like I say, we only got this gig a month ago. Only thing I can tell yer is that the building and remodeling work is going crazy slow. We keep checking to see who's moving in so we can offer security, but so far, not a soul. Now. You gonna answer my question? Seeing as I'm being so ameanaming."

"I think you mean amenable," I replied, not entirely sure of the word myself but knowing Kenneth had totally got it wrong. I still decided to give him an answer. The relationship between Portolans and Newton would always be strained, but I didn't have to make it worse. "Because they're big moves. Because land is more valuable than money once you have enough money, and there's a lot of land changing hands in areas we control. You guys are drawing a lot of attention, too. That doesn't look good."

He bristled at that. "Drawing attention! No more than you killing all of those elves. Don't think we don't know the order came from Portolans, Unara. You know how much heat we took off ACE for that?"

I ignored the accusation. There was no way they could really know if it was us, so I pushed on. "We're gonna need you to stop clearing the buildings."

He planted his hands on the desk. "We're toeing the line with you, but this is a good money spinner. I still have a district to run, and refusing the work doesn't help me one little bit."

I leaned over the desk to match his angry glare. "It helps you by not pissing me off."

"But why does it matter!" he barked out, smacking his meaty fists down on the desk this time.

I might have been threatened if he didn't lean back in his chair as he did so. "Whoever is trying to move into Newton is no friend of ours. Which means, they're no friend of yours. Haven't we been good to you since Oshbob killed Grant?"

"You have," he said with a pained grimace. "But we need that money. At least sweeten the fucking deal a little here."

Empire of Oshbob

I was about to tear into him. But my own mention of Oshbob had me thinking. What would he do? Technically, this wasn't even my direct problem. The properties were for 360, so it was Asala's. As proud of my skills as I was, this kind of thing wasn't really one of them. *What would they do?*

With a rub of my chin, because I'd seen Oshbob do it a thousand times when he was trying to present a certain image, I hmmm'd. "Here's an idea. When you get new buildings, you do what you need to do with them. You get your money."

His eyes widened.

"BUT! You let us know first. Then when the building becomes available, we can put our own offer in."

He scowled again. His face was like a damn disco. "Why do you want buildings in Newton?"

Stifling a sneer, I wrangled it into an innocent smile. He didn't know we already owned twenty percent of the damn place. "We don't want the buildings. We just don't want your new clients to have them."

The furrowed brows of confusion this time. "But you don't know who it is."

"We don't need to. Sometimes knowing that your enemy wants something is enough to know you don't want them to have it. You can buy them yourself if you have the funds." Which I knew they didn't. "Or we can buy them."

"You have the funds?" he asked, suddenly interested.

"Not necessarily. But we know people who would happily buy, and that at least keeps it out of certain hands."

"Ah, hell. Okay, I'll do it, but don't make it obvious that I'm telling you… and I want something for it."

"What do you want?"

"Five k per property."

I snatched the dagger out of the table. Kenneth flinched like I was going to use it. Truth be told, I wanted to. But I kept Oshbob and Asala in my mind. "Five k it is. Don't mess me about on this, Kenneth. I want every single building, and I'll decide whether or not we move on it. You only get paid for the buildings we move on."

His chest swelled up with indignation. He was about to protest. I spun the knife in my hand and stared at the vein in his neck that I would open up if he uttered anything other than an affirmative.

Whether he noticed my expression or had some kind of sixth sense, his shoulders sagged. "Five k for those you take. Got it."

With a wide smile, I leapt up to the opening in the ceiling, grabbing it with my fingertips, then hauled myself in with one fluid movement. Once inside I scurried as silently as I could away, pausing only to hear his mumbled words.

"Creepy bitch."

My smile grew wider.

Once I was well away from Newton, I contacted Asala.

She answered immediately, "Unara. How did it go?"

"Kenneth has no real details, but he has account numbers which he's sending me, and I've made him tell me each time he's contacted to take a building down. I figure we get in before whoever's paying him and take the property off their hands before they even know what's happening. With a little tact, of course."

"Of course. I'll set up a list of buyers who could purchase the buildings without it linking to us. Play them at their own game."

"Perfect. Is everything else okay? Any more trouble?"

"None at all. I think perhaps our recent victories over our unknown assailants are finally getting to them."

I wasn't convinced. I expected a lot more trouble. We needed to find out who they were and kill them slowly. But Asala was on the edge at the moment. With the constant pressure of running 360, the attacks on the tower, and Harold having finally moved into the tower to *keep an eye* on her, but in reality just giving her something else to manage, I found myself agreeing with her.

"Yeah. I think they're running scared."

"It's good to hear you say that, Unara. I've been sick with worry."

I smiled to myself. I was getting good at the diplomacy. "Still keep Meli working on finding out who we're dealing with. We need to crush them one way or another."

"Don't worry. I have a full team working on it. We'll find them. No matter how many doors we have to open to do it."

Empire of Oshbob

Partition 16

For the first month, we were jeered as we trained, especially by the APS who hated us now.

The constant abuse got to a few of the team. Lanris hung his head with embarrassment. Theta got angry. Agga got into fights. Froom and Nozz just got on with it. Over time, they all stopped caring and got on with it.

After all, the only reason we were training was to stay alive. And that was something none of these bastards wanted. Some of them had been involved in actively trying to make the opposite come true.

Yet after several months and despite the high risks associated with being in a Scrub Team, we lost not one member of our squad. We carried out our work in a diligent and professional manner, and those who mocked us gradually fell silent. After around ten months, it was becoming a point of pride for the base that we didn't lose people and nor did the other teams when we were on missions with them.

By that point most of the soldiers who now made up the Scrub Teams were almost entirely different to those who'd been involved in the altercation. Turnover was still depressingly fast for the other Scrub Teams. The APS however, in their ridiculously overpowered mech suits had barely changed personnel at all. And those bastards were still hostile toward us, even if they were much quieter about it now.

I was beginning to believe that the trouble was over. It was around that time that Captain Parraway came marching into the barracks, late at night.

"Sergeant Oshbob. Call for you at headquarters."

As this had never happened before, I was confused. "Call? Who is it?"

"Why don't you go and take the call, and find out? What am I? Your goddamn secretary?"

Stifling a growl, I jumped up from my bed and followed the arrogant asshole out into the dark. I suddenly got a sense of danger, and looked around warily, but we made it to the floodlights of the central base without trouble.

Parraway led me to a room and ushered me in. On the table was a video display. On the screen was Asala, and while she rarely showed emotion, I could feel the sadness coming from her.

"Is everything okay?"

She shook her head. "I'm afraid not. I'm limited with how much I can tell you, but Harold is dead."

I knew it was coming. But her words hit far harder than I would have expected.

"We've already arranged for you to be granted dispensation to leave the base and attend the funeral. It will be held two days from now. We're all looking forward to seeing you."

"How... was it bad? Painful?"

She shook her head, fighting tears. "It was very quick. This may sound odd, but I believe he died how he would have wanted to. I..." She looked off to her left. "I should go now. Sorry to have to deliver the news like this."

"Don't be sorry for anything, Asala." I was about to say more, but the communication ended. I looked up to the door as Parraway entered.

"You got the message. Transport leaves tomorrow night at nine. You know your own way back to the barracks, Sergeant."

I left the room, feeling cold and lost inside. Memories sprung to mind of the old man, and raced in swirling images across my mind's eye. I never expected to feel such pain. I had a burning desire to speak to my friends, people who knew him. But I was trapped on a base that might as well have been a prison, miles away from them all.

Entering the barracks, everyone was asleep now, snoring loudly as always. Only Umak was awake and watching me from his bed.

"Everything okay, Osh?"

"I don't know. An old friend has died. I'm being given permission to go to his funeral."

"Ah, that's rough. I'm surprised they're letting you out. Normally, they only do that for family."

Empire of Oshbob

I thought about that for a moment, it was unusual. True, I was a sergeant which came with some privileges, but not many. "I suppose it's because he was military as well. He still knew a lot of people."

"How did he die?"

"I don't actually know. He was unwell anyway, but something tells me there's more to the story. I'll just have to wait until tomorrow, I suppose."

Umak let his head fall back. "You looking forward to getting out of here? Even if it's just for a day?"

I thought on his words and grimaced. "Dunno. It'll probably just make it harder being here when I have to come back."

He chuckled. "Were you always this much of a miserable bastard, Oshbob?"

"I think so, yeah. It's gotten me this far, so I don't intend to change now."

"Oh hell no. Don't ever change. And you're out of here in a year, right? You got this. I'll be waiting in that club of yours ready for all the free drinks you're gonna buy me."

"You don't have to wait for me, Umak. Another month and there'll be free drinks and a warm welcome for you at the Prestige. My friends know to expect you soon."

"Damn. I gotta admit, knowing I'll have work to go to when I get out, it's hell of a weight off. You're too kind, Oshbob."

"Don't be saying that shit out loud. Anyone knows there's a decent orc in here and my business is screwed."

He burst into laughter. "Your secret's safe with me."

I was transported back to Artem in a windowless transporter. They really didn't want me to know where the base was, which was pretty pointless seeing as though I'd known everything about it within the first month of being here.

As the ship landed, one of the transport soldiers entered the hold. "You do the funeral and then you're back on the ship. Keep chit chat to a minimum. I'll be escorting you."

I raised an eyebrow at him. "I'm a goddamn sergeant in the Artem Military. Not a prisoner."

"Doesn't matter. These are the rules. You can always decline and we can just head straight back. I won't complain."

I wanted to wipe the sneer off his face as he said it. Instead, I turned away and ignored him, waiting for the ramp to open. I expected to be in the nearest military base, but I had been transported directly to Portolans Crematorium.

I don't know who was more surprised, me or the soldier when the gathered crowd all erupted into a roar of cheering.

It took a beat or three before I could accept that the adulation was for me and waved an arm back to acknowledge their greeting. There must have been two hundred people there, most whom I recognized. There were a number of humans I didn't know, though they had *veteran* written all over them. From the straight-backed posture, to the cold look in their eyes, modded or not, you could still tell when someone had seen shit.

I tromped down the ramp, feeling self-conscious as all eyes were on me. I almost shouted, *This is Harold's gods damned funeral, not a welcome party.* But Unara, seeming to materialize from nowhere, dove into my arms and ceased anything I had to say.

"Ah, I've missed you," she said, tears in her big green eyes.

"I've missed you too, Unara."

She barely listened, looking behind as she pulled back. "What's with the guard? Why are they treating you like a prisoner?"

I shook my head. "Because I am, for now. You live legitimately in this damn city, then you're no better than a prisoner anyway. You break out and get caught? You'll end up a prisoner."

I cast an irritated glance back at the soldier with me. He pretended not to notice.

With a sigh, I turned back to Unara. "So? What happened? Asala didn't tell me anything, but I'm guessing it wasn't natural causes?"

"No, it most certainly wasn't," a slim, regal looking human woman with an immaculate black dress and pale make said as she approached.

Her black hair was tied up tightly, pinned against her hair with an ornate black hair ornament. It took far too long to realize that it was Asala. I damn near gulped under her steely gaze.

"I'll let Asala tell you exactly what happened," Unara said. "She was there."

Empire of Oshbob

I put a hand on her shoulder and turned back to the CEO of Portolans 360 with a sad smile. "Good to see you, Asala. I'm sorry for your loss."

She gave a slight bob of her head, no sign of affection between us that could tie us together too tightly in the eyes of those watching. Unara and my own connection to the company was supposed to be severed, and in every legal sense, it was. Severed and buried. But our mutual attachment to Harold was still a link to be exploited by our enemies. Now it was gone.

"As you are aware, my uncle had been staying with me, and I was glad of his company. No one told a story quite like him, and I will miss him deeply. He would often accompany me to the tower once we had moved into our new residence, even though he was deeply unwell.

"Four days ago, we entered the tower as we normally do. All was just as it should be. Like any other day. I took my place at my desk, and he took up his spot on his favorite couch and napped from the exertion of getting there. Within an hour of getting down to work, a cacophony of sirens filled the air. I rushed to the window to see fire. Our border with Turan was ablaze."

I spun on Unara. "Has there been trouble with Turan?"

She shook her head. "Not yet. We're working on how the fire started, and so far Burrel is being helpful."

I spat at the mention of the Turan gang lord's name. I was sure he was being helpful. I wrestled daily with just letting Unara go and kill him and take over the gangs in Turan, but I wanted that honor. I wanted to feel his skull cracking between my palms.

The mental image disappeared as Asala continued to speak.

"The fire spread into Portolans, which is terrifying considering the protections the city is supposed to have. But conveniently the fire suppressors were not working on those streets. I questioned the district council about how this could have happened. Initially, they tried to dismiss it as scheduled maintenance. However, with a bit of pressure, it emerged they had been hacked. We are currently investigating to determine the origin of the hack. Though, as we are finding repeatedly, the trail will likely lead us around through several possible sources before going cold. To combat the threat without fire suppression, someone in their infinite wisdom decided that to stop the fire spreading everything should be shut down."

"Because we all know how turning off the electricity stops fire spreading."

Asala nodded. "As dubious as it sounds, that is the official line from the council. But within seconds of the power going down, a missile struck the top of the tower, followed by several unmarked AV's carrying paid mercenaries into the hole they'd created."

I held up a hand to stop her. "That glass is supposed to be bombproof. It should be able to withstand a couple of missiles."

"Indeed. But only when it has an electrical charge. Otherwise, it is just extremely durable glass."

"And the tower is reliant on the Artem Grid for power?" I said, grinding my teeth at the oversight.

"We use it, as it's the most efficient source of power, but we have our own backup generators. The problem in this case was the delay between the power going down and the generators firing up. It takes them a full minute to bring everything back online and fully operational. Which is the window of opportunity our assailants took to attack. It was a well-orchestrated attack which cost me my entire security team, though they fought valiantly.

"They used an EMP on my safe room, but we have the three backup shields in place, and they worked admirably apart from the slight lag between the next shield activating. It's only a second, but that's long enough to shoot, or in this case, throw a grenade. I thought that was the end for me until Harold knocked me to the floor.

"The grenade went off, and Harold died covering me as best as he could. I have received skin replacement therapy, but I am otherwise in fine health. My uncle, of course, didn't survive the blast, and although I would never have wished for him to sacrifice himself, I can smile in the knowledge that nothing would have given him greater pleasure knowing he saved my life. I think he would have wanted you to know he left the world in battle, protecting those he loved."

Her deadpan delivery of the story had me staring at her longer than I should have. Both fighting back my emotions and trying to work out if she had any. I knew that was unfair on her. She just processed things a little differently to almost anyone I'd ever met. I finally nodded.

"I agree, Asala. It's a fine and fitting end, though his loss will leave a hole."

"A hole we'll fill with vengeance," Unara casually slipped in.

"Of course. There'll be full payment..." I looked over my shoulder at my shadow. "Not just for the loss of Harold, but everything related to it. I assume we're thinking it's the same people? Did they leave any clues?"

She stared at me, communicating that she'd rather not say through her eyes alone.

Unara touched my arm and answered. "Possibly a mid-level Corp looking to take over the business side of things in the surrounding districts. Can't say too much yet."

"A name?"

"Just signs that point in a certain direction."

I felt my whole body tightening. It took all my willpower not to let loose the primal roar of rage and frustration that so desperately wanted to break free. The soldier off to my side seemed to sense how furious I was, and raised his gun a fraction as he took a step toward me.

"Cool it or you're going back."

It was too much. I spun on him, batting the gun away with the back of my hand. "You step the fuck back to where you were, now. Or you'll draw your last breath where you're standing."

He suddenly looked uncertain but didn't step back, so I stepped forward again. This time closing the distance so that there was only a hand's breadth between us.

I roared in his face. "I said back to your spot now! You only get to come that close if you want a hug or you want to die."

My proximity gave him no choice but to step back. As he did, I eyed him and his rifle carefully. All eyes were on us now, including all of Harold's army friends. The guard fidgeted uncomfortably, but didn't bring his rifle back up.

"Good. Do your job properly. Follow, but keep a respectful distance, or I will be putting a complaint in against you."

"And I will make sure it holds," Asala added with chilling neutrality.

The tension was broken as Effa and Wolski made their way through the crowd to me. Both wore huge grins on their faces. Wolski powered into me.

"By all the orc gods of old, you're looking damn good, Osh. Damn good. Not long till you're back out with us stomping the streets, eh?"

"You better believe it," I agreed.

Effa didn't go for the hug; instead, he thrust out his fist. "Causing trouble already?" he asked as I bumped the offered fist with my own.

"Not even close to what I intend to do when I get back properly."

Effa was interrupted from replying by a commanding voice from the front of the crowd. I looked over to see a white-haired human standing on a raised dais.

"Come, friends and family of Harold Mishokin. Let us all join each other in a moment's silent reflection before the ceremony begins."

He was definitely ex-military. I was a little sentimental that Harold had made such good friends in the military, just as I had. Despite my hatred for the institution, there were some damn good people in it.

My minute of reflection was filled with our first meeting, and more so the meeting when I had lain blind in the hospital bed before rejoining the army. Of his words over Asala and the warning he gave never to turn on her even if she messed up. A tough promise to give, but I'd given it all the same.

Then the world turned to hell, explosions from nearby, gunfire, screaming. I scanned around, Unara was already shouting at Effa.

Wolski put up a hand. "I think… we're all good. Nobody got through the perimeter."

I glanced over to Asala, she was surrounded by heavily armored 360 guards.

"What's happening?" I asked, while the soldier beside me decided it was time to try and pull me away back to the ship.

"We need to get you out of here," he snapped over Unara's response.

He was lucky with all the chaos going on around us that she hadn't seen the altercation. I glared at him until he released his futile grip. He attempted to say more, but I turned away to listen to Unara.

Empire of Oshbob

"With us all here, it's the perfect opportunity to take us all out. It was still a risk holding the ceremony outside, but we have a full security perimeter in the Undercity, and Asala has posted a full guard around us."

"Trouble to the northeast," Effa growled, pushing a rifle in my hands before setting off in that direction.

Again, the soldier tried to stop me. And again, I resisted.

"If you wanna get me back in one piece, you better put your own rifle to good use," I said, breaking free and following my friends.

"Go any further and I *will* shoot you," he snapped.

"You're supposed to be protecting me. Shoot me, and you don't make it out of here alive, and you create an even bigger problem in the city."

He continued his desperate rant, but I was running again. Up ahead, there was commotion. Armored soldiers from 360 were fighting other armored soldiers, though they wore no identifying marks. The result was already clear as we approached, though our rifle fire helped turn the balance.

If not for the sudden appearance of actual military vehicles, we'd have finished them off completely.

I turned to the soldier. "Did you call in backup?"

"I tried. There's a lot of old soldiers here, and one of them beat me to it, which is good for you. Because I would have sold you down the river. Now get back on the AV, it's time to go."

I listened to him as I watched the military somehow manage to allow all of our attackers escape under the pretense of keeping the peace.

"Why are you trying to get me back and ruin this day for me?" I asked simply, looking back at the soldier. "Is it just because I'm an orc and you didn't want the assignment? I'm here to see my friend off and mourn his passing with others who cared about him. I was given permission to do so, and it seems you just want to ruin my day."

He fell silent, scowling, he looked away and said no more. It took over an hour for everyone to settle back down after the attack. An hour later, we all sat in the crematorium, listening to people speak.

Unara nudged me as I listened to one of the old soldiers tell a story about being pinned down in the wilds on a rescue mission that went wrong, and how Harold had managed to save them single handedly with his sniper rifle.

As fascinating as that was. Unara's whispered words were even more intriguing. "We might not have the power to dig too far, but the military have arrested a few of those who attacked us."

"We have a lead?"

"Asala got it from the general who was speaking last. A company called Ferris Property Management. Leo and Meli are looking into it now."

"Ferris?" I asked, utterly confused. "Where the hell are they from and why are they trying to take us out?"

"That's what we need to find out. They're from the inner districts. Not Central, and they don't border us either. At the minute, that's all I know."

"It's something, I suppose. Keep me informed of anything else. This was a big attack. It might be just an opportunistic attempt to get at us, but it might mean they're starting up again."

"It doesn't matter if they are or not. We have a lead now. We're going to find them and hurt them so badly that they won't know what's hit them."

Empire of Oshbob
Partition 17

When I returned to base the following day, I didn't have any more information on Ferris other than they were buying up properties across a number of the poorer districts like ours.

It was frustrating, but not as frustrating as what lay in store for me at the base. As we dropped, the place seemed quiet. No missions running out, just a few soldiers here and there were running around.

I entered the barracks, and the whole team was there.

"Oshbob! You're back," Theta cheered as Umak stood up from his bed.

"You all right, Osh? Did the funeral go okay?"

"Nope. We were attacked just before the ceremony. We have some leads now, so I'm hoping we can put an end to it."

"Don't be so sure," Theta said, and my heart sank. "Commander Gullan has suddenly decided some changes need making."

"What changes?"

"We don't know yet," Umak replied. "We've gotta go out later today to meet up with them. In an hour, actually."

That hour passed quickly, and before I knew it, I was glaring at Commander Gullan and Commander Poulson along with the entire number of Scrub Teams, as well as a number of soldiers of all different ranks waiting behind them. I didn't recognize any of them, but I noticed a couple of elves among their ranks.

"Soldiers of Outpost 361. It has come to my superiors' attention that there have been many oversights in the running of this base, and they are not happy with me, because it's apparently my fault."

He didn't look like he believed that for a second. "For instance! Unbeknownst to me, it's standard practice for there to be *three* Scrub Teams supporting the APS squads, and not two as has been the case here. Each of those teams should also be assisted with drones. This is now the standard operating protocol of Outpost 361. Furthermore, your teams should always consist of eight members, and some of you have been operating below that number for quite some time."

There was a murmur of both confusion and hope among the Scrub Teams now. I remained highly dubious of the sudden and unexpected interest in running our base properly.

"We have brought in additional Scrub Teams, bringing our overall number of squads up to twelve. This should mean that we can maintain the same schedule as before and each team will receive two days off per week. As for the missions, it will feel a little different out there. I ask you to be open minded and work with the additional team and drones. If this works as intended, we should see a drastic reduction in casualties and fatalities. So, without further ado, Scrub Team 4! I believe you have been down to seven men for over a year, so we will start with you."

He gestured for a soldier to step forward—a big human, with over half his face and skull fully covered in some kind of mod. He was around the height and weight of K-Dog, and he looked just as mean, carrying most of that bulk in disproportionately large shoulders and arms, which, while not full replacements, were heavily modified. They gave him the look of gorilla-type monsters we had to face on occasion.

"This is heavy weapon specialist Gorka, and he is quite the soldier. Any issues with being overwhelmed by Leptos or some such vermin will soon be a thing of the past."

"How so?" I asked.

Gullan scowled. His cold gray eyes fell on me, and I saw anger there. "What do you mean, how so? Because he is a highly skilled soldier."

"As are we," I replied emotionlessly. "What I mean is, how will Specialist Gorka prevent us from being overwhelmed? Is he coming out with an APS suit on?"

"Are you trying to get on my bad side, Sergeant Oshbob? Because if you are, you're doing an excellent job. Gorka is a heavy weapon specialist. He will be able to kill many more of those C-Rankers than a standard soldier. Do you understand now? It's in the title of his name."

"But he won't be able to take heavy weapons out, sir. Scrub Teams are limited to the standard rifle-pistol combination, with the allowance of one grenade per team member, per mission."

Empire of Oshbob

Gullan's face blossomed red. Whether through anger, embarrassment, or a combination of both. Especially when Theta snorted. Thankfully, he couldn't see her as she was smart enough to crouch behind me as she did it.

"Uh… This is another area we will be addressing. Scrub Teams will be better outfitted."

"Perfect. We could do with more options. No offense to Specialist Gorka there, but with heavy weapon options, it's unlikely we'd have found ourselves in half the life-threatening situations we've been in."

There was a solid murmur of agreement across all of the Scrub Teams at my words. I fought the grin fighting to take over my face and instead nodded to Gorka as he approached.

He glared at me with open hostility, and even produced a little warning growl.

"You can knock that off, specialist. We've got a good team here and we don't need any assholes causing problems."

"I don't need no orcs getting me killed," he snapped. "Just stay out of my way and we'll be good,"

Agga laughed. "You're so fucked, Gorky."

Rather than give the angry human any more of my time, I turned back to the base commander. He was busy filling the other teams with new recruits, but he spared a withering glance for me.

When he addressed us all again, it was with more unexpected news.

"As we are embarking on new, more efficient procedures, it has been decided that preventable disruption to our teams should be avoided. With that in mind, could Sergeant Gara Shimley, Corporal Eden Winter, and Corporal Umak please make their way to the front please."

I met Umak's worried eyes, but there was nothing to be said. We had no idea what was going on and no power to stop it.

"Thank you for your service on Outpost 361!" Gullan said as they reached the front. "You three are all to be discharged at the end of this month. Rather than have you learn the new protocols only to then leave, you have been granted more sedate assignments within the city until your service is over. There will be a transport for you later today, so make sure to say all of your goodbyes as this will be your last day on this base."

Of the three there, only Umak looked troubled by the sudden change in circumstances.

"What do you think they're up to?" Nozz hissed.

"Nothing good," I replied. "But he's in the city. At least I can have him watched over. So don't worry about him too much."

Once Gullan had finished speaking with the three of them in a much quieter voice which none of us could hear, he then sent them directly to their respective barracks and turned on us again.

"So! We have two new corporals and a new sergeant to install." As he spoke, three soldiers walked forward.

I grimaced at the sight of them. All fucking elves.

"Scrub Team 1! Please welcome your new commanding officer, Sergeant Jeram."

The well-decorated elf made her way over to her new team. I only had eyes for the two remaining elves, wondering which one we would get. Not that it mattered.

"Scrub Team 4, may I present Corporal Elantra."

The elf in question stepped forward. The brown-haired woman looked to be average height and build for her kind, with typical, smooth, nondescript elven features.

I was caught off guard when she offered us a deep bow. When she rose her words were loud and clear.

"It's an honor to be joining your team! You've made quite the name for yourselves. The most competent Scrub Team in all of the Outpost bases. From what I hear, you haven't lost a single soldier since you, Sergeant Oshbob, turned up. Is that right?"

Her manner was friendly and positive. It was hard to find fault with the introduction, and I found myself questioning if this was a set up after all. I nodded back. "That's right."

She grinned and came to stand alongside me as if she belonged there, which she most certainly didn't. "You're building quite the legend for yourself, aren't you, sir?"

"I don't know about legend."

"Oh yes! The orc that kills A Rankers. Quite the buzz around the military. I'm insatiably curious to see how you go about such fantastic feats of military prowess."

"We ain't got no show boaters or unnecessary risk takers here," I grunted in response. "We work as a team. Trust our guts and get the job done."

Empire of Oshbob

"Captivating!"

"Yeah. Real captivating. So why the hell have they put an elf with a half-orc squad? It sounds like there's a story to tell. It's not often an elf wants to work with our kind."

"Oh I don't mind your kind at all! To me, you're either an elf or you're not. I have no more time for any of the other races as I do for yours." She lowered her voice. "As for why I'm here. I'm not just a soldier, but a research scientist of sorts. I have a keen interest in specters."

That caught me by surprise. "You want to ask me about specters?"

"Indeed I do. I have solid reports that you were responsible for taking out a team of mercenaries who were on the cusp of turning. *And*, as the stories go, you apparently defeated a Banshee in single combat! The spine of which you used to save your friend?"

I froze up now. Talking about Unara and about things she shouldn't have known about set my teeth on edge. "I'm not in the business of divulging valuable information to strangers."

"Come on! Hardly valuable. And I'm sure it won't take long for us not to be strangers."

"All information is valuable," I growled back, hoping she took my tone as a warning that she was treading dangerous ground.

"Then I shall endeavor to persevere on your good nature until we are no longer strangers, sergeant."

"Where did you say you came from before here?"

"I didn't."

I stared at her waiting for more.

She stared back, looking nonplussed by my questioning gaze. After a moment, she tried again. "So, about the specters you faced. Were they lucid at the time? Did they understand and interact with you?"

I continued to stare.

She sighed after a moment, a slight smile on her face. "You're not going to make this easy on me, are you?"

I continued to stare.

Partition 18

Things were awkward back in the barracks. Gorka took his bed and scowled at anyone who came near or made any attempt to speak with him. That, I could get behind.

Elantra, however, was a pest. She talked incessantly, and when she wasn't talking, she strummed on an old-looking stringed instrument. The high-pitched twanging that jumped from it set my nerves on edge. Especially when the irritating corporal began singing along with her playing in a voice equally high pitched.

"What I don't get," Theta said, placing her hand on the neck of the instrument to stop its ear-splitting sound, "is why you aren't an orc or a half-orc?"

"Inclusion!" she said happily. "The military is attempting to be more forward thinking. We need to divide same-race groups up to reduce interracial prejudices. Just think. If the military leads by example, our society could be so much healthier in the future."

"Bullshit," Theta replied, echoing my own thoughts. "Why are you really here? Changes like this don't happen unless something big has happened, or someone's pulling strings."

"I am but a humble soldier. I go where I'm asked and do what I am told."

"Well shut the fuck up with that whining," Nozz said.

"Watch it, Green-skin," Gorka snapped. "You filth don't get to talk to our kind like that."

Nozz spun on him, surprised. "You're an elf?"

Gorka said nothing more, but glared at Nozz warningly.

Agga moved over to him. "Call us green-skins again and I'll break every bone in your body."

I was just trying to work everything out. It suddenly became clear, to me at least, that Gorka was here as a bodyguard for Elantra.

"Try it," Gorka replied.

"Don't," I snapped at Agga as he raised his fists.

Empire of Oshbob

He looked at me with something akin to betrayal on his face.

"Specialist Gorka is going to apologize to us all for the slur, or I'll be reporting him to the base commander."

Gorka snorted and went back to polishing his arm mods.

"So you refuse to apologize, specialist?"

He ignored me.

"Okay. That's two warnings. One for the slur and one for ignoring a commanding officer. One more and you're off the squad."

"My apologies, sergeant, were you talking to me? I could hardly make out the words, grunted as they were."

I smiled at the big elf. "Well, this should be fun."

"Did you say something?" he replied.

"Specialist Gorka," Elantra said sternly. "You will speak to your teammates with respect, or I will report you myself. Sergeant Oshbob's grunting is perfectly decipherable." She turned to me with a wide innocent smile. "Please allow me to carry the report of Specialist Gorka's misdemeanors. I will bring you back written confirmation that the warning is recorded. It's the least I can do, and hopefully the action will allow some smoothing of our relationship here."

I didn't buy a word of it, but what could I do? I knew without a shadow of a doubt that any difficulties with my new corporal would land trouble directly on my doorstep. Not hers.

"That would be helpful, corporal."

Despite not seeming to rush, she crossed the floor of the barracks with amazing swiftness and was out of the door in a few heartbeats.

I turned back to Gorka. "Who sent you? What's the game plan here?"

He slowly looked up to meet my eyes. "I'm a soldier. Who do you think sent me? An Undercity goblin?"

"I think a corporation who has an interest in seeing me dead sent you."

His face was unreadable with the heavy modifications, but I swear I saw him smirk. "So you're a paranoid orc. Didn't think you lot were bright enough to be paranoid."

"Whatever you've been sent for, Gorka, whatever you think is going to happen here, you're wrong. You will toe the line until I work out what you're up to and I get you out of here."

"By running to command and telling them how I hurt your feelings?"

"Depends on how much trouble you cause. I might just kill you."

"You and your little gang of half-orcs? I'm terrified."

"I'm guessing, like our newest corporal, you know exactly what I'm capable of by myself. Let alone with this fine team around me."

He snorted. "And you have no idea what I'm capable of."

It was actually true. But I wasn't worried. He might have spent a fortune on making himself bigger and more threatening. There was no doubt he was dangerous. But violence… that was the ocean I swam in. My calm was a thin veneer. Like the rubber of a balloon, stretched and tense, with only a precarious hold of what pushed it into shape.

"You've been warned, Gorka."

He glared at me for a long moment as if weighing up whether to say something else, then returned his attention back to his work.

I sent another emergency message to Leo. There was a lot to unpick and I wanted them working on who these two people in my squad were. They had names, they were part of the military. There had to be something to dig up on them.

The next day we were called out for a mission. The others were hopeful over what surprises would be in store for us at the weapon's lockers. I had a good idea already and when we arrived I was proven right. Our available weaponry had not changed at all. I consoled myself that at least Corporal Elantra had the same as us. Gorka had a gods be damned minigun.

I kept my thoughts to myself. The others didn't.

"What bullshit is this!" Theta snapped. "Where are our miniguns?"

"You're not trained to carry them." Gorka smirked, hoisting the massive machine over onto the mag clip on his back.

Empire of Oshbob

"And!" Elantra said loudly over the grumbling. "From what I gather, you really don't need them. You are Scrub Team 4! The best there is!"

I ignored them all and marched out of the locker rooms.

Theta was by my side a moment later. "This stinks, Osh. You know he's gonna try and kill us all with that thing, right?"

"Eventually, but not today. There'll be a set up planned further down the road. Hopefully, I have more information on them both when it comes."

"How can you stay so calm?"

"I just imagine myself ripping Gorka's arms off and beating him to death with them."

She looked at me, the fear evaporating to be replaced by humor. "Now that is a plan I can get behind. Will you give me one of his arms when you rip them off?"

"I certainly will. Now come on, focus on the mission, and keep your eyes open and on the swivel at all times."

Scrub Teams 1 and 6 were with us at the back of the AV. There were plenty of teams, but even after all we'd been through now, the two other teams still sat with each other along one side, rather than with us. I was at least comforted that both teams were ones we knew.

As we disembarked and moved into position at either side of the ramp, three of the drones that flew out before the APS moved to join each of our teams. Another addition I wasn't enthused with.

As usual, we were asked to take rear guard. It was all but expected now, and it was fine. We were good at what we did, and as long as no A Rankers or armies of C-Rankers showed up, then we were all good.

When our time came to set off, Elantra stuck by my side. It was odd moving with the elf. She talked a lot more than Umak, or anyone else for that matter.

"You don't track the high points?" she asked innocently as we entered a dip in the land.

"No. It would make sense, but our orders are to follow straight in. The APS get notifications from drones about anything incoming from the sides."

"But not you guys?"

"*Us* guys," I corrected. "If you really are part of the team and not a plant of some kind. And no, we don't, though," I said, pointing to the sky. "We've never had drone support before, so who knows."

"That's pretty interesting. And you still haven't lost anyone?"

I ignored her and spoke to Lanris and Agga, "Stay close to me. Keep eyes to our rear."

They nodded and did as I asked immediately.

A few moments later, firing ahead alerted us to trouble. Nozz and Froom went running off to the left to crest the nearest slope and try to get a vantage point, while we moved forward, weapons ready.

It didn't take long to see the problem. Scrub Team 1 were under serious attack by Arachnids, a hundred at least. Nothing they shouldn't be able to handle.

"See anything?" I shouted back to Lanris and Agga.

"All clear," Lanris answered.

"Alright then. We're moving in to assist Scrub 1."

Gorka had already run forward, spraying dangerous bursts of fire from the minigun that could easily kill members of Scrub 1.

I opened the team channel. "Gorka, cease now. You're gonna kill one of ours."

He didn't listen and kept firing.

"GORKA! I mean it! Stop it now!"

"Just leave him," Elantra said, lowering the power on her rifle. "He's on his last warning. Just report him when we get back and he'll be gone."

I raised an eyebrow that she'd never see behind my helmet. She raised her rifle and fired. Only a single shot burped out at the pull of the trigger. I caught sight of her target and marveled as the shot took out one of the arachnids.

She was already firing again, once, twice, seven times in quick succession. Each bullet found not just a home, but a critical one too. I couldn't hope to achieve that kind of accuracy. But it was always good to see a professional in action and hopefully learn from them.

I opened fire myself and killed just as many in the same amount of time, but I wasted a lot of my gun's charge. It didn't matter right now as we had plenty of charge, and given a little time, the guns charged up themselves from sunlight, but there might come a time when I needed to conserve ammo.

Once the arachnids were cleared, Scrub 1 continued without barely a thank you, and continued on while we held ground.

I spun on Gorka and marched over to him. "You're done. That's your third warning within twenty-four hours."

"We'll see. You know what they say, it's not what you know, it's who you know. I'd be willing to bet that I don't go anywhere."

His words gave me pause. It wouldn't surprise me at all if that was the case. With a grin at my troubled expression, Gorka walked off.

The rest of my team looked at me questioningly, wondering what I was going to do. Solutions whirled through my mind. Relying on my superiors would be about as much use as sticking my face in an Arachnid nest. Walking up and ramming my rifle into the crease of Gorka's helmet and firing would see me at best imprisoned, at worst executed.

I made sure the record function on our squad chat was working. I considered linking in Colonel Poulson, but decided against it. For now, the recording would be enough. Then I shouted after the elven monstrosity.

"You think your *friends* in high places will save you?"

He stopped and turned slowly, a sneer etched on his face.

"You think you can put my team and others at risk because you know a few corrupt high-ranking officers?"

"Yeah. I do actually. They don't give a fuck if you lot die, and neither do I."

"I'm going to give you this last personal warning. The next time you disobey my orders in battle and put this team at risk, I'll end you."

"Sure you will. You know what will happen if you so much as raise a rifle in my direction? You'll be through."

"Unlikely. But you *will* be dead, and even if I have to explain my decision in a court, I'll be content with that trade."

I did know the rules, and while technically I should be able to deliver justice to an offending soldier in my company, the truth was often far removed from the reality. My main hope was to get him to attack me, then I'd be clean and clear. I just had to get him to bite without doing anything that could be considered inciting.

"I already ignored your cowardly orders. So kill me. See if you can."

"There are rules. You've been given your warning. Follow orders or suffer the consequences."

Partition 19

Over the next few days, Gorka kept himself to himself, only coming into the barracks to sleep. The rest of the time when not on mission, he hung about at the main headquarters. I didn't know what he was doing over there but I doubted it was good.

On mission, he continued to needle us all, apart from Elantra. But he did follow orders, which was damn frustrating as he grinned at me each time he did something I asked.

Elantra caused very little trouble beyond her incessant babbling and constant movement around the barracks. She seemed to talk more and more with each passing day. But to give her her due, she also added to the effectiveness of the team with her near perfect aim.

In reality, it was going about as well as I could have hoped with the two obvious plants in our team, and it was really just a case of watching them carefully, while they watched us.

That of course meant that I couldn't collect any nanites. If Elantra or Gorka weren't watching me, our ever-present drone was. That chafed, and I had to send a message to Leo not to send a drone.

"Can I ask you something that's been bugging me?" Nozz asked after I griped privately about the whole thing. "You obviously have a lot of money back home. How important are these nanites to you?"

"They're really important. They make sure we can pay the gangs. Most of the wealth we have is tied up in… legitimate business. But the money we make with the nanites greases the wheels of business quite nicely. We have other sources than me of course. Gangs of goblins roam the Undercity taking out specters, draining them and stripping them for parts. But it's damn inefficient."

Nozz's eyes went wide. "You take from specters? But they're corrupted, right?"

"Yeah. The nanites have to be cleaned. We lose most of them in the process. Probably need to kill a hundred standard specters to match one vial of nanites I take from a C-Ranker."

Nozz nodded. "So what happens when you head back?"

"I have a few people collecting outside the city walls. I hope you guys still will, once we're not being watched so closely. I get the feeling this is what they're looking for."

"What? You collecting nanites?"

I leaned back and took a long drag from the cigar. "Exactly that."

"But who would go to this much effort for that?"

"My people, back in Portolans, are fairly certain it's a corporation with aspirations to expand and pick up cheap property in our district and a few others we know about. We're getting in their way. That's why they've been trying to take me out. Unara too. If I had to guess, they've had enough of getting bloody noses. If they know 360 is backed up with ill-gotten nanites, they'll want to stop the supply. Which is mainly me. They'd also like to get me locked up or dead, which if I end up in a military prison, I'm as good as dead anyway."

"It makes a lot of sense. So how do we get rid of them?"

"I'm trying to get Gorka to do something stupid. One more dick move from him and I can finish him. But he's on his best behavior."

Nozz stoked his chin thoughtfully. "And we can't go too hard on Gorka, or it won't stand up if you kill him."

"Exactly. I'm running a blank at the minute on how to deal with them."

"I have an idea!"

"You do?" I asked dubiously.

"They're watching and waiting for you to collect nanites. Why not give them something to react to. Let's at least see what they're about?"

"So what? I just pretend to collect them?"

"Yeah. Sneak off a little. Make it look like you're up to something. Might smoke them out. Better yet! I'll do it. They watch you too closely and you're not stupid. They'd suspect a trick if you tried it in front of them."

"Well, Nozz. I haven't got any better ideas, so let's give it a go. Let the others know. And the moment Gorka goes too far, any threat to any of us, you all have my permission to end him."

"I know Agga would love the chance," Nozz said wistfully.

"Wouldn't we all."

When we were next called out, I made an effort to talk with Elantra. I noticed the look she gave me when I began to reply to her questions. There was suspicion, but also hope. She kept the conversation light, at least until we were attacked by a dozen Leptos.

They weren't so big, and they'd come from a small burrow in the ground. Which meant it probably wasn't too big of a nest. Gorka's minigun sang out first, killing three in quick succession. The rest fell to our rifles before they even got close.

"Shall I frag it?" Nozz asked.

I shook my head. "Save your grenade in case we need them later. Just keep an eye on the burrow exit as we move off."

"Is this what it's like to kill specters in the Undercity?" Elantra asked as we started moving across the sparsely covered grassy plain.

"Not the same at all, really," I replied casually. Then I opened my command channel to Colonel Poulson. "Small Lepto nest, sir. Doesn't look like it'll be an issue."

"Good work, sergeant. Keep moving."

Instead of turning the command channel off, I just muted Poulson's voice.

Satisfied I had finished my conversation, Elantra began again. "So how is it different? They hunt in packs, do they not?"

"C Rankers?" I laughed. "Not at all. We've come across tons of loners."

"Specters," she said lightly. "I hear they always congregate. Having never been into the Undercity, I've no idea."

"Hmmm. Congregate is probably a better word than packs. And that's only the lower leveled ones. If they manage to develop and become stronger, they tend to go their own ways."

"I see. And what do you do with them once you're finished with them?"

"Finished with them? What the hell do you think I'm doing, using them as a pillow?"

"You know what I mean," Elantra said, riveted by the conversation.

Gorka was out front again, and the drone was to our west scanning some shrubs. It was the perfect time for Nozz, who'd taken the rearguard and was hanging back, to carry out the ruse. A quick glance over to him told me he agreed.

"What do you want to know?"

"I want to know how you cleaned the spine for your friend amongst many other things. The mods themselves are corrupted, are they not?"

I shrugged. "What do I look like? A carver? I just killed the Banshee, I don't know nothing about the science of it."

"You know more than you're letting on."

"What about you? Are you keeping your own secrets? Why are you really here?" I watched her carefully as I asked.

I saw a brief flicker of something across her face and thought she was going to answer. Instead, her head spun around to where Nozz was crouching over the body of the last Lepto we'd killed.

He made a show of really fidgeting with it. I was about to say something when a shout went up from Gorka. The freakish elf was storming back. His eyes flickering between Nozz and Elantra.

She set off too as Gorka barked again. "What are you doing?"

Nozz stood up with an innocent expression on his face and his hands clasped behind his back. "Specialist Gorka! There something I can help you with?"

"What were you doing!" Gorka snapped again.

Nozz looked at me as I arrived a second behind Elantra.

I was the first to speak. "What the hell is going on here, Gorka? Why did you leave your position at the front?"

"Because," he said, thrusting a finger into Nozz's shoulder, "he was up to something with the Lepto corpse."

I squared up to the elf. "And what business is that of yours? You have a job to do, specialist. To lead the line."

He bunched his fists, and fish-mouthed for a moment, before Elantra held up a hand. "Sergeant Oshbob is correct, Gorka. Well done for spotting the anomalous behavior, but remember, you must follow orders."

Empire of Oshbob

I was such an odd exchange, and so obvious that there was something between the two of them. They certainly weren't treating me as you would a sergeant.

She turned to Nozz. "What were you doing?"

"Minding my own fucking business, corporal. What were you doing?"

"She was talking to me," I answered. "Until both she and Gorka received a message from the drone about whatever it was *you* were doing."

Gorka bristled at the accusation, while Elantra stared at me with an icy expression before speaking to Nozz. "Show me your hands, private."

"Let me think," Nozz said. "No, I don't think I will. Not unless my *sergeant* orders me to. You remember our sergeant, yeah? The one in charge."

"Answer her," Gorka growled, bringing his minigun up to point at Nozz.

"Lower the goddamn gun, Gorka. Corporal Elantra. You need to stand down too. You don't get to question my team like this without good reason."

"Gorka! Keep your gun exactly where it is."

"You betcha, captain," he barked back.

It didn't escape my notice that he called her captain. I also didn't care. "That's the last order you ignore from me, Gorka!"

My team had already circled the heavy weapon specialist. Froom opened fire, striking the mini gun which pushed it to one side.

Theta lunged forward, pushing it to point down at the ground as Gorka opened fire.

The bullets pounded into the dry barren soil as Theta fought to keep hold of the gun. We'd never learn who would win that battle as Agga whipped his arm around the elf's neck, pulling him backward and causing him to stumble with a bent knee.

"STOP!!!" Elantra barked in the most commanding voice that I'd heard from her. She tapped something on her wrist and a sigil came up.

I turned away quickly, I could later argue that I didn't see what it was. Even though I'd recognized it. Instead of listening to her, I whipped up my rifle one handed, using every last ounce of agility it possessed, and fired at the drone.

It dropped from the sky as Elantra continued to yell that she was a Captain SEPCO. Artem's secret police.

I turned to Gorka first. Agga still had him locked up tight. Lanris and Froom were tying his hands while Theta had her rifle glued to his head. I finally turned back to her. She had her pistol pointing at Nozz and her rifle pointing at me.

"You think you could kill me before I kill you?" I asked honestly.

"You kill me, then you're going away for a very long time. The punishment for killing a Member of the Military police is worse than death."

I took a deep breath and calmed the raging beast inside of me that only wanted blood. "See, I don't think it is," I said a moment later, walking casually over to her. "And if you did fire, you'd both die and I wouldn't. So stop pointing the gun at me and let's talk."

"Free Gorka and we can talk."

"No," I said flatly. "Start talking now."

"Have your man show me his hands and I'll talk."

"Go on, Nozz. Show her your hands."

Nozz raised them from behind his back and gave a double-handed wave.

"Where is it?"

"Where is what?" Nozz asked.

"We know what! You're stealing nanites! Show me your equipment now or I'll have you hauled in front of the high council."

"Kinky," Nozz said. "I normally don't show my equipment until at least the second date."

"Seriously, Nozz?" Theta snapped.

He shrugged and looked back to Elantra. "I don't know what you think you caught me doing, but I'm pretty sure I didn't break any laws."

She jerked the gun in his direction, a hint of concern creasing her face. "What were you doing then?"

"Just checking it out. Sometimes my orcish blood calls for me to skin and eat what we kill. It's just meat after all, and who hasn't eaten raw meat in the hard times."

She wrinkled her nose, attempting not to show her revulsion. "You can't be serious. That's your story, you were considering eating it?"

"Better than schmeat," he replied. "Sadly, they don't let us take anything back to the barracks to cook up."

"I call goblinshit. You were stealing nanites."

"Stealing them?" I asked. "How can you steal something from a dead creature? They don't belong to anyone."

She sneered. "You use military weapons, follow military intelligence, during a period where the military is paying for your time. If you can't work it out, that means any beasts killed by you during your military service means they belong to the military. And before you try to worm your way any further, we've seen recorded footage of your extractor and the vials. All we needed was to catch you in the act and now I have."

I sighed then casually asked. "Are you looking for a cut?"

"No. I'm looking for the truth which we'll get when my back up arrives. Your barracks are being thoroughly searched as we speak for the equipment. Now free Gorka and cooperate. This may go better for you if you do."

Searching the barracks. That wasn't good. My kit was well hidden, but I couldn't guarantee that a concerted effort wouldn't reveal it. I glanced over to the woozy looking elf, his helmet was on the floor now, and his eyes were struggling to remain open. I had to hand it to Agga, he might not be the sharpest knife in the rack, but he was holding Gorka on the edge of consciousness like a pro.

"Don't let him go," Theta, sulked, brandishing the minigun she'd wrestled from his hands. "I want to keep this!"

I shook my head and walked over to them. "Unfortunately, there's not much I can do about the situation. Agga, let him go."

Agga held on a little longer, reluctant to follow this particular order. "It's a bad idea," he grumbled.

"I completely agree. But at this point, I don't think any of our paths are looking particularly good, do you?"

"Argh!" he growled and pushed Gorka away.

The specialist staggered forward, toward me, and I met him with the hardest uppercut into the face I could generate. He lifted into the air to the sounds of gasps, and I leapt forward, both fists raised in the air to bring them down onto his chest and powered him into the ground.

"Stop!" came Elantra's command again.

But my right hand was already back up, held high above Gorka's face.

"Don't do it, Oshbob. Killing a member of the—"

I growled and brought my fist down into his already dented face before she could finish. As yet, he hadn't identified himself, so as far as I was concerned he was still just my specialist refusing to follow orders, threatening, and risking the lives of those under my command.

As my metal knuckles put Gorka's future to an end, Elantra opened fire on me. Plasma blasts struck my back, and it was all I could do not to sprawl face first onto the dead elf.

I expected as much from her, but the panic only hit when I heard the rest of my team open fire on her.

"Stop!" I yelled, desperately pushing myself from the body of Gorka.

Elantra was already down. Even fully armored, four plasma rifles and a minigun still made a mess.

I ran over to her, past the pale faces of my team members. "We can't kill her. She identified herself as SEPCO."

"But she shot at you!" Theta protested.

"It still doesn't matter," I replied, lifting Elantra's helmet.

"You're in… so much shit for this," she gasped once her head was free. "You better hope…" She hacked up blood "…that I survive."

I pulled the stim from her armor and jabbed her in the neck with it. "They only shot at you because you shot at me."

"You killed my partner," she replied. Color came back to her face as the nanites got to work.

"Then he should have identified himself. I promised him that he'd die if he went against my orders again."

"Wordplay, orc. You knew and you're going to pay for it. The APS and the other Scrub Teams are coming back to arrest you all."

"Well, shit, Elantra, you're not giving me any good options here."

"You don't deserve options. You deserve to die. You all do."

Empire of Oshbob

"When you put it like that, you're really making me regret the stim kit."

"It would have been worse, if I'd died," she said, getting to her feet in a swift, fluid movement that I could only dream about. Unara could have done it better, but not by much.

"Sergeant," Theta said coldly. "I don't think letting her live is a good idea. The drone's down. Gorka's down. We could set something up. Make it look like an accident."

A sharp movement from Elantra caught my eye. She had dropped a grenade between us and leapt back, turning almost invisible as she did so.

Despite the grenade, I was so angry that, rather than dive as far away from the blast radius as I could, I threw myself to where I expected Elantra to be. I caught a shimmer of light from her impressive stealth shield, but with a little luck and a lot of rage, I managed to snag one of the storage compartments around the belt at her hip.

With a sharp yank, I managed to pull myself a little farther forward and her quite the distance back. She wriggled to free herself but my grip held firm and the grenade detonated.

The explosion hammered at my armor. My legs took the brunt of the blast and a few of the fragments managed to penetrate the weak spots around the back of my knees. The pain was intense, but if I could get my Medi-Kit in me, I'd be fine.

Captain Elantra of the SEPCO, however, had not been wearing her helmet at the time. Nor, to my knowledge, did she have a Medi-Kit available after already using hers. For the briefest of moments, her invisibility mod faltered before reasserting itself in all its shimmering glory. I caught a glimpse of a bloody and badly damaged face and head. Despite that, she was still trying to get away.

"Gods be damned," Nozz groaned. "A grenade. Who just throws a grenade like that?"

As the others answered, and the sounds of the APS coming back our way with the other Scrub Teams, I kept an eye on the slowly crawling shimmer. We were so fucked, and I couldn't see a way out of this. So with no other options available I pulled up my rifle and fired at the shimmering form of Elantra. If I wasn't getting out of this alive, there was no way she was.

Elantra's invisibility flickered and showed her clearly as the bullets struck. The others seeing what I was doing raised their own rifles.

"Stop. Leave this to me," I replied, pushing myself up to my feet. "I killed Gorka so Agga wouldn't take the fall. I'm not gonna let you all sign your own death warrant with this."

I limped over, but Theta was there first. She offered me a resolute grin and emptied her rifle point blank into the elf's face until there was nothing left.

"And just like that, we've killed two Military Police, and APS are coming to kill us," Lanris said matter-of-factly. Though his specter-pale face suggested he wasn't feeling as calm as he sounded.

"The AV." Theta pointed back in the direction we'd come. "We're screwed."

I holstered my gun and put my hands in the air. "Sure looks that way."

Then I sent a message to Leo to prepare the legal teams once again, hoping they didn't just kill us.

Partition 20

"You're in so much fucking trouble, sergeant," Poulson roared at me as the APS led us onto the AV at gunpoint. "Why the hell did you mute me, you idiot? We could have managed the situation."

I felt a pang of hope. In all the commotion, I'd forgotten all about leaving the command channel open.

"They weren't allowing the situation to be managed," I replied. "Had I known they were SEPCO, it would have been a lot different, but after causing so much trouble, Gorka was too quick to react and too slow to identify himself."

"Save it for the commander and whoever is sent from SEPCO, because they will send someone," Poulson said tiredly. "Once we're back at base, you'll all be confined to your barracks until we get this sorted out."

"Not the cells again?" Lanris asked.

Poulson shrugged. "At the moment, no. Luckily for you all, it was Oshbob who killed them both, and as sergeant and commanding officer, he's the only one who can get away with it. Depending on how the evidence is tidied up, I still wouldn't hold your breath."

I was confused. I expected hell for what we'd done.

Poulson saw the expression. "We have the mission logs. You didn't know about Gorka. They were both too slow in telling you who they were. As far as I'm concerned, you had every right to do what you did."

"But?"

"But it was SEPCO, Oshbob. And they were fucking elves. *You're an orc*. I don't know if it has escaped your attention, but nobody likes orcs. You won't get the lickings of a dog."

Back at the base, despite the hateful looks we received from the APS, we weren't treated half as badly as I expected. As the rest of the team were escorted back to the barracks, Poulson led me to the commander's office.

Gullan was sitting smoking an elaborate water pipe and barely reacted as we entered.

Poulson snapped out a salute. "Commander. I have Sergeant Oshbob here to report."

Gullan looked up bleary eyed at me. "Thank you, colonel. You can leave us now."

Poulson was clearly relieved, and hightailed it out of there faster than I would have thought possible, leaving me, Gullan and his ridiculous pipe alone.

I ignored the smoking, steaming contraption, but he felt at liberty to explain.

"It helps with the PTSD."

"What's that?" I grunted.

"When you've seen the shit I've seen, sergeant… it changes you. I've been in some dark places. Been responsible for some horrific things. They haunt me."

"And that's PTSD?"

"Fucking dumb orc," he chuckled softly to himself. "You'll know it when it comes for you."

"I'll look out for it." I replied dubiously. Having already done and seen more horrid shit than most people could count in a lifetime, I suspected it was a human condition. I looked at every death and dark place I found myself as a step forward on my path. I'd never view any of those moments with anything but pride.

"So what happened?"

I took a moment to get my thoughts in order before replying. I doubted this conversation would be recorded, but I did want Gullan on side if I could manage it. "Private Nozz was investigating one of the Lepto corpses. Gorka screamed at him, asking what he was doing. We all turned to see what was going on. Gorka was charging him, looking ready to kill, so Elantra and I ran over."

"What was Nozz doing?"

"He was inspecting the Lepto, sir. They were quite young, the meat would be decent. Can be hard to pass up on fresh meat when all we get is schmeat."

Gullan wrinkled his nose. "So you weren't collecting nanites?"

Empire of Oshbob

"Absolutely not."

"This isn't the first time you've been suspected of collecting nanites though, is it?"

"As far as I know, it is." I shrugged. Casting my mind back, I couldn't remember a specific accusation from a higher up.

"Captain Elantra had identified herself prior to you killing her?"

"She had, yes. But we were out in the wilds and she was putting us all at risk. She had her weapons drawn and was threatening us. I had no choice."

"There's always a choice. And right now, I'm choosing to be tired of this bullshit. We're going to have SEPCO crawling all over this, I hope you realize. We're in for a horrible few days. I just hope you can keep your story straight, because it won't go well for you if you don't."

"I can keep my story straight," I promised.

He nodded, satisfied. "Off with you then. You're confined to barracks until this is cleared up."

I stood, and with a salute, I left his office trying not to show the utter bewilderment I was feeling over how this was playing out.

The SEPCO investigators came later that night. I hadn't expected them till the following day at the earliest, so I saw no reason not to make the most of the day with what spirits we had around the barracks.

I wasn't too worse for wear, but the rest of the squad were slurring, and in Agga's case, snoring loudly.

Two of them came. Both elves, one male, one female. Commander Gullan led them into our barracks. He looked surprisingly fresh considering the state I'd left him in earlier. I suspected some other kind of drug was responsible for the rapid turnaround as he was wired.

The two elves, however, were serene and almost robotic in how they moved into the barracks. Both of them wore long, brown leather-like coats and dark sunglasses despite it being dark out. It wasn't hard to work out that the glasses had a secondary purpose beyond dimming the glare of the sun.

Slowly, they swept the room with their gazes before both pairs of shades landed on Nozz. They beckoned him forward.

He pointed at himself, swaying gently from all the drink. "Me?"

The man nodded; the woman had already set back off out of the door. Nozz stumbled after them, glancing at me with an unworried expression. For some reason, that made me even more nervous than before. I had no choice but to trust him not to fuck it up.

Around ten minutes passed before he came back smiling. "They did some mind trick thingy where they could tell if I was lying or not. They couldn't find anything…"

"Private Nozz!" the woman scolded. "Our investigations are private until they are complete. Please refrain from discussing your experience."

With a shrug, he went and lay on his bed while they called Theta out.

As soon as the door was closed, I turned on Nozz. "You all right then?"

"Yeah. They pushed on the nanite thing they're trying to blow smoke into, but I wasn't using nanites. I've never collected nanites." His face went serious. "I think they can really tell if you're lying though, Osh, so you need to nail down what you're going to say."

"Well that's gonna be difficult, isn't it?"

"You could tell them…"

I held up a hand to stop any more of Nozz's drunken rambling. "I'll think about it, Nozz. Thanks, though."

He fell silent as did the rest of the room.

Theta walked back in soon after. She had a similar story to Nozz. Thankfully, the only other person who'd ever taken nanites had been sent to work in the city. Umak would have been caught.

Each of my squad mates were taken outside until only I remained. They wanted me last for some reason. I left the barracks and discovered they'd set up a table and had an odd-looking lamp illuminating the seat clearly meant for me.

"Sit." The female elf gestured.

I did as asked.

"Sergeant Oshbob?" she asked.

"If you don't know that already, you're in the wrong job."

"You are Sergeant Oshbob?" came the cold, calm reply.

"Tough crowd," I said with what I hoped was a believable chuckle. "But yeah. That's me."

"Ex gang lord in Portolans?"

"More gang coordinator. I keep them in line so that they don't cause too much trouble for the little man out there."

"Interesting take," said the man. "Do you intend to twist the truth throughout the entire interview?"

"Do you really need me to answer that one?" I asked.

"We have spoken to your men," the woman said. "They all have the same story. To them, it appeared Specialist Gorka attacked for no reason. Is this what you saw too?"

"I saw Private Nozz investigating the Lepto corpse. Gorka saw and charged at him. I didn't know what to think. I assumed it couldn't be purely because he looked at the corpse."

Her eyes lit up at that admission. "Yet you still killed him."

I leaned back in my chair and looked at the two of them. "You're damn right I did, and I'd do it again even knowing what I know now."

"Knowing he was a SEPCO officer."

"Even so," I replied. "Just like I did with Captain Elantra."

She looked at her partner. "Is that enough?"

"Not even close. Sergeant Oshbob here isn't finished."

I gave him the thumbs up. "The wilds are the most dangerous place in the world. We go out every day knowing it might be our last. Scrub Teams have a disproportionately high number of deaths."

She held a finger up to stop me like she'd won yet another victory over me. "It's well known that your team does not."

"No. Because my teammates listen to me. We work as a unit and watch each other's backs. We don't do anything that could cause harm to each other out there. Specialist Gorka would not listen. He was abusive and offensive to the rest of the team. I had five verbal warnings against him when three should have been enough to have him disciplined and moved to another team. I gave Gorka an explicit warning that should he attempt to disrupt a mission again and put my team at risk, I would end him. He did, so I did. End of story."

"You get off with Gorka," the man said. "But Captain Elantra, let's hear how you get yourself out of this one."

"Nothing to get out of. She blew herself up with her own grenade."

"We have recordings of you telling your people not to kill her. But one of them did."

"She was already dead from the grenade. If anything, it was a mercy."

"We'll be the judge of that."

"Surely the facts will be the judge of that. If you don't have a helmet on and you're three meters away from an exploding frag grenade, what happens to your head?"

"We only have your word for that, sergeant," the woman said.

"And the damage to Captain Elantra's armor," I pointed out. "And the fact that her helmet wasn't caught in the blast."

"We do not know what damage the armor already had," she replied with a hint of smugness showing through.

The man next to her groaned. "We do. The armor is repaired every evening. The only combat they saw was against the Leptos. She also threw a grenade at Artem Military personnel."

I almost felt like he was trying to help us which was a weird feeling.

"Who was trying to kill her!" the woman protested.

"Is that why I administered her Med-Kit?" I asked, neutrally. "We're a team of trained killers each with pulse rifles and handguns. If we'd wanted her dead prior to the grenade, she'd have been dead."

The man clapped. "Very convincing arguments, and very lucky that the pieces fell into place for you. You seem unusually charmed. Quite the oddity for an orc, too."

"Don't feel much charmed," I grumbled.

"Oh it's a scale, though! I mean, if you look at all of the things you've had to face in life, and all the things you've done, I think the positive far outweighs the negative."

"Maybe. Is that us done here?"

"Just one more thing," He pulled one of my nanite vials from his pocket. I guessed it was the one I'd lost fighting the Syniat. "Would you care to explain the purpose of this?"

"Looks like a canister to store things in."

"So you don't recognize it personally?"

"Should I?"

"Well at least one of your team should. It was found where you fought the Syniat. The Syniat that was notable for being unusually low in nanites despite being a healthy specimen. Does that fire any of your circuits?"

"Can't say it does?"

"The light flickered to red." The male elf grinned.

"Looks like that was a lie, sergeant. Did you take the nanites?"

"It could have just as easily been someone with stealth, like your Captain Elantra."

He smirked. "What about the consistently lower yields of nanites in any team you're involved in. Oh yes, we have full access to your full history."

"Feels like a set up to me. I think it's time we got my legal counsel involved."

"Have you sent your contacts a message yet?"

"Contacts?" I asked, trying not to make it obvious I was squirming like a fish on a hook.

"Go on. Try to send your people in Portolans a message."

I suspected they would be able to tell if I did, so I refrained. "My lawyers, please. Even SEPCO needs to follow rules."

"Indeed we do. Did you try to send a message?"

"I can't send messages to anyone. Just like anyone else on this base."

He laughed. "I suppose you didn't get this far without having a healthy dose of paranoia. We weren't attempting to track it. You would merely have discovered that the base is in lockdown. Your message wouldn't have been sent."

"Assuming I could send a message."

More head shaking. The woman was looking like she was enjoying the interview again now.

"You know," I added. "You never gave me your names. Pretty sure that's part of the procedure for questioning people."

"Why? Will you have one of your people try and drum up information on us?" she asked happily. "We're secret police, not giving our names comes with the territory."

"We could give you fake names," the man interrupted.

"I'll be happy if you just call my lawyers, thank you."

"You think they can get you off for stealing nanites? For killing the two investigating officers?"

It was time to stop speaking. He was a wily customer, and I felt myself being guided with each word now.

"Silence. A good option. As for your lawyers, I'm afraid that's not going to happen. The base is in lockdown."

"The base is in lockdown? For this?"

"Absolutely! Stolen nanites are a huge problem."

My tongue got the better of me and I snapped. "Bullshit. Who's setting all this up?"

He grinned. "Ooh, interesting. What makes you ask that?"

I mulled it over then figured there was no harm. "The military cares about nanites. I get it. It's big business. Hell, it probably keeps the whole thing running. But they're not fucking efficient at it. Not in the slightest. Every single raid we make, there are C-Rank beasts left undrained. Hell, they don't even always take the full load from some of the bigger monsters. Just whatever quota of drones they send out.

"Which leads me to my point. If someone was able to steal a few nanites here and there," I said, lifting the vial up and waving it at them, "the military wouldn't notice. And if they did, they wouldn't give a fuck about it. The shit half of the people in here are up to? The whole damn place is corrupt. Which means someone else is involved. This is about me. Or it's about my interests outside."

As I spoke, it hit me, I'd been going about this entirely the wrong way. Everyone was out for themselves. SEPCO and the Artem Military were government institutions. But the goddamn government was Corp owned. Everything was private. Everyone was out for their own interests. Just like ACE.

The man eyed me with a glint in his eyes. "So you think this is a ruse to take you out?"

"I know it is," I replied bluntly. "I just can't work out who's been paid. SEPCO or the military."

"This is even more fun than proving your guilt," the woman said with a shark-like grin.

"Who do you think it is?" the man asked.

Again, I really thought about it properly for the first time. He was pretty much admitting someone was paying for this. My suspicion was right. If I was a Corp and I wanted to get to me, how would I do it?

First, I'd engineer getting me to a post somewhere I could kill me without too many questions. They'd already done that and people in the military had been paid to see to it. I'd outmaneuvered them. They'd shut it down, but I knew the old base commander and mission commander had gotten into trouble from higher up.

If I was going to try and set myself up again, I'd want to be as far away from it as possible after the last debacle.

"Someone in the military is getting paid to get rid of me by a mystery corporation that wants to bring down Portolans 360. They can't do it directly because of Harold's connections in the military and the connections 360 have made. Which means they need to have an independent party come after me. The big question is, are you guys getting paid anything at all? Or is this just doing your duty?"

"That's a lot of wild accusations being thrown around," the man said. "The officers of SEPCO always do their duty."

So they weren't getting paid for this. "I'd be pretty pissed off if I was being used in some big scam and I wasn't seeing any creds. Fuck, you guys lost two people as well."

"Good people," the man said.

"I wish there was some way I could ease the pain of their loss. And for your time out here, running in circles."

"I wish there was a way too," he added. "It's starting to feel like we've been sent on a wild specter chase. We've done our background work as well. Even spoke to an old colleague of mine earlier when we received the call to come out and investigate. Superintendent Hersch. I believe you are familiar with her?"

"Superintendent, eh? Sounds important. I don't know what's going to happen here, but if you can pass on my best to her, I'd greatly appreciate it. Seeing as the base is in lockdown and all."

"Any special message you'd like to give her? Maybe a snippet of something only you two would know about? You know, so she knows that any message came from you."

I smiled. "Tell her I've gotten tougher from my time in the military and I'm still not going into the street fighting circuit for money."

The man smirked. The woman offered me a genuine smile.

"We will continue to pour over all of the information you've given us and your statements, and we will deliver our findings with your commander." He then lowered his voice. "Should our conclusion be favorable for you, then I suggest you prepare for…

some form of backlash. They know about your communication mod too."

"That bad?"

He nodded. "Run along now, sergeant. You've wasted enough of our time."

Empire of Oshbob

Partition 21

On returning to the barracks, Commander Gullan went outside with the elves to talk. I could only guess how the conversation would go, and I could only pray that any conversation the SEPCO officers had with Hersch was fruitful.

As for the warning about my communication mod, they were wrong. It wasn't a mod, at least not a full one. It only allowed for simple messages out and no ability to receive messages at all. It was buried in the big toe of my right foot. Accessing my keystone first, I called the local extension to the communicator.

Doing so was the failsafe. When it responded, a cascade of irrevocable changes occurred that would wipe the communicator of all information beyond basic, preset information. If this inquisition I was facing found it, I wouldn't have a chance at defending myself.

Once it was wiped, I gestured for Nozz to grab me a knife from the kitchen area, and I began loosening my boot.

"What's going on?" he asked as he handed me the knife.

"I have a hunch I'm going to be thoroughly inspected, if they find this comm, it'll be enough to screw me over until they can get something big to stick." I hauled my foot up to rest on my other leg, and forced my foot around to operate.

"You look like you're about to bust a gut, Sarge," Theta said. "Here let me. You want something to bite down on?"

I ignored the question and handed her the knife, propping my leg up on the bed. "It's on the underside of the bone at the end of the big toe. The comm itself is small, but it's coated in plastic."

"Right. Let's have a look then."

I had to give Theta her due. She didn't mess about. The knife cut straight in, striking the plastic coating on her first incision. I winced a little as she wriggled the knife around. I'd had worse, but it wasn't pleasant.

"It's bloody welded to the bone," she grunted in frustration.

"Just pry it off. If you don't get it off in the next minute, I'll take the hole fucking toe off myself."

My words spurred her to action again. A sickening pop later and the bloody little package flew free. Nozz was there with some healing spray and some bandages, quickly tying the toe up, while Theta washed the knife and Lanris picked up the communicator.

"Huh," he said, inspecting it. "Tiny. You think they'd have picked up on it if they did search you?"

"It's been missed before, but I've only had sweep scans and walkthrough scans. It was put there because it's unlikely to ever be seen. The plastic protects it from scanners up to a certain strength. If they look this time, they'll find it, I can guarantee it."

"Where do we put it?"

"Put it on the electric hob. Melt it then smash it."

It felt like only seconds after I pulled my boot back on that armed guards barged into our barracks. Commander Gullan followed them in.

"We need to have a word, sergeant."

"In the middle of the damn night?" I growled, getting up from my bed.

"Military law never sleeps," he replied, nose twitching and brows furrowing.

"Really now. Last I heard, the SEPCO officers didn't have enough to charge me with there and then. And couldn't go any further without my lawyers, so what's this about?"

"What is that smell?" he asked, looking over to the kitchen.

"Burnt a ration packet by accident," Lanris said, holding up a burnt ration packet. "You lock us in here and this is what happens. None of us can cook worth a damn."

Gullan scowled, then turned back to me. "It's come to my attention that you have a non-regulation communication mod. We're gonna find it, and then we're gonna put you in a cell."

"I don't have any such thing. You're just wasting everyone's time."

"We'll soon find out, won't we?"

I was led from the barracks, embracing the pain of each footfall as the open wound on my toe took my weight. Escorted directly to the Carver's room, I turned to Gullan. "Getting carried away, aren't you? You haven't found anything yet."

"Yet," he said, looking tired again.

"You sound like you desperately want to find something on me, Gullan. I thought we were okay?"

He sighed. "I told you, I didn't like orcs."

"Nah, it's more than that. What's going on?"

"Honestly, Oshbob, having you on base is an absolute nightmare. I'm fielding questions about you all the time. I have some higher ups checking if you're okay and others asking me to get rid of you by any means possible. Thirty percent of my job is managing the shitshow that goes on around you."

"I don't do a damn thing! I get on with the job and I leave everyone alone."

He waved me off. "I don't know what it's all about, but if I don't get rid of you, I'll be losing my own position."

"What! I assumed they would at least be paying you to screw me over like this."

"Nope. Just threats, and unfortunately, the people who are interested in your safety seem to have reduced in number since the death of your friend Harold. They provided a little balance to this shit show. Now…"

"So you openly admit you're going to see me dead."

"Prison, Oshbob. Prison. And you should be thanking me for sending you there. You have enough enemies that want you dead; it will be a nice break for you."

The guards approached with scanners now. I ignored them as they got to work, and continued with Gullan. "You don't think I'll be killed in prison?"

"Honestly?" he sighed. "I don't care anymore. I just need you out of my hair. If you're in prison, you're somebody else's problem."

"At least I know where I stand," I replied, trying not to let the whole thing get to me.

Gullan just shrugged then watched the guards scanning me.

"Nothing," one of them eventually said.

"Strip him off and try again," the carver suggested. "If it's well hidden, his clothes might be enough to obscure a reading."

"If anyone tries to undress me, I'm gonna go off. Full berserker. I might not kill you all before you bring me down, but I bet you I'll be close."

It was a point of pride that they all looked as though they believed me. With a sigh, and knowing they couldn't stop searching, I removed my clothes myself, down to my underwear.

"The pants are not coming off and that's final. Find a stronger scanner if you need to."

Half of them were mesmerized by the amount of scars on my body. Gullan was looking at my toe.

"What happened there?"

"Shrapnel from the grenade," I lied easily. "Tore the backs of my knees up good too."

"You took a Medi-Kit."

"A small. It ran out before it completed the task, and if you remember, I didn't have time to ask for a second."

Gullan fell silent and I was searched again, lifting my arms, opening my mouth, and offering up the soles of my feet.

"Nothing sir," one of the guards reported after over half an hour of vigorous scanning."

Gullan rubbed his face. "This is not good, Oshbob. Not good at all."

I felt differently, but said nothing.

"Get dressed and get back to your barracks."

"Is that it?" I asked skeptically.

"Oh, I very much doubt it."

Empire of Oshbob

Partition 22

Captain Poulson arrived at our barracks around ten the next morning. He stood upright, a severe expression on his face. His attempt to remain professional only served to highlight his discomfort.

"We've received word from SEPCO. They have closed their investigation. Somehow, you have managed to kill two of their agents and get away with it."

Despite silently rejoicing the perks of having a little power in this strange game being played, I couldn't help having a niggle at Poulson.

"If I was SEPCO, I'd be pretty pissed with the people who put their agents in that position in the first place."

"Oh, I think everyone's pissed at someone right now. As you have been cleared of all charges from both SEPCO and the military, you're free to get back to work. Prepare for a call to action."

He didn't even wait for a reply. Turning sharply on his heel, he spun and exited the barracks.

"How the hell did you get us off?" Agga asked bewildered.

"I think that's the least of our worries. Did Poulson seem odd to you?"

"No more than usual," Agga replied.

"He was avoiding making eye contact as much as possible," Theta offered. "He's up to something. Or someone is."

I shot her with a fake bullet from the fake gun shape I'd made my hand into. "Got it in one. They're going to try something."

"Again? How many times do we need to beat them at their own game?" Lanris grumbled. "Why can't they leave us the fuck alone?"

"'Cause we keep surviving," Theta said. "These types only stop once they've won."

When the call came, we reported to the hanger. All six of us. The two Scrub Teams waiting to board the AV were 9 and 11. Neither of which we'd worked with before, both of them new teams brought in at the same time as Elantra and Gorka.

They pointedly ignored us as we flew there even when I asked them a question.

"You guys are not SEPCO as well, are you?"

Around half of them glared at me, the rest pointedly ignored me.

"I don't think they are," Theta whispered loudly. "The SEPCO agents were much friendlier, and I include Gorka in that."

"Just military like us, then," I answered for them.

"We're not like you," the sergeant of team nine spat. "Fucking orcs have no place in the army. I include all half-orcs in that as well," he added with barely concealed rage as he eyed the rest of my team. From the looks of the other members of nine and eleven, it appeared they agreed with him.

Theta turned to me and whispered loudly. "I think they've made the new Scrub Teams up with orc haters."

"I think you're right, Theta," I replied calmly. Inside, I was a torrent of emotions. I couldn't even send a message home to give them a heads up that this would probably be my last day.

A plasma sword would struggle to cut the tension in the air as the AV touched down. And Poulson addressed us through the announcement channel.

We've got an A-Rank Snake type today. We need everyone focused.

I didn't like the sound of that, but I was still more concerned about the people around us. As we started walking off the AV with the other teams, I slowed and turned back to the others. "Be ready for anything. I don't know when it will come, but I know it's coming."

They were all pale faced, but nodded. I led them down the ramp and eyed the land around us looking for possible cover. We were in luck. It was a rough, uneven terrain, with rock outcroppings and a number of small hills. It looked like a place Leptos would love.

Empire of Oshbob

Lining up at the left side of the ramp, Poulson spoke over the command channel as the APS tromped off, drones spinning around their heads.

> *Scrub 4, you're covering guard. Wait until the APS cover a hundred meters, then follow in after. Maintain visual contact at all times.*

"Understood," I replied, then cut the mic for that channel as Theta spoke.

"Nearly two years as rearguard, yet today they change our position. What the hell are they planning?"

"We'll find out soon enough. I want your damn head's spinning like disco balls. Odd behavior from the other teams, surges in monsters, and places to defend and hunker down. Watch everything in every direction like your life depends on it."

"Because it does," Theta added.

I got a solid affirmative from them all and then we were off, moving after the hulking figures of the APS.

> *Scrub 9, you're up. Follow in. Maintain 300 meters from Scrub 4.*

"Sweet fucking Schmeat balls, this is stressful," Agga grumbled over the group channel.

"Focus, Agga," I replied. "The more you're thinking about the problem, the more likely we are to find a solution."

"There's a cave up there," he said, pointing up the rise to our left.

It was a shallow bank, but he was right. There was a cave or tunnel entrance. Most likely the home of something we didn't want to meet. And I was certain I could smell Lepto in the area.

"Well spotted, Agga."

We fell silent again and kept on moving.

"Scrub 9 seems to be closer than three hundred meters," Theta warned.

I glanced back to see she was right then unmuted myself on the command channel. "Poulson. Scrub 9 are closing on our position!"

"So they are. I thought you'd be glad of the extra help, seeing as though you're under-manned."

"We're good as we are. Call them back so that we have space to work if we need it."

"Last I checked, you weren't mission commander, sergeant. Keep the line clear for serious concerns."

I muted him again. "Bastard," I hissed. I was furious, but I'd also allowed myself to become distracted.

Theta brought my attention back. "Up ahead, sarge, the APS."

I looked up in time to see the fast plodding of the APS carrying them out of sight around the verge that ran along our left side.

"We were told not to lose sight of them. Everyone, double time now."

We set off at a jog after, but they didn't come into sight as quickly as I'd suspected though gun fire up ahead suggested they weren't too far away. When we rounded the corner, the APS were at the entrance to a cave or tunnel and they were dishing out a lot of fire power.

"Must be the target?" Theta suggested hopefully.

Then Poulson made another command channel announcement.

Scrub 4. APS have found a Lepto nest. And they report you are nowhere to be seen.

"We're here now, Colonel. They got out of sight where the path veers left."

Convenient. Now get in there and take over from them. They have a job to do and they're currently wasting ammo doing your job.

We raced over to support, and one of the APS turned to face me. "Don't you know anything about how escort duty works?"

I ignored him and looked into the cave. There were a few dead Leptos but nothing that warranted the level of gunfire they'd unleashed.

"They wouldn't have even scratched your armor," I noted. "But rest assured, we'll keep your backs clear as you move on."

The compact missile launcher on his left shoulder swiveled to face the cave, and a missile whistled out from it deep into the tunnel. There was a massive explosion and a large section of the tunnel inside collapsed.

The APS sergeant looked back at me. "Well I don't fucking trust you to do the job properly."

Then he turned and led his team away. There was gunfire behind us now and Poulson spoke again.

Leptos. Hundreds of them on the western slope. Be on your guard.

The APS moved off again; we held back a little, allowing them to regain the distance.

"What the hell was that? Why missile an empty cave?" Theta asked.

"To stop any more Leptos getting out," Agga assured her.

"They already killed the five Leptos in there with enough ammo to take down a B Ranker. If they wanted to drop the tunnel, they would have led with that."

"They were making a point," I muttered. "If I had to guess there were no Leptos in the tunnel when they came across it. They… got their attention."

"Well it's sealed now," Agga said. "Let's go see what else they've got in store for us."

We followed again, and again the path swerved away and we lost sight of them. Gunfire still sounded from behind us, creating a surreal experience. When the path straightened out again, the APS were nowhere to be seen.

"What do we do?" Theta asked. "This isn't an accident."

"No. I don't think it is. They're probably wanting us to speed up and run right into some kind of ambush. One second."

I cut Theta off and unmuted the channel to Poulson. "Sir, APS have sped up and gained a sizable lead. We can't see them anywhere."

"Then I suggest you find them, and do it fast!"

His words just added to my sense of doom. "Why don't you tell me how far ahead they are? As our mission command, tell them to slow down. We don't all have rocket boosters."

"I'll let them know of your concerns. Now get after them. If they're overwhelmed and you weren't there to help them, then you're in the shit again."

"You lot are just waiting for an excuse, aren't you? After all this time, you still keep fucking with me." I cut the comm so he couldn't hear or reply, then raised my visor. "He said follow faster."

"Do we?" Theta asked.

"What choice do we have?" Lanris snapped. His eyes were wild and he looked like he was about to freak out completely.

"We go forward. Agga, Froom, Lanris—you're with me. Nozz, Theta—head up the slope. We'll go steady, try and match our pace. Everyone spread out a little. Try and keep some distance between us."

They all nodded silently, hope in their eyes that I knew what I was doing. I had no idea. Visors went back down and we all moved off again. When I reactivated the command channel, Poulson was shouting.

"I'm here," I replied. "And we're moving."

"Move faster! We haven't got all day."

"All day for what, colonel?"

No reply.

Agga had moved out to my left and Froom to my right, each around five meters from my central position. I held my gun up ready to fire and kept a steady pace.

"I said hurry," came Poulson's voice again.

"Understood, colonel," I replied, not moving any faster at all.

"You notice there's no drones watching us?" Froom said, looking all around.

We moved around the next bend just as Theta shouted a warning across the squad channel. "APS are waiting around the next corner."

"What are they doing?"

"Standing with their weapons out, trying to look innocent."

"Gotcha."

I spoke to Poulson again, "Why are APS no longer moving? What are they doing?"

"Waiting for you to catch up!" he yelled.

"We've caught up now. I reckon there's fifty meters and a rocky verge between us. We'll wait until they move on again."

"You'll move now and back them up."

"Against what? There's nothing here. What's the plan? Have us run into them and they get a surprise and kill some of us, *mistaking* us for monsters? What an excuse for later, huh? Scrub 4 got too close while the APS were tracking an A Ranker. It's a terrible tragedy brought about by the incompetence of orcs?"

The line crackled, then went dead from Poulson's end. Not only that, but all comms to our helmets were deactivated. I had no choice but to roar.

"EVERYONE BACK UP NOW!"

Agga, Froom, and I began walking backwards quickly. Guns and eyes aimed forward. I just had to hope that Theta and Lanris had heard me.

"In five, turn and run. Five… four…"

The APS had reacted. Using their jet packs to boost each step they took, they pounded around the corner. The sergeant, his voice amplified by the suit, barked orders at us.

"Traitors! You would leave us undefended?"

I shouted back, my voice amplified only by anger. "Leptos behind. We're just checking on them."

"Goblinshit!" he roared.

"Fuck the count. Run!" I yelled and turned tail.

The truth was, I wanted to rage, I wanted to kill them all. I wanted to let out the feral orc. But I kept him locked away. Just one of those APS suits would be enough to kill the three of us. With eight of the bastards, we'd last seconds at most. Even retreating as fast as we could we'd be run down, and I now realized why they'd missiled the cave. And why they'd wanted me to see it.

From above, Theta screamed, pointing at something up the bank that only she could see.

There was no time for questions. I angled my run to the slope, put my head down and sprinted for all I was worth. I didn't look back. Not even once, for as much as I wanted everyone with me to survive this, if one of them fell and I tried to help, that would just end up with me being dead in short order too.

I had to trust in their abilities and keep going. The only deviations I made were to zig zag when necessary. I was still hit numerous times, but with the armor, my body took no damage, and I was able to use the propulsion from their plasma rifles to push me on to greater speeds.

I'd made it a good chunk of the way up the bank before I heard the landing of heavy metal feet behind me accompanied by the gentle buzz of a plasma sword.

A quick-fire thought came unbidden. Seven of the eight APS held their guns right-handed. I'd assume the same was true with the swords. I went with the odds and dove to the left in a roll, finding my feet at the end of it.

The air crackled with energy only centimeters above my head. I had no idea how close I'd come to death, but I suspected it was too close.

I kept my momentum from the roll and kept running forward. I heard a cry of a half-orc in pain, and it cut to the core of me, but no matter what I could learn by looking behind me, it wasn't worth the risk of slowing or stumbling and being cut down.

I still hadn't seen this tunnel or cave, but Theta and Nozz reappeared, sprinting as desperately as me with two APS in pursuit.

Just when I thought it couldn't get any worse. Scrub Team 9 came into view, charging toward us, guns up and firing.

I saw Nozz go down from their fire, shot in the side of the leg. Knees and ankles were always the best place to bring well-armored troops like us down, especially if we were running. The bullet didn't need to penetrate as long as they could bring us down. I resigned myself to that eventual fate, and promised myself that I would stay upright, no matter the pain or unbalance. I shortened my strides, but pumped my legs faster.

I tried to ignore his plight, too far away to help him even if I could.

Empire of Oshbob

Any thoughts of assistance fled my mind as Nozz pushed himself up, attempting to scrabble back up to his feet. An APS trooper came hurtling down toward him from a mighty, jet-boosted leap. Plasma sword held high, he buried it into Nozz's armored back.

Don't let it get you, I chanted internally. *Move, move, move!* I was hit. Felt like a missile had struck my back. There was no keeping my feet, despite my earlier promises. I went airborne first, in a blossom of fire and pain. Then I slammed into the ground.

After what I'd just witnessed from Nozz's death, I acted fast and rolled over onto my badly damaged back. A Plasma sword struck the ground where I'd lain. The APS trooper had executed an almost identical move to the one that had ended my friend.

I rolled again, and again, growling in agony but managing to get my feet under me without losing too much time.

A plasma sword came swinging at my head, I had no choice but to go closer to the wielder or be cut in half, even though it was the last place I wanted to go. I pulled my grenade from its pouch, activating it at the same time as I slapped it on to the mag clip for his sword.

Then I ran again, diagonally across the bank, dodging another sword swing, leaping over Froom's decapitated body, and blanking out the pain that caused me. Somehow, in all of the carnage and the coming together of the APS in their attempts to kill me, I managed to remake a little distance. And through luck rather than anything else, I saw Theta disappearing into the ground, and Lanris, who was so close to her, getting smashed in the chest by an APS minigun. He went down hard, but by his screams, not dead yet.

I raced toward him and the hole.

Heavy thuds of armored arseholes landed all around me as I ran. Their proximity at least prevented Scrub 9 and 11 from firing on me. With nothing else for it, I threw myself forward. This time skidding on my armored knees, coming to a halt next to the writhing Lanris and for the first time turning back, rifle in hand.

"Get up," I growled. "We're so close."

Two APS troopers loomed over us, one swinging his sword around in a mighty arc that would kill us both. The other, holding a minigun, aimed down at us. We backed away, stumbling together.

Both of us trying to get our own guns up. But it was gunfire from behind us that saved our lives. Theta had popped up from the tunnel entrance and deflected the sword swing just enough for it to swing wide.

That didn't save us from the machine gun fire, but a grenade at the feet of the APS certainly did. The explosion pushed Lanris and I forward into the hole.

We weren't safe, but we weren't surrounded anymore. We had half a chance now.

"Theta," Lanris growled as he raised his rifle and hit himself in the chest with his Medi-Kit. "Don't ever throw a grenade at us again…" He gasped as the nanites took hold. "But if you do, make sure you do it exactly like that."

"I didn't throw the grenade," she said, patting the compartment on her hip.

At that moment, under a hail of gunfire, Nozz fell into the tunnel.

"How in all the… Tough bastard." I ran forward and grabbed his arm, pulling him deeper into the tunnel while the other offered covering fire.

Empire of Oshbob

Partition 23

Nozz couldn't stand. While that might be the least of his problems in a few seconds, I was more than happy to throw him over my shoulder as we moved back deeper into the tunnel. Blind desperation to escape took over.

"They're not following!" Theta shouted.

I looked back to see that she was right. At least as far as I could tell. The tunnel wasn't straight, so I could only see around thirty meters behind us.

"What do you think their plan is?" Lanris asked across the comm.

"No idea," I groaned as I lay Nozz down on the floor for a moment. He was in really bad shape. We all were but he was by far the worst. I added more anguish to my voice as I stuttered out more of a response. "Nozz is dead, and us three are so close it hardly matters what they do. This is a Lepto nest. The bastards will smell all the blood and we'll be finished."

I whipped up my visor and gestured for silence and for them all to cut comms. They all did as I asked, including the barely conscious Nozz at my feet.

He offered up a strained bloody smile. "Am I really dead?"

I shook my head. "Not yet. But it really isn't looking good. I need all of you to speak directly from now on. Turn comms off entirely unless I say otherwise."

I pulled out my Medi-Kit and looked sadly down at Nozz. He desperately needed one, but so did I, and if I didn't take it soon, I wouldn't even be able to carry myself.

I noticed Lanris eyeing it with longing. I met his eyes and offered a sad smile. "Sorry, Lan. It was a toss-up between taking it myself and giving it to Nozz. But when you've been used as missile target practice by the APS, there's only so much mother nature can do alone." I turned and showed him my back.

"Hurgh," he replied, painting a vivid picture of what my back must have looked like.

"That bad, huh?"

He opened his mouth to answer, said "Hurgh," again, then vomited.

Theta managed to use more words. "We can see your actual spine, Oshbob. And ribs."

"I might never be able to see my spine, but by all the gods of old, I can feel every fucking millimeter of it." I depressed the button on the Medi-Kit and grimaced as the nanites got to work. It was too much damage for one medium to heal, but it would keep me on my feet.

Theta pulled her own Medi-Kit out. "I haven't used mine. But if anyone gets it, it has to be Nozz. Sorry, Lan."

Lanris looked down at his chest, then over at Nozz. "Fuck! Of course he should get it. But we need to find somewhere safe as soon as we can so that I can clean this shit up and try to get it to stop bleeding."

"There's only one direction for any chance of that," Theta said as she gave Nozz her Medi-Kit. "Deeper into the tunnels."

"Of course our only chance of safety would be inside a damn…"

A massive explosion behind us cut him short. The back draft, channeled by the tunnel, knocked us all on our asses and we were plunged into dust and darkness. As the light dropped to nothing, our light sensitive helmet torches activated.

"They blew up the entrance, didn't they?" Lanris groaned.

Another explosion rattled the ground around us. Which in this case included the ceiling. Soil and rock began to rain down on our heads.

"We need to move. No more complaining, Lanris. We made it this far, we're going to survive."

"In a Lepto nest?" he replied, coughing with the dust.

"I'll take a thousand Leptos over eight APS any day of the week. Add in sixteen heavily armored Scrub Team members, forty assault drones, and an AV, then I'll even face the A-Rank fucking Snake that's supposed to be lurking around here."

Lanris's face went ashen. "I clean forgot about the snake. You think it's close?"

Empire of Oshbob

Another bombardment brought more of the tunnel ceiling down around us.

"I don't fucking care. Move, move, move."

I gripped the back of the slowly recovering Nozz's armor, and set off running.

A voice reached my ears. "You think the snake's down here?"

I looked down to see Nozz looking up, tired and pale, but with a smile on his face. I dropped him back on the floor. "I think, if you can talk, you can walk."

He got unsteadily to his feet, a sheepish smile. "Seriously though. I really don't like snakes. You think it's down here?"

"Look around." I gestured down the tunnel ahead up us. "We're not swarmed with Leptos in a Lepto nest. There's a giant snake in the area, the math is simple."

"The snake ate them," Theta clarified.

"Fuck," Nozz resolved.

"Look on the bright side," Lanris said, changing the subject. "At least the bombardment isn't dropping the tunnel this far in and they haven't followed us. We could probably rest for a minute." He then looked at me pleadingly. "I could really do with a rest."

I didn't want to stop. I was too damn angry to stop. Hell, I was devastated, and stopping would just open up the floodgates of what had happened. I wasn't sure if I was ready to let all that shit in yet. But one look at Lanris and his bloody chest told me that I really didn't have any choice. It was stop or lose another one of my team, and I'd really grown to love my team.

"We can stop for a minute to check everyone over, but I want to get somewhere we can set up safely for a few hours at least. We all need proper rest and sustenance."

Even Theta looked grateful as she hunkered down against the curved, muddy wall. She didn't lower her rifle, though she also didn't know which way to point it.

I watched the other two sitting on their arses, guns over their laps, completely unready for action and looking ready to die. I had nothing but sympathy.

"I saw Agga die," Lanris said after a few minutes of silence. "Damn missile hit him square in the head, and an APS swordsman jumped in and took his damn head off clean. I mean, at least it was swift, but damn. It hurts, doesn't it? I know we're all different, but in the military... I thought there was a brotherhood even if you didn't like your brother."

"There is a brotherhood," Theta said. "It's right here, for us. The rest of them can go burn."

I felt like I'd failed them all. Like Froom and Agga's deaths were my fault, and I almost said as much. Almost let my anger and self-pity out. But I caught it before it leapt free and made matters worse. This was our reality. The world we lived in. When you scraped away all of the bullshit, all anyone really wanted to do was for them and their nearest and dearest to survive.

That was almost everyone's biggest fear. Not freedom, nor the loss of it. But the loss of themselves or their loved ones. Sure there had been points when I didn't care if I lived or died. But even then I'd still raise the world for the ones I loved.

I cleared my throat and stretched out my neck, getting their attention. "We lost two brothers today. I feel like a part of me died with them. I feel like a failure."

Nozz opened his mouth to speak, but I hushed him. "But they're dead and I can't change that with all the time, money, power, and influence in the world. They're gone but they'll live on in here." I touched my chest. "But only if we survive. I intended for us to survive."

"Good. I'm all ears," Theta said with a tired smile.

"There are a million little things to worry about, but right now, we need to focus on that. Survival. We're trapped in a Lepto nest, which may or may not have Leptos in it, but we can all but guarantee something will be living in here. So what I need you all to do is to shut your human sides off. Orcs thrive on this kind of shit. We're built for it."

"Whaddya mean?" Nozz asked.

"What do you think orcs would do in a nest, before the fall, huh? Before the cities sprang up and we were all trapped inside of their stinking walls?"

"Die?" Theta suggested.

"An elf or a human would. I told you to think like an orc."

"Probably go hunting," Nozz said with a grimace.

"We're trapped in fucking tunnel. Out of contact with anyone, and two of our team have just been slaughtered by the APS, and you think the answer is hunting Leptos?"

He shrugged. "It's not like we have anywhere to be."

"Not yet," I agreed. "Until we work out what we're going to do in the long term, we need to survive. Think of all the real meat that could be down here."

Theta looked at me like I was mad. Nozz just looked surprised that he was right.

Lanris was looking down the tunnel. "I don't think we're gonna need to look far to find something to hunt."

There was scuffling and snuffling coming from deeper down the tunnel. The sound quickly grew, and a Lepto appeared in the torchlight cast by our helmets. It froze for a moment, then let out an ear-piercing screech.

I put a small burst of plasma in its forehead. It died with another screech. "Dinner is served."

No sooner as I had uttered those words a series of screeches went up further down the tunnel.

"Okay," Theta said. "Did anyone else get the impression that those screeches were a call to action?"

She was right, that was a lot of noise. I stepped past Lanris who was furthest forward, and grabbed a rock that was jutting out from the mud ceiling. It was well wedged in there, but with a wiggle and a yank it came out along with a shower of soil. I dropped where I stood. The others stood, rifles pointed past me as more Leptos appeared.

Theta was in the best shape of the three, so I pointed back up the tunnel. "Lots of debris fell from the bombardment above. Grab what you can and help me build a barricade. You two, keep the fuckers back."

Theta ran off to the nearest free boulder, Lanris fired past me into the next squealing Lepto to appear.

Nozz looked at me uncertainly. "Sorry, Sarge, but... They're Leptos. They can burrow quicker than we can drink beer."

"They can, but they're simple and work on natural instinct. As long as we leave a route through to us, they'll use it."

"We're so fucked," Lanris grumbled.

"I never said it would be easy. But I say it's possible. Depending on how many come."

"See," Nozz grumbled. "You almost had me…" He paused to fire down the tunnel. "…believing until you added that bit at the end."

I didn't bother to answer, instead focusing on pulling a boulder from out of the ground a few meters behind our new barricade.

Their gunfire became almost constant, pushing Theta and I to work ever faster. So far, Nozz and Lanris had managed to keep them back away from our barricade, but Nozz was looking unsettled.

He turned back, a desperate look on his face. "The rifle's gonna overheat and dry up if I don't give it a break."

"Same," Lanris shouted over his own gunfire.

"Nozz, swap out. Lanris, swap out with Theta when she gets back."

They both nodded grimly, and Nozz staggered off towards where the tunnel had collapsed.

Looking down the tunnel, I saw the mass of Lepto bodies that were forming a secondary barricade of sorts. Though, it was heaving, almost pulsating with the crush of bodies behind it. Bodies were being dragged away too as the Leptos desperately tried to get to us.

"Throttle back firing," I snapped at Lanris. "I'll take over the brunt of the attack. Only fire if anything breaks me."

My words were futile as Theta came jogging back carrying a massive boulder. "Get the fuck out of my way, Lanris!" She growled, struggling with the weight and momentum she'd built up.

Lanris jumped out of the way as she reached the barricade, not in control of her run at all, but she did manage to get the boulder in a decent position.

She dropped to her knees, gasping, but still trying to get her rifle off her back. "Let's kill some Leptos then, Sarge," she raggedly shouted over my plasma fire.

"I think the days of me being a sergeant are long gone, Theta. Just call me Oshbob."

She opened fire in the ever-reducing gap in our barricade. "If it's all the same to you, even if we aren't in the military anymore, I'd still like to keep the group hierarchy as it is until we get out of this. We all know where we stand with each other if we keep that together."

"Probably wise. There's been enough change."

Considering we thought the nest might be empty, it seemed like there was no end to the Leptos. It took another ten minutes before the barricade was suitable but I was starting to worry about how many were coming. All of our guns were starting to get low on charge, and without sunlight, they'd soon run out.

As Lanris and Nozz took back over from us, Theta looked as troubled as I felt.

"We're going to need to dig out at this rate."

"We have no idea what's going on out there," I muttered. "They're likely to watch the tunnel until dusk, which is still hours away. Until then, we can't risk it. If the Lepto numbers drop enough, we might be able to find another one of their exits."

"Drop?" Nozz shouted back desperately. "There's more of them than ever. They're widening the tunnel! And I have about another minute before the rifle is completely dead and you know what that means."

"Same here," Lanris said grimly.

"Ah shit." I ran forward to look through our gap. Nozz was right. The tunnel was widening, and using the bodies of the fallen, they were inching ever closer to the barricade.

"Once they run out, they're useless. We can use the pistols, but that's what? Twenty bullets each?"

Nozz nodded. "Yep, and one bullet isn't gonna stop a Lepto. Not unless you get only eye shots."

"Better to save the last bit of charge on the rifles in the hopes we make it out of here alive. Pistols next, then we block the barricade off completely. It'll be back to basics after that. Fists and knives. Swap out with me and Theta. We'll take over. Be ready with pistols."

Theta tapped me on the shoulder. I turned to her and saw she was holding up her grenade.

"That could bring the whole place down."

She met my disbelieving stare unflinchingly. "Do we have a choice?"

"Probably not." Without overthinking it, I nodded. "Do it."

She threw it without hesitation, hurling it as far as she could beyond the hole.

"DOWN!" I screamed at the other two. Admittedly, we probably should have discussed the decision with them before going ahead and throwing it.

The tunnel walls trembled, the air filled with heat and deafening sound that was amplified within the confined space. That was quickly replaced by ringing ears, the death screams of countless Leptos and airborne debris.

I forced myself to stand the moment it passed. If the grenade wasn't as successful as I hoped, and the Leptos were still coming, they couldn't find us lying on the floor.

My head torch barely penetrated the dust and smoke still hanging in the air, but apart from the occasional movement of loose earth, there were no sounds coming from the other side of the barricade.

I peered through the dramatically reduced gap in our barricade, and waited until the sight I'd been hoping for came into view. The tunnel had caved in. We were sealed off from the Leptos. For now.

Partition 24

"We're safe for now. It's all sealed off."

"Thank the old gods," Theta said, slumping down on her ass against the tunnel wall.

Nozz bent over and rested his hands on his knees. "I could do with a break around now."

"Just one thing," Lanris said, rubbing his chin and looking at the barricade. If those sides are sealed off, and behind us are sealed off… what about air?"

It was a good point that I hadn't even considered. "Anyone even know how long the air in here would last?"

"Well," Theta said thoughtfully. "The area of the tunnel we have available is around seventy meters long. Three meters high and three wide. So if we take the rate of oxygen each of us needs per hour, and calculate the overall volume of the tunnel, and divide it between the four of us, I estimate that I have no fucking idea how long we've got! I'm a half-orc who's best option in life was to be used as cannon fodder for the corpo nanite collection machine masquerading as a city military! Now sit your ass down and rest while we have the chance. Better still. You're carrying the Skillistove, aren't you?"

It took Lanris a long second to recover from the onslaught. His face twitched between surprise, wrinkled fury, and finished on a depressed grimace. I suspected the grimace was an attempt at a smile. I knew that feeling well.

"Yeah I have it," he said, producing the self-heating, self-expanding skillet from its compartment on his belt. It was a rectangular block of metal no bigger than a human hand. The only detail other than smooth black metal was the handle, inlaid in the shape.

Lanris flipped the handle out and the block of metal activated, growing both in temperature and size. He set it down on the ground and looked at Theta.

I spoke first. "Nozz, you've got the Water Generator. Set it up, and get me a drink of water. I'm gonna go grab us a Lepto."

"You won't fit through the hole, Sarge," Theta said. "Let me go through. You can skin it, though. That's not really my thing."

I held out my fist for her to bump. "You've got yourself a deal."

She obliged, striking my fist with her own, then pulled out her handgun and climbed through the hole.

I leaned in after her with my handgun to offer back up and the extra light from my helmet, but it wasn't needed. After clearing away some rubble, she got to hauling the uncovered carcass back. She pushed it up so its pointed brown head poked through. I grabbed it on the back of the neck and did the rest.

I pulled out my Viber knife about to get to work, when Nozz offered me a cup of water.

"Drink it and fill another." I was more interested in getting the Lepto butchered and food in our stomachs. Not because we were starving, but because we could well be in the next few days, depending on what we decided to do.

I cut into the Lepto's hide and got to work, ripping the fur away in long, ragged cuts.

Another five minutes passed, and Nozz offered me another full cup of clear cool water. This time, I drained it, then refocused on the half-skinned Lepto.

I'd removed the fur from the neck down past its arms. It was time to get the skillet earning its crust. I cut into the flesh down to the shoulder joint, before snapping the joint back as far as I could. I plunged back in with the Viber knife, and cut the last few resisting sinews away.

"Get the starter cooking, Lanris."

He was already watching me, and was prepared to catch the first leg as I tossed it over. He used his own knife to slice the meat off the joint, letting it drop straight into the pan where a satisfying sizzle could be heard immediately.

By the time I got the second arm free, the air was already heavy with the sweet smell of charring flesh.

Lanris took each joint I handed over and butchered them down further while watching the meat in the pan. Nozz continued to provide everyone with water each time the cup slowly filled.

Empire of Oshbob

While I kept butchering and skinning, I sent Theta through to get another carcass.

She looked dubious, but I wanted to cook up a ton of meat to carry with us. We'd need plenty of both meat and water if we were going to survive. I wished there was a way to collect the water from the generator, but we only had the one cup that came with it.

Agga had carried the comfort pack. No bigger than the shelter I carried, but it contained sleeping bags, waterproofs, canteens, and plates. They would be a miss but not a great one. Theta carried the emergency rations that could be invigorated with water, but they'd be kept for a last resort. Froom, may the land take his soul, had carried the boat. We definitely didn't need a fucking boat, and I couldn't see a time we would need one.

We managed to eat the full first Lepto and got most of the second cooked up. I was in the middle of gutting the third when Theta hissed for us all to be quiet.

She pointed to her ear and pointed to the hole. We all listened intently. There was definite movement.

"Times up then," I snapped.

Nozz grumbled. "Didn't even get a nap."

I stormed past him to the gap. Part of me screamed it could be the snake, but as I reached the hole, a Lepto appeared from the darkness.

Despite the pistol in my hand, surprise saw me punching the damn thing instead of shooting. The straight right was a rapid solid blow with the Tier-Three arm that sent the D Rank rat flying back through the hole. I got my bearings quickly after that and fired after it.

The hole was only big enough for one of us to cover, but it was also a tight squeeze for the Leptos, meaning we had time.

With two magazines for each MQ-10 handgun we carried, I emptied my first one, then moved out of the way for Nozz to take over.

The change went smoothly, and while I reloaded my gun, Nozz fired off into the gap at a steady rate. He'd pulled his knife out for the few that managed to get up close before he could shoot them, plunging the Viber 3.1 into their heads with the kind of wild efficiency only an orc could achieve.

I preferred crushing Lepto skulls with my Tier-Three fist, but once the bullets ran out, I'd be putting my knife in my off-hand. Then things would get really interesting. A dark part of my soul actually relished the thought of the bloody grind.

Theta soon took over at the gap, stabbing and shooting with grim desperation. As she approached the end of her first ten bullets, the flow of Leptos began to slow. As Lanris moved into position, they stopped completely.

"Looks like they've blocked the way to us with their bodies," he said, peering through. We might have a little reprieve here."

We all stood around the hole, alert and ready for anything for over twenty minutes. There were no noises other than the stinking sounds of the dead as their muscles relaxed and they let go of everything.

"You think we killed them all?" Theta asked.

I shook my head. "Unlikely. They must have just had enough. There's only so many times you can stick your head through a hole and get it blown off before even stupid Leptos get a message."

"Or something else scared them off," Lanris said.

Theta sighed. "You had to go there, didn't you? You couldn't just be positive for one minute."

"Hell, I'm not complaining," he replied, hands held defensively. "Just think it's best to consider everything. You think it's close enough to dusk to get out of here yet? I'd really like to get out of here."

"I'd say a couple of hours yet," Nozz answered. "I could really use a nap, so I don't mind hiding a little longer, as long as we're left alone."

"Get a nap then, because I don't think they'll leave us alone deeper into the tunnel."

"Which is why I know you're absolutely not about to suggest it," Lanris said horrified. "I mean what possible reason could you have for suggesting something like that."

I stared back the way we came, intently, mulling over our options. "We need to find another exit."

"No," Lanris half-pleaded. "What happened to dusk?"

"What do you think?" I asked bleakly. "You really want to go back out there even at dusk? Even if they've gone, they'll most likely have left a drone or ten in the area watching for us. If they think we're dead we have time to do something about this. If they discover we're alive then they will definitely do something about that."

Theta and Nozz looked sick at the thought of our immediate future but remained silent.

Lanris wasn't finished. "You're talking about desertion?"

I smiled grimly. "I'm not, actually. I've been down that road and it didn't work out well. But, trapped in a collapsed tunnel full of Leptos, miles away from anywhere, deep in hostile territory with not even a full array of survival gear between us, I'm guessing they'll consider us dead or as good as dead. Unless we're stupid enough to dig ourselves out the way we came in. I want them to think that as long as possible."

"But we're all those things you just said. How are we gonna survive?"

"One day at a time, Lanris. Just like always. But right now, we can move forward in control of our own immediate future, rather than Commander fucking Gullan and whoever is paying him to fuck us over."

"You can get your lawyers again if we get taken back, right?"

"Listen to yourself, Lanris, we can't go back there," Theta snapped. "I don't know what we can do, but…" She turned to me. "I'm with you, sergeant. Till the end. Whatever that may be."

"Me too," Nozz added. "If anyone can lead us out of this, it's you, Sarge."

I was conscious that I'd just lost two close friends and teammates. I couldn't promise they'd survive whatever came next, but I knew going back out the way we came would be the single worst thing we could do. "It's going to be tough. Really damn tough. Things will turn to shit once or twice along the way, but we can survive this."

Lanris's expression soured further. "I've told you, I've got family serving. I can't ruin my military career."

Theta slapped her forehead then gestured to the route the APS had collapsed. "Go fucking die then. Just… when they question you, before they execute you, tell them you didn't see us. Okay, Lanris?"

He looked back the way we'd come, seriously considering it as an option. Nozz looked from him to me, his face one of dismay. I suspected he knew what would have to happen if Lanris made the wrong decision. I had plans forming in my mind. I couldn't let them be ruined by one scared half-orc.

With a petulant stamp on the ground, he turned back to me. "Fuck it, I'm with you guys. They're literally just gonna kill me out there, aren't they?"

We all nodded and I spoke. "They can't take you back. You know what they did, and if it gets out, they're screwed. What we need to do is survive for as long as we can and get word to Artem. If we can find someone in the military who's interested in screwing Commander Gullan over, then we're good. And I guarantee there'll be someone looking for an excuse. There always is."

"What about who paid him?" Nozz asked.

"Last I heard, we're closing in on them. Sounds like it's another corporation who wants to move in on what we have. When we find out who it is, I'm not just going to hurt them. I'm going to burn them to the ground. Nothing left. Any other corporations looking to move in on our businesses will think twice once this is over. To do that, I need to be free, so everyone, head down and get some rest. I'll take my first watch."

Partition 25

I should have woken one of them to take over guard duty, but I was too angry to sleep and too eager to get moving. Instead, I dragged the Lepto blocking the hole through so that I could see beyond.

I skinned, butchered, and cooked as I stared through the dark hole. It seemed a waste to leave it when I had time and the equipment to cook it.

Around three hours later, my eagerness to move got the better of me, and I woke them all up.

"Time to get moving. We have a lot of digging to do."

"You didn't rest," Nozz protested.

"I can do that later, we need to move."

"No way." Theta said, folding her arms. "I'll trust you and follow you but not when you're delirious with tiredness. We three can start clearing away, you go sleep."

I argued a little more, but all three were so unanimous in their resolve that I gave up. It probably wasn't the worst idea.

As much as it turned out I needed the rest, I woke up stiff and grumpy when Theta shook me from my sleep.

"How long have I been out?"

"A little over three hours. It took that long to dig and clear the way through the mud, rock, and corpses. We didn't even clear it fully, we'll have to crawl in places, but we can get all the way through and there's been no sign of any more Leptos yet."

"Or snakes," Lanris added.

Beyond the cave in and the pile of corpses was a long straight tunnel which we traveled with slow caution. The only signs of Leptos was the occasional dropping, but of the beasts themselves, there was nothing. After a short distance, it branched off into three. Two of them were a similar size, the third was much smaller.

"Which one?" Nozz asked.

"Hang on a second and I'll get my map of this particular Lepto nest out," Theta offered with a disappointed expression.

"Go left, Nozz," I answered over Theta's bullshit. "It seems to stay level rather than dropping deeper. I think we can all agree that we don't want to go deeper?"

Nobody answered, but Nozz moved off again. Twenty meters or so, we came to something different. It was droppings, but not Lepto. It was much bigger, and far lighter in color.

"Snake shit," Lanris said immediately.

"You know what snake shit looks like?" Theta asked.

"I know it's bigger and different in shape and color to all the other Lepto shit we've seen."

"We should have identification mods," she replied. "At least someone in a squad should."

"Well we don't," I snapped. "But Lanris is probably right. We know there's two types of creatures sighted around here."

"Should we try the other tunnel then?" Nozz asked.

"I'd rather continue this way, but we can check it before we get too far. If the other tunnel doesn't have any droppings like this, then we'll stick to that one. Otherwise, we come back.

Lanris was looking around nervously, as if the snake was as likely to burst from the walls as it was to come along the tunnels. He was already moving back down the tunnel as he replied. "Sounds like a solid plan to me."

We didn't need to go so far to get our answer. A strange sound from behind us, reached our ears. As one, we spun around to face what was coming. Between that and just sprinting off, we made the wrong decision.

Glowing yellow orbs with black slits like axe wounds appeared in the darkness. It didn't pause to gloat. It shot forward like a bolt of plasma, a huge green and brown head that filled close to the full height of the tunnels. Sweat beaded on every inch of skin I owned at the sight of it. I felt fear even greater than my first meeting with the Banshee.

With our earlier turn around, Nozz was now at the rear. Right behind me. One second, he was there, the next minute he'd disappeared and the maw of the giant snake was practically touching my nose as it snapped down.

Empire of Oshbob

Fight or flight kicked in, and I headbutted the giant bastard. It barely flinched but it was about as surprised as a giant snake could be. And in that moment, I made some space to send a right hook into its snout.

As metal met very rigid scales, something cracked. I had no idea what, and didn't have the time to check as Theta screamed, "Get out the way, you fucking idiot!"

I dove backward while the baffled snake recovered. As soon as I was out of the way, both Lanris and Theta opened fire with their handguns.

"Use rifles if you need to."

The snake recoiled from the gunfire for a moment, but it was tough enough not to die from the attacks and made its decision quickly.

We were all going to die.

"Run!" I roared, scrabbling back up to my feet as they covered me.

The snake let out its own roar and came after us again.

All I could think as I ran was, *fuck, we lost Nozz again. And gods be damned, I'm a slow piece of shit.*

The snake agreed and lunged at me with a sudden burst of speed. Its mouth wrapped around me, and as its lower jaw hit my trailing foot, I stumbled but I wouldn't go down easily.

With the dexterity of my modded leg, I managed to keep my feet inside its mouth, I braced my back immediately and pushed up with all my strength as its jaws snapped closed. I was an orc in the mold of our ancestors, not some weak half-starved city rat orc.

The snake's jaw folded me up like an envelope. I'd never had my face so close to my knees before. My back screamed that I wasn't flexible enough. The snake continued to disagree as it clamped me in that position for the longest thirty seconds of my life.

When the jaw eased up again and I rolled back deeper into the snake's throat. It didn't take an Artisan Mod crafter to work out why I'd been let up as I caught sight of Theta being devoured.

"Oshbob," groaned a voice from behind as the snake's muscles constricted all around me. "Try and keep your arms free."

Too fucking late. I was trapped again. This time in the throat of the snake. I knew immediately why Nozz had suggested it, but he was too damn slow. I wouldn't be for Theta.

"He'll let up when he eats, Lanris, Theta! Keep your arms free and your gun at the ready!"

She replied with no more than a groan, which was understandable given the awkward situation she was in. My head light was able to illuminate a position that was even more uncomfortable than my own. She wasn't as strong as me, and while the armor offered some support, she wound up with one leg forward and one leg bent at an awkward angle pointing backward and to the side.

If that had been me, I'd have snapped.

As the snake opened its maw again. Theta rolled free, and to her credit, she started firing immediately as a ripple of muscle carried her deeper.

That's why I fell backwards, I realized as the snake's throat convulsed again and I moved deeper down its throat.

Soon Theta was clamped in the throat in front of me. I couldn't see what her situation was, but I hoped she was still shooting. Even with that hope, I couldn't rely on her alone. My arms were pinned to my sides which put them close to my knife. If I could just reach it…

When the muscles around me were locked tight, it was hard to breathe in what little air we had. When the muscles rippled to move me further into the snake body, they eased up ever so slightly. Enough for me to slowly move my hand around to the Viber. It was painstaking. Minutes must have passed and I was starting to grow dizzy from the ever-decreasing availability of oxygen.

When my hands finally wrapped around the hilt, I rejoiced. With painstakingly small movements, I managed to turn the blade towards the muscle, and activate the vibration function on it.

Despite how good the knife was, the A Rank snake's flesh was tough as hell and made it feel like I was cutting with a spoon.

But it was still cutting, and soon I'd given my hand and forearm a little extra room to move in. When the snake moved me further down again, I held the knife firm and managed to make a deep cut all the way down the route. That allowed me quite a bit of freedom. Freedom into which I raged and thrashed. I could have reached my gun now, but it was too dangerous and I was making headway with my knife.

The moment I cut through to the outside world, I let out a roar of delight. Then I was moved deeper, away from my beautiful opening and there was nothing I could do about it.

Never to be defeated, I kept up my woke rate, sawing with the Viber blade like an orc possessed. I only stopped when Theta's feet that had been consistently in front of me disappeared. She was now hanging out of the hole I'd started.

The sound of the snake hissing wildly in pain reached my ears. I started cutting again, even more wildly. Theta didn't climb all of the way out, just enough to avoid being carried deeper. From her new position, she started cutting down toward me.

The snakes inside retracted again, and I plunged my knife in and held on for dear life. I was carried deeper, but not as much as it had before. The damage we were causing was clearly having an effect. And now, Lanris was free. He took a second to recover, then set to work trying to cut me out.

"It sped up," Theta gasped, fear etched on her face.

"Wha?" Lanris grunted "Shit, it's trying to get out the tunnels so that it can get at us, isn't it?"

Her answer was to start cutting even more desperately. Once I was free past my chest, I was able to wriggle free. As soon as I unblocked the hole, Nozz's pained screams reached our ears.

"Nozz, what's wrong?"

"My feet, they're bur, argh… they're burning."

It hit me quickly that it was too tight for all three of us to work on freeing him. "Cut him out," I growled at Theta and Lanris.

Before they could answer, I wedged my knife into the scales of the snake above the hole we'd created. Once there was enough of a gap I got my fingers underneath . Then I used the knife to pry up the next scale I could reach.

Like that, I made my way slowly up the snake's back as it hurtled through the tunnel. Its head was only meters away from me when it burst out of the dark tunnel and into the starlit night beyond. It twisted its body and I was thrown from its back into the night sky.

We were in so much shit now. Though, as I rolled to a stop and regained my feet, I did wonder how the snake could eat us again with a massive hole in its side. It slithered around on the dusty surface, a black writhing shadow with luminous yellow eyes that glowed in the limited light.

"Come on, you bastard!" I roared, pulling my rifle back out. Out of our group, I had the most charge left, I now peppered the massive head with plasma.

It reared back with a hiss-roar combination. I cheered in victory, surprised my attack had such an effect but relieved all the same.

But I was wrong. Apparently, this was how it was going to kill me without eating me. Bright blue liquid ejected from the sides of its mouth. I dove out of the way, only narrowly avoiding the attack, but where it hit the ground, it smoldered, and the ground burned.

I considered running, then ditched the idea. Running would put me at its mercy. Instead, I fired up at its massive head again and waited for the next attack, keeping my weight light and ready to move from my modded leg.

When the attack came, I was ready, and for a second time, managed to avoid it, rolling and firing again. Two more times, it repeated the attack, and I managed to evade it, but my plasma rifle wasn't causing enough damage. If it continued in that manner, then it was going to come down to who had the most stamina. I doubted that would end up being me, but I hoped. I'd fight until I couldn't fight any more.

It reared back again, preparing its next acidic venom attack, but this time, the clever bastard had tricked me and dove forward instead, snapping its jaws around me once more. This time, it didn't swallow. It aimed to crush. If it had caught me higher up on the back where my armor had been blown off, I would have been finished. As it was, I survived a moment longer.

From my new position, I fired into its mouth. I was causing damage to the softer flesh of the insides, but the nanite-infused beast didn't falter.

As the armor around my waist made a loud cracking sound and the pressure increased on me, I thought my time was done, only to be suddenly engulfed in flame and pain as my bare back started to cook and I fell from the snake's mouth.

Empire of Oshbob

The sounds of firing reached my ears. Looking around, I saw Nozz and Theta, handguns out, shooting the head.

I pulled mine and joined in from my spot on the floor, aiming for its eyes as it thrashed and roared. The snake attempted to get away, and then I noticed something I'd missed earlier. It was missing a body. Only the first quarter of its body remained attached to its head. I had no idea what had happened, nor how it was still alive, but it was. For now.

I regained my feet and finished the last of my handgun bullets, then pulled my knife again. "Time to die, you bastard."

I staggered over, knife held high, and when it tried to turn from Theta and Nozz to me, I jumped and buried the knife in its huge eye. It thrashed some more, but it was so much weaker now that it couldn't dislodge me.

My weight carried me down the eye, cutting all the way until I dropped to the floor and backed away quickly.

Nozz came limping over to stand next to me. "Is it done?"

"I think it is," I muttered, watching it carefully for any last-ditch attack. But it never came. "How the hell did it end up in two pieces?"

"Lanris had a grenade left. Once they got me out, he pushed it into his throat while you distracted it and kaboom."

"That at least explained the fire," I replied, watching as the snake's head dropped for the last time.

Somehow, we'd survived again.

Partition 26

Once we were certain it was dead and there was no hope it would regenerate, we headed back inside the tunnel the snake had brought us out from. Finding a wider section around forty meters inside, we tiredly blocked the tunnel off from the rest of the system, and I raised the geodome to rest in.

It was clean and fresh. It had a light inside, and it offered the pretense of safety. The moment it was up and we were inside, we all fell asleep, without even posting a guard.

The next day, just how bad shape we were in became painfully obvious. Getting the rifles outside to charge back up in the morning sunlight, I tried to gauge where we were. It was impossible, but what I could tell was that we were nowhere near to where the APS and the others turned on us. That would have to be enough of a victory for today.

We striped off all of our armor to clean and repair what we could. That went for both armor and our own bodies.

Nozz's feet were a mess from where they'd entered the snake's actual stomach with the acid in there finding each and every gap in his boots. He cleaned them up then bandaged them with scraps from his overalls. Then we spent the rest of the day cutting meat from the snake and cooking it up.

It was surprisingly nourishing, and I felt as though I was healing faster from eating it. It made sense that eating nanite-rich food might allow increased healing. I had no idea, but on the off chance it did, I made sure to eat plenty.

"So what's the actual plan?" Theta asked, breaking me from my thoughts.

Lanris and Nozz were both looking at me like I was about to do a magic trick. Unfortunately, I had no magic tricks up my sleeve for them. I had been thinking about it a lot since we were first attacked, and I felt as close as I would ever be to laying out an idea.

"We need to find a way to get in touch with my people. They can make sure all reports of what was done to us will be reported. They can bring up all the files and get our legal team involved. Hopefully, they have people in the military we can work with by now."

"That's the plan? Get to Artem? It has to be hundreds of miles away," Lanris despaired.

"It's not safe to go straight back yet. Gullan or whoever's paying him will be keeping an eye out for us."

Lanris looked hopeful. "Which means?"

"Which means we need to find somewhere out here to lie low. Somewhere with water and wildlife."

"Out here?" Theta asked skeptically.

"Good to see you can still hear. We could go back to Outpost 361. Get ourselves executed. Which we're not going to do," I added flatly. "I have around nine months left. If I can find a way to clear our names, I can get discharged and be clean and clear from the military forever. Which means I'm not in a hurry to go back and clear our names. Because as soon as I do, I'm back in their hands."

"We could stay out here for four years," Theta suggested. "Then my time would be up as well."

"It's just under seven years left for me to get through," Nozz said, clenching his fists with frustration.

"Five for me," Lanris said.

"Yeah. I know how long you've all got. That's the problem. Once I'm out, there're gonna still be a lot of pissed people with us. Even once we're cleared, the chances of you surviving till the end of your service are shit. You all have family waiting for you?"

"Yeah," Nozz said ruefully. "Yours. You haven't forgotten that you promised me a house and a job, did you?"

I chuckled. "No I didn't." I turned to Theta. "You? I remember something about kids."

"Yeah. I've got two of 'em. My ma's watchin' after them for me."

"How old?"

"Why so interested now?"

"Because I want them safe before I start pushing back. So, how old are they?"

She looked slightly suspicious but more worried. "Eight and twelve."

"You want them safe?"

"Of course I do. How?"

"You all died in the battle. I already said Nozz died over the squad comm and only three of us remained alive."

"That's why you did that," Theta said, slapping her head. "I thought you were taking the piss at the time."

"Nope. And the rest of you died in the Lepto nest. Only I managed to scrape my way out, but your dying wish to me, Theta, was that I'd look after your kids. So I'll bring them to Portolans. They're gonna be calling you something different when you see them again. I'll make sure no one can trace you."

"Didn't they trace you? That's how you're back here, right?" Lanris asked, his doubt over my plan apparent in every word from his mouth and the deep crease in his brow.

"They did. But I was stupid. I trusted the wrong person, and they set me up and screwed me over. For you guys, we're gonna change your names. I have a hacker who can make old you disappear and new you have a full and healthy history in whatever we choose to go with. I also have a cosmetic carver to change a few obvious identifying features, and a carver who'll change all your mods as soon as you get back. No one will ever recognize you. As long as you can keep your mouths shut and don't tell a single soul apart from those you absolutely have to. In your case, Theta, that'll be your kids and your mother. No one else, though."

"I'm game if you think you genuinely think you can get me out of the military. And keep me out."

"Me too," Nozz replied. "You think your cosmetic carver can give me a broader nose? Mine's a skinny human one, and it looks stupid with the rest of me."

I raised an eyebrow at him. "Do what you want, Nozz. That isn't really the conversation we're having right now."

He gave me an embarrassed grin and said no more.

"I need to go back," Lanris said glumly. "My mother got me in here, but I wanted to do it all myself. With everything happening, I clearly can't do it alone. But she'll be able to protect me."

"That's right. You said she was a City Guard Commander?" I asked.

"She is. But nobody knows I'm her son. If they did, they probably wouldn't have tried this shit."

"We could have really done with her help when they lumped them elves with us," Theta snapped.

Lanris looked away to the horizon. We all thought he was collecting his thoughts for a response, and gave him time. After about a minute, we realized he really was just staring off into the distance.

"You realize that makes it a little difficult for us, Lanris?"

"No, it won't," he said, turning back to me. "I'll keep schtum about all of this, I swear."

I nodded. I didn't like it at all, but I'd trust him. And I supposed it would help my story when I returned with another survivor.

"You better die with the secret, Lanris. I like you, but you cross me on this…" I let the unsaid threat hang in the air.

"You know I never would, sergeant. I expect to be coming cap in hand when I get out as well."

I looked at the other two. "You both up for this?"

They both nodded with as much enthusiasm as was possible given the circumstances.

"Alright then, tomorrow we'll make tracks."

"Where too?" Lanris asked. "I thought we were hiding out for a while."

"We are. I want to find somewhere decent to settle for a week or two. Closer to the city, but mainly closer to the road."

"Road?" Theta queried.

"There are ancient roads that link Artem to other cities."

"I've seen the roads," she said with a little irritation. "You wanna travel one back to Artem? From what I've heard, they're exposed."

"They're straight and flat, but I mainly just want to watch it for trade caravans."

They all looked confused by that. I'd only read of them by chance in one of Soba's files. He hadn't actually managed to trade with them as they were exclusive black-market traders in the upper echelons of power within the city. But if his records were to be believed, they were heavily armored ground vehicles that traded between cities. I explained as much to my friends.

"Never heard of such a thing. I thought the wilds out here were unpassable."

"Now you know differently."

Partition 27

Using the first rays of light to guide the way, we set off south. The sun was also our only guide for direction. While not accurate, it would serve well for the first couple of hundred miles or until we reached the road.

We all carried as much grilled snake meat as we could, which allowed us to avoid any beasts at all. I didn't care if they were F Rank right now, I just wanted to cover ground and break down the distance to Artem.

The closer we got to the city, the fewer big monsters we'd face as they'd already been culled. But that didn't mean that A Rankers didn't still wander into the city zones either. With that being said, we were still a long way from where that would make any difference to our safety.

We stopped traveling around noon when the sun became unbearably hot. Finding shade in a little patch of dry woodland that nestled in the shade of tall outcropping. Once settled in to rest for the hottest hours of the day, we had the Water Generator working overdrive.

A few hours into our break, Nozz, whose turn it was to keep watch on the border of the trees, came back to our little clearing.

"Military recon drone just whizzed by a few miles to the east. Nothing to worry about, but just a heads up that I saw one."

"I wonder if it's looking for us or for more A-Rankers to harvest," Lanris said.

"Both," was my obvious answer. "We need to be really careful about the drones spotting us. Right now, I'm more worried about them than the monsters out here. I'd be tempted to travel at night if the place wasn't so damn inhospitable."

We waited there for another couple of hours before risking moving again, and this time, we walked long into the night.

With the geodome, it was easy to stop when we were ready, but I still looked for decent defensive positions, preferably where we could get a couple of approaches blocked.

The second morning while traveling, we encountered an Arachnid nest. It was around midday when we planned to stop, but once the black mass of hungry giant spiders saw us, they soon put a stop to that.

"Let's get to that ridge in the east," I barked. "Keep gunfire to a minimum. We don't want to draw any more attention to ourselves if we can avoid it."

Together, we bolted across the hard-packed land. A quick glance back told me we were being closed down steadily, but not by all of them. Only half of their number had bothered to follow.

"Say the word," Nozz said desperately. His rifle held ready to use.

"As soon as we shoot, the rest of them are coming after us. We really don't need that." As I spoke, an idea popped into my head. "You think they'd attack the Geodome?"

"Probably. They're monsters," Nozz replied.

"Can it withstand their attack?" Theta asked.

"It's not ideal," I said with a wince. "And I really don't want it damaged if I'm wrong. But, it does have strong resistance to physical damage."

"Then I'd say, as long as they don't see us going inside, they probably won't attack."

"Yeah, that's kinda what I'm thinking too. Let's look for somewhere to give us a few seconds out of sight. Everyone be ready to dive in when I throw it up."

Along the bottom of the ridge was a tree line. I'd hoped for a spur or an outcropping around the base to get behind, but I could see nothing.

We entered the trees without thought; for some reason they offered the pretense of safety. It turned out to be a huge mistake, and one I'd not soon forget. All the trees offered was a terrain that was much tougher for us to navigate while being easier for the spiders. It also meant that they could get above our heads too.

After a little more stumbling run and the sound of branches creaking above and behind us, I had a change of heart.

Empire of Oshbob

"Back out of the trees!" I roared, changing course. At least out of the trees, the terrain suited us. I had no doubt we could kill the Arachnids, I'd just really wanted to avoid the battle and the attention it could potentially draw.

We burst from the tree line and made it about twenty meters before I brought us to a halt. "This is it! Hit them as they come out into the open. Let's have some accuracy. Short bursts, unless we have no choice."

No sooner as I'd finished speaking as Lanris opened our account. One of the meter-tall Arachnids leapt out from the tree tops and would have covered half the distance to us if not for Theta and I shooting it at the same time. It spun out of control with a spray of black ichor and fell to the floor lifeless. More leapt out like this, as many more ran out along the ground like a carpet of hate and venom.

We kept firing and killing with abandon, and while their numbers were pushing us back, we were making good headway in reducing them.

"Drone," Theta snapped. "Off to the north east."

I kept firing but looked and saw the small speck, notable for a steady flash and unnatural flight pattern.

"Shit. Everyone, move southward quickly, we get in line with the trees and we go back in on my command."

They followed my instructions, and we swung around, managing to give ourselves a clear line back to tree cover.

"Theta! There's enough of my rifle mag clip to attach yours to. Lock on my back, and when we run to the trees, you're covering fire, got it?"

"That's insane, Oshbob."

"I know. But you're the lightest, so you get to try it out. Now do it quick!"

She moved around my back as I continued to fire.

"You'll have to crouch you big bastard."

I did as she asked, and felt the moment our clips locked together. I rose back up taking her weight.

"Back to the trees now! Don't fire, just run."

And run again, we did. The hardest thing about running with the firing Theta on my back wasn't the weight. That didn't even slow me down. No, the hardest thing was trying not to bounce all over while she tried to cover our retreat.

She didn't complain. In fact, her only words over her gunfire was to let me know about the drone. "It's definitely picked up the disturbance. It's flying toward us now."

"Nozz, Lanris, if you can run faster, do it. Get back, outta sight of that damn drone.

The two of them picked up speed and pulled away from me.

"Was that wise?"

"Two of us are going back," I replied, through gritted teeth as I pushed onward.

"Fair. The drone probably wouldn't even know what it's looking at with us like this."

I didn't answer, I instead broke through the trees, ran past Nozz and Lanris who were firing past me into the spiders. I kept going toward the back of the strip of the trees. Finally, I threw the Geodome, and to hell with the consequences. It popped up in seconds, and I all but dove in through the door. Nozz and Lanris came in after me, firing till the last before slamming the door shut.

The Arachnids poured over the dome. We could hear their foot falls all over the roof. I lay flat on the floor still, breathing heavily, until Theta unlocked from my back and rolled off laughing.

"Hell, even if we do die here, that has to go down as one of the best escapes I've ever even heard of. Using the mag clips like that. Genius, Oshbob."

"Desperation," I replied. "You did good keeping them off us, though, so well done."

Lanris was looking at the ceiling full of fear. "You sure they can't get through this thing?"

"Not at all," I mumbled, pushing myself to a sitting position. "I just didn't know what else to do.

We sat for an hour like that, eating some of our rations and drinking water until the sounds of the Arachnids slowly died away.

"What now, then?" Nozz asked.

"I want to be as far away from here as I can be today in case the military comes to inspect what the drone may or may not have seen. I don't know if we've been made or not, but I don't want to be here if they come. Let's stick to the trees and continue following this ridge south till nightfall. Keep our eyes open for somewhere that can't be seen from above."

They all nodded. What else could they do?

Kevin Sinclair

Partition 28

We moved fast for the next few days, hugging the base of the ridge and trees that found haven in their shade for a good portion of that time. This led us further west than I'd have liked, but right now, I was content just to be moving.

When the ground leveled out and the trees disappeared, it was both a blessing and a curse. We could push southward again, but we were out in the open with very little cover for miles around.

Thankfully, we'd seen no more military reconnaissance drones since the fight with the Arachnids, and the few sightings of D rankers roaming the wilds were no problem.

Now that I knew that they wouldn't bother with the Geodome, on the few occasions we were chased, I simply put the emergency shelter up and we took a break while we waited for them to lose interest. I didn't think the tactic would work on the higher ranked monsters, but so far, it was ideal.

Travelling this way, it took around ten days before we found the road I was hoping to come across. I felt a surge of hope at the sight of it. Not only did it represent a clear path to Artem, but it also meant I was happy to camp up somewhere more permanent while we waited for one of these mysterious caravans.

A set camp meant that we could work on our food situation, which was dire now that all the snake meat was gone. It had been gone for a couple of days, but I refused to slow down to hunt until we found the road, or we had no other choice.

The road itself was covered in the soil of the surrounding land. But raised up, wide and flat. The four of us walked down it for the rest of the day, just to make sure it was the road we needed and made much better time by using it. But we were too exposed, so when I turned off the road again, despite everyone's disappointment, they all understood why.

Off the road, we continued to follow it in a southeastward direction, looking for somewhere suitable to hide out and watch the road. That was easier said than done, for the plains stretched out ahead of us flat and unbroken as far as the eyes could see.

As the others grumbled about their empty stomachs and aching legs. I pushed on, ignoring it all. Two long days it took before we spotted the shadow of a mountain range in the distance. I hadn't spoken for most of the day, but now I stopped and pointed.

"That's where we need to get to. You can rest those empty legs and fill those empty stomachs to your heart's content once we're settled."

Despite the distance, having something visible to aim for buoyed all of our spirits.

"How long do you think before we get there?" Nozz asked.

"Two days at most," Theta answered. "Less if we pick our knees up tomorrow."

She was wrong. With great mountains came greater numbers of monsters. At the end of the next day, we encountered a Lepto nest. Small but large enough that we had to hide in the Geodome, but not before we'd killed a few of them.

When we finally came out of our hiding hole, we spent a few hours preparing and cooking the two Leptos. One we ate immediately, the other we carried with us.

I was willing to spend the time on that, as we all needed the energy.

Within an hour of setting off again, we had to stop for roving Arachnids. That happened twice that day. The following days were the same, and it took a grand total of five days to reach the true start of the mountains.

Once there, the numbers of critters died off, which was a relief. I assumed it was because of the rugged terrain, which saw us climbing up steep slopes on all fours as much as we were walking. But as dusk began to settle on our first day in the mountains, a terrifying roar told me different.

We all froze in position, looking around and feeling hunted.

"What the hell was that?" Nozz mumbled.

"Big," came Lanris's terrified response. "Just stay still, it might not be anything to do with us. If it roars again, let's work out a direction and head away from it."

As I finished speaking, a B Rank Kyzior, a huge bear-type monster that stood at least three meters tall while on all fours, ambled into the clearing below us. It looked up, opened its mouth, and removed any doubt as to what made the noise.

"Ah shit," Nozz groaned as it set off running toward us, pounding up the slope with only one thing on its mind. "Can we set up the Geodome here?"

I shook my head. "No Geodome. Get your rifles up."

"You wanna fight it?" Theta asked, surprised.

"It's a B Rank at least. It's not going to be fooled by the shelter, and it definitely won't be stopped by it. We'd just be gift wrapping ourselves for it. Anyway, I'm getting hungry. If we can kill it, we'll be good for food for a long while."

Nozz snorted. "Yeah, I could do with a bite to eat as well. You think we can take it?"

"I don't think we've got any choice," I replied, lowering the power on my rifle to increase the accuracy like I'd seen Elantra do. At this range, it was the right decision, and my very first shot struck the Kyzior square in the forehead as it started up the slope.

It made no difference other than to piss it off further. But we weren't done yet. I fired again, and this time, I aimed for its leading leg as it ran. I missed with my first shot, but my second hit the paw, and the bear stumbled, sliding back down the bank. The others all opened fire now, moving back down the bank to finish it off until I barked at them to move back again.

"You guys not see how it took those first shots? Keep your range. Let's bring it down at a distance."

As if the bear heard my words and disagreed, it regained its feet and began coming at us again once more. Only this time, rather than using a direct line toward us, it began using the natural cover.

As it reappeared, we shot at it, when it disappeared, I pushed everyone back. We kept that up for a while until it suddenly didn't reappear.

"Where the hell has it gone?" Lanris growled as we all looked around nervously.

"We should get higher quickly," Theta offered, pointing behind us. "If we can get up that scree slope, there's not many ways to reach us apart from the direct route, and that will be easily defensible. Hell, we can shoot the rubble at its feet as it tries to follow. If it hasn't already lost interest."

"Agreed," I replied, and as one, we all dashed up the incline we were on, toward the much steeper scree slope beyond.

The moment we hit the scree, I knew we'd fucked up. Never mind the Kyzior getting up, we barely could ourselves. The loose gravel underfoot slid away as we tried to climb.

I'd come to the bank last, and began my ascent. Watching the difficulties of the others, I kicked my modded foot deep into the scree on each footfall. I attempted to do the same with my other foot, but it wasn't nearly as effective, yet out of the four of us, I was having the most success.

As I broke level with Theta and Lanris who were next closest to me, I buried my foot once more and helped them both up a couple of meters before I set off again.

While I'd do anything for my squad mates, I had a pang of regret that I'd stopped and put myself last again when another huge roar went up behind me. I turned to see the Kyzior right there at the bottom of the slope. The others looked around and Nozz, who was in the lead lost his footing and began to slide back down. As bad as that was, he knocked into Theta as he went, causing her to slap into the slope and begin her own descent.

"Nozz!" I screamed and threw my rifle at him, before swooping down and snatching Theta's legs and Lanris's arm as they went past me.

Sadly, both hands were full as I watched my rifle sliding down toward where the Kyzior was beginning its own attempt on the slope. It was at best ten meters below us, and I really wasn't fancying my chances against it anymore.

"Sorry," Lanris shouted down, after fumbling the rifle catch. I didn't really blame him and at least he had the sense to start firing at the Kyzior.

Nozz soon joined him, once he'd fully regained his feet and free of my grip, which left me free to help get Theta upright.

Once she was standing without my help, I turned back toward the Kyzior and pulled my knife. I had no idea what I would do with the damn thing as I didn't intend to get anywhere near it. But as the bear couldn't get a foothold on the scree, not while under such heavy fire, they all focused mainly on shooting at its feet and the ground in front of it. I just had to stand there prepared for anything.

After a long few minutes, it seemed that the Kyzior was stumped. It couldn't get near us, and if it stayed, it would die. It seemed to realize the same thing not long after I did, and with a roar of irritation, it stalked off.

"Damn," I hissed. "That's really not what we needed."

"We didn't need it to leave us alone?" Lanris asked, confused.

"We're looking for a home around here. If it goes, it can heal and come after us another day. I'm guessing this is its territory, and this was our chance to bring it down."

"I doubt it'll be back soon," Theta offered. "Maybe we can find somewhere to hole up and prepare some defensive fortifications?"

I huffed. "Sure. We don't have much choice now. I'm going to get my gun, and then we'll try and get up this damn bank. If it's not dead, I'd like this between us," I said, patting the slope that had probably saved our lives. Then I slid down to the base to retrieve the rifle.

The moment my feet hit the ground, the bear came pounding out from a small spur to my right. *Clever sneaky bastard!* I thought as I looked longingly at my gun. It had slid too far away, and if I went for it, I'd have a bear on my back before I had a gun in my hands, so I pulled out my knife, activated the vibration on it, and readied myself for impact.

"Run!" Theta screamed uselessly as the three of them opened fire.

But it was no use. The Kyzior braved the onslaught with eyes only for me. As the meters diminished in seconds, the Kyzior, easily twice my size, rose up to its full four and half, maybe five meters of height and pounced.

Physically, it was about as far out of my league as a goblin was with me. So I got to thinking what would a goblin do fighting me, apart from die. There was only one answer. I'd have to use my movement.

As it swiped at my head with its huge paw, I ducked. The main difference between me and goblins was that I had size and they had speed. This damn thing beat me on both. My duck failed, and it clipped me on the side of the helmet, rattling my brains and scoring a deep gash across the visor.

Empire of Oshbob

Somehow, I managed to keep my feet for a few heartbeats longer. Until its shoulder hit my chest and I went down like I'd been hit by a mag-train. I flew back a few feet, but before I could even send a signal to my body to get back up, the thing was on top of me clawing at my chest.

Its slavering maw opened wide, and it lunged to take a bite at my head. If not for a desperate thrust forward with my right arm, which tickled the bastard's tonsils with how far into its mouth it went, then I would have been finished.

Instead of chewing on orc head, however, it choked on my fist and recoiled. That freed my left arm to slash at its throat. The fur and skin on the thing was so thick I barely drew blood, but it took another step back and I used the momentum of my slash to roll away.

It followed my futile attempts at escape with its angry eyes the color of Undercity water. I tried to reassess my options as it readied to attack again. The plasma shots were hurting it, but it could be another fifteen minutes of constant barrage before they wore it down.

My time was up. It charged on all fours and smashed into me, bowling me from my feet. As it fell on me for a second time, I managed to stab into its stomach, and because the hilt of the Viber blade was braced against my armor, the blade penetrated far deeper thanks to the bear's own weight.

It roared in pain, rose up and slammed down with both its paws on my chest. My armor buckled with the force and snapped ribs underneath.

A howl of rage pierced the air that definitely didn't come from the Kyzior, as its face was only a few centimeters from mine, but the massive beast reared back again.

I could hardly breathe, my chest felt like it was about to implode from the pressure of the dented chest armor. Yet still, if I died here, it wouldn't be because I lay there bitching about a little suffocation. No, I'd keep moving until I really couldn't go on.

As I made a couple of meters distance, I was surprised that the Kyzior didn't hit me straight away. I turned to face it while I loosed the buckles of my armor off a little. The relief was instant as I drew in a painful but oxygen-filled breath.

From my new position, I saw that Nozz was now clinging desperately onto the Kyzior's back. His Viber blade was buried to the hilt between its shoulder blades. The beast was thrashing to get him off, but it had slowed a lot since first meeting it.

Against all of my better judgment, I charged in. With my knife in my left, I launched a full force right hand into its ribs which brought a loud crack but unfortunately not the snap I was hoping for.

I followed up with a knife thrust under its ribs before where I hoped to reach a tenderized organ. Instead, I was smacked in the head by a back swinging paw. Staggering back, I managed to rip my knife free to the wonderful sight of a gout of blood gushing from the wound.

My sight went hazy for a moment, but I managed to keep my feet, only to see the Kyzior bolting away. With Nozz still on its back.

I might have still followed even if Nozz wasn't hanging on for dear life, as I knew it was badly hurt and the rest of my squad were still relatively unharmed from the fight. After all, we still really needed to eat, and this thing was too clever and too dangerous to be left alive to hunt us later.

"Keep hold!" I half-screamed, half-gasped at Nozz.

Then to Theta and Lanris, I beckoned them after me. They both slid down the bank to join me as I lumbered off.

Theta caught up quickly. "Why tell him to keep hold? Are you insane?"

"Slow… Kizior… down," I forced out. "I… want it… dead. Get after it… Shoot legs only."

I looked back to the escaping bear and the bouncing Nozz who flapped around like a cape in the wind, and focused on running. I refrained from firing as I'd more likely hit Nozz with the way I was feeling. Both Theta and Lanris had pulled away from me now, and their shots were far more accurate.

For around five long minutes of chasing, watching the Kyzior becoming ever more ragged but not giving up despite the damage it was taking to its powerful legs, I was beginning to lose hope we'd ever bring it down.

It seemed possessed by some kind of healing power to take so much abuse. But finally as we went higher in the mountains along a narrow track just wide enough for the Kyzior to traverse, we approached a cave.

Nozz wisely dropped off the back as the bear powered onward, disappearing into what I guessed was its home. If it wasn't for the danger still present and the injuries I was carrying, I would have rejoiced. As it was, there was still some unpleasant work to do.

Lanris and Theta stopped with Nozz, and they all watched the bear cave with dread.

I reached them then barreled straight through them. "Come on… you lot," I croaked out. "Jobs not… done yet." I started firing into the cave. Full power, long bursts. The time for selective shots was over. "Come on… all together!"

They joined me quickly whether they wanted to or not. The Kyzior roared in pain and anguish inside the cave.

I felt no pity, but I did feel something akin to respect. It was a clever, powerful beast and a worthy adversary. But it had failed, and this was the price. A heavy reminder for what awaited us all. Both Predator Prey. The end was only ever one mistake away.

We entered the mouth of the cave in a line, firing constantly. And I waited for the moment, shouting over to my friends. "Be ready for anything. If I read this tough bastard right, it'll make one last charge before it's done."

A few more meters into the cave and my prophecy came true. The Kyzior surged forward again. I almost ran and I could feel the same from the others who all took a step back. But the beast was so injured and exhausted now that it faltered, then fell before ever making it to us.

As the others cheered and whooped, I turned and headed back out of the cave. Outside, I looked toward where I thought the road ran. Trees lined the way, but I thought I could glimpse a small stretch, and with a little woodland work, we could certainly craft a clear view to the road.

The others had followed me out.

"Everything okay, Sarge?" Theta asked.

"Better than okay," I replied, loosening my chest armor off so that it hung free over my shoulders. "It seems to me that we've found more than a meal and a great victory. We've found a home until we're ready to move again."

"Stay here?" Lanris asked, surprised. "In a cave in the middle of a monster-infested forest?"

"Where the hell were you expecting us to lie low in the Wilds?" Theta mocked. "A luxury corpo hotel?"

"Just not a damn cave," Lanris protested. "Cold and damp. Are we not better making our shelter somewhere safer?"

"Safer than here?" I asked. "We already killed the monster who lived here. This was its territory, so there won't be anything else to cause us too much trouble for a good while. We have high ground, and a highly defensible position, and trust me, once we start getting some fires raring inside, the place will warm up nicely enough. The rock will hold the heat.

Lanris finally shrugged, his shoulders dropping in defeat. "Those're actually pretty good points now, if I think about it."

I gestured to the tree line as well. "I'd say if we chop a few of these down closest to us, we should get a good view of the road as well. I don't think we'll do much better than this. Welcome home."

"I *could* do with a lie down, after that," Nozz agreed.

"What do you mean?" Theta protested, with the slightest of smirks. "You got a ride all the way here! We had to run. The poor sergeant there got flattened!" She turned to face me. "I forgot to say, thanks for the save on the scree slope back there."

"Yeah," Nozz added, scratching his head, and looking embarrassed. "Good hands."

Lanris suddenly looked as though he wanted to be anywhere but there.

I wasn't going to say anything, but Theta burst out in laughter. "Which is more than can be said for Lanris, grease fingers over there. Dropping the sergeant's gun while he saved us."

Despite all of our injuries, we all laughed and headed into the cave to inspect our new home.

Partition 29
Unara

"You really don't get it, do you? That's not how Oshbob works," I mentally hissed across my keystone, adjusting my grip on the cable tray as I did so. The gap between the false ceiling and the concrete above was narrow, and my hold was awkward. Once settled, I added. *"He doesn't just die."*

"I'm just telling you what the official reports say, Unara. It's hard for me to read... I know he's clever and he's tough. Probably more so than any orc has a right to be from what I know of these things. And if you think he's alive, I'm content to go with that."

"He is. And once I'm done here, I'm going to make sure it stays that way. Tell me again what the report said."

"An A Rank Snake type cut off Oshbob's Scrub Team from the rest of the group. They hid inside an active Lepto nest to survive, but the whole complex collapsed in the battle with the A Ranker. APS did everything they could to save them, but it was too late."

"And no bodies?"

"Two of six that were killed by the A Ranker. Specialist Agga and a Private Froom."

"And this is just after the issues with the two elves in the team and the payment to SEPCO?"

Asala's voice was cold as she replied. *"It was. There is no doubt in my mind that whatever travesty has befallen Oshbob and his squad, it came about from our enemies."*

"Well if this works out, we should have some answers today."

I could almost hear her headshake. *"You shouldn't be putting yourself into these situations, Unara. You're too important. We could have had drones follow."*

"This needs a personal touch. I hear voices, Asala. I need to concentrate."

She managed to slip out a, *"stay safe,"* before I cut her off.

"It worked... just," a miserable male voice said. "I managed to tap into the new camera system in their textile factory. It's just a bunch of fucking goblins being goblins though."

He fell silent as someone must have responded. I couldn't hear, but there was plenty of time to find out who it was.

"I'm sending you a link to hand over the feed, then I'm out, Jarren. I was too close to getting caught today, and they don't treat people working against them with kindness and compassion."

You were caught, you little snake, I thought as he listened to a response. *And no. No kindness and compassion for you."*

"I said I'm out! I've seen the bodies that turn up. Tortured, with everything cut off! Nobody can tie it to 360, either. They've got a gang in their pay that does all the dirty work and they're literally everywhere around there."

I smirked at that. *Damn right we are, and the only thing you're out of is luck.*

"You got it working? ... Good. Don't call me again."

It seemed as though the call had ended, which was my cue to act. I didn't want this Jarren to know I was onto him, but I also didn't want the meat sack below to wipe the data.

I dropped from my perch, smashing through one of the polystyrene tiles before landing on my feet. "Daen!" I said happily, before shooting him.

An arc of blue light shot from the chunky little silver gun I had pointed at him. As his body seized up and his eyes rolled back, I looked back at the gun with a smile. I had no idea where the name Hogtie had come from, but I liked it.

Moving over to the asshole's rigid body, I saw his eyes following me, somehow managing to convey fear despite none of his facial muscles working. My smile widened as I jumped lightly onto his stomach. A gust of breath escaped his mouth but he remained otherwise paralyzed but from those eyes. I leaned over to stare into them. "I want to know who sent you. Would you tell me once the stun effect wears off?"

I waited a moment for an answer I knew couldn't come.

"Ah, so sad. That was your last chance." I pulled out my plasma sword, and stabbed it into the crook of his elbow. "Looks like we'll have to find out the easy way."

Empire of Oshbob

With a few wiggles of the glowing sword, the arm soon separated. It seemed my new stun gun didn't paralyze blood either.

I kicked the arm away. "You should get that looked at. Seems unnatural to have such a valuable body part rolling around like that."

He remained silent of course. It was creepy and not at all what I was used to when out looking for answers.

"You're being incredibly calm," I added, stepping up to his shoulders. "A lot of people would have lost their heads by now, but not you. Lying there all cool, calm, and collected. Staring at me like there's something wrong with me!"

I dropped to my knees, and lowered my face until my eyes were only a few centimeters away.

"You have snake eyes. I don't like 'em." I pushed the thumb from my free hand into one of the accusing eyes. It popped, full of juicy eyeball goodness. I found myself frowning. "I swear, I expected that to be a mod. But it couldn't be, could it? It would have locked up with the rest of you otherwise. I'll leave the other one for later. I've still got work to do and having fun popping eyeballs is not gonna save my Oshbob or reduce whoever you're working for to a pile of ash on the ground. So be a good sport and roll over."

I jumped from his shoulders, and flipped him over so that I could access his keystone. Then I inserted the jack from a small, specialized nano-drive which cost a pretty penny, but ripped every last iota of information from its target. In this case, a keystone and attached extensions. The nano-drive didn't break passwords or failsafe, it took them all whole including what information they protected.

Once the upload finished, I pulled out the jack and removed the asshole's head with a few heavy-handed hacks from the sword. Ever since Thorn had made me an honorary member of the Oka clan, I carried it with pride, and it had come in handy on multiple occasions. I quickly put the head and arm in a plastic sack, tied it up and headed off out of his scruffy apartment satisfied with a job well done.

Once back into the Undercity, a group of goblins waited for me led by Sig. We could have used drones to transport the goods, but I didn't trust them half as much as I trusted Sig and his boys.

"Get it to Leo as fast as you can. Tell him to let me know as soon as he has a rough location."

"Quick as a flash, boss. You want me to come with you? Might be a second hand could help you out."

"I already have two hands, Sig, and it does help a lot. Thanks for the offer, though."

He cocked his head at me curiously. Then turned to the other goblins. "Go get a package to Leo."

They all ran off immediately at his command.

"At least some people listen to orders," I said to Sig. "This is recon only, and for that, I work alone."

He shook his head. "You never just reconning. You always with the killing, and this will be in enemy territory. I can keep back. Stay out of the way, but be there close by if you need me. And if you need help, I can give it or get it."

I wound my neck around on my shoulders, loosening up neck muscles as he spoke. Part of me wanted to stab him for not doing what he was told. But I actually quite liked Sig, especially with the new optics. The oversized one he had had before that always looked upward had always unsettled me. I could tell from his demeanor and that he was even risking to back up his offer of help against my refusal meant that he genuinely just wanted to help keep me safe.

"You stay back when I tell you."

"You'll not even be knowing I'm here. Or there. Wherever there is."

"I better not. And we need to be fast and quiet through the Undercity as we go further. I've not been much past this point, but I know it's like what the Undercity of Portolans used to be like before we got to work on it. So specters, goblin tribes, other gangs, homeless people with nothing left to lose, mercenary bases and who knows what else."

"Sounds fun."

"No fun. We aren't stopping to sight see either. We run, sneak, and hide. All that matters is getting to this location. There's a lot of work gone into getting this information."

"Lucky we don't have Oshbob here for this one then. Worst sneaker ever and very hard to hide."

Empire of Oshbob

"He's a good sneaker," I snapped. The soreness over Asala's news was still just under the surface. "He just sneaks different."

Sig snorted. "Diving through walls!"

"And ceilings," I added, smiling at the memories. They served to remind me that he was still definitely alive and I was suddenly glad to have Sig here to talk about him while we waited.

We were on the northern border of Portolans. The apartment block that was considered rundown in the Ashway district would have been seen as average in Portolans. I walked with Sig deeper into the Undercity here, staying alert and figuring wherever we had to go would be toward the center. If not, then it was a good scouting mission for future takeovers.

It didn't take us long to find a small group of specters that looked frozen in the darkness of the tunnel ahead. I sensed them before they sensed our mods, and pulled Sig back.

"We'll find a way around. I can't see how many there are, and…"

The beep of my keystone filled my mind. It was Leo.

"Hey Unara! We got a hit. Where are you now?"

"A couple of miles into Ashway."

"Okay. That message was sent to a weapons tech company in Riwol—it's to the east of Ashway. I'm putting a marker on your map now. I know we need to strike fast, but you might want to back track and go through Turan to reach it. I'm gonna contact Meli and have her pull up everything on the building and this Jarren figure. I'll tell her to get in touch with you first when she finds something. I'm gonna keep working on the nano-drive. See what I can find."

"Good work, Leo. I'll get straight there. Let's get to the bottom of this once and for all."

I turned to Sig once I'd finished. "It's a long run and I'm going full out. You won't be able to keep up with me and I can't risk matching your pace."

He scratched his head. "Go then. But give me the location. I'll be around."

I shrugged and sent him the information before patting him on the head. "There you go. Don't get killed."

Despite Leo's words, I didn't take the long route around to the location. It would take close to three hours. The direct route using an old subway station a few levels beneath me could have me there in half an hour. Yes, it was more dangerous deeper down, but with the stealth coating on my skin active, and my clothes already having a similar function that was permanently active, I was eager to run through unfamiliar territories and see if I could make it there without any trouble.

With a quick plan of my route, I set off running to an elevator shaft I marked out in my keystone map. It didn't open into the storm drain I was traveling through, but as I hoped it had an inspection hatch from this Undercity level.

An inspection hatch which was both locked and rusted shut. Whipping out my dagger, I hacked quickly at the rusty to create a small opening between the frame and door. Then I produced a small ball of Expla from my pouch. Forcing the moldable explosive into the gap, I inserted the detonating rod then moved back a few paces.

With one last check to make sure no one was about, I detonated it. The hatch opened as a chunk of twisted metal that I could easily slip through and into a free fall.

I only allowed myself to drop a dozen meters before kicking out and bringing myself to a sliding stop. From there, I briefly flicked a torch on to see how much further I had to go. Another ten meters at best.

Memorizing a safe spot to land, I turned the torch back off and dropped again.

Landing lightly on the abandoned Elevator car roof, I dropped into the car itself and entered the subway from there. The moment the doors opened, the stench of specters hit me—decay and the off-metallic scent of badly maintained mods.

I could see them all as they turned to face the noise of my entrance. There were hundreds I could see through my own regular vision, I suspected possibly thousands beyond my limited view. And I wasn't turning back.

I sprinted forward toward the first. When it lunged for me with an outstretched robotic arm, I jumped high, stepping on the decrepit thing's elbow and finding enough purchase to take a step onto its head.

Empire of Oshbob

From there, I leapt again, snagging hold of an old subway sign. With one swing, I launched myself into the air with nothing but hope that I'd find something else to catch a hold of.

It came in the form of an old announcement speaker. I only just caught hold of it; the metal pole that held it disintegrated and the speaker dropped. I almost let go to prepare for landing in the center of the boiling mass of specters, but the light of hope shone through in the form of cables that ran through the now broken pipe and into the speaker. It halted my fall a couple of meters above the hands of the specters and then ripped from the ceiling to drop me lower again but also carry me towards the track.

My eyes were on the swivel looking for options. A hand grabbed my leg but failed to get a grip.

I pulled my legs up, and with the momentum I had, I let go of the speaker. I was airborne once again and spinning, barely in control. I saw the charge rail that used to provide the old-style subways with power. It was a few tantalizing meters away from me, and I was never going to reach it as my wild descent took me barreling into the hungry crowd below.

As my luck ran out, I knew I had to make my own. Almost ripping my back muscles as I forced them to contort in an unnatural position with my Tier-Four spine, I managed to find my feet more quickly than should have been possible. Then I ran up the mass of bodies which I'd knocked over in my landing to give me half a chance. The specters moved in for me, clawing wildly. I took a hit on the leg as I stood on a shoulder and then I was off again. Relying on the dark tunnel air to lead me to salvation.

The subway power rail came into view. To my surprise, I hit it higher than I'd expected, but all that mattered was that I got a solid grip.

It stretched out in front of me down the subway tunnel and to freedom. Hand over hand, foot over foot, I moved quickly toward my target, hoping to rid myself of my pursuers so that I could drop to the ground and run again. If I wasn't running, my half an hour estimate was never going to come true.

An hour later, and I was still clambering. Meli and Leo had both gotten in touch with me with more details, but with the specters following me relentlessly, I didn't have time to process it all properly. There were at least a thousand of them and they just wouldn't quit. It made me realize how lucky we were that we actively hunted them across Portolans, Turan, and Newton.

Thankfully, we weren't alone down there. A tribe of around a hundred goblins had made their home in that tunnel. They had defenses set up against specters. Just not the amount I'd led toward them.

It finally allowed me to create some distance as they were sidetracked by them. To the sound of an entire goblin tribe being wiped out, I dropped to the floor and set off running again. I was around ten minutes away from the building.

The rest of the journey was fairly uneventful. My stealth carried me past goblins and other violent types looking to make a life for themselves under the city. It was only the specters that noticed me because they could smell the mods. Thankfully, there were no big groups like the last, and I navigated them easily enough.

It took another ten minutes to traverse the layers of the Undercity and come up under the weapon development building. It was owned by Ferris. But we'd already worked out that that company wasn't real. There was a CEO of the company, sure. But he didn't exist.

Workers in the company knew nothing other than their day-to-day operations. We'd checked their pay slips and everything. It all went through multiple accounts with no traceable account holder and would finally end up at a dead end.

But we'd never found this building before, despite our huge efforts in searching, so I entered the basement with real excitement.

The moment my hand popped above ground level inside the building, the alarm went off.

"Meli!" I hissed down the keystone a second later. *"You said there was no alarm down here."*

"There shouldn't be, Unara. It's not showing up... unless they have an AI in there."

"An AI?" I snapped. "You mean you don't know?"

"Of course I don't, I'm a hacker not a magician, Unara. I do know you need to get out of there. If it's an AI, we need to be properly prepared."

Empire of Oshbob

"If it's an AI, it means we've found something that needs an AI. They'll know we've found it too. I'm not going anywhere and neither are you. Get Leo in on the call and let's get this done."

"I... but..." she sighed. *"I'll get Leo."*

I didn't have time to wait for Leo to answer with the alarm blaring. Company would arrive soon, and I needed to find somewhere to hide before that happened. Across the other side of the basement were rows of empty shelves that offered my best hope of remaining undetected, so I sprinted across the metallic floor and leapt as high as I could reach. From my grip on the fourth shelf up, I was able to propel myself up another two shelves. I climbed a couple more levels until I reached the second from top. I remained there for cover from any cameras that might be watching the room from the ceiling and navigated the rest of the room at that level to find a way out of the basement. It didn't take long for the sound of heavy booted feet clomping into the room. Their arrival brought me to a standstill. I dropped flat on the shelf I'd made it to and settled my breathing.

"Who's in here?" a gruff voice shouted.

I managed to catch a brief glimpse of a guard, armored from head to toe. I moved deeper onto the shelf until I definitely couldn't be seen.

The voice shouted again, "Show yourself, now!"

Leo's voice blared to life as the man shouted. *"Unara! An AI? You need to get out of there."*

"I already did this with Meli. We're doing this now. It's gone on long enough. Now, find me a way to navigate the building and find out what we need to know."

"That's just it! The AI is blocking all our attempts to breach the building's security," Meli said with more heat than usual.

"So how do I make it so that you can get in?"

"You'd have to find the AI CPU," Leo said. *"It's gonna be the most guarded place in the building, and the AI itself will make sure you never reach it."*

I fell silent, my mind racing.

"We have an AI in 360, right?"

"It won't help us here, Unara," Meli said.

I ignored her. *"Why doesn't it attack our own people?"*

"Because it has scanned the biometrics of every single person that enters the building as part of the reception process."

"So is stealing the armor of one of these soldiers crawling around beneath me a no go?"

"Of course it is!" Leo said. "Biometrics mean—"

"Wait a minute," Meli cut in. "They're fully armored? Helmets and everything?"

"They are."

"It might work, Unara. If you can get one of them back into the Undercity and take their armor… it might just work."

"Then that's what I'll do. Bear with me. I'm gonna cut the call while I work. Call me if you have anything that'll help and do what you can while you wait."

I called Sig immediately after. He answered quickly.

"Sig, where you at?"

"Not far away. I have a few friends with me. What do you need."

"What's not far? Are you near the basement entrance? And what friends have you got?"

"Well I was gonna try and go around till I realized how long it was, so I kinda gave Wolski a call to see if he'd give me a ride."

"And he did?"

"Not at first. Told me to go shit my brains out and leave him alone."

"What have you done, Sig."

"Well, I might have said I was in a hurry to meet you and that I'd fallen behind. He asked where you were and I told him in a roundabout way. He said he'd pick me up but arrived with six cars and a bunch of orcs. Effa's here too. We're parked a block away."

I wanted to shout at him, yet an orc would fit this armor far better than I would. "Sewers now. Don't get seen."

"Just me?"

"No. All of you. Leave a guard for the cars. In fact, get more goblins here, too. Have them watch the car, but be ready to help here."

"Will do, boss!"

He was far too cheery but I had to admit he'd done good. I always tried to go it alone, but Sig had called it right this time. I remained where I was while the others got into position.

Empire of Oshbob

The armored guard continued to shout, loud and threatening. "We'll find you. There's nowhere for you to hide. A full scan of the room is being prepared. It'll go a lot easier for you if you give yourself up now."

If the scan was worth shit, they wouldn't be trying to sell me on giving up. I figured I'd take my chances and remained hidden. Conscious that I'd be warming up the metal shelf with my body heat, I slowly slid along the shelves until someone contacted me.

When Leo spoke again, he sounded daringly hopeful. *"You have help there already! If you can distract the building security, get yourself some of their armor, and get to the control room, we have a chance."*

"Where is the control room?"

"I'm guessing here from what little I can see of the building and old floor plans I've found, but I'd say fourth floor. There's a room in the center of the floor. It's technically right in the center of the building. The safest place, I'd say. Be prepared for it to be highly secured."

"I'm always prepared."

I had to wait a short while, but Sig arrived with the others before I was discovered. He contacted my keystone and an image of his face appeared in my mind. As much as his scratchy voice was a relief to hear again, the image of Wolski appearing in the chat was even more welcome.

"Unara. We're coming up. What numbers have we got against us?"

"Don't come up!" I replied urgently. "They'll shoot you to shit. Try and lure them down into the sewers."

"Will do. What will you do?"

"I'll be helping out from this side. I need some armor. Might need to get a couple of you inside some armor as well for what comes next."

"You think this is it? The fuckers who've been messing with us?"

"I think it's the furthest we've gotten and we need to act quick before they burn any link to them."

"Got it. You're not within ten meters of the entrance hatch to the basement, are you?"

"Not yet, no. What…"

A massive explosion filled the room. Noise heat and shrapnel. I wasn't within ten meters. It was closer to twenty meters, and if I hadn't been protected by shelves, I would have died or been badly injured. Someone had seriously miscalculated.

"What the hell!" I shouted through my keystone.

"Bit of a miscalculation there," came Wolski's strained voice. *"Fucking goblins."*

"The whole damn building's gonna have felt that!"

I peered over the edge of the shelves as I spoke. Smoke and injured groans filled the room. Both were good things. The smoke would help speed the situation up. Leaping down, I heard gunfire immediately and dove to one side, but it wasn't directed at me. The fighting had started in the sewer.

"They've bitten," came Wolski's voice. *"We're gonna fall back and try to lure them."*

"Good. I'll wait to join in until most of them have followed."

I activated my thermal contacts to check the numbers. Of the fifteen guards who had entered the room, three were down and not moving. Ten were standing around the large hole we'd made. I guessed the other two were already on the other side of it.

My body ached to go killing, but I could do more damage being smart. I moved to the smallest looking heat signature on the floor. Their armor would be mine.

"Garrggh!" came a desperate cry. They were still alive.

My rondel in their throat soon fixed that as I lay flat on top of them.

"Hang on in there," one of the guards snapped back. "We'll get you fixed up soon enough."

As they turned their attention away, I sighed with relief. They didn't notice my heat signature lying on top of the soldier. I rolled off, then dragged the body away from the others. It was risky, but the smoke and dust was beginning to clear in the basement, and I didn't want to get caught short.

Once I had them behind some shelves, I worked on stripping them down. A shard of steel door had pierced their thigh which made the leg armor difficult but not impossible to remove.

I donned the helmet and upper body armor first, then set to work cutting the shard out of their leg.

Empire of Oshbob

Soon I was fully dressed. A quick glance over told me only four remained in the hole, rifles held high, pointing out of the room. They must have thought whoever had set the alarm off was still out in the sewer after not being able to find me. They'd pay dearly for that mistake. I raised the dead guard's rifle and with great care, moved silently over to stand with the other soldiers.

"Sig, Wolski. If you get back to the hole and start firing, I'm the small guard on your right-hand side. Try not to kill me."

"Got it boss," they both said almost in unison.

"We need them to retreat if we can get them to. Have you guys taken any of them out yet?"

"We have. Big human. I'm having to send in a half-orc. Dondo. He's the only one that fits, and even then, he's too tall."

"Fucking Dondo. Oh well, he'll have to do it. Link him into the conversation."

A few seconds later, the soldiers alongside me turned and ran. I guessed they'd been given orders to retreat through their keystones, so I just ran with them.

"Where's Dondo?" I snapped through my own conversation.

"They just called the retreat. He's following behind them."

I was about to reply, when Dondo's voice entered the channel. *"I'm here. I'm coming, Unara."*

I followed the others up the stairs and through a heavy-duty security door. I slipped to the back of the group and waited. I felt surprisingly calm, yet ready for anything as I waited to be discovered. I thought the gig might be up as the surviving guards from the sewer ran up the stairs.

"Throw a grenade," the one in the lead shouted as they practically dove through the door.

I saw Dondo at that moment reach the bottom of the stairs. I tried to lower my voice as I shouted, "Hold."

It was risky but no one seemed to notice I wasn't one of them and the grenade thrower paused as Dondo dashed through the door. I only knew it was him because he was so tall and the armor didn't fit quite right.

I made a slight hand gesture and moved half a pace off to one side. *"I'm here."*

Thankfully, he noticed and moved to stand with me as the other guard threw the grenade into the basement while another closed the door and locked it.

"Shine a light, that was intense," one of them said. It was a male voice, slightly distorted by the helmet. "Where the hell did they come from?"

"Apart from the sewer?" a feminine voice answered.

"Word from above said they're from 360," another man said. It was the one who'd shouted to throw the grenade, and I took him for the commander. "It's bad. They shouldn't know about this place. We need to hold the door until they wipe the building.

"Why don't they send reinforcements and we can kill them?" the woman replied.

"Because if they know about the place then this won't be all they throw at us. We need to wipe and we need to do it fast. Now shoot up and stay alert."

I contacted Wolski and Sig. *"They're waiting outside the door. Don't bother coming up, but if you can find any other routes into the building, then find them."*

"Will do, boss," Sig replied. *"I called more goblins in case."*

"Good. If anyone can find their way into where they're not supposed to be, it's goblins. I'm gonna call Meli and Asala now. Speak soon."

I cut the call and brought up Meli first. *"Get Asala in on the call."*

A moment later, Asala appeared.

"Listen up. They're worried about us getting information from here. They're expecting more from us than just our Undercity attack. I'm inclined to not disappoint them. Asala, do you want to make a thing of this with 360?"

"I've been working with Meli to assess the security, layout, and history of the building. There are some interesting gaps that I'd very much like filled. I have mercenaries on standby, say the word and they'll be on their way."

"The word," I replied easily. It took a moment for Asala, but Meli laughed.

"I've given them the signal. They should be joining you soon."

"Good. Hopefully, it will move us from this door because right now we're stuck here."

Empire of Oshbob

"It will be twenty minutes at least until the first of our troops can get there," Asala added.

"As long as they're coming," I replied, feeling eager anticipation rise. *"I'll leave the channel open if you need to speak."*

"Okay. We'll not fill it with chatter so that you can work," Meli added, falling silent.

I was conscious we were missing a load of conversation between the guards through our keystones, but there was nothing I could do about that. I just had to hope that we didn't look too obvious. We continued to stand staring at the door for another five minutes before the commander spoke aloud again.

"Looks like they've gone. The SecuSystem isn't picking them up at all. No movement after the grenade."

"We checking?" the female asked.

"Nope. We're going up to help with the wipe. That door will hold long enough for us to return if we need to."

They all seemed relieved as the group leader led us off.

"I can't believe they haven't worked us out yet," Dondo said across the keystone.

"Me either. Just be ready for when they do. Close the distance quickly, fists and knives into armor gaps. We won't win a firefight if that distance opens up."

"Gotcha, boss."

We fell silent again, and I quickly let Wolski and Sig know that the door was now unguarded if they needed to make an effort on it. Then I put all my effort into moving like the other soldiers, stomping my feet down in an unnaturally noisy way as I followed along.

When we reached an elevator, I suddenly felt vulnerable. Dondo and I entered last and ended up with our backs turned to the other guards. The door closed, and I tensed up.

Silence for a moment then I was prodded in the back with the butt of a rifle.

"Mitchell, why you not on squad chat? I can't pick up your keystone."

I had to breathe and try to relax my chest and diaphragm to get my voice lower again. "Took a knock in the explosion," I said simply, not wanting to embellish for risking saying something Mitchel wouldn't.

"Why'd you not say anything?"

"I just did," I replied as the doors slid open on floor five of eight. I stepped out, hopeful Leo had gotten it wrong and that we were on the right floor as I answered.

"Asshole," he grumbled and I smiled. It seemed as though I'd just played Mitchell to perfection. We all stepped out, and I moved to the side with others who allowed the group leader to go first.

We set off at a quick march.

Dondo spoke again, *"Didn't even notice I wasn't in the channel. Just as well. I don't think I would have done as well as you."*

"*If it happens, you will,*" I replied flatly, uninterested in talking about failing before it had even happened. It was a sure path to failure with that attitude.

We finally arrived in a large open office space. Other guards were there, rifles primed and looking stressed.

"What's happening?" our group leader asked.

"Armored AV's have been spotted leaving Portolans. They're coming in force. Protect the control room until we can go. The AI is destroying everything, then we need to get it out of here no matter the cost."

"*They actually brought us to the control room,*" I told Dondo, before realizing he was the wrong person to tell. I spoke next on the channel with Asala and Meli repeating myself.

"*Can you get access?*" Meli asked immediately.

"*Not without being target practice for over forty armed guards. Once your people get here, we should be able to slink in no problem. I saw a suit heading in earlier. We'd just need to wait for our moment.*"

"*Our forces are three minutes out. Get ready for that moment.*"

"What should I do with the AI once I'm in there?"

"*It will have an automated defense system. You need to take that out first. Then the guards, and finally whoever's working with the AI. Even if they've wiped the building's system, the AI will still hold all of the information. We need the AI. Keep it safe and intact until I get there.*"

"*You're coming?*" I asked, completely surprised.

Empire of Oshbob

"Of course I am. It's not just you desperate to work this out, Unara. These bastards have had me run ragged for over a year. That on its own is embarrassing enough to want to burn them to the ground. With the attempts on our lives, well, let's just say I want to torch them twice and piss on the ashes."

"I will happily piss on the ashes with you."

Meli laughed, then spoke again. *"And Unara... I'm with you on Oshbob. I don't think for a minute they've killed him. If it was anyone else, maybe, but the things I've seen that orc survive. It would take the full military, not just a bought and paid for base commander."*

Despite her words being positive, I still tensed up again. It took me a long moment to reply. *"We'll find out after this. I intend to go and find him if we haven't heard word."*

"If I can help, I will, now get ready. We're coming in."

"Ready, you worms!" the team leader said.

It was only at that point I realized he was the leader of all the guards here. They all tightened up their rifles grips, staring terrified out of the windows in a wide circle around the control room.

"Dondo, move back but don't make it obvious."

I watched him as I spoke. He did well not to look over. Instead, he set his feet as if he was changing his position to a more comfortable one. I was watching for it and could barely tell that he'd taken half a step back as his shoulders and gun remained in almost the same spot. He then slowly straightened so that he could repeat the move.

"Nicely done."

"Your turn now," he replied, seeming to enjoy the challenge.

I went about things a little differently, stepping slightly to one side and then back to my position, only a full pace further back.

"Ah! I might try that one next."

"You should. Mix it up a little." I cast a glance back when I heard the door open and close. As the suited man let go of it, I counted how long it took to close. Three seconds. It was fast. Clearly assisted by a door closer of some kind.

"Dondo. When we move, you need to move fast. I can make the door, and hold it for you, but you need to get in quickly. Try to be calm when we enter. There's a chance we can still keep the fake up

and scout the room properly but only if we look like we're there for a reason."

"Gotcha. I can totally do that."

I groaned. I liked confidence. Oshbob carried it, Wolski and Effa carried it. In a completely different way, Asala carried it. Dondo's tone was smug and overconfident, and that worried me.

"Dondo, I'm serious. Don't fuck this up with your big head, or you'll get us both killed, and if by some miracle we don't die, I'll skin you alive and feed you to the rats."

"Understood."

I breathed a sigh of relief as he lost the cocky edge to his voice and sounded serious.

We both edged back a little more, when the 360 AV's appeared. Ten all told, but they were monsters, each capable of holding up to twenty people.

Meli's voice came through the keystone. *"And we're firing in 5... 4..."*

I turned around to watch the door. Dondo looked around too. I snapped at him on our channel. *"Eyes front, dickhead."*

"2... 1..."

The AV's opened fire. The door didn't open as I'd hoped. *"Move back to the door,"* I yelled at Dondo amidst the plasma rounds.

I fired out toward the AV's though not directly at them. But I had to make a show. Then I banged in the door to the control room.

The door peaked open. A suited guy peeked out. "What's happened?"

"They're on the floor already," I snapped back. "We need to protect you if they get in the room."

He looked uncertain.

Dondo growled at him, almost repeating my earlier words. "Don't fuck this up. They can't get what they came for. And if they do and by some miracle we both survive, I'll skin you alive and feed you to the rats."

The man nodded, and I shook my head at Dondo and spoke briefly into his keystone. *"You can't come up with your own threats?"*

Empire of Oshbob

I saw his armored shoulders rise and fall in a shrug as we both entered the room. *"It worked on me, and it worked on him. Why fix it if it's not broken?"*

The room was large and bright. A number of suited corpo types worked on individual terminals. They were almost all elves. My blood soared as I dreamed of killing them all. But Meli's words had dug into my mind. Automated defense systems.

"What are they doing in here?" someone asked.

I didn't see who because I was too busy looking around the room. There were three automated turrets, one on each side of the room and one above what appeared to be the AI unit.

"This is gonna be tough," Dondo said. *"We can take one each but that one in the middle is going to shoot us to shit."*

He was right, but I had a plan. *"I'll go to the other side of the room and find cover from the central turret. You do the same here. If we can throw everything at just one turret each, we have half a chance."*

I didn't wait for him to respond before moving. I heard the pleading tone of the man who'd let us in explaining our presence. To be fair, he was doing a better job of it than I could, so I left him to it while I scoped out a hiding place.

Unfortunately, there was nothing on this side of the room that would cover me from the central turret. Apart from one thing.

"Ready?"

"Fuck no. But I'll do it anyway." Dondo's voice was light and carried humor, but I could hear the nervousness he was trying to hide.

"Go!" I shouted through our communication, then leapt, planting a foot against the back wall and leaping up to grab the back of the turret.

It tried to spin its gun to face me and almost knocked me off. More worryingly, it very nearly carried me around so that I'd no longer be hidden from the central turret.

As I hacked into the armored power cabling that ran into the ceiling with my knife, some of the suits had pulled handguns and had started shooting at me. Other than the armor, I couldn't protect myself as the turret continued to resist my attack.

I heard Dondo roar with rage as he opened up with his rifle. He'd already managed to deactivate his turret, and from cover, he was mowing down *my* elves.

I hadn't realized I needed any extra impetus, but seeing that, I got to yanking and twisting even more violently than before, and finally I managed to damage enough of the cable to deactivate it.

The moment I leapt away from the turret toward my first victim, the central turret hit me. It hit hard. Compared to the fly bites from the corpo's handguns, it was like being punched by Oshbob.

My trajectory changed, and I smashed against the wall and slid to the floor, gasping for breath. The only thing that saved me was the corpo bodies in front of me. Bodies that were being annihilated by the AI. Clutching my damaged side, I used the distraction to sprint off into cover. The turret followed but didn't manage to hit me again as I dove behind a terminal.

"Fuck you, turret!" Dondo screamed, firing wildly.

I finally pulled my own rifle again and peaked out. The turret had turned to attack him now. There were still elves alive, so I couldn't run out. I couldn't give them the up close and personal touch, so I started picking my targets to clear the room. There were only four of the bastards left and they were all taking cover now.

At least they weren't helping the AI, I thought as I kept them in their positions.

"You all right?" Dondo asked. *"That was a hell of a hit you took. Damn thing hits like a hover car, don't it?"*

"I'm fine," I lied. *"Did you get hit too?"*

"Yep. In the godsdamned groin. An inch higher and my friends would have had to stop calling my tripod."

As he talked, I'd timed the movements of one of the remaining elves and managed to get a head shot as he popped his head out from cover.

"Even now you're an idiot," I replied. *"There's only three left."*

I heard his rifle fire. *"Two. And I feel better after the Medi-Kit. Back pouch pocket on the armor if you're wondering."*

I ground my teeth at the annoying half-orc, then pulled the Medi-kit from where he'd said. Once it flooded my system and healed my side up, I felt good to go again. *"We're gonna have to make a move on the turret. Screw the corpos with their handguns."*

"Definitely. Any ideas how?"

Empire of Oshbob

"You distract it, I'm going to jump up on its back side as it fires at you. Cut the power then kill the two elves."

"Sounds like a plan!" he roared again, and fired a burst.

I didn't waste any time and sprinted from cover, leaping up on a desk and throwing myself through the air at the turret.

It sensed my approach and swiveled to face me. If it had been a second faster, I'd have been done for, but I managed to stick the landing and moved straight for the cable again.

I heard Dondo firing, and I sighed as he spoke. *"Both elves popped up to kill you. They're both done."*

"Good work," I replied through gritted teeth, finally ripping the cable free. *"Meli, the control room's secured."*

"We're almost finished out here, but the door is high spec security and the AI will keep it locked. Can you see any other way in?"

Most people didn't think about walls being weaker than the actual doors, but I'd spent enough time around Oshbob to consider walls, ceilings, and floors as minor inconveniences.

"Have you tried the walls?"

"Yes. Blast proof."

"What about from above?"

"I'll send someone now, so clear to one side of the room and take cover. I expect to have the same problem."

"Okay then, can we override the AI."

"It doesn't work like that. We need to disconnect it and reboot it in a safe environment."

"Talk me through it then."

Meli sighed, which fired my irritation. *"I might as well explain quantum physics to a gerbil, Unara. It's not something I can just talk you through."*

"Hey, Unara." Dondo shouted, distracting me.

"What?" I snapped back, already fuming with Meli.

"The machine..." His face was a mask of worry and he was inching steadily away from the AI unit. "It's making a really weird noise."

I took notice of what he was saying. It was making a funny noise and my instincts told me to run, So I ran, diving over the nearest terminal to relative safety. I joined a dead elf there, and as I waited for whatever it was about to transpire, I noticed the elf was wearing a name badge.

And as the AI Unit exploded, filling the room with fire that barely troubled me with the armor I wore, I spoke again to Meli. *"One of these idiots had a name tag on. Run up a corporation called Aspire."*

Partition 30

Cave life. Foraging and hunting. Despite living life in a city for so long, it suited me down to my bones. Even if the hunting was of crazed mutated animals ten times bigger than they should be, I was in my element. Only the need to get word to Unara weighed heavily on me.

That the military was out to kill me? That some corpo was out to see us dead and move in on 360? Well that was just part of my life from the start. Maybe not with corporations in the past, but certainly with other gangs, and in my head, there really wasn't any difference between the two.

Despite having the skillet to cook, we used fire inside the cave more often than not. It was easier to cook our hunts whole, and it dried out the damp cave. More than that, it was comforting. Staring into the fire at night spoke to the inferno in my soul.

Days turned into weeks, and in that time, we saw not one military drone and not one caravan, despite having cleared around twenty square meters of forest so that we could see part of the road.

As predicted, there really wasn't a lot of trouble in the Kyzior territory. The B Ranker had clearly hunted everything that was worth hunting in a three-mile radius, meaning we had to travel a little for food. On the plus side, that meant there were no A or B Rankers in the area.

At least not at first. On our third week hiding out there, an A Rank moved into the area. Our discovery of it would have been mildly amusing if not for it signaling the end of the relaxing rhythm we'd found.

It was a wolf type which prowled like a hunter. Unlike the Syniat which could go almost invisible and move with genuine stealth, this thing was so big that the trees cracked and splintered in its path. Yet still it tried to move undetected.

It was around two times the size of the Kyzior we'd faced, and it was completely out of our league to fight. Even if we had a full squad fresh off the base, I would have chosen running over fighting.

One thing this monster had over the Syniat was an unnatural speed burst. We saw it from our vantage point, high in our mountain overlooking the forest. It accelerated from its steady prowl to move blindingly fast, and the maneuver was followed by the death scream of its victim.

"What do we do?" Theta asked.

"Please don't say eat it, please don't say eat it," Nozz muttered behind me.

"We have enough of a reserve of food for a few days. I say keep an eye on it and hope it moves out of the area. Until then, avoid the fucker at all costs."

"Maybe block the route up?" Theta suggested. "We have all those trees we dragged up for fire, we could sharpen the ends and set them pointing out to keep it away."

I wasn't convinced. I liked the idea, but Lanris articulated my thoughts. "The trees that the thing is walking through and smashing like they're dry twigs? And won't us making a barricade like that draw attention to us?"

"Shit," Theta hissed. "What then? Just hide and hope?"

"We can block the entrance off so it's only big enough for one of us to squeeze through. There's loose rock about the place and we can do most of the work inside the cave."

"Better idea," Theta grumbled.

"Lanris, you watch the road and the A Ranker, youse two help me. Grab whatever loose you can find and let's get to work."

"Typical!" Nozz said, laying down next to the fire, dirty and tired. "Work all through the damn night to protect yourself and it just wanders off!"

"You'd have preferred it to attack?" Theta asked, equally exhausted and unamused.

He gave a dry chuckle. "Of course not! I'm sure there'll be plenty more stuff along to kill us any day now and…

Empire of Oshbob

The sounds of distant gunfire reached all of our ears at the same time. It was followed by an impossibly loud howl. I jumped up and ran to the mouth of the cave, squeezing past our new wall.

Most of the night had passed, but it was still dark outside, which could well have been a blessing as the lights from the firefight gave us a direction. It looked to be around the area of the road, just not in the window section we'd made in the trees.

"You think military?" Theta asked as she joined me.

"I don't know. Could be, but to my knowledge, the middle of the night is not their usual time to go hunting."

"What if they're hunting us?" she asked.

I thought about it for a moment and decided our escape had definitely been missed. If they had any notion of us traipsing the wilds, they'd have been on us like a swarm of flies.

"It's something else. Possibly even a caravan that we've missed."

"We go then?"

"Lanris and I do. You and Nozz need to stay here."

"But…"

I held up my hand. "We've talked about this. If it's a caravan, they can't see you. If it's not a caravan, then we'll be heading straight back."

A scowl stretched her face, hands thrown into the air. "What if it's a caravan that can't kill an A Ranker?"

"Then we come back."

"Hunted through the forest. Just the two of you."

What could I do but shrug. "This could be it, Theta. No one said it would be safe or easy. The opposite is true until this is all resolved one way or another."

"I don't like it either," Nozz said, hands on hips as he looked out toward the light show. "We should come with you until you've checked it out. If it's a caravan and they look like they can beat the Wolf, then we come back. If not and everything goes bad, then we fight as a team to get out of there, as always."

"Fair enough," I grumbled, knowing when I was beaten, and knowing in the same position, I would say what they were saying and do the same. "Just don't be seen. And be careful coming back if it's just the two of you. The forest is still dangerous."

"All the more reason why you shouldn't head down there alone," Theta replied, pulling the rifle from her back.

The forest was damn dark, forcing us to use head torches as we moved closer to the sounds of fighting. I didn't like how much of a target they made of us, but the one bonus of having such a dangerous A Ranker in the area, howling and snarling for all to hear, was that the other smaller monsters remained hidden wherever they lurked.

It took over half an hour to reach the edge of the tree line. I worried constantly that we'd be too late, but I needn't have bothered. Whatever was going on between the wolf and the mystery gun wielders was turning out to be an epic battle.

We slowed our approach and crept up to the last line of trees. The ground beyond sloped gently and the first rays of dawn gently illuminated the carnage below.

My hopes of a caravan were rewarded with around sixty dusty chrome wagons positioned in a ring including a few that had been overturned. Inside that ring were around a hundred men all fighting the wolf.

They used the ring as a fortification, and it seemed on the whole to be working, as the wolf stalked the perimeter. One of its legs looked to be injured, and we saw no sign of its speed boost as it looked for an opening.

"What's the play?" Lanris asked.

I looked to where Theta and Nozz crouched and offered them a pained smile. "I'd say this is it. We're going down to help. You two need to get yourself back to the cave and wait. I'll have someone come out and get you as soon as I can."

"You really think they're gonna hold out down there?" Theta asked, her angry expression suggested she thought otherwise.

"Once me and Lanris roll in and help out, sure. The beast's limping and it's slowed right down. If we wait until they've beaten it, they probably won't give us a ride back."

"I don't like it. We'll hang here until we're certain it's dead and you two are accepted."

"I won't argue with you, Theta. But make sure you look after yourselves. No unnecessary risks. I don't want my people to get here and find you both dead."

Nozz slapped his hand on my shoulder. "We'll be waiting for the boss. I promise."

I couldn't help but grin at him. "You both better, or I'll dig up your corpses and give them both a right earful."

I touched the fingers of my right hand to my chest and then to Theta's and repeated the gesture to Nozz. I'd already taught him the Onia, and he returned it full of pride and sadness at our parting. Theta looked confused but repeated the gesture.

I nodded. "Until next time."

Kevin Sinclair

Partition 31

Moving away from the tree line at a crouch, we closed the distance on the battle, coming to a stop behind a rise in the land.

"Lower the fire rate on your rifle and we'll crawl up the bank. We should be able to get some decent shots from here. Aim for that damaged back leg, and if you can't hit the leg, hit…"

"I know. I know," he snapped, messing with his rifle. It was an uncharacteristic response for him.

I looked back to see his pale complexion was from more than just the wan morning light. He was terrified.

"We got this, Lanris."

"What if it comes for us, Sarge? There's nowhere to hide."

"Run, survive. Get to the caravan if we can, it'll be safer for *all* of us than heading back to the forest." I eyed him for a moment, making sure he was listening then continued. "With the amount of firepower the caravan guards are laying down over there, it really shouldn't notice us."

I didn't wait for another worry-filled response and set to crawling to the top of the rise until I could rest my arms on the ground and take a shot at its rear left leg. It would be vulnerable in its eyes and ears, but those were much smaller targets.

I opened fire immediately once I was set in position. Lanris crawled up a few minutes later, and without another word, began firing. As ineffective as we were, I hoped that people on the caravan would notice our efforts.

Two more caravans went over before it fell, but that didn't mean it was finished. Apparently, wolves could walk on three legs without too much of a problem.

Focusing on its other back leg as it continued to snap and barge into the caravans, I felt a pang of sympathy for the monster. I admired its ability to stand there and trade even after such a grievous wound. It was a beast after my own heart, but today it had met its match.

Empire of Oshbob

As it staggered on its remaining hind leg, I stood up. "Come on, Lanris. This is our time to make a little show."

"Are you fucking insane?" he snapped back, wide-eyed.

"What's that then?" I asked but stepped away before he could answer, slowly increasing the power of the rifle as I moved closer.

It took a while for the wolf to see me as it had its back to us, trying to cover its leg with its body as it barged into one of the vehicles. But when it felt the increasing firepower smacking into its leg, it turned and let out a bone trembling howl. Then it turned and came after me.

"Gah!" I heard Lanris squawk a few meters behind me before reducing the rifle power once more, taking a knee and firing at the wolf's eyes. Lanris fired wildly at its face as terror took over.

I just prayed silently that the caravan would take the opportunity to take that leg out now they had a clear shot.

"Get close," I barked at Lanris who was still a few meters away.

To his credit, he did as I asked, and soon we were shoulder to shoulder. It was a strange thing, but just before the wolf reached us, I swear I felt him relax. As if he accepted his fate. His rifle fire suddenly became more accurate and less desperate.

"On my count of three, dive to the side as far as you can."

"Sir," was all he said, and I began to count.

"One…

Two…

THREE!"

As I jumped I could feel the wolf's breath. Then I could feel its gods-be-damned paw as it trampled me. There was a surge of panic as I cursed myself for overestimating how far I could jump, before I realized the wolf had fallen.

I told myself it wasn't because it tripped over me. That you couldn't bring an A Ranker down that way. But as I jumped up and got running toward the caravan, roaring for Lanris to do the same, I had a sneaking suspicion that I had indeed just tripped a three legged A Rank wolf over.

I stored away the disbelief I felt over that and focused on running. Not just towards the caravan, but toward the caravan guards running towards us. At their head was an orc at least as big as me, carrying the most wonderful hammer I'd ever seen.

I didn't even see the dwarf by his side until they were almost up to us.

It was he who spoke though. "You two look like shite. Get to the perimeter and we can talk once this bastard's done with."

Then they were all past us, charging at the wolf trying to get up. There was no way I was going to the caravan while they still fought, so I followed slowly after them, firing at its eyes again.

I saw the hammer the orc wielded rise and fall with amazing skill and power amidst the gunfire. It was soon very obvious the beast was finished. But the caravanners remained busy with the corpse. Eventually, a group of them walked back—a rough looking mix of half-orcs, humans, and a few more dwarves thrown into the mix.

Despite the imposing orc following along at his shoulder, it was the dwarf who'd spoken to me on the way to kill the wolf that was doing most of the shouting and ordering, so I put him as the leader. He was a well-muscled block of a dwarf, standing at around a meter and a half tall and about the same wide.

As he approached, he scowled and looked up at me with distrust in his eyes. Bringing the group to a halt, only he, the orc, and half-dwarf half-human or -elf female at his other shoulder. She was a little taller than the dwarf but not as wide, and she barely had a beard either. Just a sparse goatee tied into a small plait.

"Never thought the military would stop to help the likes of us," said the dwarf. His face still angry but his voice surprisingly friendly.

"That wasn't technically the military. That was my friend and me. We're trying to get back to our base."

"How did a couple of fine soldiers such as yourselves come to be absent from your base then?" he asked suspiciously.

"Caught in a landslide fighting in a Lepto nest. We're most likely thought dead."

"And you wanna go back to that shit show?" the orc asked, surprised.

"You don't get out of the military unless your time's up or you're dead."

The dwarf nodded thoughtfully at my words. "True enough. And I won't say I didn't appreciate the help. Your luring it away and using your body as a tripwire was one of the best things I've seen all… well forever!" He suddenly burst into raucous laughter that was swiftly joined by the others. "Gave us a solid shot at that other leg. I'm Yax, by the way," he added, sticking out a hand.

"I'm Oshbob," I replied, shaking it. But I looked at the others as I gave my name, seeing if anyone recognized it. I was relieved that nobody reacted. For all it could be a good thing with my reputation, it was more likely to sour the meeting.

"Well, we don't do detours, but we're heading back to the city. You'd have to work guard as we lost a couple in that shit show, but we can take you there. You can get back to your base the roundabout route?"

It was just the news I hoped for. I wanted to dance like a goblin on fire. I nodded thoughtfully. "That'd probably be better than the route we're taking. Quicker as well."

"Then you're part of the team for the next few days. We just need to get tidied up, then we'll be back on the road."

"Just tell us what you need us to do and we'll help."

The orc behind him snapped his fingers. "You look like a good strong orc. You can help me lift the caravans. The others are too weak and need too many hands. Better they're all doing their own thing while we do this job."

The dwarf looked at him with obvious skepticism but said nothing. I met his eyes and nodded. He was a fraction smaller than me, but easily the biggest orc I'd ever seen. He was fully armored apart from his arms which remained free. But both were full replacements.

"Sure I'll help. But what's the Strength on those things? This one is weaker than my original," I said, lifting my armor-covered arm mod.

"What level of mod is it that it's weaker?"

"Tier-Three. Strength's only fourteen."

His eyes raised. "Still strong then. Your natural is higher?"

"Fifteen," I replied, realizing only afterward how much it sounded like I was bragging.

The dwarf, Yax, whistled. "You shoulda just wrestled the wolf."

I rode the shame at my own words and shrugged. "You were all firing at it. Otherwise, I would have."

Thankfully, they all laughed and the orc stuck out his hand. "I'm Karak and my arms are a Tier-Three pair. Both fifteen in

Strength. We should be good to do this together. Tier-Three and fourteen Strength is poor."

"It is, but I didn't have much choice available to me. They make up for the shortfall with fourteen in Dexterity which is something I ain't ever had before. It's a nice change."

Yax whistled again. "Fourteen in Strength and Dex. Them are some arms. Sounds like you struck lucky. Now I'll leave you two boys to it." He turned to the woman. "You coming Esker?"

She nodded and they both strode off with the rest of the group. Karak slapped me on the shoulder, then beckoned me toward the first fallen carriage. When Lanris fell in alongside us, I saw Karak give him a sideways glance. He clearly wasn't impressed but said nothing.

When we arrived at the carriage, Lanris offered to help, but Karak waved him off. "Me and Oshbob try this alone first. It is good for proper orcs to test their true strength. You watch how real orcs do business.

Lanris didn't seem offended. I just gave him a wry grin, hoping to convey, *don't listen.* Part of me actually reveled in his words. It was good to be with a full orc again. They just worked a little differently from everyone else. The natural aggression felt like a warm blanket.

Karak walked to one end of the big metal caravan, and set himself in position to lift, knees bent, hands gripping the lower of the roof rails. I copied the move and gave the caravan a little heave. It was incredibly heavy. I reckoned Karak may have overestimated us. The thing must have been loaded high with gear inside.

"Ready?" he barked.

"Ready," I answered, masking my doubt, and together we heaved.

And heaved.

And inch by inch it started to rise. No sharp powerful movements here. It was a screaming, straining, grinding movement.

Blood filled my face as I pushed up. Karak was roaring in exertion just a couple of meters to my side and that was my entire world. It was a stupid idea, but together, we managed to get that bottom roof bar up to our waists. I locked out and took a moment to breathe, though it came in ragged gasps.

It was enough for the next stage of the lift. An awkward transition from legs to relying on our biceps and backs. I worried more for my modded arm than my real one. It was not enjoying the ridiculous strain we were putting on it.

A glance over to Karak saw him trying to get his body under the carriage. It looked like he was going to do himself a serious injury, but to his credit, he managed to turn and transfer the weight from his arms to his back and legs again. He'd obviously done this before, and I was always happy to learn new things, so I copied the move.

He grinned over at me as we held the carriage in a static position again. "Ready?" he shouted far too loudly for the distance he was from me.

"As I'll ever be!" I shouted back.

"Heave!" he roared.

I pushed with all the strength I had in my legs. I pushed with my shoulders too. The caravan creaked up, and up, then finally it toppled upright. It almost toppled completely over, if not for Lanris sprinting forward, and jumping up to grab the roof bar. His weight only just prevented it from falling over the other side.

Karak seemed not to notice the save and walked over to me. He thrust his fist out. "Good work, brother."

"Good work, brother," I repeated, bumping his fist.

He brought his hands together in a mighty clap. "C'mon then. Let's do the next one! And you," he said, pointing to Lanris. "What's your name, half-orc?"

"Lanris," came the dour reply.

"You can come, too. You did a good job stopping it toppling." He then planted a friendly thumping slap on Lanris' back. "Not bad."

Kevin Sinclair
Partition 32

We settled into life on the caravan well. Though I kept speaking to a minimum for those first few days. We saw nothing like the A Ranker wolf again. Though, there were a number of smaller attacks. The caravan guards were good at dealing with them and went about their business with more efficiency and impetus than any military raid I'd ever been on.

Yax, I learned, was very precious about his cargo, and no matter how small the trouble was, he looked fit to have a heart attack.

Karak, whooped with joy and jumped down with his massive power hammer to destroy anything in his path. I hadn't seen anything like it, though according to Karak, they really weren't common unless you had a very good dwarven friend who knew some of the best weapons manufacturers in the city.

As we came to the end of a particularly rough Arachnid attack, Karak, knowing how interested in it I was, shouted over. "Oshbob!"

I turned and he threw the monstrous weapon at me. Snatching it awkwardly with one hand, I quickly stowed my rifle away on the new caravan guard armor I wore. Though, new was a push. It was a spare of Karak's.

As the rifle locked into place I got my second hand on the weapon, swung it around with a grin, and brought it down in an overhead smash. The approaching Arachnid, died with an epic explosion of guts and exoskeleton, and that was without activating the power thrusters on it.

An activation pad on the handle created propulsion in whichever way the hammer was moving and from watching Karak, it gave the blow considerably more force.

On my next attack, I swung horizontally in a wide arc and activated the power as I struck the first Arachnids. Four died in that one swing, and I was almost taken from my feet with the speed.

Empire of Oshbob

Karak let out a boisterous laugh. "Takes some getting used to! Well done for staying on your feet!"

I grinned, but the last wave of Arachnids were closing in on me, so I focused on that instead of telling him he could have warned me. I repeated the same swing, but this time deactivated the thrust halfway through the swing. It helped a lot, and a short minute later, I reluctantly handed the hammer back to Karak. He took it back with great pride and I couldn't blame him.

"Come on then," I asked in the mess caravan that night. "How do I get one of those hammers?"

I was asking Karak, but it was Yax who answered. "Join my caravan. Work hard for five years, and I'll make sure you get one."

"That's a good deal," Karak agreed eagerly.

"If you think after ten years in the military that I'm joining a caravan to fight out in the wilds, you got another thing coming! I want to buy one. Or do a deal. How much?"

"You don't pick something like that up off a shelf," Yax replied. "I know people, but I'd have to get it made custom. You're talking big creds."

"How much?" I asked again.

"Maybe a hundred thousand," he said, hedging.

"Worth it. I'll have one off you when I finish my military service."

He barked out a laugh. "And where's a retired soldier gonna find that kinda money from, eh? I know the kind of numbers they pay you in pension. Even at sergeant rank, you're miles away. Unless you already got some good merc work lined up? If you have, it won't be nearly as lucrative as working on my caravans."

I chuckled at his determination, but shook my head. "I won't be leaving the city again once I'm back inside. But I have a few side hustles going that see me alright."

Yax leaned forward, suddenly very interested. "I do love a good side hustle. What are we talking about?"

"I can't say too much, you know." I smiled. "None of it is exactly legitimate. But I have money, and as interested as I am in the hammer, I'm very interested in what you've got going on with these caravans, too."

"What do you think we've got going on with the caravans?" Yax asked. His bushy brows furrowed suspiciously.

Even Karak looked suddenly mistrustful. But I saw a business opportunity here that could pass up. I'd been working up to it as I gained their trust and now seemed like the ideal time to broach the subject.

"You're transporting weapons and mods at the very least. I don't know what my people are shifting at the minute because I'm out of touch on account of my current situation. But we deal in a wide range of the same things. There's business to be done."

"I like you, Oshbob," Yax said. "I'd even consider working with you after a few extra checks. But I don't know anything about the people you work for and we need to keep our… less legal side of the business quiet."

I sighed. "I don't work for anyone. My partner and I, we're the gang lords of Portolans. A district in the south of the city that borders on the industrial strip." I paused as the mistrustful looks deepened.

"A gang lord in a slum district?" Yax said. "You're not exactly selling yourself here, Oshbob."

"It's not really a slum district anymore. While it might look it to a casual observer. We have control over it, Turan, and Newton in all but name."

"In all but name?" Yax laughed dismissively. "So you *kind* of run three slum districts from your precarious perch within the military. I'm not hearing anything of substance here."

Karak slapped me on the shoulder. "We work with one of the big boys, Oshbob. Still, color me impressed that you can pull a hundred thousand together."

I leaned back in my chair and laughed my own laugh. "I can do a lot better than that. I don't think you're understanding the scale of what I'm talking about. I have thousands of people working under me, including highly skilled hackers and carvers. I have deals with ACE in all three districts. Plus, I have strong ties to a fast-growing corporation."

My last words seemed to pull Yax back into the conversation.

"How has an orc achieved such things, and why would he be in the military if such a thing was true?"

Empire of Oshbob

I saw no harm in giving them a recap of my life. There was no harm they could cause me from the information. I wasn't the best storyteller in the world, but they all listened with rapt attention. Even Lanris, who knew most of it, but had never heard the full story before. I left out a few details. Particularly anything about my direct involvement with Portolans 360.

"Damn," Lanris said. "That's... well if it was anyone else, I might not believe it, but you're a special kind of orc, Sergeant Oshbob."

"He is," Karak agreed. Then he looked at Yax. "I say we trust him."

"I know you would, you daft sod. Anything that's orc and you're all for it."

"You better believe it. Us orcs gotta stick together."

"Well, I'm no orc," Yax said. "And I've got to be careful who I deal with. Seeing as we're being honest with each other..." He took a long look around those in the carriage, "I have ties with Anvil Corp. Familial ties. This isn't just any operation. So while I always enjoy extra personal funds, Anvil corps sponsor this caravan. It's how I'm able to come and go as I please. Every trip, at least a quarter of my carriages are for them, the others are... available for discussion, but anything I do can't get back to them. You get me?"

"I get you," I replied thoughtfully. "The eyes of the big corporations is something I'm always looking to avoid. We already have enough trouble with one in particular."

Yax's lips drew back in a grimace. "See, that's the kind of shit we can't be having. Who's got you in their sights?"

"Don't know. We're fairly sure they're not part of the central corporations, but they have far reaching resources."

Yax clicked his fingers together and pointed at me. "That's why you're out here!"

It was a statement more than a question, but I answered all the same, "It is. And while we're on the subject, I won't be going all of the way into the city. I need to see my people before I present myself properly back to the military. I'll be jumping out of the caravan before we reach the gates."

"But you're still going back to the military?"

"I am. You can't escape the military. They're relentless for deserters. I'm gonna go back and see my time out. But I have some legal protection."

Yax rubbed his beard. "I get you. Clean break or you'll have it over your head the rest of your life. Do you have a way to sneak into the city?"

"You already know I do." I grinned. "The way I got in after my first stint in the military. It's a well-used route by my goblins, so I'll probably find friends pretty soon after leaving you.

"Alright then. Take Esker with you. And Karak for that matter. They'll come and scope you out a little and make contacts with your people. We need to know who we'll be dealing with while you're not there."

"You want them to travel all the way through the Undercity with me?"

"You better believe it. Need to know who we're dealing with and get an idea what kind of operation you're running. You've seen ours after all."

"I don't mind," I replied quickly, not sure if I minded or not. It would mean taking them to the unit where Leo was.

"Then we have a deal. We should be seeing the wall tomorrow."

I rested back in my chair, trying to hide my pleasure at how this had worked out. We were still completely in the shit, but if I did manage to navigate it, this meeting could be huge for us in the future.

My mind was more working over the benefits of possibly having a connection with a big corporation that kept itself apart from the others. A corpo that wasn't run by fucking elves.

Partition 33

It was early dawn when the four of us dropped out of the caravan. We came right up to the towering bridge structure which defended the pit crossing. Two large steel doors blocked access for the land-based vehicles that passed through.

Vicious steel spikes, similar to those that lined the pit below, jutted from the walls of the tower, making a formidable sight. Armed sentries with heavy mounted weapons lined the walls above.

Using the caravan as cover, we were able to slip down into the pit without being spotted, and in its shadow, we hurried west.

"Do these even work?" Esker said, pointing at the towering spikes.

"Not much," I replied. "It's the landmines on the other side that do the real damage."

"Thought as much. There're no remains anywhere."

"Ah, well it still kills some. There're a lot of creatures in the tunnels that lead to here. Quite a few specters and goblins lurk around these parts. They strip *everything*."

Her face wrinkled. "Dirty bastards."

"It's not much of a life for them, but it's life," I grumbled, not feeling quite the same. "Just keep your eyes open. Unless there're any Banshees roaming around, there shouldn't be much we can't handle down here."

"Banshee?" Lanris said, slowing.

"Did I not mention that in my story," I chuckled.

"There's a fucking Banshee down here?" Esker growled, slowing alongside Lanris.

"You cowards!" Karak boomed far too loudly.

"If there is, it's not the one that hunted us. We killed it good."

They seemed relieved by that, but not entirely convinced. I kept walking, and they eventually realized that, of all the options they had available to them, keeping up with me was definitely the best of them. They walked in silence a while longer, their eyes darting to the occasional tunnel that opened up into the pit.

Until Esker, attempting to hide her nervousness, spoke again. "How much further is it?"

"I was about two miles from the bridge when I was blown up, so it shouldn't be too much longer. I can't remember."

"And it took you three weeks to get back to the city from here?" Kakar asked, suddenly second guessing the plan.

"With one arm and one leg among a few other little issues. I've had goblins out searching all of the tunnels, all the way out to here. It takes them two days when they're hunting. We can do it in that or less."

When I finally saw the tunnel entrance, I looked around to see if I could see the spike that had skewered me. I couldn't. But entering the tunnel, I had a pang of painful nostalgia mixed with a hint of pride at how far I'd come since my last visit.

I found myself moving faster in honor of my old, ruined body.

Small, luminous blue streaks now marked the fastest route to the wall breach in the wall. The very same one the goblins had once dragged me through.

The gap had now been widened, and a camera had been installed that linked back to the control center in the unit. It was to watch for monsters and assholes we didn't want in our section of the Undercity, but it would also alert them that I was here.

We continued to move well, eating up the distance and only resting occasionally, nothing more than a twenty-minute nap and a quick snack before setting off again. And after around ten hours to reach it, which was definitely an improvement on my last run, we had actually found the codes for the Undercity wall gates, but an alert was sent to the military any time they were open.

"So your people will have spotted us now, right?" Esker asked as we entered the Undercity proper.

"They will. Should be three hours to reach the unit from here, so we should see someone soon if they're doing their job properly."

"I look forward to seeing this place. We're always looking for ways to make our trips more productive."

"Have you traveled with Yax for a while?"

"Twenty years," she said thoughtfully.

"That's a long time. You don't look that old."

She planted hands on her hips. "And how old do I look?"

"Maybe thirty?"

"Ha! A baby. I'm fifty-eight this summer. How old are you?"

I suddenly felt uncomfortable answering the question, then brushed it off. What did I care. True age wasn't measured in time, it was measured in hard experience. "I'm twenty-six,"

"You are a baby!" She chuckled.

"He is not a baby," Karak replied for me. "Orcs don't get to live two hundred years like Dwarven folk. We grow up fast and mean."

"Huh," she said absently. "I have no idea about how long orcs live."

Karak looked at me. I shrugged, then he shrugged. "Don't know. Oldest I know is maybe fifty?"

"That's about as old as I've heard of," I agreed.

"I know a couple of half-orcs in their late fifties," Lanris offered. "None above sixty, though."

Esker pulled a face. "How utterly miserable. Well if we do make deals, I hope you have good people to take over from you."

"I do," I assured her.

I thought of Unara, but I didn't know how long a half-goblin elf would last either. Neither of us had a good start to life. Then I realized I didn't really care. When I was done, I was done. I'd be happy enough knowing I left the biggest orcish skid mark across Artem as possible. Maybe even elevate what it was possible for orcs to achieve in our fair city.

Esker chattered a lot as we walked. It seemed to be another difference between dwarven kind and orcs. She finally stopped when the pitter patter of little feet reached us. They all raised their weapons alert, but I'd recognize the sound anywhere.

"It's all right. It's my people."

"You sure?" Karak asked uncomfortably.

"I'm sure," I replied, then watched as Bagri came burning boot rubber around the next bend.

"BOSS!" he screamed.

I was taken aback by how happy he was to see me. He came screeching to a halt a foot away, stopping just short of jumping into me for a hug. I could see in his eyes that he'd thought about it.

"We all were told you was dead, but no one believed it."

"Thanks for the faith," I replied, happy to see him.

"So, are you back? Back for good? I have ideas. I want to expand, but no one will listen to my ideas."

"I'm not back properly yet, Bagri. I still have a little under a year left to serve. But I'll listen, Bagri, I have a few ideas of my own, but we're holding off on any growth plans until I get back. For now, just keep making sure that Portolans is scrunched up tighter than an elf's asshole."

"It is! We catch any infiltrators here and in 360, and once we take out the corporation sending them, we should be ready to take more of the city."

"Just how much of the district have you got under your control?" Esker asked.

By the way Karak and Lanris leaned in, it was obvious she wasn't the only one eager for an answer. "You said you were a gang lord with ties to a corporation."

"360 is ou…Yeow!" Retti screamed as I booted him in the backside.

"Is ou what?" Esker asked, turning on me with a knowing grin.

I thought fast. "Just a protection racket I have going on," I replied.

"Goblinshit," Karak said, stroking his chin as he looked at me. "He said it was your business."

"The head of a crime corporation, and actual corporation, and a sergeant in the Artem Military, all at twenty-six years old?" Esker added. "And you intend to expand?"

I glowered at Bagri and pointed in his face. "Not another fucking word out of you for the rest of the walk back." Then I turned to the others. "A lot of effort went into keeping my name away from 360. Effort that's ruined if word gets out."

"I'll tell no one, brother," Karak said, smashing his fist against his chest.

"Nor will I," Lanris added quickly.

I looked to Esker.

She shook her head "I'll tell Yax everything, and he might have to tell his contacts at Anvil some of it. We'll talk about what you really don't want out there, but I can't not."

I admired her honesty, stuck down here with me, Lanris, and the goblins. I wondered which way Karak would go if I killed her. I eyed the big orc, his expression gave nothing away. If he did defend her, it would be a good way to acquire a good hammer. But in the short period of time I'd known him, I genuinely liked Karak. Then there was the issue of Yax. He could very well bring Anvil down on me if anything happened to the two of them.

I weighed it all up in a long, troubled moment. Then I finally forced the words from my mouth. "I trust you both enough to not cause trouble for my operation here."

"Damn that took you way longer than I was comfortable with," Karak said with a huge sigh of relief.

I noticed that Esker sagged as well. I hadn't realized how much the tension had grown in my silent contemplation. I grinned. "We're all friends here. Come on. Let's get to the unit."

The walk was a little awkward after that. But I forgot all about it as a fresh wave of nostalgia hit me at the barricaded entrance of the unit area. It was a far superior construction than what had been here before. A solid concrete wall had been built across the entrance leaving only a few feet of clear space along the top, where four goblins guarded with rifles.

"No one's getting in here, are they?" Esker said, looking at the wall in amazement.

"You're telling me," I replied in suppressed amazement. I didn't mention that I'd never seen the wall before, either.

Bagri and the other goblins led us through a narrow, gated tunnel on the far side of the wall that I only just managed to squeeze through.

Kevin Sinclair
Partition 34

The unit had been worked on too. I hadn't expected things to be the same, but the shelves were filled with boxes, floor to ceiling, front to back. Esker and Karak's eyes goggled at the amount of stock. I only had eyes for Leo. He was fully grown for a human and had clearly continued to eat well and work out. He was with a big orc, and a much leaner half-orc, neither of whom I recognized.

"We knew you wouldn't be dead!" he gushed as we reached each other. "How the hell are you here, though?"

"Not through happy events," I replied.

"Unara, Effa, and Wolski are all on their way. Should be here soon. I didn't tell anyone else but them. Not sure who you'd want to know, but those three would kill me if I didn't tell them."

"No, you did right." I patted him on the shoulder, then looked at the other two. "You both look familiar, but I can't place either of you."

"Naru, we were in prison together," the orc replied simply.

"Ah! Of course. Damn, you've grown a lot since then."

He smiled as the half-orc grinned and bowed. "We have met once or twice. My name is Dondo! Son of Don."

"Long streak of piss!" I said with a bark of laughter. "You did fill out then. I hope you're behaving yourself."

He was unable to answer as Unara came tearing into the unit, sprinting across the shelving tops with no effort at stealth. She moved like a dark blur, leaping from the top. I got my arms just in time to catch her.

She hugged tightly around my neck. "How are you here?"

"A long story. I'll tell you once we're settled."

"Ah, I've missed you," she said, tears in her big green eyes as she dropped back to the floor.

"I've missed you too, Unara."

She looked behind me mistrustfully. "Who are these people?"

"These two are Karak and Esker. They are the owners of the trade caravan we used to get back here. They're here to talk business." I then gestured to Lanris. "This is Lanris. He's part of my squad and a part of the family now."

"So you like half-orcs now?" Dondo asked.

Unara spun and glared at him. He paled under the stare but remained confident.

"Why are you even here?" I asked. I remembered him being difficult on our first meeting.

"We're buds," he said defensively, pointing at Naru and Leo. "I'm learning shit about hacking and shit, so I can be even more useful. I helped find out who was attacking us, you know."

My head spun to Unara. "You know who it is?"

She grinned a wide, malicious smile. "We do. Found out a couple of days ago."

My blood was suddenly boiling. "Who? What are your plans?"

I totally forgot about our two visitors, which wasn't like me at all, and if not for Unara's meaningful look past me, I would have continued. Dondo missed the look and spat out the name.

"Aspire! The bastards. You should have seen me and Unara take out a room full of turrets and people."

Unara spun on him again as I stepped toward the idiot. He had the sense to look worried and took a step back.

I spoke in a low growl. "When I'm talking to you, you'll know about it. Until then, you need to keep your mouth shut. Now get out of here." I looked to Naru. "You too. It was good to see you, though."

Naru nodded and stalked off. When Dondo looked confused, Naru snapped at him. "You better follow, Dondo."

Soon it was just the six of us, including a nervous-looking Leo.

I patted him on the shoulder again. "Will you give Karak and Esker a tour of the unit and answer any questions they might have about what we've got and what we might need?" I looked back to the two caravanners. "You'll be completely safe here. I'll catch up with you soon, but we have a lot of personal shit that you probably don't want to be embroiled in." I turned to Lanris. "You can chill or go with them. I won't be long."

Lanris saluted, then took a seat in the unit reception area looking relieved to be excluded.

"I'm sure you have a lot to catch up on, so I don't blame you," Esker said. "And I suspect your man here will know a lot more about the fine details, so I'm not offended to be pawned off. But now that I know who your trouble is with, it would be remiss of me not to mention that I know of Aspire. They're a powerful corporation. Upper, mid-level. Still a long way from an elite corporation, but they're aggressive expanders who deal in security and real estate. Twenty years ago, they were small fry. Now they have their own mini military, and high-grade defenses."

"What are you saying?" I asked.

"I'm saying to be careful. You're not the first corporation they've swallowed up."

"We'll be the last when we burn them to the ground," Unara replied.

"I don't know enough about your inner workings and financial clout, but I doubt you have the ability to take them out."

"If they're so expansionist, will the top corporations not take them out?" I asked.

Esker laughed and shook her head with vigor. "Not a chance. They love to see that sort of thing. They may even admit them into the center if they continue their climb. Aspire will have a number of admirers at the top already looking to make alliances with them should they take that next step."

I grunted in disappointment. "So we could have elite corporations coming for us if we take them down?"

"Oh, not at all. They might have alliances in place, but that will be with similar level corporations. None of the elite will help with their rise. If they can't do it on their own, then they don't deserve to be among them. It's a dog-eat-dog world even at the top."

"That makes a lot of sense. Where does Anvil fit in with all of that?"

"Anvil is one of three elite Dwarven Corporations. How much do you know of dwarves and how they operate?"

"Not nearly as much as I should," I replied. "That's not to say some of the people around me won't know."

Esker nodded. "We have our own district to the west of the center, Westhelm. It's actually made up of a number of incorporated districts covering around one hundred and fifty square kilometers. We're insular and our corporations keep their headquarters in the Westhelm district where they can *generally* benefit the whole of dwarven society."

"So you have good corporations?" Unara asked dubiously.

"If you're a dwarf," Esker chuckled. "They'd use and abuse anyone outside of the district just like any corporation, and dwarves work damn hard. A lazy dwarf doesn't last long."

I rubbed at my chin as I listened. A flurry of ideas for the future popped into my head from the potential alliances of companies outside the center, about how we would crush such a corporation as powerful as Aspire sounded, and also about creating an orc-only district. I wasn't sure how that would work with all the humans I employed, but it was something to consider.

"Thanks for telling us what you know, Esker. I appreciate it. If I can tie them to what happened with my squad, I might be able to cause a bit of trouble for them officially."

She slapped her hand down on my arm in a firm but friendly gesture. "Don't hold your breath, Oshbob. You want to survive the rest of your time in the military? Then relying on their official systems is like asking one A Ranker to protect you from another. Make your own deals within the military if you have any clout at all."

I thanked her again, then watched them as they walked off with Leo across the unit floor until Unara and I were finally alone.

"How long can we keep you here?" she asked. "They don't know you're alive, right?"

"Not as far as I know. I'm willing to push my stay here for as long as I need to get things ironed out. If we can take Aspire out while I'm here, that'd be great too, but they sound powerful, and I really need not to be seen. The longer I can stay here, the less time I need to serve when I get back."

She hugged me again. "I'm so happy you're here. None of this is the same without you."

I patted her head softly. "I know. We're a team. We should be doing this together. And speaking of teams, I need you to do something for me. We had two other squad members survive the attack. We left them in a cave to the northeast so that the caravan didn't see them. They have years left in the military, and I don't think they'll last long once I'm gone, so they're going to desert. I need someone to head out and pick them up. They'll need to be slipped into the city quietly and given new, watertight identities."

"We can do that. We should do the same for you, too. Don't go back," she said hopefully.

"Not possible and not worth it. I'm too visible with too many enemies. You can guarantee one of them will find out I'm still alive. So no, let's just do this properly and get me free of them once and for all."

Shouting from across the unit reached our ears, heavy booted footfalls practically running. Finally, the overjoyed faces of Wolski and Effa came into view.

"About damn time!" Effa roared, outpacing Wolski to come crashing into me with a mighty hug. He stepped away a moment later to let his older brother have a go at crushing my ribs like it was a competition.

"Gods be damned, it's good to see you, Osh. We knew you'd be alive. We all did."

"It seems to be the one area where I really excel," I chuckled. "Staying alive when I really shouldn't."

They both nodded in unison and Wolski spoke. "I take it you're intending to go back?"

"I am. We don't need a repeat of last time, do we?"

"We definitely do not. Thankfully, they put you back together pretty well. You took enough stims to kill a whole district. Is the head still okay after you ripped the keystone out?"

"Thankfully yes. I gotta hand it to the military, they patched me up good."

"Good to hear," Effa offered. "What you going to say to the military when you get back? Are you just going to roll up to one of the city barracks?"

"They'll want to know how I got inside of the city. That's gonna fuck my story, so Lanris and me, we'll head back out the tunnels and approach the main gate, I reckon?"

"The half-orc?" Wolski asked, nodding over to where Lanris sat.

Unara spoke before I could. "Why is he going back when your other two teammates are deserting?"

"He has family in the military. His mother's a human city commander, and he has a few years left of service."

Empire of Oshbob

"You sure you can trust him?" she asked. "Especially once you've left. If he tells anyone about being here, or the desertion of the rest of your team, then… it has trouble etched all over it."

Her words hit me harder than I cared to admit. I'd grown to trust Lanris, and while it would never be absolute, he was a brother. But I was giving him a lot of power over me letting him reenter the military. Even if he didn't want to give me up, they had ways of finding the truth. But what were my options? Let him go back, imprison him here, or kill him?

After a lot of internal wrestling, I shook my head. "I have to trust him. We've been through hell together, and he trusts me."

I saw Effa and Wolski nodding, but Unara shook her head. "It took you too long to answer, Oshbob. You have doubts, and when you have doubts, you're normally right." Her fists clenched as she spoke. I knew what she was thinking. She didn't need to say it. But the words came out anyway. "I'll do the deed. He won't feel a thing."

"That's a huge betrayal," I replied. "I'm certain he won't intentionally give us up. My doubts lie in that they have ways to extract information."

"There are ways to wipe people's minds," Unara said. "Asala told me she was thinking of trialing the tech for people who leave the company. Only problem is that the equipment is expensive *and* incredibly difficult to get a hold of."

That caught my attention. "Is it effective? Does it wipe everything, or just selective memories?"

She shrugged. "No idea. I just know the tech exists and if you really don't want me to kill him, then it—"

"We need one. Hell, we should have something like that anyway. Any ideas on who to see?"

"No one I know. You're looking at corpo gear, and even Asala was struggling to find a supplier."

Wolski cleared his throat. "What about your new caravan friends? They're tight with a corporation, yeah?"

I snapped my fingers together. "That's a damn good idea." I looked back to Unara and then to Effa. "I'd asked Unara to arrange collecting my teammates from the wild, but she's gonna be busy working on our Aspire problem, so can I leave that to you? Ask Asala, take what you need to stay under the radar. We didn't have too many problems between here and where I left them traveling along the road."

He thumped his chest. "Leave it with me. They'll be back before you know it."

"Make sure to take the best fighters you can and that you're all well equipped with armor and weapons."

Wolski patted him on the shoulder. "I'll help you get set up."

I watched my two favorite orcs walk away, then beckoned for Unara to follow me.

Esker and Karak were in Leo's base of operations. The old control room had been expanded, knocked through into the four of the surrounding rooms and now filled with far more high-end looking gear. They all looked up as I entered.

"Esker. We have a problem."

"You still don't trust us?"

"I trust you as much as I can. All business involves risk, but I think we could be good for each other."

"The half-orc," Karak said. "He's too quiet."

I couldn't fight my look of surprise at his insight, proving once again that, despite appearances and vocal tone, orcs were not stupid. Just different. "I used to distrust him because of that, but he's a good one. That doesn't mean his mind won't be inspected when he returns. He's a weak spot for us in the future. But Unara suggested there's tech that would wipe memories…"

I left the thought hanging.

"Ah," Esker said, twiddling her plaited goatee. "And you think we might be able to get one for you?"

"Can you?" I replied hopefully.

"I don't know. Yax is the man to ask for that. It'll definitely cost you."

"I know," I grumbled. "Ask him. See what he has to say."

She closed her eyes to contact him. I wondered if her keystone was different, or if she just liked to shut out the world around her.

While we waited, I spoke to Karak. There was a lot I wanted to know about him. "How long have you been with Yax?"

The big orc had been watching Esker, but he looked across to me thoughtfully. "Ooh, ten years at least."

"And he was happy to take on an orc?"

"I killed four of his guards. I was about to kill him when he made me an offer I couldn't refuse."

"What offer?"

"He'd call off the other forty-six guards surrounding me and let me live."

I chuckled at that. "How did you end up in that position?"

"A couple of us were trying to steal food from their caravan. We'd fallen on even harder times than usual."

"You lost people?"

"I did. But it's all water under the bridge now."

"It took about three years to break you, though," Esker said, having returned from her conversation.

Karak snorted. "Nobody breaks me. I chose a better life. Nothing more."

"Sure, sure," Esker replied, then switched her gaze to me. "We might be able to help you. I've spoken of your operations, as far as I know them. I've told him that I trust you as far as I'm able. That you didn't kill us, and that you're making an effort not to kill Lanris, are both strong factors in your favor. Yax thinks he can arrange something, but as I said, it will cost you."

"What are we talking about, because as much as I don't want to kill Lanris, I don't want to be in the pockets of a corporation."

"Who isn't in the pockets of a corporation?" she replied, shortly.

"We aren't," Unara answered for me. "And I'll kill Lanris right now if we can't reach a favorable deal."

Esker held up her hands. "I'll be honest, direct cred-wise, you won't have anything to worry about. Big deals are normally handled in trade and deals. Which means you'll have stronger links with Anvil. You've talked about Aspire and your problems there. You may not want anything to do with corporations, but corporations want something to do with you. Friends are strength."

Unara looked ready to kill Esker, but I smiled gratefully. "I'm happy to hear what Yax comes back with and strong allies are not to be turned away."

Esker nodded curtly, side-eying Unara but speaking to me. "He thinks he should have something for you within the hour."

"So we have time to talk?" Karak asked Esker.

"Of course. I still have a number of finer details to hammer out. What did you have in mind, Karak?"

He looked to me. "This district you run above us. Portolans. Can't say I've heard the name, but I lived miles away from here. In the district just southwest of dwarven-hold, orcs are treated like gutter shit there."

"Same as everywhere else then," I replied.

"Except in Portolans," Unara added. "Orcs are respected here. We make sure of it."

Karak's brow wrinkled at her words. "Yeah, I was wondering about that. I still have family back home. I'm on the road most of the time, and I send them money and stuff, but, you know… it's still bad for them. They're part of a small community. Maybe around three hundred orcs, maximum."

I grinned at him. "Have they ever thought about relocating? If so, then they'll be welcomed here with open arms. They can move freely around the district. They'll get the same protection all orcs get, and there will be homes and work for them."

His eyes widened. "You can really offer all of that? It sounds like a goddamn paradise."

"Paradise, it is not." Unara replied. "We work hard here, and we're surrounded by trouble. But if they want to come, and you need help bringing them, we can arrange it."

Esker seemed troubled. "Won't you alienate the people already living here if you make it too densely populated with orcs?"

"Anyone offended by the new ways here have already moved out," Unara offered, before adding, "Or have been removed. There're more goblins and orcs in Portolans than any other district, I'll wager. We have orcs traipsing in every other day now, including a good few from Newton."

"We do?"

"Absolutely. Ever since your fight with Grant, they started coming. Hi-Shone Tower is practically entirely orcs now."

"Hmm." It was good news, but something snagged at my mind. "How many orcs are in the tower?"

"Probably a few thousand," Unara answered. "We put them all there."

"That's a hell of a target," Esker said, speaking to my own reservations. "If I wanted to strike against the orc gang lord of Portolans, that'd be the first place I'd hit."

"We had thought about it," Unara said. "Some of 360's new acquisitions are being refurbished to accommodate them. It just takes time. Like I say, we have new groups coming in all the time."

Esker suddenly held up her hand. "One moment. Yax is calling back."

We all fell to silence while she spoke. It was only a few minutes this time.

She looked thoughtful as she ended the communication. "You said you've killed people from Aspire?"

"We did, yeah," I answered.

"What happened to the mods from the bodies? Did you loot the corpses?"

I had no idea and looked at Unara.

"When time allows, we strip every corpse we make down to the bone. We run a mod and nanite business after all. Why?"

Esker answered the question with a question. "So you've sold them on?"

Unara gave a vigorous shake of her head. "We've sold a lot of them on. The only ones we kept were the unmarked ones. Most of which we found during our raid on their factory workshop. We have people working on them now, trying to find their source. We suspect Aspire has their own mod manufacturers, but they're high quality. Not one of them under a Tier-three."

Esker nodded with a grim smile. "They're not from Aspire. I told Yax about your troubles, and he looked into them. They have a high-level corpo sponsor. A sponsor which Anvil has had a long history with. Bottom line is that Anvil wants those mods, and they'll pay market value for them. If you're interested, then draw me up an inventory, and we can bring the Mindwipe. They'll also pay well for any mods you can get from their agents going forward."

"Who supplied the mods?" Unara said coldly and without any form of agreement to Anvil's deal.

"It probably won't mean much to you, so I can't see any harm in telling you, but a corporation named Living Earth."

The words hit us both like a slap in the face. It could be a coincidence, but it was a very close coincidence.

"You've heard of them?" Esker asked.

"We have, and we don't like them either." I turned to Unara. "You think they're the real force behind this?"

She looked angry. "Part of me hopes so. But why would they go to such lengths to screw us over? Surely they're powerful enough to just come after us directly."

"They are," Esker said. "I know you're doing okay down here, but why would a company like Living Earth give a damn about you?"

"That's a long story," I replied. "They wanted a mod in our possession and they came after us to get it. We hoped that would be an end to the trouble, but what you just told us… it sets alarm bells ringing."

"It does," Unara added. "Just as we thought we found the top of the pyramid, it goes higher."

Esker rubbed her chin. "Hmmm. They can't be that invested. It could be a coincidence, or they could have given you up to Aspire as a kind of test. It's not uncommon. Something like: *Prove you're worthy of a place in the center. Get rid of Portolans 360 and everyone attached.* Bear in mind, most of what I know is second hand information, but it checks out. I'd personally focus on Aspire for now, but keep your eyes open."

"Thanks for the insight. I'm curious, though. What's Anvil's business with them?"

She bobbed her head as if she expected the question. "There're limits to what I can say, but let's just say that Anvil and Living Earth are on two sides of the same coin. Dwarves and elves do not get on, and they operate in a similar area. Namely high-level tech."

I grinned at her words. "We can definitely do business."

Partition 35

That night, I slept like the dead in the unit bedroom I'd claimed for myself so long ago. Unara's own still adjoined mine via the rough hole I'd punched and kicked in the wall that first night here. Despite all of the other changes, Unara had made sure our rooms remained the same. Completely untouched, other than to be cleaned.

I rose up stiff from the bed and peered through. Her eyes opened the moment my head appeared around the corner.

"Were you awake already?"

"No. Your change in breathing woke me."

"You must have been light then. Short of a building falling on me, I wouldn't wake up for shit."

"That's why you have me. And I sleep well. I'm just sensitive. In fact, I would say that's the best I've slept in four years."

I grinned at her. "You big softie."

She smiled back. "I never got to tell you this face to face. And… I didn't want to say it in front of anyone in case they think I'm weak, but I'm sorry."

"Sorry for what?" I asked, amazed.

"For trusting Raven."

"Bah!" I said, wafting my hand at her. "She was a very clever woman. She gave us everything we needed and she played on our weaknesses."

"Exactly! I shouldn't have been so weak. You weren't."

"Goblinshit. We both learned a lot in that year. I let her have way too much power over us and don't forget it."

"You warned me constantly."

"I didn't like her," I replied simply. "I could be just as easily fooled if someone gave me exactly what I wanted and I liked them as well. Hell, Harold could have turned on us just as easily."

"But you got that right. I got it badly wrong."

I put a hand on her shoulder. "Shit happens. It was damn hard to live through, but we're both still alive. And if I manage to survive the last of my military service—which I fully intend to—then it's all been worth it. Easy times make weak people, and we're not weak, are we?"

"No," she said, her face still, expression firm, like a porcelain figurine. "We're not. And I will never be again."

I patted her shoulder and removed my hand. "You've still gotta bend, Unara. Become too hard, you'll break."

"You don't. And you're the hardest person I know."

"Oh yeah. If that was true, I'd just kill Lanris and be done. It might turn out for the best, but if the decision was between death and taking the risk of letting him go, I made the wrong choice."

She let a small smile cross her face. "Yet here we are, gaining from the decision. The link with Anvil, the enemy of our enemy… We gain so much more than we lose. And I'm still not convinced you wouldn't kill him in the end despite your words. No matter what bond you formed, he's still not your family."

A pit of shame enveloped me at her words. "No, he's not," I agreed. "But you are."

I wrapped her up in a hug and my merciless monster snuggled in more than I'd expected. I got the feeling she'd missed having someone who genuinely cared for her.

After a moment, I backed up. "Come on then. We have a lot to do today. And a lot to work through. I could eat as well. My stomach thinks my throat's been cut."

"There's plenty of food here with Leo, Dondo, and Naru hanging out around here all the time. Those three idiots don't let themselves suffer."

"Let's go have a look at what we've got then," I said, heading out of the bedroom. "Are Naru and Dondo behaving themselves? I don't like the idea that they're distracting Leo from his work."

She sighed. "Honestly, as annoying as Dondo is, he's useful and capable. He really did help me infiltrate the Aspire building, and any wrong move could have given us away. Naru spends more of his time with Effa. Leo doesn't get out much with all the work he has to do, so it's a good thing those two come and see him."

Empire of Oshbob

I hadn't thought of it like that, and it seemed that I'd judged the three of them too harshly. I hadn't said anything to them yet, but I was now glad I'd spoken to Unara about it first.

We made our way to the common room where Esker sat alone eating a small bowl of cheese porridge. It smelled great and set my stomach to rumbling.

Unara heard and punched me in the arm. "I'll go get us some food. You grab a seat."

I happily did as she suggested, a minor pang of joy at being here mixed with sadness that it would soon end.

I sat down across from Esker. "Where's Karak?"

"Still snoring, I imagine. He'll be up soon enough. Yax will be here within the hour."

That caught me by surprise. "So soon? That's fast."

"His contact in Anvil is very keen to get their hands on the mods you picked up."

"Is there something special about them?"

"Maybe. Probably not. Beyond Living Earth mods being difficult to get hold of by the general public or other corporations in direct competition."

We chatted a while longer, but she didn't have a great deal more information to give, and when the scent of seared meat hit my nostrils, I didn't much care to listen any longer.

It took every ounce of my willpower to stay where I was seated and wait. And when Unara finally walked in with two steaming plates of real white meat and a few real looking vegetables of orange and green, my mouth filled with saliva.

"Where did we get meat from?"

She put the plate down in front of me with a smile. "I think you're forgetting how much access we have to things now."

"I think you're right," was all I managed to say before I inhaled the plate of food. Once finished, I wiped my mouth and sighed. "It was worth coming back for that plate of food alone. Did you cook it, Unara?"

She snorted. "Yeah. Sure I did. With a little help from the chef."

"We have a chef down here now?"

"Auto chef. It gives you a selection of meals to eat from what we put in its storage. Then it picks, prepares, and cooks it. I did press a button twice, though."

I chuckled and lay back content until Esker suddenly sat bolt upright.

"Yax is here," she said after a moment. Clearly, Karak had gotten the same message as he appeared in the doorway moments later.

"You ready?" he asked, then paused to eye the two plates and sniff the air suspiciously.

"Where is here?" I asked, more to Unara. "I know we're linked to the surface now but I haven't seen how or where yet."

"We bought out Abdo's Autos directly above us. It's right in the center of the industrial sector."

"No trouble from Aspire there?"

She shook her head as she led us from the room. "We didn't buy it through the usual channels, so it has no links to 360, or you and me. It was actually Leo who found it and picked it up from the previous owner with untraceable creds. I'll not lie, it wasn't cheap. But it *was* worth it. We're still running it as a chop shop under the same name, and all of Abdo's old staff still work there. Well, apart from the few snakes I had to get rid of. Those left are all on the books for us now."

"What about Abdo?" I asked as we reached a very unfamiliar elevator.

She smirked. "If it's any consolation, I gave him the chance not to talk to anyone about the deal, like we'd agreed. He failed miserably."

"So it didn't cost that much in the end?"

She rubbed her chin. "In the end…? I think we actually turned a profit."

I laughed, but Esker didn't seem quite so comfortable. "Ruthless lot, aren't you?"

"It's not ruthless if he went back on his word. It's just business," Unara replied with an evil glint in her eye that told us all she'd enjoyed her little hunt a little too much.

"Wait for me," a tired-looking Wolski shouted, running across the factory floor. I put a hand on the elevator door to hold it open.

"We probably should have gotten Leo too," I said as Wolski barreled in.

"He'll already be up there," Unara replied.

Empire of Oshbob

The chop shop was exactly as I'd imagined, only much larger, running off in one direction as far as the eye could see above a host of broken-down vehicles of every variety under the sun.

Through the massive shutters at the front of the shop, a heavy-duty hover van of dark gray and black pulled in and landed on a raised platform.

Yax jumped out a moment later and greeted Esker with far more affection than I'd remembered ever seeing on our travels. After they'd removed their tongues from each other's mouths, he spun on me, a wide grin on his face.

"I never thought we'd be trading quite so soon!" He slammed a button on the side of the armored van and the rear doors slid open. "Esker did tell you this was just a loan, right? One shot use?"

"She did not," I replied, looking at the half-dwarven woman.

She was too busy punching Yax in the chest with a solid blow to notice my glare. "That's because I was never told that!"

I held my hand up to stop the movement of mod crates from our side. "What's going on, Yax?"

"Too valuable to give up something like this. It takes crazy creds to buy or make one of these. And I didn't tell Esker because I knew you'd be pissed. I also didn't tell her one more requirement and... I'm sorry to say it's non-negotiable. As in, even if we never speak again, this needs to happen or you'll have Anvil so far up your arse, I'll be able to beat metal on you."

I got a bad feeling about what the true cost was going to be for this agreement. "Spit it out then, Yax, for fuck's sake."

"If you're going back into the military, then you need to use this too and wipe everything since you met us."

"You can't be serious," I spat.

"It's not me, Oshbob. This is entirely from Entrax. I don't need this kind of shit in my life."

"Entrax?" I asked, unfamiliar with the name.

"Director at Anvil. He's basically the most powerful person in Anvil who isn't a CEO, and he's not the type of person you want to piss off. If it's any consolation, you can record all of your memories on a mem-core and re-upload them once you're back out."

I heard Unara tearing a strip off Yax, and then Esker joining in the argument, but it all sounded very far away as my mind swam over what was being asked. It hit me how selfish it was to ask Lanris to undergo the mind wipe for Theta and Nozz's safety and not do it myself. If I was to go after Commander Gullan, then SEPCO would be called in again. If that happened, a mind scan of the incident was all but guaranteed. And if I was Anvil, I would absolutely make me do it too. The information I had on the caravan and the fact that they supplied this machine, how could I not?

I refocused on Yax. "I'll do it. I understand the need."

Unara spun surprised and I put a hand on her shoulder. "Think about it from their perspective. Hell, think about it from ours. No one can know I came back here first."

"If it's any consolation," Yax interrupted with a wide grin. "I've got a deal sweetener."

I eyed him with interest. Who didn't like a deal sweetener?

Yax brought a crate from the van. It was long and narrow, and I assumed it was the deal sweetener. I couldn't fathom what it was, but as he unclipped the lid and revealed what was inside, I was about as excited as an orc could be. A Pulse Warhammer, just like Karak's.

It took some effort to pull my eyes away from the glorious weapon, and meet Yax's grinning face.

"It's not custom, but it's damn epic and as far as I'm aware, there's only been five made of this particular model," he said.

"Well it looks like you've still got yourself a goddamn deal, doesn't it?" I said, lifting the weapon reverently from the crate. It was beautiful. Around six feet long, the haft was as thick as my wrist. The head was a mix of panels, red and gold and silver and it was as heavy as Karak's. It felt perfect in my hands.

"Give us a demo then!" Wolski grunted.

I looked over to Leo. "How valuable are these cars?"

He looked confused. "Until they're fixed up, they're not valuable at all."

"Good." I swung the hammer up above my head as I leapt toward the nearest car, then thumbing the activation panel on the handle, I brought it down full force in the already damaged car. And into the concrete floor of the factory.

It crushed and punched almost the entire way through the car body. "Perfect," I beamed.

Empire of Oshbob

"There's a mag clip for it too," Yax said, pointing at the crate. "It should fit on most any armor or it can be tied to your back if you're not wearing any."

"This is worth the Aspire mods alone."

"I hoped you'd see it like that. Now shall we get this Mindwipe unpacked and get you and your pal sorted?"

"You can set it up if you want, but I still have things to do, so I'm not wiping anyone's mind just yet."

"I'm back out on the caravan at the end of the week, so it'll have to be done by then."

"Is there no one else who can come back with it?" Unara asked, much to Yax's amusement.

"You lot are my find. Any interaction with you and Anvil goes through me, and trust me when I say this: You really wouldn't want it any other way. I'll look after your best interests, and I reckon we can form a pretty good relationship here if you're willing. That or you get a visit from the private army of an elite dwarven corporation carrying weapons you've never even dreamed of."

I really didn't enjoy being cornered this way. All of my orc instincts rebelled against it. But those instincts would have seen me die in a blaze of glory a long time ago if they lived alone in my head. The rational side, the side that had carried me this far, told me to shut up and accept it. That this was an amazing deal which I was lucky to have found. My eyes flickered down to the hammer, and then to Yax's fancy ship. The price was steep but the rewards could be immense.

"So I have a week?"

Both Yax and Esker breathed a sigh of relief. The meaty hand of Karak landed on my shoulder. His eyes filled with… gratitude perhaps. I wasn't quite sure.

"A week. If you want me to come back sooner with it, just let me know and we'll get you set up."

"So are you the one operating this bit of kit?" I asked dubiously.

He puffed up indignantly. "I'll have you know that I'm sublimely talented with all things technological. But! If you want to bring your clever hacker in to lend a hand when we go through the instructions again, I won't hold it against you."

His words didn't exactly inspire confidence, so I nodded. "We can definitely do that. I'd rather not have any accidents. Can you leave the instructions here so that he can study them in the meantime?"

"I think... I'm not actually sure. But I doubt anyone will notice, so why not."

He beckoned for one of his workers to bring over a data pad from the box that held the machine. He took it, then handed it directly to me, meeting my eye. "We good, Oshbob?"

I pushed out my fist. "We're good."

He bumped it with his own then turned back to the ship and began shouting at his men again. I took the moment to escape the chop shop floor, heading back to the elevator with Unara and some space to think.

"I hope this is worth it," she said as the doors closed. "Is a week even going to be enough?"

What could I do but shrug? "It's going to have to be. There's no point in stewing over it. Right now, we need to focus on Aspire, and clearing my name."

"I've arranged a meeting with Asala at her home. I guessed you'd want to speak with her."

"Great work. As long as I'm not spotted."

"Oh, you won't be."

Empire of Oshbob
Partition 36

We'd been walking through the Undercity for a while, before Unara led me to a narrow grate that I only barely fit through. I looked at her skeptically as I forced my chest though.

"What is this? I thought we were going to our new home?"

"We are," she replied with a guilty expression. "I thought it would be wide enough. I'll have it widened immediately."

"I'd say so, if I'm expected to live here. Not very high tech either," I added, looking at the rough and rusty metal.

"It's intended to dissuade people coming further down here."

"It would dissuade me," I chuckled as she set off again down the dark tunnel beyond. The walls were so narrow that my shoulders touched on either side, and I was soon glad to have a guide as it wound, twisted, and split into multiple, equally unappealing offshoots. We finally came to a rusty iron door that barred our way.

She pulled a brick from the wall that slid out easily, then peered into the hole.

Retinal Scan Complete.

The immensely thick—not nearly as decrepit as it looked—door swung open. The rusty metal part of the door was just a thin veneer. The back was thick, reinforced steel with multiple solid locking bars.

Beyond was a wide, light, open space that had been painted white. A half-orc guard sat there watching live feeds of tunnels.

"Hey! Welcome to your new home," he said as we came in. "Good to see you again, Oshbob."

It took a second before I recognized Don. Dondo's father. He was looking old, but well. I walked over to bump fists with him. "Don. How are things?"

"Good, good. I've got a cushy job watching dark tunnels all day and responding to any threats which have so far amounted to nothing. Still, I get well paid so I'm not complaining."

"What idiot is paying you for doing that?"

He shrugged. "Some jumped up orc. Thinks he's the next king of Artem so I've heard."

"Hmph. Sounds like an asshole."

Don shrugged noncommittally, but grinned. I slapped him on the shoulder and we said our goodbyes as Unara led me down the tunnel to our right.

"So this is our new home?" I asked, a little confused. "I knew you'd been busy making a safe place down here, but this is pretty amazing."

"It's a complex. We haven't started work on our home yet. I planned to have it ready for you leaving. Asala's main residence is down here as well. There's about ten square kilometers of tunnels that are reinforced and locked off from anyone who isn't permitted. Which is everyone but me, Asala, Wolski, Effa, Bagri, Leo, and Meli. The tunnels incorporate our house, Asala's house, access to Prestige, and Harold's shop which is yours now. We're going to expand to Leo's unit in time. Just a long shot tunnel completely sealed up and hidden."

"It's amazing," I muttered, marveling at the work. The brightness seemed wrong considering our location. Even the floor gleamed with shiny metal floor tiles. "I'll tell you one thing as well." I pointed to the shiny metal floor. "That would have been a damn sight easier to drag myself along, wouldn't it?"

She smirked. "I could have wet you up and slid you along in record time. We're planning transport down here to move around faster eventually. Right now, it's still in the planning process."

"So does this go near the 360 tower?"

"Yep. Nice and close for Asala. We had to get her down here first. She was too vulnerable at the top of the tower."

I nodded. We'd already discussed that at Harold's funeral, but the reminder wasn't unwelcome and my imagination of what was being created down here wasn't even close to the reality.

After a few kilometers of walking, passing multiple doors that broke the tunnel up into segments which I assumed was for security or fire, or both. We eventually arrived at an open space with another desk and another half-orc guard whom I didn't recognize.

She stood up as we entered. "Unara, Oshbob, it's an honor to meet you, sir."

"You too…"

"Arik," she replied quickly. "I was only young when you had to go and serve."

"Good to meet you, Arik."

"Lady Asala is waiting for you both." Arik hit a panel on the desk and another set of doors spun open, widening like an iris.

Inside was a clean, light hallway which led to a sparsely decorated living area. Asala came bounding over, a wide smile on her face and looking far less severe than I'd seen her at the funeral. Her voice, however, was still the consistently soft monotone that never changed.

"I haven't been able to concentrate on my work all day knowing you were coming. I can't tell you how good it is to see you again, Oshbob."

It wasn't part of either of our comfort zones, but just this once, I hugged the slender woman. "It's amazing to see you too. Sorry you have to live underground. That's not what I would have wanted for you. Once we deal with Aspire, we can move you back out if you want."

"I accept my lot down here, and I am content. Even if we are able to deal with Aspire, both my own and 360's rise to power has not gone unnoticed, and while we might still be considered a small corporation, competition is fierce."

"Amazing work. So… we're actually considered a corporation now rather than just a business?"

She nodded with pride. "We certainly are."

"What kind of money are we talking here?"

"A lot. But the question is not so simple. We have a great deal of money tied up in property. A lot of that property is run down and derelict and practically worthless as it is. Once we take over all of the facilities, managements, and everything else in Turan and Newton, and set our regeneration projects into motion there, we will hold a considerable amount more power. Enough to reach middle tier."

"That big of a jump?" I asked, trying not to show my overwhelming surprise.

"It is one of the things I wished to talk to you about while you were here. If we pushed on those two districts and brought them fully into our circle, we would have a lot more financial power to push back against Aspire. It would also give 360 a huge bonus in bargaining power with other important powers within the city."

"What are our chances in direct action against Aspire right now?"

"In all-out warfare, we have a very slim chance if we use everyone at our disposal. I don't know what would be left of Portolans afterwards, even if we did win. My honest opinion, now that we know who they are, is to begin by undermining them while strengthening our own position with the means available to us."

I nodded along as she spoke. "How long before we can act?"

"A year. Perhaps longer."

"I have five months before I'm free, perhaps I can help speed that up."

"You have four months and three days," Asala corrected. "And a lot of our progress will depend on how quickly we can turn Turan and Portolans around. From there, we can start making favorable deals. The only thing holding us back is your insistence that you're there when we take them."

"Wait a goddamn minute. I thought we were okay? Neither you nor Unara said taking them would make any difference to our progress. If I'd known, I'd have said to unleash hell years ago."

"It hasn't been an issue at all until now," Asala responded dryly. "We were taking the slow and steady approach. Putting things into place but not drawing too much attention to ourselves. Now that we know our enemy, we can push."

"The main reason you wanted to be here when we took the districts was because you wanted to kill Burrell yourself and show the orcs of Newton it was you who took them over," Unara said. "And you're here for a whole week!"

"That's not exactly low profile, is it?" Asala pointed out.

"It's not," I muttered. "But I don't have to announce my presence, as long as Burrel sees my face as the light drains from his eyes, that will do for me. The Newton orcs will see me even if they don't know it's me they've seen. They'll have to wait four months and three days before the truth hits and I can live with that. You should hear more from Anvil as well. Has anyone told you about them yet?"

Her face brightened at the name. "Yes! An elite dwarven corporation. A very good acquaintance, I must say. I will endeavor to flatter them as we rise."

"Do it! They don't like Living Earth, so they can't be that bad. We might be able to get more tech from them."

"Even without their aid or tech, I have faith that, when you come out of the military, Portolans 360 will be a true force to be reckoned with. And I want you to know…" She frowned. "I've thought about how best to put this, but it's hard to say well. But, in my eyes, you are and always will be the true CEO of Portolans 360. If there are any concerns about my place and the power I'm accruing…"

"Bah! I trust you, Asala. You're the best person to be where you are."

"As long as you know. I am still entirely in your debt and will be until the day I die. This life you have handed me is more than I could have ever dreamed of, and if I have it in me, I will take your corporation to the center of Artem."

I smiled and laid a hand on her shoulder. "Just keep doing what you're doing and enjoy it as best as you can, Asala. And know that I'm as much in your debt as the other way around. I could never have done what you have."

She shook her head. "But you did do all of this. You hired me. You provided the base for everything that's been built. You've supported me, and both of you have done everything in your power to make sure I'm safe." She gestured around herself. "I doubt there's anywhere in Artem more assassin proof than this place."

"I thought that had stopped," I growled, my fists clenching automatically as I imagined breaking necks.

"I don't think Aspire has sent any for a while, but this is still Artem. There's always someone lurking around looking to cause trouble or make a quick cred. I killed this one guy last Thursday," Unara commented. "Cut his throat while he was still looking down his rifle sight. It was brilliant. Not even a murmur from him and definitely one of my finest stealth kills yet. Had to cross five roofs that had hardly any cover."

"And I thank you for your diligence, Unara," Asala said, unaffected by Unara's story. "I think now we should discuss how we keep you alive. Another advantage of knowing our enemy is that I have been able to find others who have enmity with Aspire. All corporations that I intend to approach in the near future when we face off against Aspire. Some of them will have their own contacts within the military. I will devise a package of incentives for the ones I deem powerful enough to pull strings within the ranks that will keep you safe. It may be best to let bribes and coercion fix this mess, rather than direct legal action."

I didn't like what I was hearing. I ground my teeth in frustration and Unara, sensing my unease, patted me on the arm. "Don't worry. We have the names of every single soldier involved on that mission. We'll make them all suffer."

That brought a grin back to my face. "Oh, I'm gonna have fun with that list as each of them leave the military. But I still think there's room to maneuver on the legal front. Asala, make sure we have lawyers researching everything we know and what we can prove. Killing a whole squad of soldiers isn't something the military can take lightly, and we can get evidence out there circulating. Then the military will have to act. If they have to act, then how much damage could that do to Aspire?"

Asala nodded. "It's incredibly risky as you're putting yourself in the lion's den, but you're right. If we could swing it, I imagine there would be severe penalties for them. I will get to work on those contacts and look at different ways we can play this, while you get to work on Turan and Portolans?"

"That sounds like a plan to me." I put out my fist to bump, but Asala surprised me by going in for another hug.

"It's so great to have you back. I'm elated that Harold gave his shop to you too. It meant everything to him, after me."

"I consider him part of the family," I replied, feeling uncomfortably emotional.

"We consider you family too," Unara said, joining in on the hug.

I expected Asala to recoil, but she didn't mind at all. In fact, the two women seemed to have grown very close in my absence. As we left the basement I questioned Unara on it.

Empire of Oshbob

She gave a nonchalant shrug. "To start with, I trusted her because you trusted her. I decided that, from now on, I only trust people you trust. Unless I don't trust them, of course," she said, looking confused by her own words. She waved it off and continued. "But Asala's proven herself so many times that she's now the person I trust the most after you. It's almost like that bit of humanity that would allow her to consider double crossing you isn't there. I'm serious. She has an almost psychotic need to prove her worth to you and you alone. All of 360 is her trying to prove herself to you to repay your faith in her."

I wasn't sure how I felt about that news. "You as well, surely."

Unara shook her head firmly. "Nope. Definitely just you. I'm a trusted partner, but you are something else to her entirely. After a lifetime of being overlooked and dismissed, you accepted her exactly as she was and both saw and rewarded her usefulness. She's talked with me about it before. You've made a follower for life, and I personally don't blame her at all."

Unsure how to respond to that, I fell silent to think it over.

Kevin Sinclair

Partition 37

"Plan?" Unara said with obvious disbelief as Wolski, Leo, Lanris, and I sat around one of the tables in the Prestige. "What's to plan? We tell Newton to follow us or else. Then we roll in and take Turan. You want Burrel dead anyway, and the man's a snake. He pretends to toe the line with us, but he's always hiding what he's doing and sending us a shitty cut from his turnover."

With four and a half years in the military, I could now see just how bad our planning had been historically. In the past, I would have done exactly what Unara was suggesting and we would have bludgeoned our way through it. Not this time.

"I still want detailed plans of exactly where Burrel's located. I want to know how many men he actually has and what they're packing. Whatever armaments, drones, hackers, and allies he has. Are Turan ACE still in his pocket or are they sick of him as well?"

Leo pulled up his data pad and jacked in. His eyes flashed blue and he began speaking. "We keep close tabs. He has six hundred fighting men. No notable assistance, and his average tech level is basic, Tier-Two across the board. Weapons, drones, and mods. He still pays Ace, but it's a lot less than we pay, and he suffers for that when his men are caught."

He threw up a map of Turan for us all to see. Red lights began to jump up across the display. Then a similar number of green lights. "The red are all Burrel's buildings. You will notice some glow brighter than others. Those are safe houses, the rest are storage units and the likes. This one here," he said, pointing out one of the brighter spots. "Is the base he uses eighty percent of the time. It appears to me he's grown lazy and complacent."

"That's good information. We can match that number of people, right? What are our numbers?"

"Not counting gobbos, we have around three thousand we can call on for a scrap. As for gobbos, well, we can't keep count of those little bastards, but you're looking at around the six thousand mark. Their numbers just keep growing."

"Right, that's a lot of people. I'll need you to take charge of the orcs, and who's our best for the half orcs?"

"Probably Don, or, and this pains me to say it, Dondo. He's making a bit of a name for himself."

I was about to automatically pick Don, when my eyes fell on Lanris. He was no good to lead, but seeing him pushed a name into my head. "Umak! What about him?"

"The half-orc from your squad?" Unara asked, surprised. "He's no use for something like this. He works transport for us now."

I eyed her with confusion. "How well do you know Umak?"

"I know he has no interest in fighting."

"That doesn't mean he can't. Get him here to look over all of this stuff. Tell him he doesn't have to fight, he just needs to direct the half-orcs."

"He probably will fight though," Lanris added with a smile for me. "You know what he's like once his battle sense flares up."

"If you're sure," she replied simply, her eyes glazing over.

I looked back to Wolski and Leo. "Once Umak and Bagri are here, we'll organize properly."

"What about the mercs we've got?" Leo asked.

"Any military leaders among them?"

"I'll find out."

While Leo looked into that, Unara spoke. "Umak is on his way. He sounded a lot more interested than I expected him to."

I wasn't surprised by that at all. The man was a fighter through and through for all of his words to the counter when he retired.

"We have two ex-military teams on retainer," Leo added.

"Perfect. Involve them but don't bring them for this planning session. I'm not supposed to be here. When it comes to the fight, I'll just be another orc along for the ride as far as anyone else is concerned."

"You can be my bodyguard," Unara added. "No one's ever seen you with a hammer before, and if you have a helmet on, there's no way for anyone to tell if you're not barking orders out loud."

"We can definitely keep your presence quiet," Wolski added. "But will Newton agree to fall under our control without you making your presence known?"

"Only one way to find out," Unara replied, looking eager. "Shall I do it?"

"Do it. I don't expect them to fold without trouble, but we might as well get the ball rolling. Can we use an external comm so that I can hear?"

Leo grinned and pulled out a small device from his bag. "It just so happens that I have a comm link I've been messing with. It connects with your keystone to give you an extra layer of defense when contacting people you don't trust. Your chances of being hacked or traced with this thing in are so slim it's basically unhackable. Not that Kenneth is gonna have much of a chance at hacking you."

"Will he be able to hear us?" I asked.

"Absolutely not. Unara will still speak through her keystone, but both their voices will be amplified so that we can listen in. You could sing an old orc battle song if you wanted and Kenneth would be none the wiser."

"Let's do it then."

Leo talked her through how to use the device and a few minutes later, Kenneth's voice sprang to life for us all to hear.

"Hey, Unara. I was gonna contact you today."

"This is convenient then, isn't it. What did you want?"

"Well, you know how we're not getting any requests to turnover property anymore?"

"I do."

"Well, two days ago, we got a new chief of ACE in Newton. He's an asshole. Sent me a message that all bribes are off. Then he sent a message to all the gangs under me that anything we're caught for we're going down for."

"Sounds like a plant to me," I said as Unara looked up and scowled.

"ACE not taking bribes? That's got to be Aspire's work."

I nodded in agreement. "Tell him we're taking over Newton and we'll deal with it."

Unara repeated my words exactly as I said them. I cringed at the lack of tact, but couldn't help a little smile as Kenneth fumbled over what she'd said.

"Wha...? Taking over? What's wrong with our current deal?"

Empire of Oshbob

"Oshbob is out in four months. If Newton isn't fully in the fold by then, he's gonna be pissed and he'll probably want to come over there. I don't want that shitstorm in my hands, so either fall in, or we'll be heading over there to deal with you alongside the new ACE chief."

"Sweeten the deal a little," I said as she finished. "No need for bloodshed if we don't need to."

"You come here fighting and killing ACE, then the power you have in Portolans isn't going to mean shit," Kenneth snapped back at Unara.

"Don't worry about us. This is happening one way or another. You've done a good job as gang lord there and we'd want you to continue exactly as you are. We just need to merge the districts if we're going to keep growing. This is happening one way or another, and trust me when I say, you want to be along for the ride."

"What about Turan?" he half stammered.

"They will be falling in line soon enough."

"You're gonna give that rat, Burrel the same offer?"

Unara looked at me, the question in her eyes.

"Do we trust him?"

She shrugged, which wasn't a no.

I looked over to Wolski, who looked similarly uncertain. "Hard to say. I don't trust no one and he's human, but we've not had any trouble from him in the four years he's been in charge. He's kept the district running smoothly, and paid his dues."

"I wouldn't like to put my neck on the line for him," Leo added, "but I've never found a reason to distrust him apart from the burning of buildings for Aspire, but I believe him when he said he didn't know. He hasn't given us an outright no to coming into the fold yet either. He's doing his due diligence to see what his competitor is getting. And by competitor, I mean Burrel."

"You still there Unara?" Kenneth said with a nervous sound to his voice.

I nodded at her. "That'll do for me. Tell him, but warn him to keep it quiet for now."

With a thumbs up she spoke through her keystone again. *"Can you keep a secret Kenneth?"*

"Er, sure."

"Burrel has no future here. Like you, we think he's a rat. Oshbob in particular doesn't like him. There are no offers of a peaceful transition for him. Turan will be taken by force. We like you, and you've done an excellent job so far. Please don't force my hand."

My eyes widened at Unara's words. She'd changed a lot in the past four years. That was definitely the first time I'd heard her say please to anyone but me in all of our time together.

"What's gonna change exactly?"

"Good question. There will be a number of businesses that are opening up in all of those derelict buildings. They will be part of Portolans 360. Those businesses are to be protected at all costs. Any businesses set up in those buildings you arranged to be available get wrecked. They don't survive more than a week."

"You know this new ACE guy isn't going to stand for that."

"We'll sort the ACE guy out. Don't worry about that. There'll be a new chief on the take with us soon enough."

"I don't have much choice, do I? We can't match you in a fight."

"You wouldn't want to. Think of this as a good thing, Kenneth. A promotion even."

"Fuck it. It's not like we're not working for you anyway. Done. I'll have to ease the lads into it, though."

"If you have any trouble and need some support, let us know. I guarantee that the orcs left in Newton will back you, and we can have our Oka clan branch speak to the one in Newton to help."

"You can do both of those things. I should be all right with everyone else."

"Okay, Kenneth. We'll be along to Newton in the next few days to pay a visit to this new police chief. Do you have a name?"

"Chief Jardin."

"Perfect. I'll be in touch later." She ended the call while Kenneth was mid-sentence in his own goodbye. Then clapped her hands together. "Well that went both better and worse than I expected."

"Yeah, that police chief isn't good. Leo, start digging. Unara, get Hersch on the line. Use the comm again. I want to hear what she has to say."

Empire of Oshbob

Leo was already messing on his Data-pad and only offered a thumbs up in response. Unara hovered over the comm device. "I take it we're pushing for this Jardin's information."

"And let her know we're toasting Turan today, and if she can ease the way with Turan ACE, that would be ideal."

Hersch's voice filled the room moments later. *"Unara! How are you doing, dear girl?"*

I saw Unara's face wrinkle with irritation. *"I'm fine thank you, we need to talk."*

"Of course. We're encrypted on my end. Have you heard any more on the details of Oshbob's demise?"

What little color Unara's face had drained. Her voice grew stiff and cold. *"I haven't heard a thing."*

"I've had a few snippets through from my contacts. It seems there was a clamor from others about the famed unkillable orc being killed. They've sent out teams to clear the tunnel."

"They should have done that immediately. But I'm willing to bet they won't find anything."

"So certain? I have to admit I was surprised to hear they'd finally brought him down."

"Either way, that's not why I called you. With Oshbob gone and our discovery of Aspire acting against us, we need to move. We need to gather our strength. So tonight, I'm planning a raid on Turan. Can you have a word with their district ACE to make sure they're not involved? I'd like to extend our offer of a fruitful relationship to them once the gangs are under control."

"That's a brave move," Hersch said, sounding genuinely surprised. *"I was sure you'd go after Aspire."*

"They're too big. We need to build our defenses. If, and I mean if, Oshbob is dead, then all of the scavengers and opportunists will flock. We need to send out a message to all. We mean business."

"What of Newton?" Hersch asked.

"What of Newton?" Unara replied meaningfully. *"Is there anything we should know about the place?"*

As she spoke, Bagri arrived. I beckoned him to be quiet while we listened.

Hersch barely paused as she quickly did the math and understood we knew about the new change in Newton ACE. *"There's a new chief and they're not going to fold so easily. They* were apparently sent to Newton a few days ago. The day after you discovered who Aspire were."

"You think they're an Aspire puppet?"

"I can't say too much, but yeah, I'd guess so. I can't actually find anything on a Lance Jardin. Chief or otherwise."

"So not even ACE?"

"If he is, his name is either protected, or it's been changed to protect him."

"Okay. Thanks, Hersh. We'll tread carefully around Newton until we have more information."

"So she wasn't much help with Newton ACE, but at least she told us," I said once Unara had cut the line.

She looked at me with a troubled expression. "So what do we do about him? He has to die."

"We could bully him out," Leo offered. "I couldn't find a Lance Jardin anywhere, so I searched high-ranking ACE officers around the center, including Riwol and Ashway who've moved on from their roles recently. I could be wrong but I'm figuring that in an institution like ACE even a high-ranking corpo can't just walk in as the chief for an entire district."

"You got anything?" I asked eagerly.

"Fifty-two who'd fit the bill."

My heart sank, but it was a start.

"Forty-six of them already have new roles."

"Better," I grunted.

"Of the six remaining, three of them retired."

I was up paying real attention now.

"I told Meli what I was doing. She started hunting slightly differently. She sent a drone to check out the new captain's home and his vehicle. Nothing back from the home yet, but the vehicle was registered in Holwell."

"And are any of your three from Holwell?" Unara asked, leaning forward with even more anticipation than me.

"Nope," Leo replied with a smile that suggested he had more to come. "I did run a full background check on the three of them, including parents and romantic partners. One of them has a wife named Suzanna. Suzanna Erias works for none other than Azure Corp. And she's originally from Holwell but lives in Clemence now, the district between Ashway and the center." Leo then slapped his brow, laughing and shaking his head. "And get this. Her maiden name? It's only Jardine."

I snorted. "Idiots."

"That does seem too easy," Lanris said suspiciously, but Leo shook his head.

"We've gotten good at this sort of thing over the past few years and we've expanded our network of infiltrated systems tenfold in the last year alone. Police databases are something of a specialty of mine might I add."

I gave the young hacker a disapproving look though it was tinged with humor. "Hacking ACE databases was how I ended up meeting him in prison in the first place," I explained.

"Trust me," Leo continued. "We just make it look easy."

Lanris nodded, satisfied with Leo's confidence. The two of us were distracted from further conversation by the entrance of Umak.

I didn't stand for many people, but I jumped to my feet at his entrance.

His eyes widened as he spotted us. "What the fuck are you two doing here?"

"We're not here," I said with a wink, then embraced him. "As far as our righteous Artem Military are concerned, we're both dead."

"So you're out? For good?"

"Sadly not," Lanris said, getting an embrace of his own. "We need to go back. We just couldn't go back to base. They tried to kill us again, Umak. This time, they thought they were successful, and they were in part."

Umak paled. "Are you all that's left?"

"Theta and Nozz survived. We've got people out there now bringing them in. They will be deserting, though. We can hide them."

Umak's eyes darted briefly to Lanris, and I could see the worry in his eyes. "And you're staying there for your full time?"

"I have no choice if I want to stay in touch with my family. I'd rather not, but I have a duty to others."

Umak slapped a hand on Lanris's shoulder. "I understand, lad, but understand this. If you give Theta or Nozz up, on purpose or by accident, I'll hunt you down, cut your balls off and feed you them,"

Lanris gulped like he was swallowing a goblin whole. "I wouldn't dare."

"I know, lad, I know. But I mean what I say, and I can't not give you a warning. You give 'em up, it's a death sentence for them, you understand?"

He nodded mutely, as if the full weight of his decision to go back and remain had only just settled on him. I said nothing about the Mindwipe. That would have to remain a secret for now. Instead, I changed the subject back to planning.

It was the general assumption that we'd be going mob-handed into Turan. I stamped that out quickly. It would work, but it was a sure path to carnage and an unnecessarily high body count. I wanted to take Turan as quickly and as cleanly as possible, so I had our numbers divided into manageable teams ranging from ten to twenty people.

Each team had their own leaders, with instructions to enter the district from different points. They were all ordered to stay mobile, maintain good lines of communications and work toward the center. There would only be two sizable clumps of people entering Truan. Those coming with me to draw Burrel and ACE's eyes, and the goblins, though they would be out of sight.

Once our forces were all set up, I focused on Bagri. "Take all the goblins you can pull together and flush the Undercity below Turan. Avoid specters where you can. If you absolutely can't, use grenades to clear them quickly."

He nodded happily. "Use grenades to clear the Undercity. Got it."

I groaned and spoke slowly. "No, Bagri. You *only* use grenades to clear specters. You need to avoid specters at all costs. If you use the grenades for anything else, then ACE has to act against us."

He nodded again. "Got it, boss."

I had no choice but to accept that he understood. "Good. Be ready to come up when I tell you."

He clapped his hands together happily. "It's good to be back in action with you."

"As long as Burrel hasn't managed to get his hands on any rogue mechs, I'll agree with you."

"If there is, you won't be fighting it alone this time," Unara said, nudging me in the shoulder. "I'm not leaving your side."

I laughed at that. "You mean I'm not leaving yours. This is your battle, I'm a silent partner."

"Then if there's nothing left to plan shall we get armored up and get moving?"

Kevin Sinclair
Partition 38

I never liked to use the word smart because it meant so many different things to so many people. But as I jumped fully armored into the back of an impressive looking armored hover truck, I felt confident our planning and effort would work well.

As the truck moved off smoothly, I felt a strange mix of excitement and wonder. It felt very much like I was heading out on an APS mission. Especially with Lanris there. But on this mission, the back of the truck was filled with people who worked directly for me. And then of course there was Unara. I'd have to be careful swinging my wondrous new hammer about as Unara's fighting style generally involved fighting off me as a base when we worked together.

In the back of the truck was a display that showed us a few different angles of what we were heading toward. The main view was from the driver's position. But it was the drone views I was most interested in. It showed the movement of Turan's gangs. They'd clearly gotten word of our approach.

It wasn't a surprise when Unara got a call from Burrel a few minutes later. She fed it through the comm Leo had provided earlier.

"Hey, Unara! What's happening? I'm getting reports of you mobilizing your people and heading this way. I hope it's Newton you're heading toward. I didn't tidy the place up for company." The thin veneer of confident humor wasn't enough to hide the tremble of nervousness in his voice.

"No, Burrel. It's not Newton we're after. They've already officially handed over their district to us. Now we're taking Turan."

His voice rose to reasonable anger quickly. *"Hey now! We're at peace. I dance to your tune when you want me to. What's all this about?"*

"Turan remaining free of us was only ever temporary."

Empire of Oshbob

"Then why not give us the same deal as Newton?" he half screeched. *"Come on, Unara, there's no reason for this."*

"We'd give Turan the same deal, but we won't give a snake like you anything. Your betrayal hasn't been forgotten, Burrel. You signed your own death certificate that day."

"It wasn't like that!"

"It was, and we know you've helped Aspire place infiltrators inside of Portolans, so don't bother pleading. It won't help. If you want to do one honorable thing before you die, hand yourself over to us so that we can kill you and offer Turan a deal. Otherwise, it's suffering time."

His voice changed again. This time, true anger came out. *"You think I don't have friends? Come, see what happens when you face the might of Turan."* He ended the communication, leaving us all bemused.

By the time we reached the Turan border, Leo contacted us through the truck's communication system. "I don't know what drone feeds you're all watching, but Burrel is trying to make a run for it."

"I expected as much. Do we have his exits covered?"

"We do. I have people watching all the players in this thing; we'll keep tabs on him no matter what."

At the first physical sight of Turan gang members, we brought the trucks to a halt. I jumped off and walked around to the front of the vehicle. I was joined by the three hundred people we'd brought with us. We were outnumbered but not by much. Our equipment, however, was far superior, and that couldn't have been more obvious as I pulled the hammer free of its mag clip.

I grinned inside of my helmet at the fear I was about to strike into the heart of our enemies all while completely anonymous.

"Right, you lousy bastards!" Unara yelled. "We're here to claim what's rightfully ours. This district. You're more than welcome to run and hide. You can come and beg for your lives once we're done. But any who stand in front of us today, dies today. This is not a threat. It's a fact. We have plenty of people to fill the gaps you leave in Turan."

I expected some to leave, and by the way a few feet shuffled, it looked as though it was going to be an easy evening's work. Until a big man stepped forward with a big old rail gun. It didn't look pretty but it looked dangerous.

"You want Turan? Come and take it."

His confidence strengthened the wilting resolve of the others.

Umak's voice came through my keystone. *"Oshbob. We've not met any resistance yet. Leo tells me we're in a position to hit those you're facing off against from the rear. You want a little help?"*

"Yeah. Let's send a message to anyone paying attention to this, huh?"

"I'd say so. And if we crush this lot, most of the rest will run, I reckon."

With that agreed and the message quickly passed on, Unara waved us forward with a roar of rage that was met in kind by those with us.

The guy with the railgun was my main target. It seemed as if I was his, as he opened fire on me as I charged. If not for a well-placed shot by one of Leo's drones into his helmeted head and the distraction it caused, I might never have closed the distance to him before someone else took him down.

But as his head snapped back for a brief second and he sprayed bullets wildly into the air, I closed the distance and leapt. Hammer held high, I pulled it forward as I landed, using strength and momentum, and finishing with a strong pulse from the weapon itself.

In an explosion of blood, bone, and gore, my hammer struck the ground as the man disintegrated. I expected him to die, but that one strike alone had horrified all of those lucky enough to watch the move. At least thirty people bolted.

Right into Umak's waiting gunfire.

I continued with my own assault, leaping deeper into their ranks, with a power swing left and a power swing right, which spoke to my fears as Unara had to leap out of the way. To her credit, she did so with ease and impressive agility.

Then it was over. It had taken at most five minutes, but that was being generous to the now dead and broken gangsters.

A cheer broke out, which I ignored as Leo spoke again across our comms. *"Perfectly done. The other splinters of Turan's defense are spread out. Our other groups should clear them easily. For you guys, Burrel has moved to a safe house in a high rise.*

Empire of Oshbob

Near the center. We've not seen this one before. I suspect it's a real last resort. He has around a hundred men there protecting him. Unara, I'm sending the coordinates to your keystone now."

"Thanks, Leo. We'll get right on it," she said, before shouting across the heads of our people. "Everyone, back in your vehicles and follow us."

At a slow pace, we drove deeper into Turan, the streets were deserted but curtains and blinds flickered all around us, and I wanted to make sure everyone saw our arrival.

The street where Burrel was hiding out was lined with high rise buildings, forty floors high at least. Gunmen hid all the way along the street, and they fired as we passed. They were more of an inconvenience, offering very little in the way of danger to our armored trucks. At least until we reached the building itself where each and every window had a shooter inside.

"Leo, which floor is Burrel in?"

"The highest," he replied immediately.

"Typical."

"We could just blow the top of the building. We have the ordnance to do it but it might raise eyebrows."

"Yeah, we're not going down that route yet. It'll bring heat we don't need, and this needs a personal touch."

Leo's reply sounded amused. *"Just thought I'd offer, boss."*

"How do you want to do this, then?" Umak asked by my side, though he directed the question at Unara as well.

"I see two possible choices, seeing as though we aren't using explosives," I replied. "Try and pot shot everyone at a window until we get enough of them to reduce the danger. Or…"

I set off sprinting for the door, surprising not only all of my people, but Burrel's too.

By the time they started firing in any great number, I was already at the entrance to the tower block, and with my hammer raised, I smashed a mighty dent in the steel doors that created a gap wide enough for me to get my fingers in.

Then the doors just opened. If awkwardly.

"I probably should have mentioned that I've already hacked the codes for all of the doors in the building," Leo offered. *"I was just waiting for you to reach the entrance first."*

"That's good to know. Next time, mention it in the planning stage."

"I'm pretty sure I did."

I burst through the last of the broken doors that now couldn't open all the way because of the damage I'd caused.

Unara reappeared by my side as I entered the hallway beyond. "That was funny," she said with a smirk on her face.

I'd have preferred her to use a full helmet, but she insisted her survivability was increased without armor and would have no more said on the subject. I did need to get her a proper stealth mod, though, the kind Corporal Elantra had access to.

Still, I thought idly as someone ran out of the next room in the hallway. *That is something to work on at some other time.*

I thrust the hammer out from where I carried it across my chest. With the angle I had to strike from, using the pulse function wasn't possible, but it still made a pretty mess of his unprotected face. Unara leapt past him, flashing on her stealth cloak and skin mod, before stabbing the next in line in the eye. Then she pulled a gun and shot a third still in the room.

More of our fighters were swarming into the building now, so I moved past her, jabbing with the hammer in the narrow corridor as enemies appeared. I should have used a gun, and it was probably foolish not to, but I loved the hammer so much. It spoke to a primal part of me that couldn't help but listen.

It didn't take long to reach the stairwell, where gunfire rained down from above. Keeping to the wall side, I began my ascent, pulling out my shotgun but keeping the hammer ready in hand just in case.

A face appeared above me on the next flight of stairs, and a bullet from his plasma rifle followed shortly after. I was hit in the chest, but hardly moved with the wall at my back. He was not so lucky as I returned fire instantly, causing his head to disintegrate with the close-range shotgun attack.

He was my only assailant before I reached the next floor up. I held the door until the rest of my people came up the stairs.

"First twenty in here," I ordered.

Umak was around the eight back in the line and he shook his head as he passed me. "I wasn't supposed to be fighting, Osh."

Empire of Oshbob

"You're not," I agreed. "I only told you to give your team instructions. I don't know why you're one of the first up the stairs and into the trouble behind me."

He grinned. "Well... maybe I missed it more than I expected. And I couldn't let you have all the fun, could I?"

I slapped him on the back. "So there is still an orc in there somewhere. I knew it!"

"Asshole," he managed to growl and smile at the same time.

"Get in there. I'm going up again, follow when the floor's clear."

He nodded, and I clomped off up the next flight of stairs.

We followed this pattern as we continued our way up, with our fighters rejoining the back of the line as they cleared floors. By the time we reached the forty-eighth and final floor, my shotgun had barked out death fourteen more times.

I was fit from the military, but forty-eight floors in full armor had me sucking in air like a power-vac. Most of those who'd followed me were roughly the same, but Unara was scanning the door.

"I'm going to need a second," I gasped at her, but the urgency of my breathing was already subsiding as I leaned against the banister.

She raised an eyebrow at me. "Your second is up."

It was a joke, but she also wasn't wrong. We needed to keep moving and get this done.

"Leo, we're at the safe house door. It's solid steel. Can you do..."

The heavy door slid open for us.

And a grenade flew out.

Unara reacted like lightning, batting the grenade back in through the door with speed I could never hope to match.

She then grinned at me. "Is it okay if I use their..." She paused as the air filled with the sound of the explosion and we were buffeted with heat. "...grenades against them?" She continued once the sound had died off.

"It's not like anyone's gonna see it from inside there, is it?" I answered, peaking around the corner. "I just hope, after all this time, you didn't just kill him with a grenade."

She waved off my concern. "He won't be in the dog fight. He's a rat. He'll be hiding in a corner somewhere, deeper on the floor."

"Let's go find him then," I replied, holstering the shotgun and resuming my double-handed grip on the hammer.

Unara followed behind, using my armored mass as cover, she leaned around to shoot now and again as we encountered enemies.

There were far fewer than I'd have expected after we stepped over the ten or so lying dead from the returned grenade. I figured that move had put Unara's kill count above mine for the day but as long as I got Burrel, it didn't matter.

"Burrel!" I yelled at the top of my voice. "Where are ya, you sly bastard! Come out and I'll make it quick. Stay hidden and I'll make it real slow."

A voice replied from a distant room, "Oshbob? Is that you?"

"Shit," I hissed at my idiocy. If he passed on that news, I was ten kinds of screwed. Rather than reply, I set off running toward the voice to manage my mistake.

"Oshbob!" he shouted again. "It don't have to be like this! We can work it out, man. I'm way more useful to you alive than dead."

As stupid as I'd been to give myself away, he was even stupider to keep talking and lead me right to him. I came face to face with another solid security door.

"Leo? I'm at his safe room door. Would you do the honors?"

Leo's voice came back confused. *"There shouldn't be any more doors. At least..."* There was a long pause. *"Ah shit. He's got a secondary system I missed. I should have checked, but I didn't think he was savvy enough to have something like this. Must have cost a pretty cred, too."*

"How long?" I asked.

"Give me five."

I shook my head more to myself. It was too long. Instead, I took a step forward past the door and hefted the hammer. "People always put their faith in these unpassable doors and forgot about the walls." I grunted then swung.

Whoomp!

I brought the hammer down and around in a mighty swing, working the push button at the last second. It was a jarring blow, and the crater wasn't half as big as I'd have expected, but the cracks radiating out look promising. I went again, hitting higher this time and then a third time lower. The third time worked and the wall I'd softened up, now came crumbling down.

A grenade flew out. I was fully expecting it after last time, but before I could even react, Unara dove past me, grabbed it this time and threw it down the corridor rather than back in the room. It was clearly to save Burrel for me and I appreciated the thought, but she could have been badly hurt.

"You need to stop doing that. You could have lost your hand."

"I can afford a new one," she said casually as the grenade exploded and yet more screams reached our ears.

Once the worst of the noise died down she continued. "It's not every day you take over two districts. If losing a hand is the worst that happens I'll consider it an excellent day's work."

It was hard to fault her logic and she'd survived this long. "Fair enough," I replied, then strode in the room.

There were only four other people in the room. They all shot at the big, armored monster in the armor, which left Unara and Lanris free shots.

I had eyes only for Burrell and soon he was the only one left alive.

"Is it really you?" he asked, cowering on the floor, in the corner just like Unara had predicted.

He didn't wait for an answer as his pulse pistol reloaded and he sent another shot at me that glanced harmlessly off my helmet as I closed in silently.

"Stop! You don't need to do this."

"It's judgment day, Burrel. Your betrayal hasn't been forgotten."

"It wasn't a betrayal if I just didn't turn up, man. I was late, that's all."

I swung the hammer from its place near the ground. No pulse needed as it clattered into his hands and gun, breaking the former and sending the latter skittering across the floor.

Only then did I remove the helmet to look in his eyes. The waste of breath pissed himself. If he was hoping for sympathy it had the opposite effect. He enraged me with his weakness.

I clipped my hammer onto my back, then grabbed Burrel's leg. With a sharp yank I pulled him out of the corner and then I stood on his chest. He put his broken hands up to try and dislodge my leg but it was futile.

It did, however, help me with what I planned. Grabbing one of his arms, I slid my foot closer to his shoulder, and with a sharp, full-strength pull I ripped it free of his shoulder.

His screams and cries were ear splitting, but for a moment of silence when he blacked out. I woke him back up with a solid hit of his arm around his head.

"I've been dreaming about this for four and a half years, Burrel, and it's exactly as much fun as I thought it would be."

I removed my foot from his chest so that I could better swing the bloody stump of an arm at his head. Which allowed the blood to pump from the wound in short powerful squirts.

A quick look around showed me that most of the people in the room were looking the other way as I worked. Even Lanris, who'd seen some bad things. His face was pale, and for a brief moment, I wondered if I'd gone too far. Then I saw Unara's beaming smile and felt peace.

"Wanna go?" I asked her.

She seemed uncertain at first. "But you wanted to kill him yourself."

I shrugged. "It's the blood loss that'll kill him, and it wasn't just me he betrayed. It was you and all of Portolans."

She grabbed the arm gleefully and dealt a few well-placed whacks before Burrel stopped moving completely.

"Was that necessary?" Lanris asked once we were done.

"Very," I replied seriously. "I don't make a habit of doing things like that, but I needed to send a message. Do you know how many people died from Portolans because of his setup with Grant?"

Lanris's pale face shook from side to side.

"Let's just leave it at too many and move on from this."

He swallowed deeply, but seemed to accept it.

"Okay, everyone. It's clean up and secure time. Let's get Turan locked down and brought into the fold. Unara, will you speak to ACE here? Let them know the new state of affairs and find out how they want to proceed."

Empire of Oshbob

"On it!" she said, still beaming. "It's great to have you back. Even just for this week. You're so much better at all this than I am."

I couldn't help but laugh. I barely had a year running Portolans. "You've done it yourself for almost five. I think you've got this, Unara."

"I definitely wasn't alone. I had help. Asala, Harold, Leo, Wolski, Effa. Even Bagri!"

"Same as me, then. But I had you as well. Now get us our contact."

She pushed me in the chest. "One contact coming right up. But you know what I mean."

Kevin Sinclair

Partition 39

It took a couple of days to get on top of Turan, but it was Newton that turned out to be the bigger problem. Word had gotten back to Chief Jardin that the gangs had fallen under our control and he was not happy.

His solution was to start arresting Newton gang members on any charges he could find and sending them to prison.

Sergeant Hersh and Senior Detective Wensley, our Turan contact, were no use. Apart from warning us not to hurt or kill Jardin, there was nothing they could offer.

We sat with Asala and Meli at Asala's house to work through our options, and none of them looked good.

"We simply must remove him from Newton. One way or another. Many of our expansion and power grab plans depend on having the land and real estate there."

"I should really just go kill him," Unara said. "I know I can get in and out without getting caught."

"That is not an option," Meli said firmly. "You're the first person they'll look at and if we can't find a watertight alibi for you, they'll find a way to make it stick."

"Can we employ an assassin?" I asked. "A high level one?"

"We can," Asala replied. "But their hiring leaves a trail. If the death of a high-ranking ACE officer is attached to any of us in any way, then we are through."

"They've played a strong move," Meli said. "But they acted quickly and they made mistakes. You know we learned who he was immediately. Well trust me when I say that we've already compiled a lengthy file on him and his family."

"Kill his wife?" Unara asked curiously.

Meli fought the frustrated sigh. "I was thinking more along the lines of blackmailing him."

"Sounds good," I said, rubbing my hands together. "What are we leading with?"

Empire of Oshbob

"I honestly don't know. There's not a lot on file that indicates a bad man if I'm honest. He appears to be diligent and hard working. His wife, however…" Meli said, sliding over a data pad to me. "There might be something you can use there."

We could have had Leo set up an elaborate blackmail plan for Jardin. But both Unara and I felt we should at least start with the personal touch. Which was how I found myself wedged in a reclined seat in the all new and improved Perfect Pout the following morning, with Clara hovering over me.

"Just a few more minutes and we're done."

"Good. This is not something I ever want to go through again," I grumped.

She patted the top of my head like a mother comforting a child. "You've done well. I expected you to be a fidgeting nuisance given your position, but you've been one of my best clients so far. Apart from you being bigger, I dare say, you'll look more like Effa than Effa."

"And this is all changeable, yeah?"

She nodded. "Completely. I can have you back to your old self in ten minutes or less. Most of it is surface cosmetics, but it's all temporary."

I lay back and sighed. In all my years, I never thought I'd be in Clara's seat. She was, despite her fiery nature, professional and very good at her job.

"I'm glad you got back out of the unit. How's the rest of the family?"

She frowned at me for a moment before relaxing. "They're good, thanks. We've never felt so safe. Our first meeting may not have been the best, but it's been good for us. And apart from you, it's been eye opening to see that orcs are not half as monstrous and savage as we'd been brought up believing."

"Apart from me?" I said, unable to fight the grin that *attempted* to stretch my face against the numbing injections I'd been given.

She slapped my chest. "No smiling or you'll ruin my work. Also, don't smile when someone calls you a savage monster. It doesn't build confidence in your more delicate friends like me."

"Delicate!" I said, moving from smiling to outright laughing. "You might look delicate, but we both know you're about as delicate as a goblin fart in an elevator."

She folded her arms, her expression grim. "You've gone and ruined the neuroparalyzer now, it's spread past your forehead. Typical man. I give you one complement and now you look more like Wolski!"

I shrugged. "Wolski will do, as long as I don't look like me."

"Well in that case, you're done," she huffed. "Now get out of my parlor, you brute. Coming in here, casting aspersions on my delicate nature."

I jumped up, relieved to be out of the chair. "Happy to help, Clara. I'll see you later to put all this back to normal?"

"I'll come to the Prestige tonight. Until then, just give your face a good massage at the numb spots and wash with ethanol solution. Unara will have some to clear her own cosmetics."

I shook my head. "Glad I don't wear makeup. Sounds like a rigmarole."

"Don't worry, Oshbob. I have a suspicion that even if you were female, it still wouldn't be an issue for you."

"Cheeky fucker." I grinned as I waved goodbye.

She smirked, then turned back to her work.

A few hours later, I was driving toward Newton District Precinct, with ten of our best people. We had close to a thousand goblins in the Undercity, but this wasn't intended to be an attack, just a conversation.

My face was tight and loose in all the wrong places but I still wouldn't have been confident in the disguise if not for Wolski's uncomfortable glances.

"We have a name for you, then," he grumbled as we crossed the Newton border.

"We were going to pass me off as Effa while he's away. Now I'm not so sure. You have any other brothers I might pass for?"

"Not that I know of."

Unara leaned over with a grin. "I've been calling him Woffa."

Wolski smiled, though it wasn't entirely comfortable. He was stopped from replying by the sound of sirens as ACE Drones surrounded us.

Empire of Oshbob

Please state your business in the District of Newton.

Unara leaned out of the window and shouted back, "Pretty sure there's no law requiring us to do that."

The drone fell silent at that, but now ACE cars were appearing down the long, wide main street that ran through the district.

I'd been expecting something like this, there was always something. But so far, there was no reason to stop and none of the people with me had any outstanding warrants on them. "Keep going, Wolski. Just drive past them."

"I will. But who warned them we were on our way?"

"They've probably been waiting for us to show up," I muttered.

"True," Unara added, pointing upward. "There're cameras and drones everywhere around here."

We had to take three detours as the police blocked off the road. In the end, we got out and walked the last couple of blocks. The city Enforcers looked uncomfortable as they followed us closely, and my disguise was feeling less and less convincing by the second. Only our Undercity presence of goblins gave me confidence that, if things turned bad, we could get out of there.

That tense atmosphere only grew as we headed up the stairs at the front of Newton ACE. We approached the desk, and Unara spoke to the human woman who stood there, bristling with righteous anger before Unara even began.

"We need to see Chief Jardin."

"The Chief isn't at your beck and call. Make an appointment and then get out of here before I arrest you and your little band of followers."

"Remind me of the ACE motto again?" Unara said coldly.

The woman scowled deeper. "Out, or arrested. Those are your two choices."

"ACE. Protecting the people of Artem since the walls went up. That's your motto. So why are you threatening myself and these fine people of Artem?"

"We know who you are. Criminals, all of you. Now out of here before we find something to stick on you."

"There are no criminals here," I assured her. "In fact. the only person guilty of breaking any laws right now is you, by threatening to unlawfully arrest us."

"And this is all being recorded, just in case you decide to do anything foolish," Unara added. "Now go get Jardin. We aren't leaving until we see him. And just in case you don't know who I am, tell him Unara is here."

The woman's eyes darted from side to side as she lowered her voice. "Look, I'm trying to help you here. I think you're good for the area but Jardin's a right bastard. He's not going to take a bribe, and if you offer, he'll have you arrested on the spot."

I was genuinely surprised that she was on our side after the greeting we'd received. I wondered how much of the police presence was trying to head us off from speaking to Jardin. I was extra interested in the man now.

"No bribes," Unara said. "This is just a short, law-abiding conversation. A getting to know each other kind of chat. Go get the chief." She leaned forward and read the woman's name badge. "Officer Perriello."

The woman sagged and hit the intercom. "Chief Jardin, we have an Unara here over from Portolans. She's quite insistent on speaking with you."

"Very well. Send her through, unarmed and alone."

Unara shook her head and pointed at me. "Unarmed yes, alone no. I will bring my bodyguard."

Officer Perriello relayed Unara's words. I heard a sigh from the other line. "I'm coming through."

Moments later, a smug, middle-aged half-elf sauntered through. I took an instant dislike to the man.

"And what does the self-titled Lady of Portolans want with the Chief of Newton today? Have I upset some of your criminal plans in my fair district?"

"I haven't heard anyone use that title for me but you," she replied sourly. "Not sure what you're trying to prove with it, though."

"I am trying to point out how pathetic it is that a jumped-up gang lord like you thinks they can come to my precinct and make demands."

"I'm neither a gang lord, nor am I here to make demands," she replied. "But there's a very good reason ACE generally works with the gangs."

"Greed and corruption," Jardin snapped back, leaning on the front desk with an intense, eager look in his eyes.

"Sure," Unara replied. "There's plenty of that. Right from the top of Artem to the very bottom. But that's not the real reason. The simple fact is that ACE can't do their jobs properly."

Jardin bristled at her words, but she continued over his attempt to interrupt her. "They can't compete with the amount of crime in Artem. There's not nearly enough of you and there never will be. So ACE does deals with the most powerful criminal elements to make sure that the crime done is mostly invisible. ACE relies on the gang lords to keep the districts running smoothly. You're basically criminal administration. Not law enforcement."

He slammed his hands down on the desk. "Oh I assure you that I enforce the law. I'm here to clean up this place from the top to the bottom."

Unara leaned forward so that her face was an arm's length from Jardin's and spoke low and forcefully. "If that was true, and you really wanted to clean up crime and corruption, you'd start with whoever employed you and put in Newton in the first place."

Jardin's face lost its red hue at her words. "I was sent here because of my proven track record. I'm a seasoned enforcer and I've worked on the meanest streets of Artem with a track record of cleaning districts up."

Unara laughed at that. "We've looked into you, and I wouldn't exactly call the streets in the central district mean streets. What exactly did you clean up? Food wrappers?"

"Whatever you've found on my past will be whatever I want you to know," he said with confidence.

"Sure it is," Unara replied. "Is that what you'll whisper to Suzanna tonight across your keystone?"

As she spoke, one thing became abundantly clear. Chief Jardin—or rather Chief Erias—did not want us to know that bit of information. All color drained from his already pale skin, and his fists clenched. I could see panic in his eyes as he worked through his options.

I decided it was time to stick the boot in. "Must be real lonely having to be away from her and that warm house in Clemence. But you're entirely right, Jacob, it was incredibly hard to find anything on you."

He spun on me. "Who the hell do you think you are?"

"Woffa," I answered easily. "And seriously, Suzanna? We found some dark shit on her. How many affairs has she had now? And the latex. Gods of old, how does she even get into that stuff."

His face blossomed into crimson once again as he squawked. "Arrest them! Arrest them now."

"Please do," Unara replied. "We have the finest lawyers money can pay for all ready to go, with some interesting insights into whatever case you call against us. As we mentioned to Officer Perriello earlier, all of this is recorded and backed up across multiple sources."

"How much are Aspire paying you to be here?" I asked as Chief Erias fish-mouthed, looking across to Perriello.

She offered no support beyond a troubled expression.

Unara pushed my arm. "Stop asking such personal questions, Woffa." She couldn't help but crack a smile when she said the fake name. "We only came here to wish Chief Erias good luck in his new position." She turned to him. "So here it is. Good luck in Newton, and if you need any help getting to grips with the more difficult residents, you just let me know, okay?"

We turned and left the building without anything else being said. It wasn't until we got in the car that Leo's laughing voice broke the silence across the internal speaker. "Well that went well! Loved how you handled it, Unara, and how you worked in the extra information on his wife, Woffa. His face… it was classic! I honestly thought he was going to start crying there and then."

"What's next, though?" Unara asked. "How do we push this through?"

"We have lawyers working on pulling out the Newton gang members imprisoned by Erias. They're going to pull apart his case on each of them and make him look like an over eager idiot to those who don't know he's been paid to go there. If he fights back, we can make things so much worse for him. I imagine it won't take him long to realize that, and it will depend on what leverage Aspire are using against him. If he has any sense, he'll run. He should probably leave his wife as well. I mean damn, some of the vids I got were… deep."

"So we're done?" Unara asked, confused.

"I reckon so. You guys have thrown the stone that will start the avalanche."

"If only every job was that easy," I replied, laying back in the car seat and massaging my face as Clara had told me to do.

Partition 40

"I can't believe you've been here for almost a week and you haven't even paid me a visit yet," Tenev said with mock anger. "Did Unara not tell you about the mods we have waiting for you?"

"It's been chaotic, Tenev. I hadn't expected to be so busy during my short stay here."

"I heard! Running around in a disguise causing all kinds of trouble. Well done on Newton and Turan, though. Exciting times."

"Newton's still a problem, but Unara and the others can sort that out from here. Right now, I'm more interested in what you've got for me. I need something to look forward to once I'm back."

"Oh well let me tell you then. First, we have your new arm!"

Full Arm (Right)	Tier: Four

Special Edition: Might is Right RA3

With a nanite-enhanced titanium alloy skeletal structure, combined with fluid joint articulation and state-of-the-art synthetic muscle fibers, you are getting an arm that fully replicates the flexibility and smoothness of an organic arm but with far greater Strength and Dexterity. To protect the organic body from these increases, shock absorbers are located throughout the forearm and knuckles to absorb and all but eliminate recoil from punches thrown.

Special function 1: Power Punch
With hundreds of micro pneumatic pistons located around the elbow and shoulder, you can call upon short bursts of further increased power.
(+4 Strength for one attack)

Special Function 2: Chameleon Skin.
The surface of the arm has adaptive camouflage capabilities,

allowing it to match the user's natural skin or any chosen pattern or color. Active time: 1 hour. Recharge time: 24 hours.

Special Function 3: Nanite Repair System.
Arm is equipped with nanites that can perform minor repairs and maintenance on the arm whilst in action. Nanites will need to be replaced and major damages will still require professional attention.

Strength: 18
Dexterity: 14

| Durability: 100/100 | Slot Cost: 4 |

"That's an amazing arm!" I said, practically salivating over the description.

"It gets better," Tenev said smugly. "The arm is part of a set and I've got you the leg too."

I immediately jumped onto the next mod.

| Full Leg (Right) 1 of 4 | Tier: Four |

Special Edition: Might is Right RL3

With a nanite-enhanced titanium alloy skeletal structure, combined with fluid joint articulation and state-of-the-art synthetic muscle fibers, you are getting a leg that fully replicates the flexibility and smoothness of an organic leg but with far greater Strength and Dexterity. To protect the organic body from these increases, there are shock absorbers throughout the leg and foot to absorb impacts from kicks, stamps, and landing from height.

Special function 1: Power Kick
With hundreds of micro pneumatic pistons integrated into the calf and thigh, you can call upon short bursts of further increased power.
(+4 Strength for one attack)

Special Function 2: Chameleon Skin.

The surface of the leg has adaptive camouflage capabilities, allowing it to match the user's natural skin or any chosen pattern or color. Active time: 1 hour. Recharge time: 24 hours.

Special Function 3: Nanite Repair System.
Leg is equipped with nanites that can perform minor repairs and maintenance on the leg whilst in action. Nanites will need to be replaced and major damages will still require professional attention.

Strength: 18
Dexterity: 14

Durability: 100/100	Slot Cost: 4

"Maybe I will just sack off going back to the military. These are serious upgrades. And thanks for finding ones that play to my strengths."

"I wouldn't be much of a friend if I didn't, would I? Now check the last one out. I can't wait to *see* what you think."

"I take it the next one is eyes?"

Tenev chuckled. "You saw straight through me!"

I had no choice but to groan.

Replacement Optics - (pair)	Tier: Four

The Visionary MK-IV boasts a wide array of functions that will never leave you in the dark.

With Identification, Thermal Imaging, and Infrared-Night vision as standard, you're already ahead of the game. When you add in Hyper-Resolution 3XR, which provides unmatched clarity up to 300 meters, Real-Time Augmentation of maps, alerts and helpful information boxes to help with day-to-day activities, and a protective shield which creates a transparent layer that automatically covers the eye on detection of harm, there's nothing to stop you from seeing the world in all its glory.

Warning: Real-Time Augmentation is entirely reliant upon Keystone quality and data access.

Empire of Oshbob

Durability: 100/100	Slot Cost: 4

"The protective shield. Will it protect against EMPs?" I asked, daring to hope.

"I'm afraid no mod will protect against those, Oshbob."

"Then I don't want them. You kept my old eyes, right?"

He nodded. "I did. They are still in storage in the unit. You do realize they are far more delicate than even trash-tier mods. Don't you?"

"I can protect them from physical harm with a helmet or eye protectors. Neither of which I can do with mods against EMPs."

"Actually, while EMP technology is still developing to subvert defenses so this wouldn't be a guarantee, we could get you a helmet which might work."

"That was the most unconvincing sales pitch I've ever heard. Thanks for the eyes, Tenev, but give them to someone else, or if they're better than yours, take them for yourself."

"I don't think you understand how much these cost. Unara specifically told me to acquire better mods for you and to spare no expense."

Unara, who was off screen but lounging only a few meters away, jumped up and strolled over. "You got them. That's all I asked. As far as I'm concerned, they're yours, Tenev."

"Then... I don't know what to say. Thank you, thank you!"

"When I see you in four months and you fit my new mods, you'll have earned them again."

His eyebrows raised in surprise. "You're going now?"

"Today at least. I have a few last things to take care of, and then I'm off."

"Oh my. Do you have a plan to return? I mean, they did try to kill you. It's not as if you can walk straight back in is it?"

"We have a few things up our sleeves. I've pulled in a few favors from some old friends and made some expensive promises to some new friends."

"I suppose that's to be expected," he replied sagely.

"It is. Now I must get moving, Tenev. I promise, in a few months, I'll come and see your new shop. You fit the mods and I'll bring the beers."

"It sounds wonderful. Apart from the new shop part. I've been here a while now. It's in need of a face lift."

"It's Artem. How bad can it be?"

That brought a knowing shrug from him as we ended the comm.

Unara was quick to speak. "Are you sure you can't stay longer?"

"I'm sure. Too many people know I'm around here now. I trust them all, but it's still a dangerous game and we both know how this ends if I'm caught."

I turned to Lanris, he looked up expectantly, and I couldn't help but grimace. "As for you, I have some not great news."

His face fell. "You're gonna kill me, aren't you?"

"Well,..." I replied, trying to phrase my words sympathetically. It wasn't a strong point and Unara dove into my pause without such reservations.

"Lanris. I was all for killing you at the start of this week, and as much as I've grown to trust you, you still know way too much, and we can't afford you walking about with all that knowledge, so we need to remove it."

He held his hands up in a panic, clearly not following her words. "I'd never betray you guys. But I know how much keeping quiet matters. Theta and Nozz..." He paused close to tears.

"Lanris," I interrupted patiently. "We..."

"I'll stay. I'll stay here. My mother doesn't like me anyway. She's probably not even missed me."

"Lanris!" I barked. "We're not fucking killing you, and your mother has missed you. Leo has spoken with her."

"He's... what? Why didn't you let me know? I could have smoothed things out."

"Think about it. We're supposed to be dead. He spoke to her as a fellow mourner of the fateful accident that befell us."

"What are you saying?"

Empire of Oshbob

"I'm saying that your mother was devastated over your loss. She's launching an investigation into your death. Leo explained my situation, and that he believed I was still alive. It's your mother who demanded the site be excavated. She's going to be one of our best bets at returning to the military unharmed. Leo has greased the wheels of a few other important parties that she pointed out to us. We just need to get out of there and get picked up."

"So we'll be safe? What about if they scan us? They'll know about Theta and Nozz."

"No, they won't because I'm having both of our minds wiped from the moment the tunnel collapsed to when we wake up, a day's walk outside the city. We'll leave flashes of memories to give some clues as to what we were doing. We're both gonna have to get a bit of carefully administered brain trauma too."

"So we're being dumped out in the middle of nowhere, alone, with brain injuries and no memories of the last seven weeks?"

I gave him a thumbs up. "Exactly. Though Leo will be watching us with drones, and we'll have people nearby ready to rescue us if we need them too. Just we won't know they're there." I grimaced at the thought myself.

"And we really won't remember any of this?"

"Leo's going to record all of our memories so that they can be reinstated afterwards. It will be a little confusing, and you don't get yours back until you leave the military and rejoin us, but they'll be there waiting for you."

"Will I remember that my mother gives a shit about me?"

Unara laughed at that. "I'm sure she'll let you know when you meet her."

He stood up full of enthusiasm. "Then let's get this done! I'm ready."

Lanris and I went and got changed into our military uniforms before heading to the medical room. I made Lanris go first. Not because I didn't trust the machine. Well not entirely. I was still practical first. But more because I wanted to say goodbye to Unara one last time. I watched as they lay him down on the table and knocked him out then turned to her.

She was already watching me. "You sure you want to do this to yourself?"

I sighed. "What choice do I have? If we go after Gullan and whoever else was involved, then they'll want my memories of the incident. We can't be having that."

"It'll be SEPCO, though. We pay them."

I shook my head sadly. "We pay some of them. You can guarantee Aspire will be in there already. We've asked them to intervene if things go too far, but a standard mind read of the event isn't too far. Not to mention that Anvil will kill me if I don't do what I've promised."

She sagged. "I know. I just don't like it. You're gonna forget everything we did here and what to watch out for. You'll probably shout at me for taking Turan without you." She chuckled, but I could see the worry on her face.

"Probably," I agreed, grabbing her in a hug. "But you can put me right easily enough if you want to. And it won't be for long."

Partition 41

I woke up with a start. My head was spinning, but I could focus enough to recognize I was inside a geodome. Memories of APS attacking us forced their way into my mind, followed by the images of Agga and Froom dying from their sly attack.

My hand touched something warm. Lanris lay beside me, but we were alone. I couldn't remember seeing Theta or Nozz die, but… it was all too blurry.

The only other memory that would surface was of Lanris and me hiding behind a shallow rise, firing on a wolf type that was attacking a trade caravan. We were trying to get to Artem! That made perfect sense, but where the hell were we now. I shook Lanris awake.

He sat bolt upright, his face a mask of alarm. "Oshbob? What's wrong?"

"I can't remember a damn thing after the attack of the APS…"

He held his head. I noticed a nasty bruise on it that really didn't look healthy. "I can't remember anything after that either. No. There was a snake. The A-Rank the APS were supposed to be hunting. It was chasing us. It ate you, Nozz, and Theta. That's all I can remember. Literally nothing after that."

I stood up and opened the geodome door. It was dark outside and cooler than I'd have expected. "I remember being in a fight against a wolf type," I said as he came to join me. "We were heading to Artem, though it's hazy and I can't remember anything else."

"Sergeant. You're bleeding out your ear."

I held up my hand to check, and he was right. A trickle of blood was flowing out. It made sense of how dizzy and disoriented I felt. "I think we're quite far south, Lanris. If we can get to Artem, I can get us inside and have someone check us both over. Then we can look at getting retribution on Gullan."

Lanris looked back at the geodome and our limited gear. "Don't think we've got much choice. We won't last much longer out here."

"No," I replied, rubbing my stomach. "Not that I'm overly hungry, mind. I must have eaten recently."

"Yeah," he said absently. "Me too. I don't like this, Oshbob. Something's not right."

I agreed completely, but I sensed that he was ready to break down into a full panic mode, so I kept my thoughts to myself, but something was definitely off about this whole thing. Had something happened with the caravan? I remembered wanting to hitch a ride. And we were really far south. I took another look around at my surroundings.

"Whatever's wrong, we need to push on, Lanris. Right now, south seems like the only real option we have." I pointed with my left arm to the distant glow on the horizon that heralded dawn to get my bearings. Then I packed up the geodome.

Half an hour later, a glow appeared on the horizon in front of us. I came to a stop and looked back to what I'd thought was east. The sun hadn't lifted any higher in the sky.

Lanris gave voice to my thoughts. "I'm damn dizzy, Sarge. So I might be wrong, but I think we've been using the wrong sun. I don't think those lights to the east are the sun at all."

I rubbed my head, trying to clear the fogginess from it. "Yeah. I don't think that's east, I think it's Artem."

We didn't really say much more. We just turned and began our trudge toward the source of light. As we drew closer, the lights grew dimmer, which wasn't a surprise.

We spent the day trudging forward. It wasn't until dusk began to settle, and the obvious neon lights of the city brightened again, that we saw the wall. Though, it was still small to our eyes.

"You think we'll reach it tomorrow?" Lanris asked as we came to a stop to admire the view.

"Depends. I'd rather keep walking until we reach the pits at least. You got it in you?"

"I feel like shit still, but sure. I'm scared that if I fall asleep again I might lose what few memories I gained today."

I nodded, feeling exactly the same, so we pushed on into the evening.

Empire of Oshbob

When the sun finally set, there was still enough glow from the city that we had visibility without the aid of night vision. But I still flicked it on whenever we approached any rises or outcroppings in the land. It must have been around midnight when I noticed the first bit of movement that wasn't caused by wind.

"Spotted something," I hissed, dropping to one knee, and pulling my rifle from my back.

Lanris copied the move a few feet to my right. "There're about fifteen of them. Different sizes, but they look small, and they're cautious."

I observed the same as he spoke, but with one curious addition. "Are they fucking wriggling?"

At the sound of my surprised voice, whatever was approaching us decided to speed up. We both opened fire on our new friends which brought hissing and piercing squealing sounds from the ones who died.

Not all of them died. No matter how much plasma we threw at the five largest ones, they kept coming.

"What the hell are they?" Lanris shouted.

It didn't take long to receive an answer as those impervious to our fire came into view. They were a lot bigger than I originally had thought, and I was hit with a sense of morose humor and disgust as they scuttled at us on hundreds of tiny, little legs. They were evolved weasel grubs.

"Just focus on one at a time and aim for the eyes," I replied as we backed away.

He picked a target quickly, and I joined him on hammering the wrinkled little face of the bulbous, creamy white monstrosity. The result was depressingly ineffective.

"Why won't they fucking die?" he grunted.

"The hell if I know." I said, pulling my handgun as I spoke. It was more to give my rifle a break as it wouldn't recharge until the sun came up, and to my surprise, it still had ammo left, so I stowed the rifle away for a moment.

"Let's see if they can stand up to armor-piercing rounds. If this doesn't work, we're just going to have to sprint for it."

Aiming for the face we'd been targeting, I fired. I whooped with satisfaction as its face disintegrated. Then swallowed with despair as a new face regenerated almost instantly. I fired again, and after five new faces and a slight reduction in body length, the giant weasel grub still continued to follow. Though, it had fallen behind its friends now.

"Run now?" Lanris asked, after firing his own handgun to similar effect.

I was stopped from answering by distant lights growing fast in the night sky.

He spoke again. "Is that an AV?"

I could barely make it out, but whatever it was it was coming directly toward us and it was moving fast. "I think so. The big question now is whether it's coming to finish us off?" I really wasn't happy to be caught out in the open like this. I needed to get in touch with Unara and the others before the military reclaimed us. "Lanris, if we're taken in like this, with hardly any memory, we'll be screwed. We need to hide."

He shook his head, firing on a closing grub. "I'll tell them to get my mother. She can help, I promise."

I wasn't convinced, but then I didn't exactly have a lot of choices available to me. Where would I even hide?

When the AV opened fire, I expected the worst. But all their attacks landed on the grubs in front of us. Their much heavier weapons caused so much damage that the weasel grubs couldn't recover fast enough. It still took them a good five minutes to finish them off.

Then the moment of truth came. How would they react to us? The AV came in to land, the rear door lowered, and an armed squad, similar to what I had been part of with Jacobs and Maddock, came marching out, guns trained on us.

"Where'd you two come from?" one of them barked aggressively.

"An outpost!" I shouted back. "One of the wild bases. The location is classified but I'm happy to report to headquarters."

"We were caught in a landslide," Lanris added, apparently unconvinced with my response. "We lost all comms and now we're just trying to make our way back."

"You were in an outpost and you came all the way back to the city?" The disbelief in the soldier's voice was clear.

"All roads lead to Artem," I offered. "You know how hard those bases are to find out there?"

"Aye. I suppose you're right." His eyes landed on my insignia and he seemed surprised. "Sergeant?"

"That's right," I replied curtly.

"Well goddamn. I think you might be the first orc sergeant I ever did see."

"There's a good chance I'm the only orc sergeant the Artem military has ever seen." I didn't go on to say I'd only gotten the position so that they could set me up to kill me and my entire squad. That could wait.

"Lucky we got here then! Else you would have been the last. You boys wanna ride back to the city?"

"We'd very much like that," Lanris agreed.

I accepted as graciously as I could. This wasn't exactly ideal, but if we could get healing and we were allowed to contact people before any big decisions were made, then it wasn't a terrible turn of events either.

The flight back to the city only took a few minutes, and the AV descended at one of the wall bases.

"We ain't got no air clearance to fly straight to headquarters tonight. You boys'll have to hang out here tonight."

"That's fine," I grumbled, just relieved that we were being treated well, even if it was just temporary. "How did you even find us? Was it just our gunfire?"

"We got a report come in from someone or other that there was a firefight out there. You're damn lucky, it did too, huh? Those evolved weasel grubs are damn tough sons o' bitches."

I couldn't even listen to what he was saying. My mind was focused on one thing only. "Who sent the report?"

"No idea, sergeant. I just got the call. Best ask the base captain when you see him. He's gunna want to talk to you. Walking in from the wilds all bust up like that. I ain't never seen anything like it. You must have seen some shit out there."

"I can hardly remember a thing," Lanris said, rubbing the dark bruise on his head.

"Aye," the sergeant said, eyeing the bruise. "You two boys don't look too good. What can you remember."

"Flashes," I replied shortly. "We both keep blacking out. We both remember the cave in. Lanris remembers an A-Rank Snake type, and I remember an A-Rank Wolf type, but nothing else."

"Shit, that sounds bad. Hopefully, they'll get you fixed up straight away at headquarters."

I sincerely hoped so.

We stepped out into a large concrete yard in the center of the base. The moment we walked off, a number of people poured out of the main entrance. They appeared to be mainly base guards and a medic, followed by a familiar man with a captain's insignia. I couldn't fight the groan. Hazy memory or not, I'd recognize my old sergeant, Turner, anywhere.

"Well, well, well. What do we have here?" he said as we were brought to standstill in front of him. He looked over my shoulder at those escorting us. "You can go now, Sergeant Briggs. I know this one well." He looked back at me with a sour expression. "What an indescribable surprise to see you again. Sergeant Oshbob now, is it?"

"It is, yeah," I replied curtly. "Why wouldn't you expect to see me again?"

"The military is massive, and we went in different directions. I distinctly remember you heading out to the wilds."

I felt my blood beginning to boil at the smug bastard. Of all the people I would have to come face to face with first, it was this useless goblin shite. "Yeah. I did go to the wilds. You wouldn't have anything to do with that, would you?"

His posture seemed to change. He sagged a little. "Honestly, Oshbob. When I got pulled away from the team, I spoke highly of you. And I meant every word. This city is a cesspit and everyone's out for themselves, but everyone in that team felt a hell of a lot safer having you around. You changed my mind on what an orc even is, and it pained me to see you overlooked for promotion after promotion. When I heard you'd been sent out to the wilds, I knew you'd been fucked over again, but my hands were tied. You were supposed to be made the corporal of the squad with Maddock moving to sergeant."

"Is that so?" I replied, not even to try hiding the doubt I felt at his words. "Well, I was fucked over. Do you know how many attempts there's been on my life since I went out there?"

"I can imagine. What I need to know is why the hell you're here?"

"Which version? The political line that I intend to use until I'm safe and have legal representation, or what actually happened?"

He met my eyes and winced. "I think I'll take the political line for now. If you don't mind."

"Not at all, Captain Turner. My squad was out on a mission and were caught in a landslide. I took a serious knock to the head and I'm now lacking most of my memories and my teammates. Only Lanris and I survived, and we could really do with medical attention."

"Of course. We have a medic here to take you to the medical bay and check you over."

"Perfect," I replied, casting my eyes around at who was listening. Then I lowered my voice accordingly. "I'd also really appreciate it if you didn't let the base I was stationed at know we're alive yet. We need to get some things in order first."

"And…" Lanris said nervously, "If it's not too much trouble, captain. Could you contact my mother? Commander Luasos. She's the Western Gate Base Commander."

Turner smiled with none of the surprise I would have expected from him learning that Lanris's mother was an important base commander. "I'll send a message to her, then follow up with a call first thing in the morning. For now, you two get to the med room for a check over. I'll give you both a guest room which will have a terminal that you can use to contact the outside world. But, I'll warn you. They will be monitored."

I understood what he was doing for us and I nodded my gratitude. "Thank you, captain. We will be respectful during our stay."

Kevin Sinclair

Partition 42

The medium Medi-Kit healed our wounds, but it did nothing for the memory loss. The medical technicians that checked us over even carried out brain scans, and they were left just as confused at the loss of memory as I was. In the end, beyond far more intrusive testing, there was little else they could do but send us off to our rooms to get some sleep.

Four guards waited for us outside the medical room. They looked irritated at the duty they'd been given. Their manner was short and snappy, which automatically put me on edge as we were marched through the corridors of the small wall base.

I watched them all closely as we moved. My trust in the military was so damaged that I expected them at any minute to either try to kill us, or take the earliest opportunity to give us up. Be that to Commander Gullan or whoever was behind his attack on us.

Yet we made it to our rooms without trouble and without seeing anyone beyond the night time cleaners.

I bid goodnight to Lanris and entered the room allocated to me. It was basic but comfortable looking. A clean, gray carpet covered the floors. Two sofas arranged in an L-shape around a small coffee table greeted me first.

Beyond them, deeper into the room, a comfy looking, if typical military style, metal-framed bed filled most of the room, and a desk with the promised terminal sat waiting for me. Despite my fatigue, only one thing mattered right now: contacting Unara and Asala.

The problem with contacting Asala was that we were trying to reduce our ties to 360, and it was the middle of the night. I also desperately wanted to speak with Unara. Making my way over, I sat and eagerly accessed the contact screen.

I found the contact details for the main bar in the Prestige and hoped fate would be kind and that someone was in the bar working.

Empire of Oshbob

Fate was not just with me but practically jumped down my throat, as the moment the communication went through, Leo and Unara's face popped up on screen. They weren't in the Prestige either. They were sitting in the unit as if they'd been waiting for me to call.

My already confused mind began doing somersaults at the implications. Especially when they both *acted* surprised to see me. I knew them both well and their, "Oshbob! You're alive!" was not at all convincing.

"I am alive," I replied slowly. "Before we get into anything, this channel will be monitored."

Leo shook his head. "Not likely. I've got it well shielded."

"Which means we can talk freely," Unara added. "How are you feeling?"

"Not good. Soldiers from the base we were stationed at tried to kill us. When we escaped into a tunnel, they brought it down on us."

"We heard about the accident that caused your apparent death, though we neither believed it was an accident, nor that you were dead. Still, it must have been terrible for you." She was speaking so slowly that the entire conversation felt awkward.

I bit my tongue a little longer while she continued, but something was very wrong.

"Leo said you're in the city now in one of the wall bases. We'll send drones over to watch from a distance, and a couple of teams through the Undercity in case you need anyone. Do those who tried to kill you know you're alive?"

"Not that I know of, but who knows what's going on right now. I have no memories and nothing feels quite right. You two are acting odd for instance. Is everything okay?"

I focused on their faces, watching for some facial cue that something was wrong. None came.

"We're fine. What's most important is that we get the 360 legal team on the situation immediately. I assume you're going to want to go after those who did this?"

I shifted uncomfortably in the small chair and nodded. "Yeah. We'll definitely be going that route. I can't talk to anyone until I have legal counsel."

Leo looked off to one side for a moment, then back to me. "Done. They know to come to your location tomorrow."

"We have a few other contacts in the military now," Unara added. "Once we've spoken to them, they'll likely get involved. I'll also contact our friends in SEPCO too. Matters like this are usually in their jurisdiction after all."

I let my head drop into my hands and cradled it for a moment. *What the hell is going on?* I screamed mentally.

Unara interrupted my small breakdown. "We also know who's been coming after us. A company named Aspire. They're a big company that has targeted 360 in order to clean up its assets on their quest to become an elite corporation. We're making moves to nullify their attempts to take us down. It'll be good to get you back in the fold so that we can properly catch up. You should also know that one of your teammate's mother's is a city Commander. She had already been looking into the accident, and 360 has supplied her with a little outside assistance."

I slammed my hands down on the desk. "You've already spoken to Lanris's mother? What the hell is going on here? How are you so far ahead of me when you only learned I was alive a second ago? In the middle of the night as well!"

"It's okay, Oshbob. We heard about you going missing a couple of weeks ago, as did Commander Luasos. She had the power to start an investigation. We started looking into how we could get revenge on Aspire. We've been preparing, that's all. But you must be exhausted?"

"Exhausted doesn't come close. I'm missing most of my memories since the tunnel and now I appear back here only to be faced with an asshole who used to be my old sergeant and for some reason he's being helpful? You two are sitting there waiting for me to call, pretending you're surprised. I feel like I'm in the middle of a dream and I don't know if it's a good one or a fucking nightmare, but I'm leaning toward the latter."

"You're not dreaming," Unara said with a firm intensity. "But you need to do me a favor."

My eyes narrowed suspiciously. "Yeah."

"Trust me. Get some sleep. Get up at dawn, and be ready to tear Aspire a new asshole. It's not going to be easy. They're gonna come for you, and we're gonna upset a whole load of people. But stay strong, focus on how you were attacked, and most of all, *trust me*."

"I do trust you."

"Good. Now go get some sleep. We'll talk again tomorrow once everything is underway."

I felt empty and anxious as the conversation ended. Unara's words to trust her were ringing in my head. The fact that she had to push that idea so forcefully put me ill at ease.

But she was right. I was incredibly tired and things might not look so dark in the morning. Deciding that sleep probably was the best option, I dove onto the bed to find that it wasn't nearly as strong as it looked. It protested loudly with my carelessly thrown weight.

With all my troubles, and the noise from the bed rocking and creaking every time I shifted, I seriously doubted my ability to get to sleep. At one point, I considered dragging the mattress onto the floor, but before I summoned the energy, sleep must have taken me.

Sadly, that sleep was short-lived as I woke up to heavy breathing and lots of pain.

On instinct, I curled into a ball to protect myself, but found I remained exactly where I was, with my hands and feet tied to the bed frame. Amid the raining blows, I blinked the three times necessary to activate my night vision. The green glow of six figures came into view. Six rising and falling arms that brought what I could only guess were batons down on my body in a violent flurry.

It was at that point that I noticed they weren't hitting my face. Meaning this wasn't attempted murder. This was a warning.

That knowledge still didn't stop me desperately heaving at the bed frame. I knew it was a poor bed, and if I could just break free, I could return at least some of the punishment. Of course, if I did break free, you could bet your ass there'd be murder.

As the bed began to bend and give a little, my assailants stopped.

One of them leaned forward and spat in my face before he spoke. "Right, you fucker. Listen up and listen up good. Scum like you doesn't get to ruin the lives of good soldiers. The charges against Gullan? The APS? You fucking drop them, or next time we visit, you won't wake up."

I continued to pull at the bed posts while he spoke, trying to mask that I was straining by spitting back. The curse of being an orc meant that the shape of my mouth was all wrong for a decent spit projectile, and the pathetic effort landed on the bed next to me. I received a baton to my already broken ribs for my attempt.

It hurt bad, but I'd distracted them enough to bend the head and footboard of the bead further, and that final blow allowed me to put in an extra burst of strength as I feigned trying to cover up again.

The bed must have been hanging on by a thread now, but they clearly couldn't see what I'd managed to do through their own night vision.

The one who'd spoken before had more to say. "You tell everyone the tunnel was an accident and you get to see your service out. You press charges, then you'll be beaten *in* court before being beaten to death out of it."

Through the pain, I managed to force out a reply. "You really don't know who you're dealing with. Tell me one thing and I'll let you live. Who sent you? Gullan or Aspire themselves?"

He lunged down, thrusting his baton under my chin and pinning it against my throat. Then he leaned in. His breath smelled of cheap Aska and cigarettes. "We had orders not to break anything too badly, orc. But accidents happen and you're close to another accident."

I chose that moment to put all of my strength into breaking the bed again. Of course, it didn't shatter the way I would have wanted, with all hands and feet coming magically free. Not at all. The bed base dropped to the floor, my feet still trapped in place, but the headboard did come free. And in a stroke of luck, shitty Aska-breath had been leaning his weight on my throat which meant he fell forward on top of me as the bed dropped. Finally, I could return an attack, and I wasn't wasting the opportunity. I bit into his masked face with primal rage.

My right tusk buried deep into his cheek, and I got a mouthful of nose in my bite. Clamping on, I shook my head like a wild dog shaking a rat. But one close to its own size. Very ineffective as a killing technique, but a bloody and brutal warning for the rat to fuck off.

As I tore a chunk of this face away, he fell back screaming, and the others attacked with more ferocity. I brought the headboard forward over my head to use it as a shield against most of the baton strikes and using it to club anyone within range when the opportunity presented itself.

When the metal frame split in two, I roared out. "I'm an orc! I've killed A Rankers, fought a mech! You think an old bed frame is gonna hold me?"

As I spoke, I saw a heavy booted kick coming in at my head. With an awkward twist, I managed to get a solid connection with the metal bar against the inside of their knee and roared again as the owner of the knee fell to the floor screaming like a dropped baby.

The remaining four now backed off, and with that short reprieve, I kicked wildly at the bed frame holding my feet.

Realizing I was about to break free, they regrouped and charged in again. Too late for them at least as the cuffs holding my modded leg tore free, and I was mobile once again.

Bloody and with a few broken ribs that fought against me taking a full breath, I forced myself up to my feet under an onslaught of blows. I'd been through worse, and a few poxy humans, or elves judging from their body type, had no answer to my strength with clubs alone.

"Shoulda brought guns," I panted out, then clanged two pieces of bed frame together.

The idiots backed off, scrabbling back across the room and colliding with the sofas and coffee table in their blind retreat.

"I'll ask you again," I shouted after them. "Who sent you? Aspire or Gullan. Or was it someone else?"

One of them was close to the door now.

I sighed, though it came out more like a wheeze. "I will find out. Even if I have to break each and every one of you." I staggered forward toward the nearest opponent and led with an overhand right that was all about power over style.

I expected them to avoid the blow and have to use my momentum to take him down but they didn't. The sweet sound of a breaking neck and cracking skull rang out with the heavy thud, and they dropped. Dead before even hitting the floor.

Wasting no time, I stalked further forward. The three left were all in full panic now as they scrambled to open the door which appeared to be locked.

"Make sure you all protect your heads now. This is going to get very violent, but I need a few of you alive until I get my answers."

Before I could reach them, the door to my room burst open. The light was momentarily blinding to my dark vision as more shouting, more soldiers, and more violence entered the room. Thankfully, none of it was directed at me.

By the time I got my bearings, the three remaining attackers were down, convulsing on the floor. Stunners had clearly been the weapon of choice.

The room lights came on, and Captain Turner walked into the room looking around, furiously. When his eyes met mine, I saw shame. "I'm so sorry, sergeant. This should never have happened, and whoever is acting against you has made a grave error with this attack."

"How did they get in here?" I asked, wheezing heavily.

"Money changes hands, you know how it goes. While rules can be bent for better corporation-military relations, there are still lines, and the attempted killing of an entire scrub team and breaking into a protective custody in a military base… those lines have been crossed."

He pulled something from his uniform, and as he handed it over, I was very relieved to see that it was a medium Medi-Kit. I took it gratefully and almost immediately felt my lung function return to normal. Most of the aches and pains around my left knee and elbow eased too.

"We'll put you in another room and we'll post a guard. One I assign personally and whom I trust."

I shook my head. "Tomorrow night maybe. Just give a stim and another Medi-Kit. A small should finish off the healing."

Turner beckoned to one of his soldiers who provided both items. I took them greedily and felt like a new orc afterward, despite my ongoing confusion over my lack of memories.

Empire of Oshbob

Partition 43

Terese Sloan and Caleb Price arrived just after 6 AM. The two lawyers who'd helped me with my first legal battle in the military were back for more. I sat and waited for them in the private meeting room and felt a weight lift as they strode in with confidence.

Terese spoke first, "Sergeant Oshbob. It's a pleasure to see you again. You have a private named Lanris with you, is that correct?"

"It is. He had a rough night and he was sleeping when I came along."

"Understandable. But it would be better if he was here if we are to push this matter along quickly. We will be holding some video calls this morning with other interested parties, and his absence will be noted."

"That's fair. I'm certainly happy for him to be here," I replied. "I've been hanging around waiting to get started since around four, after the attack."

"Attack?" Caleb asked, leaning forward. "Last night? While you were here?"

"That's right. I still don't know who sent them, but they got in my room, kicked the shit out of me, and told me that I better not press charges against the soldiers of Outpost 361."

"I'll speak with Captain Turner about it, and ask for Lanris to be brought along, too."

As he sat back in his seat, his eyes losing focus, Terese continued. "An unprovoked attack like that should help the case greatly. Especially if it can be proven the men were paid by Aspire. They will still be punished of course, but we really need to direct everything at Aspire and their bribes, rather than focusing on the soldiers directly."

I shook my head. "I know this room's supposed to be private, but can people still hear us in here?"

"Absolutely. Once Lanris is here, we can set up a barrier which will protect us from unfriendly ears."

"Then I'll wait until that's in place to speak further."

She nodded her understanding. "A wise decision. While we wait, you should know that SEPCO has been informed of the situation and they are sending agents over to begin their investigation."

"Let's hope they do their job properly," I muttered, hoping Unara was able to pay them off. It wasn't even that we should need to pay them off, as the evidence against Aspire and Gullan was going to be pretty hard to refute, but if someone else got to them first, then they'd find a way to screw us over.

Around five minutes later, Lanris was led into the room. He looked fresh, but confused.

"Come, sit, Private Lanris," Terese said. "We're all on your side here, so you can relax."

I pointed to the chair next to me. "Come on, Lanris. Let's get this shit show moving again."

The moment he sat, Terese activated some kind of shield around us. It came from the end of her modded index finger, which she then removed and placed in the center of the table.

"That is a very nice bit of kit," I said appreciatively.

"Perks of the job, I suppose," she said with far less enthusiasm. "Now back to our earlier conversation. We think it's best to target Aspire, and in some regards, that is what we've agreed to with other military investors interested in this case. No one wants to see us going after soldiers. It will affect city morale. I also don't think you want to be a target of the military for years to come."

"I disagree. What all soldiers hate the most is soldier killers. If we can spin this up and make sure the shit sticks, we'll get way more support from the lower ranks, those not on a corpo payroll. They'll be outraged that a corporation can have them killed by other soldiers with a few creds. If we can prove it."

"Oh we can prove it." She turned to face Lanris. "Commander Luasos has already looked into the situation, and with the assistance of our cybersecurity team, we've pieced together enough evidence to show that you were hunted into the tunnel system and that those tunnels were forcefully dropped by military ordinance.

Empire of Oshbob

"We just need to move fast enough to prevent any retaliatory actions from Aspire. We're already ahead of the game, but we need no slip ups. Everyone must be following the same script. We want to spin this entirely on Aspire and how their growth ambitions have corrupted an honest and dependable cornerstone of our society. We want to paint the soldiers involved as victims in this wicked game too."

"Bah, you're right. Aspire is the goal, and I don't want to risk the attention being taken off them. I can take my own revenge on the soldiers at another time. Let's just get this done."

The two lawyers spoke more, baffling me with the wealth of knowledge they already had which led me to feel even more out of the loop with my own damn story. I stayed quiet for the most part, just confirming a few details here and there. That went on for close to half an hour until the display in the room came to life.

Terese dropped the barrier at that point and took on the telltale expression of someone speaking through her keystone.

A mean-looking, middle-aged human female appeared on the screen. Her perfectly straight blonde hair was cut down to her jawline and gave the impression of being a hair helmet.

She had piercing blue eyes that landed immediately on Lanris. Her sour little mouth broke into a relieved smile that completely changed her face. Going from a bitter little beige prune to a surprisingly warm and welcoming woman.

"It is so very good to see you, son. I have been ill with worry since I received news of your demise."

"Mother," Lanris replied softly. "It's good to see you too. Can you stop me from being reassigned back to that base?"

"By the time I'm finished, that base and all of its occupants will be unrecognizable. And you will still be nowhere near it." She turned to me, her stern, sour expression back on her face. "Sergeant Oshbob, it is entirely because of your presence that Commander Gullan came after your team."

"Mother!" Lanris protested.

"Yet I cannot find it in my heart to place any blame at your feet. The average life of a Scrub Team member is eight months. On that particular base, it was closer to five months. You managed to keep all of your team alive for well over a year against all the odds, and you even walked out of a certain death situation with my son alive.

So for that, I must thank you. And mark my words, while Aspire will suffer first and foremost for setting this up and taking advantage of our soldiers, heads from Outpost 361 will roll."

"That's good to hear, commander. And Lanris is an excellent soldier who had a huge impact in us all staying alive. We made a fine team."

She nodded, the pride clear in her eyes at the compliment for her son. "You honor us both in saying so. And I really do feel we are in a strong position to push this all the way and ensure that Aspire receives a very harsh punishment. Hopefully, it will send a powerful message to other corporations to remember that there are limits to their interference."

"That can only be a good thing," I agreed. "So what part are you able to play in all of this?"

"I'm leading the military side of the investigation. My findings will be taken into account, but obviously SEPCO will be overseeing the entire case, and they *will* be scanning both your minds. I hear you both suffered amnesia?"

"We did, yeah," I replied uncomfortably.

"We can't even remember how we got so close to the city!" Lanris butted in, with a higher-pitched voice than usual. "Honestly, it's so confusing."

"I'm sure it's nothing to worry about. When SEPCO gets here, they'll take your statements and run a memory scan of the event. Just focus on the events leading up to the event. Do not over talk about your amnesia as that came after and has very little bearing on our case."

Her words were too leading. She knew something, and I wasn't about to let it go. "This amnesia, do you know anything…"

Caleb butted in over me. "That's entirely correct, Commander Luasos. We must all focus on the event and what we're hoping to achieve here."

His interruption made the situation even worse for me. They all knew something I didn't while my life hung in the balance. I stood up and slammed my hands down on the table. "Listen. I didn't survive by being a gullible fool, something…"

Terese stood quickly, attempting to put her face in front of my own. She shouted unexpectedly, "Sergeant!"

I was both surprised and sorely tempted to rip her head off.

Empire of Oshbob

She took the moment in which I stalled to reactivate the privacy shield around us. "Nobody here thinks you are gullible. You have the utmost respect of everyone in this room. But this is a very sensitive time in our work here. You are right to be mistrustful after everything that has happened, along with your memory loss. Sadly, there are parts of this case, this situation, that we cannot tell you about for powerful reasons. Once you have had the mind scan, we can talk more, but until you're out of the military, things must remain unsaid. I must ask you, from the bottom of my heart, to trust us. We are here to help. Asala sent us. You know Unara and Leo are fully involved."

I clenched and unclenched my fists, then looked at Caleb, who offered a worried smile.

"We are genuinely here to help. You have good people around you so that you don't have to do everything alone. Trust them now when they ask you too. If we give you too much information on the case we're building, it could potentially be used against us. Do you understand?"

"No. That's the fucking point. But at least you're admitting something isn't right, which is an improvement. "

Caleb nodded and sat back down. "I mean, what's the worst that could happen? We turn on you? We say that nobody tried to kill you and you're making it all up? We wouldn't have to say that. It's what would happen if you didn't have us. They'd either string you up for the accusations, or they'd send you back to base to face your punishment there."

Rather than respond, I turned to Lanris. "What about you? You buying all this bullshit?"

He looked shaken but shrugged. "Like your lawyer just said. Without them, we'd be screwed."

After an hour of back and forth and filling in the blanks, two SEPCO agents were led in. I saw a flicker of irritation on both Terese and Caleb's faces as they entered.

If I had to guess, they weren't the agents they were expecting. Two male elves, one with black hair, the other with brown, they both looked uncomfortable as they walked in. I noticed Terese's eyes glaze over for a moment as she evidently communicated with someone.

"Sergeant Oshbob, Private Lanris, it's a pleasure to meet you both," Black hair said, ignoring the face of Commander Luasos and the two lawyers. "For today, you can call me Agent One, my partner will be Agent Two. We've heard so much about this case in such a short space of time. In all my years at SEPCO and the military before that, I've never known such a dramatic response to a case that seems fairly straightforward. Nor have I known so many high-ranking officers that have something to say on the matter. All for an orc gang lord, too."

"Still," Agent Two said. "It certainly sounds like an interesting pot of trouble we need to stir. I wonder what will float to the surface."

I offered no response, for what response was there to such a heap of steaming shit. He then warned the lawyers not to speak on my behalf as the first agent began his questioning.

"What have you both been doing since your deaths were reported from the tunnel collapse?"

It was a direct question, and it was also the worst question he could have asked. For some reason, I decided not to lean on the amnesia to start with. I certainly didn't trust these two guys, and their attitude so far told me that we were definitely not paying them.

"After surviving the attack from the APS in our mission squad," I said pointedly. "We focused on survival."

"Bold accusations to throw at your fellow soldiers," Agent Two said smugly.

I ignored him and continued. "Knowing we would only be killed if we headed straight back to our base, we had to travel south to find somewhere safer."

"And you ended up all the way back in Artem. That's quite the walk where the accident happened. Did you have any help getting here."

"I'd like to know the same thing, but we both suffered severe brain damage from the cave in. Luckily, we're orcs, and orcs keep going, no matter what. Little did we realize how far the corruption goes, and we were attacked again here."

"You were attacked here?" one replied, seeming genuinely surprised.

Empire of Oshbob

"In my room as I slept. They woke me with a beating and told me to drop all charges against the base soldiers."

"So they were concerned soldiers worrying for their brothers?" Agent Two asked with a puzzled look on his face.

"That, or they were paid," I replied with my own smile.

"More hearsay. You said amnesia, what do you remember of that time between getting trapped and *before* you arrived here."

I rubbed my chin thoughtfully. "It seems to me as if you already have an idea of how you want this to play out. How do I go about getting new agents from SEPCO who haven't been paid by Aspire?"

They both recoiled from my words.

Agent One was quickest to recover. "We don't take bribes and you don't get to choose the agents who investigate you, orc. We are carrying out this investigation, and it would serve you well to listen and do as you're asked. We can kill this case dead right now if we want to."

I laughed, though it held no humor. "It's Sergeant Oshbob, and I will be reporting that alongside everything else you have done in your handling of this case so far."

He ignored the threat and turned to Agent Two. "I think it's time we set up the Mind-Sweep, don't you? Let's get this debacle over and done with."

Agent Two nodded, and they both left the room.

As soon as the door closed, I eyed the two silent lawyers "I don't get a good feeling about this."

"Nor should you. You called it right. They were not unbiased SEPCO agents. But I've called my contact in their head office. I hope the situation can be saved. Though I suspect that is why they've gone to set up their equipment so soon. They'll know they're on borrowed time to find something against you."

"Can we stall?" Lanris asked as a knock came at the door.

"Come in," Terese shouted, and Captain Turner and a squad of armed men, eight in total, filed in.

"Good work on contacting SEPCO about those two agents. I've come to leave you a guard while you wait. After last night's disaster, I didn't want to take too many chances." He turned to face me directly. "These are guards I've handpicked from the base. I trust them, and they will keep you safe while you're here. Split up into two groups, each doing twelve-hour shifts. I should be able to keep both of you safe."

"Can I have a word in private please, Captain Turner?"

"Of course, sergeant, I'll just send my men out."

Once they'd left, I spoke quietly, "I'm sure those guys are good, but I don't know them, and after everything that's happened, I'd like people I know and trust to watch over me."

"We can't bring in outsiders," he replied quickly.

I chuckled. "Oh I'm not thinking of outsiders. I'm thinking of Maddock and Jacobs. They're still based in the city, right?"

With a deep sigh, he sagged, looking dead tired. "I'll see what I can do."

Empire of Oshbob

Partition 44

No more than an hour had passed before we were led into an identical room next door. Set up in the center of the space was the vaguely familiar Mind-Sweep machine that SEPCO had used on me before. Only this was far larger and had far more to it.

The SEPCO agents were arguing with Captain Turner and my lawyers about something as we entered.

"I won't tell you again, captain, the Mind-Sweep is private, for SEPCO use only. You must all leave the room while it is happening."

"You aren't scanning me unless my lawyers and a guard are present in the room at all times," I replied.

Booted heels from down the corridor caught all of our attention. I turned to see two more SEPCO agents walking toward us. They swept past me into the room without a word, and the atmosphere seemed to chill.

It was Agent One who spoke first. "Superior. Why are you here?"

The taller of the two men—a tall, broad-shouldered human with gray hair and a gray mustache—scowled. "That is quite simple," identifying himself as the Superior by answering. "There have been compelling questions raised about your handling of those involved in the case and exactly how this case was originally assigned to you both. You could say this is an investigation of the investigation."

Agent One gulped and looked over at Two then quickly looked away again. "We received a message this morning from headquarters to come here with all urgency and assess the situation."

"Very well. I see you have the Mind-Sweep set up in record time. It is barely 8 AM. Have you followed procedure and taken full statements from the accusers?"

"We tried," Two said. "But they were difficult."

"Very well then. The sooner we get the Mind-Sweep done, the sooner we can continue with the rest of our inquiries. Please continue."

The air was tense, but I felt it was tense in a way that very much favored me. I noticed that my lawyers and Turner seemed to have relaxed a little too.

With a nervous wave of his hand, Agent One gestured for me to take a seat in the machine while Two sat opposite me and fiddled with some dials. Parts of the machine moved around, beeped, and flashed until Two nodded to One satisfied.

"Okay then, Sergeant Oshbob. After the event which precipitated your being trapped in a tunnel, you were injured from the falling rocks. I want you to focus on that moment."

"I can't. Because to my knowledge, I wasn't damaged by the rocks, I was damaged by the guns, missiles, and fists of the APS troops we were supporting. I remember vividly when and how they turned on us and attacked. And I also remember the commands of Colonel Poulson. That might be of more use to you anyway as that's what we're here about. You do remember that I'm pressing charges against either Commander Gullan and everyone involved in the attack on us, or Aspire who put them in the position where they had no choice but to kill their fellow soldiers?"

"I am fully aware of my purpose here, and if I deem a subject to be important in this case, you will answer my questions pertaining to it." He sounded confident, but I could see in his nervous eyes which kept flickering out to the side where he was being watched that he was damn uncomfortable with the set up.

"And why do you feel that is more important than the event itself, Agent One? Should we need to ascertain the events after the alleged attack, they can be asked for later. Now please do your job properly and begin with either the attack or the events leading to the attack."

Agent One rubbed his forehead, and I saw him glance at Agent Two again. Fear passed between them. Agent Two nodded as if they'd communicated before Agent One turned back to the SEPCO Superior. "You're of senior rank. If you aren't happy with our methods, perhaps you should take over?"

"Perhaps I should. Now get out of here."

They both obliged happily.

Empire of Oshbob

"And report to Director Enlan about your inability to carry out a simple investigation," he said as they passed him.

Then the female SEPCO next to him spoke for the first time. "In fact, you two can wait here and watch how an investigation such as this should be carried out. Then I will escort you to Director Enlan personally and we can discuss this some more."

They both stopped in their tracks. I had no idea what was going on and if money had changed hands, but I knew for certain that if anyone wanted to help me, all they had to do was investigate the attack properly.

The SEPCO Superior sat down in front of me with a serious expression but a glint in his eyes. "Sergeant Oshbob. There's no reason this should be such an intimidating atmosphere. You are the victim and should be respected as such unless we uncover something in our work that suggests otherwise. For the purposes of this meeting, I am Agent Truth. Are you ready to begin?"

"Good to meet you, Agent Truth. And yes. I'm ready."

"Very well. Then we should probably start at the beginning of the mission. Can you cast your thoughts back to it?"

"You bet your ass I can."

With a little focus I thought back to us being called to action—the coldness of the other soldiers in the hanger and the dour atmosphere hanging over the entire event. I went on to replay the whole ordeal in my mind as slowly as I could, trying to make sure I didn't miss a thing. Remembering Agga and Froom's deaths and their broken bodies in such forced details hit me harder than I expected, but I powered through until the cave in.

When I was finished, I felt exhausted, but Agent Truth seemed content. He offered me a sad smile and leaned forward to pat me on the shoulder. "That is more than enough to begin with. And I'm sorry for your loss. The emotion you felt at the betrayal and the loss of your friends and teammates is obvious. Providing Lanris's memories align to prove that there has been no tampering, we can move on swiftly with the charges against Commander Gullan and those involved with the assault. From there, we can look at *why* they came after you."

I was surprised at how fast the whole thing went in the end. The Superior wasn't pushy, nor did he show any interest in digging beyond the event. I was led out of the room by two of the men Turner had assigned me and led back to another room.

My room was easy to spot because it already had two guards standing outside.

"Well would you look who it is! The big green bastard, in trouble as always."

"What are you doing here, Maddock? You useless sack of shit." I was surprised to see he too now wore a sergeant's insignia. Behind him stood a grinning Jacobs with a corporal's insignia.

"Apparently, some wimpy half-orc, maybe even a quarter-orc, has been having night terrors, so we've come to tuck him in and tell him a bedtime story."

"Good one, you asshole. I can't actually believe they let your dumb useless ass become sergeant."

"I damn well earned this rank, unlike you who got it as part of some kind of equality drive."

"Is that the one where everyone's trying to kill me?"

"Yep," he said, snapping his fingers together and pointing at me. "That's exactly the one."

"Well it's good to see you both, and thanks for coming. I mean it and I won't forget it."

"We didn't have any fucking choice?" Maddock grumbled.

Jacobs elbowed him. "We both really wanted to come. And we have a good team with us. Turner checked them all out before they could come here to help, but we'd both personally vouch for them. No corpo skivvies among them, and if they get any offers while they're here, I've told them to tell me and that you'd match whatever they were offered."

My instant reaction to that was to take offense. Greedy bastards. But my more pragmatic side took over, and it would be money well spent.

I lowered my voice and spoke quickly. "Tell them I'll give them all 10k each as a sweetener." Then I spoke normally. "It's good to see you, old friend. I hope you're keeping this fool in line."

"10 fucking K!" Maddock screeched, completely blowing the effort I'd made at subtlety. "I hope me and Jacobs are included in that. I'm trying to keep him in line, but I'd have better luck getting a nest of drunken goblins to read Talette."

"Talette?" I asked, confused. Maddock laughed as if he knew what Jacobs was talking about.

"He's a famous Artem Philosopher," Jacobs replied.

"Philosopher, Oshbob. Keep up, man," Maddock added.

"You can tell me all about it inside," I said, pointing at the door. "Hopefully over a drink."

"We're on duty. We can't drink," Jacobs said to a snort of derision from Maddock. I could predict how the next hour would go.

As Jacobs finished his second glass of beer to Maddock's fifth. News came to my room. Lanris's story checked out the same as my own, and SEPCO was now moving ahead with charges and arrests against Gullan and Poulson first.

I felt an unusual wave of nerves at the news, though I was relieved things were moving along in the right direction.

"Right, you two. Unfortunately I'll need to kick you out while I speak with my people, and you really don't want to hear all the details or you'll end up embroiled in this clusterfuck alongside me."

Jacobs jumped up. "Yep. While I wish you the best and I'm happy to guard you, I definitely don't want to be too heavily tied to this."

Maddock groaned on the sofa. "If it means I get to sit on this sofa instead of standing at the door, I'll happily be embroiled."

Jacobs kicked him. "Come on, sergeant. Out you get."

"But I need a piss!"

"Nip it until I'm done with the call. I'll be more than happy for you both to come back in and guard from in here once I'm done."

Maddock grudgingly got up and left, leaving me in a surprisingly good mood as I contacted Leo and Unara. It took a little longer for them to answer this time, and when they did, only Unara sat there in view, holding a finger up for me to remain silent.

Finally, Leo popped on the screen. "Sorry, Oshbob, someone had hacked our secure connection. A lot of work went into breaking my code to access the line."

"How did you kick them out so quickly?" I asked. Though, I wasn't sure if I cared for an answer.

Leo laughed. "The simple answer? I swapped over to another secure connection I already had in place. I have ten more set up, so we can hop from one to another as they break them down, though it won't be easy for them."

I nodded appreciatively, having no idea how much effort all that was to set up, but glad someone knew what they were doing. "I'm just calling to say that the mind scans have been completed and SEPCO have moved on to Gullan now. I suppose it's just a waiting game to see what happens. Have you guys heard anything from Aspire?"

"Something like that," Unara said with a menacing grin. "We have them on the ropes across Turan and Newton now. All the properties they bought are useless to them as we've stopped all of their building work. Closed the businesses they'd already got up and running, and we're actively preventing any new businesses opening up."

"Really? I knew Kenneth was playing ball, but how is Burrell taking our interference on his turf?"

I caught the uncomfortable look that passed between them as Unara answered. "That's something I needed to talk to you about. To fight against Aspire, we needed 360 to grow openly and visibly into those districts. To do that, we needed to control Newton and Turan fully. Kenneth came onboard willingly, knowing very little would change for him, and if anything, he'd benefit from more protection and better opportunities. Burrel, however, we didn't give a choice. He's dead, and Turan is ours."

"You attacked?" I asked gobsmacked. It was always supposed to be me who killed Burrel, but I did the simple math in my mind. They needed to grow in power and I was presumed dead. I held up my hand to stop Unara trying to explain. "Excellent work. I'd have loved to see the bastard suffer under my own hands, but it would be stupid to hold off just for that."

Both Unara and Leo nodded with surprised but relieved smiles on their faces.

"But," I said, locking them both with a serious expression. "When I get out of here, you'll tell me *everything*. Every last detail."

"Don't worry," Unara said, matching my seriousness. "You're right to be suspicious. I'd be worried about you if you weren't. But

I can promise you with certainty that both 360 and our entire underworld family are doing everything they can to free you. Once you're out, you'll understand everything."

"I can't ask more than that."

Kevin Sinclair

Partition 45

The next few days, I heard very little of what was going on. Most of that was through my daily chats with Unara, though she was still waiting for solid news from SEPCO. I heard the same from the lawyers and Lanris's mother.

It was a waiting game, and it was tense. So I spent most of my time drinking with Lanris, Maddock, and Jacobs. A few of their men joined us when they weren't on duty, and as Jacobs had said, they were all good men. They even had two half-orcs on their squad. Something Maddocks openly admitted he would have complained about if not for his time with me.

Three days after SEPCO arrested Commander Gullan, we finally received news, and it was not great. Unara was the first to let me know, calling the terminal in my room.

"Aspire has been accused, and apparently, it was almost a done deal. Proven beyond doubt that they tried to have you killed by paying people in the military. But Aspire called into question SEPCO's integrity with the Artem City High council. The High Council had to act on Aspire's proof which means this now has to go through them. Don't worry too much. We have people we can rely on within the court system, but SEPCO is done with this now beyond providing evidence."

"Fuck!" I roared, throwing my glass against the wall in an uncharacteristic act of frustration. "The damn worms. How did they prove we were paying SEPCO?"

"Oh they didn't. They couldn't as we haven't yet. We expected something like this so to avoid any corruption trails, only verbal agreements have been made. Certain people have guarantees from us that they'll be looked after in the future. The only way they could prove SEPCO were corrupt in such a short time-span... and you're not going to believe this, but they outed their own contacts!"

"And the High Council bought that?

"I know. It sounds stupid, but what choice do they have?"

As speechless as I was at the audacity of Aspire, part of me was impressed. "So what now?"

"From what we've heard, they intend to move you tomorrow morning at dawn to the protective custody at the courthouse. Asala is speaking to one of our contacts there, and you'll be protected properly."

"I'm sure I will, but I'm not going anywhere without my current guard. Will you let whoever needs to know that Maddock's team will be coming with me. I'll let Turner know when he comes with the news."

"Good idea. We'll be ready to follow your transport as well. We'll have drones in the air watching you. We'll have our AVs ready to move if anything happens, and we'll have the Undercity over there teaming with goblins."

"We have AVs?" I asked. For some reason, that was what caught my attention.

She laughed. "360 do. But for this, I'm willing to take a few for personal use."

"That's good to know. I doubt much'll happen over the city, but it's good to know you're prepared."

"We are, and we still think it'll be a breeze in court. All they're doing is stalling for time and hoping they can find a way to wriggle out of this."

"And they're very good at wriggling," I replied.

Around an hour after Unara spoke to me, Captain Turner appeared at my room to give me the news. If in a slightly altered format.

"I just heard from my commander that you have to go to court with this one. SEPCO can't get it over the line themselves. There's been a transport organized for you in the morning, so get some sleep and prepare yourself. They're a different breed near the center, and if you don't have your wits about you, they'll eat you alive."

"If I'm moving, I want to take Maddock's team with me for continued protection."

He winced at my words. "I honestly don't think that'll be possible, sergeant. I'll ask around and try to arrange it for you, but I can't promise anything."

"Just do what you can please, captain. We both know how easy it is for the wrong people to get close to me."

"That we do, sergeant. That we do."

I didn't hear from anyone else for the rest of the day. It seemed everyone was busy trying to keep up with the changes happening around me. I felt about as lost and as powerless as I ever had as I sat there. I contacted Unara, but she was so busy organizing and trying to speak with people we needed to speak to that it was fruitless. Terese and Caleb, the lawyers, were knee-deep in paperwork, and Turner had disappeared from the base.

All I could do to help myself was to try and get Maddock, Jacobs, and their team to escort me to the court house. They agreed if they were allowed, and I couldn't really ask for more than that.

Later that night there was a knock at the door. "Captain Turner here to see you, sir!" one of the guards shouted in.

"Let him in, then," I shouted back.

Moments later, Turner strode into the center of the room, He looked angry, then saw Maddock passed out on the couch and looked disappointed before he finally settled on defeated. His shoulders sagged as he met my eyes.

"I just received a message from the region commander that we need to move you tonight. His exact words were: So much noise had been made about moving him in the morning, if anyone wants to take him out, they'll know exactly where and when."

I eyed Turner carefully. This was either a setup or a genuine attempt to avoid trouble. He'd been so helpful this far, and I felt like he was on my side, but I'd been wrong before. "What do you think about that, captain?"

"I think it makes sense."

I could tell from his body language that he hadn't finished. He was just working out how to say what he wanted. Probably in a way that wouldn't get him in trouble. He proved me right a moment later.

"I suggested that you be escorted by more AVs and more armed men. That was declined for legal reasons. Apparently, we can't have too many military craft flying above the city at one time unless proper notice is given through the correct channels. I also put forth the idea of you taking Maddock's squad. That was also refused. They are not courthouse guards, and they have their own duties to take care of. He suggested you should show more faith in the people trying to protect you." He gave a tired laugh as he spoke those last words.

"So it's a setup?"

"I honestly don't know, Oshbob. Nothing he said was unreasonable. It could be me just being paranoid."

"When do they expect me to travel?"

"Now."

I laughed. "Of course they do. I'll just need to let Unara know I'm moving first."

"I've been told you are not to tell anyone or it might give us away. Your Terminal has been disconnected."

I eyed him dangerously and he read it well.

"It has nothing to do with me. I'm just the bearer of bad news, I promise."

"Then help me out. Let me contact them from somewhere else?"

"I can't. We're being watched."

"Listened to?"

"Not in here. I made sure of it after the first attack on you. Ah shit," he said, seeming to decide something. He turned to Jacobs and Maddock. "I just changed the guard on the door and sent your men back to their rooms. The two guards with me are to escort us to the courthouse. You two need to go and rouse your men. Armor up and get on that AV. Move quickly and stop the pilot from communicating your presence. Be civil if you can. Just tell him you're checking for something. You have ten minutes and then we'll be along."

"Checking for what?" Maddock asked, looking like Turner had just shat in his beer.

Jacobs grabbed his arm. "We'll work it out, Sarge. Come on."

I watched them leave, wondering just what Turner had in mind. "Are you supposed to be coming?"

"I am, yes. Which is why I don't think anything will happen. I'm also certain you won't be harmed in the courthouse. But I want to be certain. Now talk to me and shout a little. Wave your arms about. We need to stall for ten minutes."

It wasn't hard to fake. I argued against going till morning. I argued that I should be able to contact Unara.

After a few minutes, Turner held up a finger. "My commander is on my keystone." His eyes glossed over.

He was unfocused for about a minute before he was back with as much anger as when he first entered.

"We need to go now. Or I have to bring the guards in."

"That's alright, isn't it?" I snapped back in a ferocious snarl for the show we were putting on.

"Not ideal. I'll hold off for another couple of minutes then bring them in. You can argue with them for a bit as well. I can't order them to hurt you because you're a witness."

"What did you tell him about Jacobs and Maddock leaving?"

"Just that I sent them away, and they weren't needed anymore."

"Fair," I mused. "How long have we got left?"

"Five minutes, but I'm hoping Maddock contacts me soon so that we can get moving."

"What happens if I actually refuse?"

"Tranquilizers," he said simply. "When a regional commander gives an order, it's expected to be followed." Lowering his voice to a murmur, he added, "I have stims on me. I can bring you back quickly."

"And you're sure I can't speak to Commander Luasos or anyone else?"

"My commander is of a similar level. She'd have no power against him, and if I went to her, I'd be in more trouble than you can imagine. I'm gonna have to call the guards in now, okay?"

I nodded mutely and he yelled. "Guards! Our guest needs some persuasion to leave."

The two guards were human. Big and mean, for humans at least.

Turner spoke again, "Don't make me have them drag you, sergeant."

"I'd absolutely love to see them try."

It seemed they'd both like that as well, as they both pulled out dart guns.

Empire of Oshbob

"Like that, is it?" I sneered. "At least you're not delusional. Definitely stupid, though. You hit me with those and I'll make sure you go down with Aspire."

And they shot.

I was so surprised that they actually did it that I stood rooted to the spot for a moment. Then the red descended and charged forward, leaping at them. I didn't go quite as far as I should have, but it was enough to catch the one on the right with a glancing right hand as he backpedaled.

I kept going, though I felt as though I was walking through knee-deep mud. The one not lying on the floor had managed to reload and shot me again.

I heard Turner speak, though it sounded like he was a hundred meters away now. "Sorry, Oshbob."

I turned to see him shooting me with a tranquilizer too.

Another bit me from the guard on the floor. They were on three sides of me now. Too far away to reach in one step. But if I was to kill anyone, it would be Turner. After everything, the bastard had betrayed me. I lunged at him, was shot twice more, tripped over my own feet, then clattered to the floor in a pile of numb misery.

Blackness fell over me like a wet blanket.

I sat bolt upright, gasping. My first instinct was to attack the nearest body to me. It was a similarly groggy Lanris. Harsh laughter seemed to fill my fuzzy mind.

"You're one angry son of a bitch, Oshie."

It was Maddock. I'd recognize that voice anywhere. Slowly, I took in my surroundings. Maddock's full team sat around me, looking worried.

Turner was there too. He offered an uneasy smile. "I told you I'd get you back with stims."

"You didn't tell me you'd fucking shoot me, though. I thought..." My eyes fell on the two unconscious guards tied up at the back of the room we were in. No. Not a room. The back of an AV. I nodded my thanks to Turner. "So what happens now? Is the pilot onboard?"

"Pilot's unconscious too. Jacobs is flying," Maddock said.

"Is he flying the same route the pilot had?" I asked, getting uncertainly to my feet. It was a weird feeling to have wooden legs and arms and a heart that was fluttering like a tarp in a hurricane.

"He's not. We're taking a different route," Turner said, then clutched at his chest and bent over. "Damn, Oshbob, this has gotta be the most stressed I've been since I joined the military."

"That bad, huh?" I asked, pretending that I gave a shit about his troubles.

"Yeah. You wouldn't believe how many death threats I've received from all kinds of people, all tied to Aspire one way or another."

"Death threats? Not money?"

"Oh the money came first, but I don't take bribes."

"You what?" Maddock asked bewildered.

"My family is most likely richer than Aspire. They wouldn't be impressed with me taking bribes from other corporations for whatever reason."

"How rich? Who the fuck are your family?" Maddock squawked.

"They're pretty well situated in Takemoto," he said casually. Then he looked at me. "Before you ask, no, I can't get in touch with them. Surviving military service is a test. If I can't do it, then I'm no good to them."

"That's sucky as hell!" Maddock replied. "All that money and you're stuck doing this shit. How come you started as a sergeant with us if you have so much money?"

"We have to start at the bottom," he said with a slight red hue on his cheeks marking his embarrassment.

"Let me guess," I grunted in amusement. "You considered squad sergeant the bottom?"

He let out a long-suffering sigh. "You're both still as big a pair of assholes as you were when I left you."

Maddock snorted. "I think you'll find I'm much worse now that I'm a sergeant."

"Me too," I agreed. "Now how long does it take to get to the courthouse on our new route?"

"Half an hour. It's on the far side of Central District and there's a speed limit over most of the inner city. Can't be having any accidents in the fancy parts, you know."

Empire of Oshbob

"I can only imagine," I replied sourly and turned to check on Jacobs.

Pushing through the cabin door, I saw the corporal in the pilot's seat looking tense. There was a copilot's chair that I sat down in. "Everything okay?"

"There's stuff flying about all over," he grumbled, his eyes darting about nervously. "So far, no one's tried to attack us, but I really couldn't tell friend from foe anyway."

I looked out through the windscreen into the neon-filled landscape ahead. He was right. There were thousands of other vehicles in the air from taxis to transport vans.

"I'll stay with you and help keep an eye out while you drive."

"Thanks. Appreciate it," he muttered.

"Can I contact anyone from here?" I asked, looking over the panel. "I need to get in touch with my people."

"Sure if you know their calling signature."

I didn't, but I hoped I could work something out and reach the Prestige from the basic interface. Minutes later, I was still looking for a way to search available business premises. It seemed, much like how the military keystones prevented free communication access outside of the military, so did their AV systems.

"No luck?" Jacobs asked.

"None. They really don't want us communicating outside the military, do they?"

"No, but let me have a look, I might be able to..."

The cockpit went dark and Jacobs screamed as the AV suddenly dropped. There was commotion from behind us and the door opened behind us.

Maddock's terrified voice burst through. "What the hell's going on!"

My stomach lurched again as we came to an abrupt stop. It didn't feel like we'd crashed and we definitely hadn't regained power. Everything outside was black, and I could barely see my hand in front of my face. I was about to activate night vision when the lights came on.

A voice came over the cockpits internal comm. "The catch was a success despite your change of course, and the AV remains undamaged. Have the orcs brought out quickly. We don't have much time."

We all gawked at each other.

"Catch?" Jacobs said in a whisper.

Turner was at the door now. "Who was that?" What's going on?"

"That was our captors," I replied calmly. "They're waiting for those guards to take me out."

"What do we do then?" Maddock asked, looking at me rather than Turner.

I thought quickly over our options. They were painfully limited. "I guess Aspire has us, but I have no idea what's happening out there. I'm gonna hazard a guess that they don't know you're all in here. So here's the plan. Cuff our hands but don't lock them, then have two of your men that are unlikely to be recognized, escort us out."

"Then what?" Turner asked.

"I have no fucking idea Turner. I just told you, I don't know what's happening out there any better than you do, but this gives us the element of surprise. Be ready for anything. If a fight kicks off I expect you all to join in quickly."

The voice came over the comm again, angry, and urgent. "What's going on in there? Get out here now!"

Turner ran over to the comm. "Prisoner is still groggy from the tranq, but we're coming." He then turned back to the other soldiers. "All of you in the cockpit now."

"Except you two," Maddock added to two of his men. "You take them both out but be ready with those guns."

"Yes, sir!" they both snapped with impressive confidence.

"Anyone got a spare handgun?" I asked.

Maddock passed his over happily. "Not like you need it," he said seriously as I stuffed it into the inside pocket of my overalls.

Seeing my plan, Lanris looked around hopefully.

Turner was quickest to react, passing his handgun over. "As soon as we're all in the cockpit, I'll lower the ramp. Get ready."

Empire of Oshbob

Partition 46

As the ramp lowered, a bright, white room came into view. It was clearly the inside of a very large cargo transporter. Only, this vehicle contained our AV on a giant but steadily deflating airbag, and around forty soldiers. They were fully covered in sleek, black armor, including their helmets which sported black tinted visors.

On the right pectoral segment of each of the soldiers was emblazoned a golden triangle with a blue ocean wave logo. My first look at Aspire's logo, and I really hoped it would be my last. They stood like statues with high-quality pulse rifles all pointing at Lanris and me.

"Sergeant Oshbob! Come forward please," a voice said.

I followed the sound of it to see an elf with the blue body armor and a golden cloak through the mass of bodies between us. All the soldiers took a step to one side, split down the middle to create a narrow walkway, giving me a better view of the elf. His golden hair and bright green eyes seemed to shimmer and sparkle. If I had any doubts about whether I wanted to kill the bastard, his aesthetically enhanced eyes and hair sealed the deal.

"We have much to speak of and limited time in which to do so if we are to remedy this situation without great cost to both parties. So please, come and sit." He gestured to a table behind him then went to sit at it himself.

"So you aren't intending to murder me this time?" I asked, not moving.

He put his hand on his chest, a look of mock offense on his smooth features. "I wouldn't dream of it. I merely wish to talk. You and your friends have been far more industrious than I would have thought possible. You have both my respect and my regret that we didn't choose an easier target. Now I wish to try and fix the situation."

"Why us?" I asked, remaining where I was.

"We use a highly reputable information broker to choose our targets, and so far, the Inside Eye have never failed us. Until your band of misfits. The message was clear: Portolans and surrounding districts are prime for the taking, and Portolans 360 is little more than a cover for a small crime organization with a lot of property. Kill the orc and the half-goblin, *who nobody will miss*, and the company will fall. I feel they undersold us on this one."

"I think you're right," I agreed. "But don't worry. Once we've taken Aspire down, we'll take out the Inside Eye as well."

"Come on, Sergeant Oshbob. Come and sit for a moment while we discuss another avenue for us to walk down."

"Not happening. You fuck with us, you pay the price."

"Ah. Effa will be heartbroken to hear that, with him being implicit in assisting with the desertion of two Artem military members—Specialists Nozz and Theta, who we are currently transporting to the trial. I will let them all know of your decision."

The news that those two had survived hit me like a wave of relief and joy. I wondered how we'd managed to lose them on our way back to the city. It wasn't like me to leave friends behind. More importantly, how Effa was mixed up with them. The questions and confusion piled up in my head.

"What did you want to talk about," I finally said, heading through the corridor of armed bodies.

He didn't reply until I pulled out the plastic chair, eyed it dubiously then sat on it gently. To my surprise, it held my weight without objection.

"My name is Premier Ullaxin, director of Aspire military affairs. It appears to me that the situation has gotten out of hand within the military, and we need to resolve the issues between us."

"Resolve the issues?" I asked sourly. "Go on then. Tell me what that looks like."

He smiled eagerly. "Of course! Drop the charges against Aspire and we will pull out of your district, never to return. You can have your friends back and they can continue with their intended desertion. We will not say a word. After that, we can go our separate ways and pretend none of this ever happened. We have plenty of other targets to pursue."

Bullshit, was the word that popped into my mind immediately. This whole thing just showed how desperate they were. If they did really hold Theta and Nozz, which I had no reason to doubt, they'd punish me and sell them both down the river the moment I dropped the charges.

If they didn't do it immediately, this prick would forever hold their lives in the balance and that wasn't a place I wanted my friends to be. Better to push the narrative that they were trying to protect themselves against those who'd attacked us. And have them rejoin a safer military once we'd fucked Aspire over. The only question was, how did we get out of this mess alive? For that, I'd need the three of them where I could see them.

"Nice try, Ullaxin. Theta and Nozz died in the attack. D'you think I'm an idiot?" I finally replied.

My ruse worked better than I'd expected as he clicked his fingers above his head. Moments later, Effa, Theta, and Nozz were led out in handcuffs.

When I turned back to Ullaxin, he grinned at me like he'd won a huge victory. "What do you say now?"

I met Effa's eyes and he shrugged apologetically.

"I'd say send them on to the military AV first and I'll drop the charges," I lied.

He laughed, though his face held no mirth. "Oh no. I don't think so, orc. I may have underestimated you before, but that won't be happening again. I'll put you through to SEPCO headquarters and you can drop the charges officially. *Then* you can have your friends and toddle off back to any base you like."

"And what's stopping you from screwing us all over once I make the call?"

He offered a carefree shrug. "You can always renege on your decision. It will be a little awkward for you, but it's in our best interests to behave."

Or you'll kill me, I thought as he finished speaking. "Okay then. Make the call."

I could feel Lanris's shocked eyes on me.

Then Theta shouted over. "Don't do it Sergeant. Don't worry about us. Take them down while you—"

The guard with her sent a savage right hand across her jaw to silence her. My anger exploded in me, and I had to fight all my instincts to keep it penned in.

"Take them out while we do this!" Ullaxin barked to the guards with them.

"No," I snapped. "If I can't see them, then I don't make the call. They'll remain quiet from now on. Won't you?" I shouted over at the three of them. "Shouting isn't going to help us now!"

Ullaxin nodded for the soldiers to remain where they were and picked up a hand-held comm from the table. He messed with it for a moment, then handed it to me.

"Make sure to drop all charges," he warned as I took it.

"SEPCO central. How can I assist this evening?"

"Hey there. My name is Sergeant Oshbob, and I need to speak to whoever is handling my case. They only gave their name as Agent Truth, but I know they were a Superior."

"Just a moment. Pulling up your records now... Ah yes. I see you on file. Passing you through now."

I waited for a moment before the familiar male voice of Agent Truth came over the speaker.

"Sergeant Oshbob?" he asked, sounding very confused. "It's very late."

"Hello, Agent Truth. I'm on my way to the courthouse now, but I've had a change of heart."

His voice darkened but remained calm and steady. "A change of heart? At this stage of the game, sergeant. There are a lot of people invested in the outcome of this case. You might want to reconsider."

Ullaxin pulled out a gun and aimed it at Theta with a sinister smile. I loved Theta like a sister... and I trusted her to survive. I'd made my decision.

"You misunderstand, Agent Truth, a few of my teammates have been recovered by Aspire, and Premier Ullaxin, their military leader, is currently threatening me mid-air with their lives."

Ullaxin gaped in disbelief.

"I just wanted you to know that if I die, or Specialists Theta and Nozz die, then it is entirely..."

Ullaxin roared in rage and shot at Theta. He didn't even wait to see if it hit her as he swung on me. I saw her dive out the way, though she still took a hit on the shoulder before landing heavily on the floor.

Empire of Oshbob

I shook the handcuffs free and battered Ullaxin's gun from his hands as he roared, "Kill them all!"

Lanris swept up the table into Ullaxin, knocking him over. He then dove over the table for cover as he pulled out the handgun. I did something similar, but I grabbed Ullaxin as a shield as the soldiers began to fire. They weren't alone.

From our AV, Turner and Maddock's squad opened fire on the soldiers. The soldiers all had their backs to my friends as they focused on us. It didn't take them long to realize they were being targeted from behind, but they lost a lot of people quickly.

Continuing to use the screaming Ullaxin as a shield, I looked over to Effa and the others. They'd killed the guards with them and managed to hide behind the loading bay control panel. I saw Effa, bleeding badly, reaching out to grab the leg of one of the dead guards, dragging them behind cover with them.

Satisfied, I pulled out Maddock's handgun and began to fire back.

I made three shots of questionable effectiveness when everything changed. The roof of the transporter we were on was blasted open, knocking all of the soldiers, friend and foe alike, from their feet.

Even crouched on the floor, Lanris, the table, and me holding Ullaxin were blown backward. Ullaxin managed to free an arm in the commotion and hit something on his hip, and an electric pulse blasted out from the armor.

I locked up for a second, and in that moment of weakness, Ullaxin broke free. I expected him to attack me, but he just ran from the room with his tail between his legs, shouting something indecipherable.

He wasn't the only one shouting as I turned back to the newly formed hole above us. Soldiers were jumping down, dressed in sleek armor not too dissimilar from that which the Aspire soldiers wore. Only theirs was dark green with a red circle as their insignia.

At that moment, I didn't care who they were as they were killing the Aspire soldiers with intensity. *The enemy of my enemy was my friend*, I thought before the biggest armored figure I'd seen yet ran over to me carrying an impressive-looking war hammer that might very well spell the end for me if he could use it.

I scrambled to my feet, tossing the handgun and setting myself to grapple. But the big soldier tossed the hammer to me. By the time I caught it, he had lifted his visor.

"Wolski?" I asked with disbelief.

"You bet your ass it's me. Careful with the thumb activation on the side. Just tap it for extra power in your swing. Got it?"

I gestured all around us. "There's no one left to kill. And where the hell did you get this from?"

"It's yours. Don't worry about where we got it from. And there's plenty left to kill," he said, waving a medium Medi-Kit in front of my face before jabbing me with it. "There's more Aspire AVs around us, and they're taking this ship down. They own this part of the city we're over."

The smart orc in me wanted to break free and go to the courthouse for vengeance. But my orc blood boiled for the old-fashioned kind. "How long till we land?"

"In about one minute," a menacing voice said at my shoulder.

"Unara!" I shouted with joy as she appeared as if from nowhere at my side.

She wore green armor too, though hers was lightweight compared to everyone else's, and it was mostly covered by her stealth cloak. In her hands she held a section of body armor and a helmet that I guessed were for me.

"How did you find us?"

"We've never lost you," she said, thrusting the body armor panel into my hands. I slipped it over my head and she handed me the helmet which I put straight on.

"Now get ready to use that hammer, because there are a lot more soldiers on the ground."

"Sounds like a good way to spend the evening with old friends," I replied, gripping the haft of my new weapon tightly.

Seconds later, the ship landed heavily. It was almost as if the pilot was in a hurry. Through the hole in the transporter's roof, we could see we were inside a large building. The back door of the transporter began to open before a few of our soldiers shot at the hydraulic hinges.

Unara seemed to be concentrating on something. I could only assume a message via keystone. So I waited patiently for her to give us some direction. While we waited, Theta, Nozz, and Effa all made their way over to us.

"Sorry I got caught," Effa said about as awkwardly as I'd ever heard him say anything.

"It wasn't your fault," Theta snapped. "It was…"

"Hold it," Wolski shouted over them. "We can keep the crap shoot until after we kill every Aspire soldier put in front of us."

I wanted to hear more. Like how the hell Effa was with the two of them in the first place, but Wolski was right. We had more important stuff to be getting on. Unara was speaking again.

"Okay, everyone!" she shouted across the cargo hold above the sound of intense gunfire and outside. "We have around five hundred Aspire soldiers out there, and they're all ready for a fight. They outnumber us two to one and our AVs are outnumbered in the air. For now. They also have a state-of-the-art security system in here which Leo is attempting to bring down now. That's what we're waiting on, so everyone get ready, and if they breach that door, unleash hell on them. Otherwise, we wait until my command. And I want to see carnage out there. If it's wearing a golden triangle insignia, it dies, plain and simple. You all ready?"

A roar of affirmation came back. Everyone looked pumped.

I was less enthusiastic and leaned forward. "Are we really that outnumbered?"

Unara looked up at me, grinned then whispered. "No one counts goblins, right?"

My eyes widened and so did my smile. "How many?" I whispered back.

"Who knows with them lot. Bagri keeps telling me there's around four thousand fighting goblins, but Leo's made an attempt at counting them and he reckons closer to nine thousand. Only half that number are here though. We need to keep our own streets safe, and they all have jobs… mostly."

"Shit," Lanris murmured. "I don't think I've seen so many goblins before."

Wolski snorted and Unara glared daggers at him. Everyone else just looked confused.

Turner and Maddock's squad came sidling over, around the green-armored soldiers of 360 to stand with us at the back.

"These all your people?" Maddock asked.

"Sure are." I clamped a hand on his shoulder and met his eyes. "Golden triangle only. If you see any goblins, do not shoot. You hear me all of you?" I said, raising my eyes to take them all in.

"Yes sir!" all but Turner replied. He did offer me a respectful nod, though.

Partition 47

"Security is down!" Unara yelled at the top of her voice. "Go, go, go."

Two simultaneous explosions rocked the transporter ship, and it took me a moment to realize that they were the charges we'd placed on either side of the door.

The door itself dropped outside, and then we were pouring out.

We were outnumbered, that much was clear to see, but once they all had their attention on us, around a hundred heavy-duty attack drones came in through the windows. I rejoiced at their arrival for a moment until around four hundred of Aspire's attack drones entered.

Within seconds our front ranks were pinned down, and I ended up asking myself, *Why the hell am I at the back?* I activated the visor and strode through our people to the front. Unara followed behind me like she always did, and when I was shot in the shoulder, I felt a needle enter my upper back, and the nanites from a Medi-Kit raced in to repair the damage.

"I have four more on me and the other soldiers carry two each. We are prepared for this. As long as you keep going, I can keep you up." She then leaned around me and shot a nearby enemy soldier in the knee. It didn't penetrate armor but he fell to the ground. "Of course I won't just be medicating you."

"Of course," I said, louder than I'd intended as I raised the hammer high above my head, and brought it down on the soldier's helmet.

I hit the button Wolski was talking about, and I made a mighty dint in the concrete factory floor. I couldn't even describe the damage I'd done to the head as only a mangled piece of black polymer helmet remained.

Unara whooped behind me as Wolski and Effa appeared, each firing their shotguns.

"We got you covered!" Wolski yelled with ferocious glee as his attack tore open a weak spot in his target's armor.

Something in the darkest recesses of my mind seemed to know how to use the hammer more effectively, and so I swung left, just tapping the pulse button this time.

It sped up, wildly blasting the nearest soldier into those next to him. He was dead on impact, the armor he wore working well for gunfire but offering hardly any protection against the swinging of a hammer built for war by an angry orc.

The next soldier in line fell underneath him, and a second later, his head disappeared in a spray of gore. I wasn't sure which one of my friends did it, only that they were filling in the blanks I left to let me really go for it. That headshot was the last bit of notice I took off my surroundings as I really got to work.

I swung right. Pulse button tap, and two crushing deaths this time. My arms strained under the force of the hammer, but it was that good kind of strain. The kind of strain strong arms were born to endure. Left swing pulse, right swing pulse, step forward. No one I hit cried for long. These were merciful deaths I was dishing out. Undeservedly merciful, but I was having far too much fun to stop now.

For a few moments, I felt like the soldiers were beginning to back off. The sensation didn't last long as the building filled with guttural snarling, high-pitched squeals, and insane screaming. The goblins had arrived, and the crowd around me was suddenly much more compact.

I took a moment to assess the result of my rage-filled charge. I'd pushed deep into enemy ranks, but my friends were still close by shooting, and in Unara's case, stabbing with vicious efficiency.

We were close to victory now, and even their drones were being taken down as goblins practically filled the entire room.

Then I was mysteriously on my back, crackling blue energy dancing across my chest. From my new position, I could see that around fifty more soldiers had appeared across the back of the unit on a second level gantry.

They were not dressed like those we were currently battling. Their armor was of shimmering blue with a large golden triangle emblazoned on their torsos. They were clearly elite soldiers with a lot of money behind their armor and equipment. One of them held a huge gun with four pincer-like projections which held a ball of the very same crackling energy that now fizzled out on my chest, leaving a deep scorch that had almost gotten through my chest plate.

He fired again, but I managed to roll to the side and avoid the second blast. I got back to my feet to see that our goblins were already closing in on the newcomers, and at first, I cheered that. Until around thirty of them each pulled out a pair of swords that sprang to life with a buzzing golden energy coating them.

Goblins fell the moment they came within range. Bagri was up there standing on a railing, screaming at his kin to fall back and shoot.

Surprisingly, the goblins listened, but it didn't help much as their bullets were useless against the expensive armor and more died as the soldiers moved like lightning, killing with abandon.

"Bagri! Get them back!"

Bagri looked over to me and did a little happy dance, waving at me before he remembered his predicament and thankfully dodged a sword attack. He did an incredibly impressive somersault to avoid a second, then hammered two bullets up into the soldiers armpit. The soldier fell from the wound, and Bagri leapt away from the fight, shouting for all of the goblins to back off.

The soldiers followed more slowly. They were clearly well trained and moved with effortless purpose. Meanwhile, I could hardly believe what I'd just seen.

Wolski must have sensed my amazement and offered an explanation. "He has some tasty mods now. Fairly sure his legs are Tier-Four, though him and Igri are keeping quiet about it, and Unara just smirks when I asked her about it."

I turned to Unara, but she was nowhere to be seen, and I didn't have time to search her out.

It was time to start swinging again. I hefted the hammer over my shoulder one-handed and walked toward them, matching their slow pace. I was ready for them to turn on the speed, but my movement was all about keeping a solid base. A cliff against the ocean. And by Artem's asshole, they would break on me.

The moment I saw one of them twitch a little faster, I swung. They moved as anticipated, but still managed to avoid my attack.

Their smug face was visible through the visor as they arrived in the space my hammer had just cleared. What they'd failed to notice was that I hadn't used the pulse. Now I did.

The hammer flew back the way it came with nothing but direction from me. I knocked the soldier to one side as the hammer clattered into them, and I was back in motion again. Swing, pulse, smack—the rhythm of the next minute of my life.

They cut me. They hurt me. I saw my people falling all around the factory, and I kept going. I kept killing, and with the help of the goblin numbers, and Unara using her stealth, we managed to whittle them down, though the life cost was horrendous. Especially for the goblins.

As a large, black Aspire AV slid in though the factory hanger door, I yelled for Bagri to pull them all back.

The soldiers on my left wing, closest to the ship, began firing, and I yelled for them to stop. "Save your fucking ammo!"

We would still fight, but right now, we were too disorganized, and it would play into their hands. We had to be much smarter. "Everyone, fall back to the rear of the unit."

As more Aspire soldiers pounded off the new AV, an amplified voice reached us. I turned to face the elite soldiers and found they'd stopped.

"Are you sure you don't want to drop the charges, orc?" Ullaxin boomed. He was in among the elites. He held two of the energy swords, and he looked ready to use them. "We'll still have to kill everyone here, but you can go free. Drop the charges, and then you'll be free to go your own way. Far, far away from Portolans as I've changed my mind about my demands."

"I wouldn't worry about it too much," I growled back. "In the next few minutes, you're not going to have a mind left to change when I chop your bastard head off."

"How quaint," he replied casually. "You are in the wolf's lair. There is only one outcome here.

"Before we finish this," I said, letting the hammer swing free in my weaker left hand. "I have a proposition for you."

"Too late for that," he said, replacing his visor and raising his swords. "I'm going to bleed you to within a hair's breadth of death, then bring you back. And I'm going to do that as many times as it takes until your spirit is broken and you beg to drop the charges against Aspire. Kill them all, but leave the orc to me!"

With that, he charged, lightning fast, with a skillful attack that saw one blade coming in low and one coming in high. It was practically undefendable, but he really hadn't considered that I didn't need to swing the hammer. He'd clearly never fought against anything like it before, and as I activated the pulse, the hammer shot up.

It smashed into his low moving blade, smashing both that and the hammer head into his thigh. I threw up my right arm at the same time, and his descending blade cut deep into it, frying the circuitry in the forearm, and leaving my hand useless.

He almost fell but fought to keep his feet which was probably a mistake as I swung my modded leg full force into his crotch. Armored though it was, he still felt the impact and then slid to the floor.

Unable to use my right arm, I placed the head of my hammer on the floor a foot away from his head, changed my hand position so that I could swing it like a pendulum, then stopped as the hanger doors were ripped off and another amplified voice filled the air.

"Drop your weapons. This is SEPCO. Anyone found with a weapon in their hands will be arrested."

I was fairly sure that the speaker couldn't see me, so I quickly swung the hammer and pulsed it, keeping my finger pressed down as it connected.

Ullaxin's helmet came off with the impact, his neck bent at a horrible angle, and I let the hammer go. It went skittering across the floor with the helmet. No one noticed the attack but somehow Ullaxin was still groaning.

"So you got yourself a spinal mod, huh, fucker? What about your skull? Is that reinforced?" I raised my foot to stomp.

"Sergeant Oshbob! No!"

I looked up to see Agent Truth picking his way through the carpet of bodies. Our eyes met and I stamped.

Ullaxin's skull was not reinforced.

"Sorry, Superior? I couldn't hear with all of our weapons hitting the floor as per your order."

"I can see why people dislike you now, Sergeant Oshbob," he said, finally reaching me. "Who was it?" he asked, looking down at the crushed head.

"Who? Oh the guy I just tripped over? That is… was Premier Ullaxin."

"Of course it was," Agent Truth groaned. "Come on. You need to come with me now. My main priority here is to rescue you, believe it or not. Now come on, we need to get out of here. You're still vulnerable to snipers."

Partition 48

The trial didn't happen. Or if it did, I wasn't invited to it. At the courthouse, I was put in a room without any outside connections, and I saw no one except the courthouse guards and the staff who delivered my meals.

Three long days I was kept in the dark, and when I was finally brought out into the main courtroom, the place was empty beyond a serious-looking man behind a ridiculously high desk, his five very heavily armed security guards, and Agent Truth.

I stood alone under their stern and silent stares. If they were expecting me to say something, we'd all be in for a long wait. I just stared back up at them defiantly.

Soon the reason for their silence became clear as Lanris, then Nozz, and finally Theta were led into the room.

The man behind the desk finally introduced himself, "I am High Judge Hasuma. You have been brought here today to hear the verdict of our fair city in the case Scrub Team 4 vs Aspire.

"We had gathered ample evidence from a variety of sources to make a decision without the need for the distractions and emotions of those involved, and so, due to the sensitive nature of the case, it was held behind closed doors."

I heard Theta groan, and so did everyone else. She looked over at me guiltily, and I nodded. I agreed with her groan. This sounded bad, and I doubted anything we could do here would make it worse short of going on a rampage.

"Aspire have been found guilty of putting honorable military members in an impossible position whereby they were left with no other choice but to carry out their heinous crimes against hard working soldiers. This puts a bad name and a black mark on our city's military. In doing so, they have upset a great many of our current investors and senior military officers.

"As such, all of Aspire's assets have been seized by the military, notwithstanding reparations to the city, and the corporation has been broken up. As the actions of Aspire were directly targeted at the districts you are involved with, all properties owned by Aspire within Portolans, Turan, and Newton have been resold through the district auction house."

I could hardly believe it. "So is that Aspire finished?" I asked.

The High Judge looked up from what he was reading to cast a sour look in my direction. "Yes. Aspire is no more."

I wanted to cheer. Hell, I wanted to dance, but I remained passive and waited to learn what they had in store for me and my friends. Where would they put us? Would we be set up again after all of the trouble we caused?

"As for you all. Specialists Nozz, Theta, and Private Lanris. For the wrong done against you, if you wish it, I give you permission to take early retirement from the military. You will receive the standard pension according to your rank."

Theta scratched her head as surprised as the rest of us. I couldn't fight the grin at her response. "I really don't know. I mean I absolutely love the military, but after what happened—you know, the strain and stress—maybe it would be best if I did bow out now. Might make other soldiers feel uncomfortable."

The judge didn't look amused, but I was beginning to suspect that was just the way his face rested.

"What she said, sir," Nozz added quickly.

I turned to Lanris, interested to hear what he would have to say with him having his mother in the military.

He surprised us all by agreeing. "I will also take my retirement, sir. Thank you, and it was an honor serving."

"Very well, you are all herby retired. You can pick your papers up at Captain Turner's wall base. As for you, *Sergeant* Oshbob."

I didn't like the way he said sergeant at all.

"In our investigations, it has come to light that you have been stealing nanites from the mutants you killed out in the wilds. What do you have to say about that?"

I hadn't been expecting that, and it seemed no one else had either. I didn't even have lawyers for this. "I didn't think I was on trial here, your honor. And I wouldn't exactly say stealing. More making sure none went to waste."

"You are not on trial. You have already been judged. All that's left to do now is for you to choose your punishment. Because while this may come as a surprise to you, the military views your nanite acquisition quite differently."

My heart sank. After everything, after watching my friends set free from the military, I was going to be screwed over at the final hurdle. I supposed I should have expected it really.

"Hit me with it then," I said bitterly.

"We have discussed three choices, which is not typical, but after the hardships you've endured, I am willing to be lenient. Choice number one is five years imprisonment."

I clenched my jaw and remained silent.

"Option number two. Five further years in the military at private rank where your light fingers can be watched."

I sensed real hatred from the look he gave me as he said that. But the hint of smile that tugged up the corner of his mouth before reading the last one told me option three was going to be something extra sadistic.

"Option three is perhaps the most unpleasant of the three. You pay reparations for the missing nanites to the value of 500,000 credits. You pay the remainder of your additional wages within the military, totaling three hundred and ten credits. You forego any rights to a military pension, and you leave today, never to darken the doors of our great institution again."

His smile had disappeared now, but I could feel the humor radiating from him. The bastard had enjoyed that far too much.

"Tough choice, but I think I'll take option three."

"Are you sure? That is quite the sum for an orc sergeant."

"Oh, I'm fucking sure," I replied.

"Very well. Contact your people and have the reparations and wages sent over immediately. Once they've cleared in our system, you can leave."

I didn't have anything left to say, so I nodded mutely and allowed myself to be led away from the room. I was given access to a communication terminal in the courthouse admin area where I was able to send Unara a message only.

She replied instantly. They'd already been told the verdict and were ready and waiting to send the money.

With that done, we were transported back to Captain Turner's wall base immediately. He was waiting for us as we descended the AV's ramp.

"Welcome back," he said to all of us, and then he approached me, his expression serious. "Are you okay?"

"We are," I said, still feeling tense.

He looked at me as if wrestling with saying something.

I shook my head and sighed. "Spit it out, Turner."

He nodded and said words I'd have never expected to hear from his mouth. "If you have any trouble raising the funds to get free of this place, let me know, Oshbob. I'd be happy to help you out."

After I picked my jaw up from the floor, I stuck out my fist for Turner to bump.

"I'm going to be okay paying it, captain. But the offer means more to me than you'll ever know, and if you ever need any help yourself, you know where I am."

He returned the gesture with a smile. "I hope never to have need to take you up on that, but thank you."

"You're a much better man than I thought you were, Turner. I should probably apologize for how much of an utter bag of shit I thought you were."

He laughed "Don't apologize. I definitely wasn't a good man when we met. But I have been trying to be ever since."

"Oh, I wasn't going to. I'm still horrible."

We laughed together at that, and he led us into the base and to the reception area.

"We have Sergeant Oshbob's papers, captain," a human clerk behind the desk said as soon as we walked in. He then rustled around on his desk, stamped four different documents with enthusiasm and then pushed them over the desk.

We each picked up our own. Mine was easy to find as it had big red letters that read Service Void rather than Service Complete. It actually annoyed me that they belittled everything I did here with this final insult, but then I looked at those around me and knew that the people who mattered, all knew what I'd achieved here.

With a few more goodbyes with Turner, we all practically bolted for the door.

A car horn beeped across the parking lot, Wolski sat in the front of a shiny, dark green hover car, looking completely out of place as he waved at us.

"There's our ride, guys. What are your plans, Lanris?"

Empire of Oshbob

"Coming with you for now if you don't mind. This has all happened so quickly, and I just want to be away from here as quickly as possible before someone changes their mind."

"I couldn't agree more," Nozz said hastily.

I led them across the road quickly, finding I agreed with the sentiment too, and we all jumped into the car. The windows were blacked out, so I didn't realize that Unara was in there until I jumped in beside her. She hugged me immediately and it was a special moment.

"Ah hell, I've missed you. It's been too long."

She let out an unusual giggle at my words. "Not as long as you might think," she said cryptically.

"Welcome back, boss," Wolski grunted from the front. "It's been too long!" Then he chuckled as he set off into the air.

"Right, what the hell is going on? You've all been weird as hell."

Unara lounged back in her chair comfortably. "Those memories you lost? We took them. You spent a little over a week with us, just before you woke up outside the wall." She looked at Lanris. "Both of you."

"You're joking!" I asked, not knowing whether to laugh or cry. "Can I get them back? The memories?"

"You sure can, but we need to go visit Tenev first and get all of that military gear off you. You need a keystone that actually works for a start. One we can trust. Then we can upload your mem-core."

I shook my head in disbelief. "This explains so much. So I take it we set a lot of stuff up before I was ever taken?"

"We really did," she chuckled. "Oh and you should know, you actually killed Burrel and took Turan."

I roared with laughter, slapping my legs. "I've spent the last week or so feeling overwhelmed, out of my depth, and completely useless. I never thought in a million years I'd set myself up!"

"Well you did, with some help from some good friends," she said, reaching under the seat and producing a bottle of Aska. "Now, shall we celebrate?"

She popped the lid off and took a swig then passed the bottle to me.

"You drink now?" I asked, surprised.

"I might have developed a taste for it since you've been gone. There were some dark days."

I nodded and took a swig myself before handing it along to the grateful Theta sitting next to me.

It appeared we were all thirsty, and the bottle barely made it around once, leaving a very disappointed looking Nozz. Until Unara produced another from under the seat.

"Don't worry I have a few for the ride. Twenty minutes is a long time!"

By the time we reached Tenev's shop twenty minutes later, we were all nice and relaxed. Wolski brought the car down on the rooftop where Tenev waited to greet us.

He came running up to me as I stepped out, a wide grin on his face. "You did it! I've been following everything that's happened. I've been barely able to keep track of my own work!"

"Well you can concentrate now," I said, grinning. "And you better be on top of your game because Unara tells me you have better mods to install on me, right?"

His face took on a brief look of confusion before something dawned on him. He snapped his fingers and laughed. "That's right! You don't remember me telling you about the Tier-Four replacements do you?"

My mind boggled at the thought of Tier-Four replacements. "No, I don't."

"Well that's what we've got, so come on, come on. I'm all set up to get you fixed up! You'll be close to unstoppable… Do you still want your old eyes reinstalled?"

The question caught me off guard, but the memory of losing my sight to the EMP was still fresh in my brain. "Depends. You got any that can withstand EMPs?"

He smiled sadly and shook his head. "I still don't."

"Then put the ones I was born with back in. I can use scopes and equipment if I need to."

"I may have something to help with that too. I had a special delivery this morning. It's something you haven't seen yet. A rather unique brain mod. While it's only a Tier-Three, I've never seen the like in all my years. It is the worst brain mod I've ever seen for general use, but for you, I really think there's none better."

"Sounds interesting. Lead the way."

Tenev led us down into the building and into his very expensive-looking lab. Seeing how much better it was than his original lab and even better than the one in the unit filled me with pride as I lay down on the table. He showed me a display of the brain mod I'd be receiving.

Brain Mod	Tier: Three
The Anvil: Miss Nothing model is a prototype model which focuses almost entirely on visual processing. In order to compensate for the increased flow of visual input, there is also a minor upgrade to information processing. This model is primarily geared towards military commanders and high-level law enforcement management who specialize in risk assessment and role assignment. Early reports indicate that the increased speed of information delivery creates the sensation of physical movements slowing down in the viewing area. One concerning development is that the Mod appears to have excellent applications in the less prestigious area of direct combat, giving a Miss Nothing mod operator a large advantage in one-on-one situations. Thankfully, the price range should keep this very special mod out of the wrong hands. Active time: 30 seconds. Rest time: 1 hour. Perception: 14 Mental Power: 12	
Durability: 100/100	Slot Cost: 3

"I don't know if I'm reading this right, but does that mod say it slows down time?"

Tenev smiled. "In a roundabout way, yes. Yes it does."

"And who is Anvil? Can't say I've heard of them before."

"It's a Dwarven corporation. They generally only supply mods to dwarves or those who live within their district. But before you ask any more questions I feel it would be better to do the work and install your mem-core where you will receive far better answers than I could ever provide."

"You know best when it comes to this kind of stuff."

"I'm glad you agree," he replied, jabbing me with the anesthetic needle.

It took a moment on waking to process my amnesiac memories and how they fit in with the restored memories. That in itself was special. It should have taken a lot longer than it did for my mind to file the contrasting information, but moments later, I sat up, feeling complete again.

I raised up my new arm and marveled at it. As I activated the camouflage, an almost holographic image fuzzed over it, clearing into an exact replica of what my right arm should look like. I goggled at it for a moment, then touched it with my other hand. My hand passed through the shallow image and touched cool metal.

"That is very disconcerting," I said, troubled at the illusion. I looked up to Tenev and he looked worried. "It's amazing, Tenev. Don't worry I'm not complaining. I do wonder what all this work looks like on my overall abilities."

I accessed the unusual keystone interface and was glad to find that, while it was different to any I'd used before, it was probably the most intuitive and reacted to my thoughts more fluidly.

Identification: Oshbob				
Species: Orc		Bonus: None		
Mod Capacity: 26		Mod Capacity in use:		
Stat	Current Points	Description	Mods	Quality
Dexterity	6	Governs agility and movement.	Right Leg Cost: 3 Strength	Tier - 4

Empire of Oshbob

			: (18) Dexterity: (14) **Right Arm:** Cost: 4 Strength: (18) Dexterity: (14)	Tier - 4
Mental Power	11	Governs swiftness and fortitude of the mind	Brain Mod cost 3 (Per 14) (Men 12)	Tier - 3
Perception	9	Governs an individual's senses and connection to the world around them.	Brain Mod cost 3 (Per 14) (Men 12)	Tier - 3
Strength	15	Governs physical strength and damage dealt	**Right Leg** Cost: 3 Strength: (18) Dexterity: (14) **Right Arm:** Cost: 4 Strength: (18) Dexterity: (14)	Tier - 4 Tier - 4

Toughness	15	Governs the body and internal fortitude		

Partition 49

As we drove away from Tenev, I played with the special functions on my new mods. Flickering the camouflage on and off, finally, I asked Unara to punch me.

"I don't think that's a good idea. I've just gotten you back and I'd like to stay friends."

"You don't have to go for a fatality!" I joked. "I just want to try the Miss Nothing Mod."

She shrugged. "Okay then. If you're sure."

I nodded and activated the ability. As the description said, it gave the impression of slowing down time. I could see the muscles bunch in Unara's shoulder and watch as the punch came at my face. I had all the time in the world to block it. Unfortunately, I just didn't have the speed, and while I set my own arm off in motion to protect myself, it moved as if through setting cement, and Unara's punch landed square on my nose.

I dropped the new skill and laughed. "Okay. It's overpowered, but not that overpowered. I could see your strike for years, but I couldn't move my own body quickly enough."

Unara nodded with smug satisfaction. "So against anyone with a similar Dexterity, you'll be fine. You just chose to practice with the fastest person you know."

"Exactly," I replied thoughtfully.

"But," she said, tapping her temple and pointing at me. "If you weren't in a car, you could have stepped back and avoided the blow that way."

"Hmm, I suppose. I probably could…Why are we here?"

She followed my gaze out of the window as the hover car pulled up outside of Harold's shop. "Two reasons. The first is that this is one of the entrances to our new home. The second is that Yax and Karak wanted to meet us, and this is as good a place as any."

"You want us to hang around?" Wolski asked.

"No. You all go get settled in." She looked in the back of the car at the three soldiers. "Wolski will look after you all. We'll catch up tomorrow."

With that, the car sped off, and I turned back to the shop. "Can't believe he's gone. I wouldn't be here without him."

"He was a good find for us," Unara agreed. "Need to tidy up this shop front, though. It looks like goblins have taken it over. I just wanted the underground area done first."

I laughed at her description of the shop. "You know that's the point though, don't you? It's supposed to look unassuming. If it's all the same to you, I'll probably keep it exactly how it is."

"Typical you!" She grinned. "You must be the only super wealthy corpo to have their old eyes put back in."

I spun on her in mock fury. "You wash your filthy mouth out. I'm no corpo."

She chuckled some more then pointed to the rough wood door. I looked through the hole she pointed at, and a red light flickered.

The door opened up automatically, and the lights came on inside. The place smelled the same as it always did. Gun oil, dust, and the earthy smell of the wood paneling all around the walls.

"Can't believe you want to keep it like this," Unara said.

I ignored her and entered the back area. Nothing had been moved at all to my eyes. All the weapons Harold had in stock remained where they were stored, there were even a few bottles of his favorite whisky under the counter.

I headed over, ripped the top of one and raised it in the air. "To you, old human." Then I took a swig, feeling a deep sense of loss.

All that was swept away a few moments later as Yax and Karak came bustling into the shop.

"What a shithole," Yax said, eyeing the place.

"Looks are deceiving," Unara answered for me. "What did you want to speak about so urgently?"

"We could do with a little more privacy," Yax said, looking back at the open door.

I hit the secure room activation under the counter, and the thick metal security door dropped down to cover the door. Turrets came out, but I deactivated them quickly.

The two caravanners looked around nervously. Karak knocked on the walls while Yax spoke. "That'll do, I suppose. So what we wanted to talk about. It's sensitive. We were sent so that you didn't get the wrong idea."

"Not a good start," I pointed out. "I'm already getting lots of ideas why you're here, so some of them have to be wrong."

"Funny, Oshbob. I'll lay it out flat for you. I know you tried to distance yourself from 360 before, but this whole shitstorm has dragged you back into some people's minds as something to do with it."

Unara leaned forward toward the dwarf. I could tell she was getting a little agitated.

"Well, Entrax, the director at Anvil that I deal with, he likes 360. Hell, he likes you both. But he can't work with you. An orc street thug and a… I don't actually know what you are, Unara, but neither of you look like good business partners for an elite corporation. Asala, however, she is perfect, and she's the visible CEO."

"Cut to the chase, Yax," I said tiredly. "It's been a long day."

"Alright, alright. This isn't easy. He made clear that you would always be known to the powers that be at Anvil as the real owners of the company. But if you distance yourselves again, and maybe remove as many other people who know about your links outside of your own people of course, then he has this offer for you." He paused for a moment. I suspected for dramatic effect. It was lost on Unara and me.

"With your demolition of Aspire and consolidation of Turan and Newton, you've pushed 360 up to a lower mid-level corporation. People are starting to take notice. Anvil certainly has, and they're willing to sponsor 360."

I wasn't stupid. That was a huge deal. It was an incredible opportunity, and a pathway to incredible power within the city. Unfortunately, we weren't welcome as part of the deal. Not only were we being pushed out, but we were being asked to push ourselves out.

My eyes met Unara's. "What do you think?"

"I think we're being pushed out of our own company."

"No," Yax protested. "Absolutely not. They know who you are. You will always be part of it. They just need you to be… less visible."

Kevin Sinclair

I planted my hands on the counter and glared into Yax's soul. "It's a good deal, but we're gonna need some assurances."

"Name them," Yax said confidently.

"Oh I will. Once I've thought about it a little more, we'll be in touch."

The End.

Empire of Oshbob

I've loved writing this series and honestly? I could go on forever! But my purpose in writing was to see Unara and Oshbob fight their way from nothing, to proving themselves as a real power in Artem.

So while this book marks the end of Oshbob and Unara's rise, they do still appear in other Artem Universe books where they're involved in the adventures of other great characters.

Check them all out!

[Revenant](https://mybook.to/Artem) by Jez Cajiao
https://mybook.to/Artem
Underdog by Lars Machmüller
Tailspin by Dawn Chapman

Kevin Sinclair

Reviews and shoutouts mean so much to authors like me. They increase visibility and encourage others to pick up my books which allow me to keep writing. So please, take a minute and help me out! Leave Review.

I also love to hear from people who have enjoyed my work, so here's a bunch of ways to get in touch. Join my Facebook Group or Discord where I hangout. I also lurk on twitter and Instagram to a lesser degree. If that doesn't entice you, then you can always have a peak at my website for new releases and even sign up for my Reader Group newsletter where you can grab a free companion novella for my Condition Evolution series.

Empire of Oshbob

Printed in Great Britain
by Amazon

c941fcb7-777b-487f-bcd5-7e879ccacec3R01